Unplugged

The Return of the Fathers

Robert Egby

Three Mile Point Publishing
Chaumont, New York

Copyright © 2013 Robert D. Egby

Published by:
Three Mile Point Publishing
Chaumont, NY USA
609-315-5878

Book formatting and cover design by Jera Publishing

All rights reserved. No part of this book may be reproduced in any manner whatsoever without the written permission from the author, except in the case of brief quotations embodied in critical articles, reviews and books with suitable credits.

First published: August 2013
Three Mile Point Publishing, Chaumont NY

ISBN: 978-0-9848664-4-1

Library of Congress Control Number: 2013943134

Printed in the USA

This book is dedicated to:
All those who believe and all those who know.

Many thanks to my partner Betty Lou Kishler for all her patience and dedicated help in proof reading this book and for her continued support.

Novels by Robert Egby

PENTADAKTYLOS: Love, Promises and Patriotism in the Last Days of Colonial Cyprus

THE GUARDIANS OF STAVKA: The Deadly Hunt for the Romanov Gold in Canada

CATACLYSM '79: The Day the River Stopped.

UNPLUGGED: The Return of the Fathers

Non-fiction by Robert Egby

Cracking the Glass Darkly

The Quest of the Radical Spiritualist

INSIGHTS: The Healing Paths of the Radical Spiritualist

HOLY DIRT, SACRED EARTH: A Dowser's Journey in New Mexico

Autobiography

KINGS, KILLERS AND KINKS IN THE COSMOS:

Treading Softly with Angels Among Minefields.

Author's Foreword

Unplugged: The Return of the Fathers is primarily a work of fiction based upon the discovery over the past 150 years of more than 30,000 clay tablets found in the Cradle of Civilization which was Mesopotamia, land of the Sumerians now known as Iraq. While the historical background is condensed and accurate, the novel is primarily a work of fiction. All of the characters are fictitious and therefore creations of the author's mind. Most of the places where the action occurs are real except the Anasazi Resort Hotel in Taos, NM and the Elks Head Valley Ranch in the heart of British Columbia.

Two news stories occurred while the novel was in production. The surprising and critical discovery at Edinburgh University in Scotland of a new and unique gene called miR-941 and it is mentioned as a news item. The other news item came from central Europe early in 2013. In essence it said the World Economic Forum meeting in Davos, Switzerland turned its attention to space. The Huffington Post reported "World Economic Forum Ponders Consequences of Contact with Alien Life." A subhead declared: "ET discovery could happen within 10 years." The article told of NASA's current planetary explorations and then added: "The risk factor of all of this comes with the long term psychological and philosophical implications that will accompany the discovery of alien life." That is exactly one of the problems indicated in the novel. How does authority introduce real alien existence to a public that has routinely been told they are big, ugly and threatening?

This novel *Unplugged: The Return of the Fathers* is one scenario.

Robert Egby
Chaumont, NY USA
August 2013

Unplugged

The Return of the Fathers

1

THE WHITE DACIA DOKKER rental car made its way along the tortuous dusty track that winds along the tops of the deep red and burnt umber ragged cliffs of southern Morocco. Occasionally the wheels kicked up a dust cloud and every now and again the couple would stop and peer at the deep blue Atlantic Ocean as it sent magnificent towering white caps crashing endlessly on the narrow sandy beaches. Sometimes the car would disappear briefly as it navigated behind clumps of rich acacia trees with gnarled sun-bleached trunks and roots searching for succulence in the dry sandy soil.

The driver finally stopped the vehicle on a dusty white plateau atop a rugged headland overlooking this vista of rich blue sky and even bluer water laced with elegant surfs born far out to sea and driven by the strong fresh breezes from the north-west into towering fifty-foot tall whitecaps. The sounds of these monster rollers crashing on the beaches and the subsequent chuckles of sand and rocks as the water quickly resided, appealed to the couple as they stood by the car and stretched their arms and bent their legs to relieve the travel stiffness. It had been a long drive from beyond Tiznit in the south.

The barefooted young woman looked around and finally slipped the old Pentax from her pocketbook.

"When are you going to trade in that old film camera and go digital?" asked the lithe energetic young man as he moved to her side and flashed a grin.

"Jean-Pierre, you're the professional." The gently tanned face threw a mocking sniff and she tossed back her long ash blonde hair. "Paris Weekly! You can't beat that! I'm just a secretary from West Kensington."

"Ah, but you're part of me. You're writing my life story."

"Is that why you married me?" she said with a faint frown.

"Oui! Absolutely!" the Frenchman cried defiantly.

"You're a bum!" she cried, jabbing him in the ribs with a long finger.

He laughed lightly and she liked that.

"Are you going to take a picture?" he asked quietly. "We need to be in Agadir for dinner."

"It's such a fabulous Martian landscape framed by a beautiful Atlantic and an even bluer sky," she said holding up the Pentax. "No wonder the Berbers love this place. It's home for all sorts of creatures – gazelles, wild boars, jackals – and that ugly old bald ibis you photographed this morning. It would be a great place to build a home."

Jean-Pierre frowned. "Now I know you are nuts, Angie. Loco!"

"All right, two shots."

The young English woman held up the Pentax and took two pictures. "D'accord!" She called out as her hand wound the film.

"Mon dieux!" he responded with a grin. "You're almost a polyglot."

"Bum!" she called out. "I'm learning. Have patience."

They climbed back into the car. Jean-Pierre leaned forward to start the engine when a large shadow suddenly appeared and blocked the woman's window.

"Oh, God!" cried the Frenchman. Angie shrieked in sheer terror.

It was the face of a young man, perhaps a teenager. Colorless glassy gray-green eyes stared from a skull cloaked in white bloodless flesh. The lips mouthed something but they failed to hear. A hand flattened itself against the window and then slid away as the figure slumped onto the dust.

The next few minutes were a complete blur. Jean-Pierre felt the urge to escape from whatever was out there but the woman cried out "No, he needs help." Together they picked up the limp body and pushed it onto the back seat. Angie gave the youth some water. "Drained of all fluids. We'd better get him to a doctor," she cried.

"Look," cried Jean-Pierre. "That must be the boy's back-pack over there." Immediately, he ran across, picked it up and tossed it into the car.

Angie seated in the back seat with a water bottle turned to her husband. "He looks bad. Really bad! Incredibly dehydrated! I don't think he'll make it."

"There's a village east of here," Jean-Pierre cried and turning the car they sped off towards the buildings. Several Arabs pointed to a well presented, one level adobe building where a gendarme helped carry the youth into the office. They placed him on a long divan next to a cool clay water chatty. Speaking in Berber the policeman briskly ordered a young boy to fetch the nurse.

"This young man is an American student," exclaimed the gendarme knowledgably. "Peter Singleton. We understand he recently attended university, unhappily he said. He was here only two days ago talking about hiking, studying shells – sea shells – the conches, you know."

The nurse, a slim middle-aged woman dressed in a tired white uniform entered and kneeling beside the youth examined his body. She spoke in Berber to the gendarme then glancing at Jean-Pierre and Angie she broke into English: "He's physically and mentally exhausted. Suffering acute dehydration. It was lucky that you found him."

Hearing the woman's voice the youth struggled to get up. Staring at the people then peering round the room as if there might be others, he muttered in shaky voice: "Where am I? Are they gone?"

The nurse placed a comforting hand on the young man's shoulder.

Jean-Pierre stared at the gendarme. "Two days ago. Was the boy all right then?"

The gendarme nodded.

"Then how did he become so physically and mentally disabled in so short a time?"

"C'est une excellente question, Monsieur"

Sitting at his desk the gendarme took down a statement from the French photographer and his wife then offered them coffee but they shook their heads and said they must be going.

As they stood at the door, Jean-Pierre asked if he could take a photo of the nurse and the young man. For a moment the nurse hesitated then called for the gendarme to be in the picture too.

As Jean-Pierre finished, the youth suddenly sat up and in a cool straight forward voice gazed at the nurse. "Have the Egyptians gone?"

The question froze the group.

"What Egyptians?" the gendarme said quietly, moving to the youth's side.

"The ones..." the boy started to say, but hesitated because he suddenly realized the quiet. "The ones...the ones in the pyramid. I assumed they were Egyptians." A feeble hand tried to catch the policeman's uniform. "They were Egyptians weren't they?"

The gendarme ignored the question. "What else did they say?"

The boy gasped for air then blurted: "They claimed they were expecting me."

"Expecting you?" "Jean-Pierre frowned.

"They knew my name. Peter Singleton. How did they know my name?"

The gendarme and the nurse both shrugged as they looked at each other.

"Where was the pyramid?" asked the nurse.

"Out there!" he cried throwing his hand up. "Didn't you see it? It was out there. In the desert...they said...no, they didn't...I assumed they were Egyptians because of the pyramid." Suddenly the youth started screaming and as the gendarme held him down the nurse stabbed his arm with a hypodermic needle. Within seconds all was quiet.

"We'll move him to the clinic and notify the American consulate in Agadir. They will know what to do."

Jean-Pierre fetched the boy's back-pack from the car and gave it to the gendarme. The policeman peered inside. "Not much, just a few clothes, a passport, a notebook, a bottle of water and this," he said and pulled out a hardcopy book and read the title. "The UFO File: Fact, Fiction or Mass Hysteria by David Rowan." He tapped the book. "That's strange. Two weeks ago several fishermen from the next village spotted several UFOs – how do you say? – flying saucers hovering along the coast."

Angie looked across at the boy now lying quiet. "Do you think he was here looking for them?"

The gendarme shrugged and rubbed his moustache. "Qui sait, peut-être le diable?" Then he grinned. "The Devil knows all such things."

As they turned to leave, Angie turned back to the gendarme. "Excuse me, Monsieur. What is the name of this town?"

"Oh," said the gendarme with a brief smile. "It is Tikiout," he said, pride much in evidence in his voice. "Tikiout, Morocco."

They found the N1, the National Highway of Morocco and as they drove the 45 kilometers to Agadir they discussed the strange incident of Peter Singleton and the book he was carrying.

"The author of the book – David Rowan," said Jean-Pierre. "I was on assignment at Cannes last year. I spent a day with him taking shots for Paris Weekly. He enjoys debunking things like UFOs and aliens." He paused as if in thought. "But that doesn't account for what happened to the kid at Tikiout. How could he see Egyptians?"

"Maybe he was in the sun too long," suggested Angie.

And suffered hallucinations perhaps," he added.

Angie thought for a moment. "But the curious thing is the boy's condition developed all within two days. Less than 48 hours in fact. All he had was what he was standing up in and a small back-pack. The gendarme said he had a bottle of water in the bag so how could he become seriously dehydrated? How could it happen in so short a time?"

Jean-Pierre shrugged. "It's one of those weird events for my autobiography that you're going to type."

Angie poked him in the ribs. "You never give up do you?"

Three days later they were back in their Paris apartment settling in, showering and washing the desert sands from their bodies and laundering their clothes. Later, Angie went shopping and returned with prints from her film. As she started to flick through the prints, she stopped and stared.

"I took two pictures of the same spot on that headland near Tikiout," she said.

"Just before Peter Singleton turned up…?" he asked as he peered over her shoulder and caught sight of the two prints.

Both showed the reddish brown rocky landscape with the Atlantic and the blue sky beyond. Except one. Superimposed on that was the shimmering but distinct image of an Egyptian pyramid.

2

DAVID ROWAN SPOTTED ALISON Simonian when she first entered the crowded bookshop on London's Charing Cross Road. While the place was thronged with Saturday afternoon tome-lovers, she stood out, head and shoulders above the crowd. First, she was tall, at least six feet plus. Second, her slim, very erect and smoothly shaped body was clad in an ivory white suit while a red silk scarf draped her shapely neck. Third, most people move from side to side as they walk or wander, but this woman seemed to glide effortlessly across the floor and for several seconds he was sure this impression was a creation of the imagination. Fourth? Well, her face could easily have been chiseled from high grade ivory. Her dark green eyes behind gold-rimmed spectacles glanced briefly at him with a slight hint of a lurking smile. Then somehow this sleek high fashioned goddess disappeared, lost in the milling crowds that flocked about the tables of two other authors. For a while he was busy signing books, chatting with passers-by and completely thought the woman had gone.

The summer heat blew past the bookshop's air conditioning and after an hour of signing books and making polite conversation with potential readers and trying to fathom what his fans were asking, he desperately wanted a break.

An ice-cold beer, perhaps. Brits don't know the meaning of ice-cold so he shrugged and looked at the youngster.

"Hallo there. 'ave you seen one of them alien things?" asked the seedy long-haired cockney kid suffering a bout of acne that made his face appear like a lunar surface.

"Sure! They're all over the place. Look, there's one over there by the cash register."

The acne kid turned away. A space appeared in the line-up. Breathing a fast sigh of relief he tossed down his pen, stood up and started to walk to the washroom.

"Mister Rowan!" The voice was soft but firm. "I'm ashamed of you. Saying silly things to that young man. He's a believer, you know."

The writer stopped and stared at the woman. It was the tall, elegant creature he had spotted an hour ago. Now she was leaning against a bookshelf while her long delicate fingers fondled a Greek version of Lawrence Durrell's *Alexandria Quartet*.

"Alien's come and alien's go," he said mustering a tired grin. "When you write a book challenging the entire UFO fraternity, the existence of the greys and life on other worlds, they get all bent out of shape and hot under the collar and start buzzing."

"They seem to like your book. It's a best seller on both sides of the pond," she said easily, removing her gold-edged spectacles as if she wanted to get a better view of the writer.

"There's a group that hates the book so they buy it to argue against me, and there's a group that loves any solid argument that shoots down the UFO theories," he said shrugging his shoulders. "So they both buy books for different reasons." He grinned. "It's an all-win situation if you know what I mean. Now, do you like Durrell?"

"Oh, he's wonderful."

"You read Greek."

"Yes, but this doesn't have the articulated finesse of Durrell's English. In English Justine is a vibrant moody lass enjoying her loves and friends. In Greek she appears as a common whore. It's probably in the translation."

"Wow!" Rowan stood back, a little surprised by the comparison. "Look, haven't we met somewhere before?"

"Brussels!" she said quickly. "The U.N. Forum on arts and culture and world peace. You were with the American delegation and I was a replacement translator shipped in from London."

"You speak?"

"Russian, Greek, Arabic, Turkish, Armenian and some others not so well known." Her shoulders shrugged slightly as if the subject was of no importance.

"A regular polyglot," he said warmly. "Care for a drink and a bite after this?"

And so started a relationship between David Rowan and Alice Simonian. It was nothing special in his mind. As he explained to her in various oblique ways, it was purely platonic. It was simply boy meets girl, so enjoy.

After dinner they walked along the Thames Embankment and when David told her about the riverside cottage at Bourne End, she agreed to come for the weekend.

"We're still at the platonic level?" she added and he nodded.

"My father's friend rarely uses the place and so I have a place to stay when I'm in England," he said as the Renault swept west on the M4 to Maidenhead.

In the true sense of the title the cottage was olde world. It gave the appearance it had been there since the Boadicea passed by with her hordes of Ancient Iceni to battle the Romans. Its recently re-thatched roof hung over aged white walls covered with vibrant all-clinging ivy, while a spectrum of rose bushes bloomed profusely in the garden beds on either side of the lush green lawn that swept magnificently down to the gently flowing Thames. An old wooden boathouse with a cock-eyed weather vane bent out of shape hugged the bank and overlooked the river.

Inside the cottage were stone tiled floors covered with heavy mats while sturdy wooden beams supported the paneled ceiling and the bedrooms above. Alison slipped into gear and was immediately at home and offered to make some herb chamomile tea. Then her sharp eyes discovered Scottish shortbread biscuits – cookies in America -- in a picturesque jar dating back to 1952 and the coronation of Queen Elizabeth.

David sat at his laptop on an old oaken desk by the window and tried to check his email but his eyes watched her movements indiscreetly as if he feared being found out. There was no doubt about it, he enjoyed being in Alison's company. One, she possessed a vibrant nature, totally curious, always ready to ask questions and she listened intently to what was being said. He liked her slim, well maintained figure which was sexually very attractive, although the idea of opening the subject at such an early stage was abhorrent to his way of thinking. "Guess, I'm old fashioned when it comes to women," he once admitted to his stepfather.

Alison's face was clear and sharp with a slight tan and her dark green eyes always flashed as if she enjoyed being mischievous. He guessed she was about his age – mid forties -- and he wondered if she too had been born in the wild days of the hippies.

"Father is of Armenian stock," she said as they sipped tea. "A languages teacher at a prestigious school on the Island of Cyprus, he lost his home in the Turkish invasion of North Cyprus and together with my mother immigrated to the United States. He's a professor at a university languages lab down in Virginia. Mother is not well. Her heart is always in Cyprus where she had many Armenian friends."

As if on cue her dark eyes peered across the room. "Are you married, David?"

The writer sighed and stared out of the window with its old diamond leaded panels at the elegant what swans standing on the river bank. "Her name was Carla. A Philadelphia girl, she had a love affair with the piano and played anything from traditional jazz to elegant classics. The critics and many others recognized her as a talented concert pianist but her career ended abruptly. Three years ago one wintry night while driving home on the turnpike she ran into a blizzard and slammed into a multi-vehicle accident. Severely burned, she died in a Princeton hospital." He turned to face the woman. "So the answer is no."

"There's a touch of anger in that statement, David."

"Carla should have stayed with her parents that night and not tried to come home," he said. "Katherine, our daughter, took it badly. Spent a year hiking across America and I hardly heard from her. But she's fine now. We moved and bought a cottage out on Puget Sound in Washington State."

After a pizza and red wine supper they wandered across the lawn and stopped by the old wooden boathouse. There was nothing inside and their voices echoed in the hollowness.

David stared at the slow flowing Thames and reflected. "Last weekend I spoke to a UFO group in Buffalo and afterwards an elderly woman confined to an electric wheelchair cornered me outside the hotel and in thick voice muttered: I have a message for you."

"And?" Alison peered curiously into his face.

"Guess I was blunt," he said. "I told her I don't believe in all that Spiritualist stuff and started to walk away." The writer smiled lightly. "Well, her finger stomped the accelerator button on her wheelchair and trundled after me."

"And?"

"She called out: Watch for the woman of many tongues. She loves another but she will lead you to find the truth and the destiny of the world on a mountain far away."

"Sounds ominously cautious."

"Well, it's happened, hasn't it?"

"Was there something else?"

"She told me to count the pyramids and carry a candle."

"Are you heading to Egypt?"

"There are no plans," he said, then pulling an iPad from his jacket pocket, he said: "A photographer I know in Paris sent me this just before the book signing. His wife took the picture in Morocco a week ago."

Alison appeared stunned and as Rowan later reflected perhaps embarrassed.

"A pyramid! But it doesn't look real."

"That's just it. At first I thought someone had rigged the picture, done some computer hocus-pocus or used Adobe Photoshop but I know this couple," he said quietly. "They are not the sort to create a fake."

They started to walk across the lawn towards the cottage.

"From your books I see you are very skeptical about metaphysical things, crop circles, UFOs and things that go bump in the night," she said slowly.

David made a grimace and nodded. "A lot of bunk."

"It might be worth your while to research pyramids, especially the Great Pyramid at Giza," she said with words that contained some urgency.

"Whoaa! I've been to Egypt several times and was never impressed."

"On your list of things to do," she said, "make sure you get round to spending some time with a man named Geraint-Jones. Hugh and his wife Chloe are both excellent archaeologists and they will steer you into a story that will make an excellent book. Probably a best seller. Put it at the top of your things to do file. They have a wonderful seaview location at Nehalem, Oregon." She reached into her pocketbook then placed something in his hand. "It's their business card."

"My immediate plans are to visit a so-called UFO observers group in Taos, New Mexico for a day or so or until I get lynched or burned at the stake," he said with a grin.

The woman nodded. "Yes, it's on your website that you will be attending," she said quickly. "But keep the Oregon couple in mind. It's important."

Rowan frowned. He disliked people who kept track of his movements. "Anyway, Alison, I must tell you that all good pyramid books have already been written," he added with a tone of mild protest. "By some excellent authorities too."

"Not this one. It'll be a best seller," she responded with a simple smile.

"What's your take on this?" David was a degree suspicious.

"Take?" she said it with a light laugh. "Oh, I love pyramids."

The cloak of night enveloped the couple and they returned to the cottage. Pleading tiredness, Alison started to go to her bedroom but then she turned back: "If as the woman in Buffalo indicated I am the woman of many tongues, I think it's fair to say our paths will cross before you write your next book. By then you will have found the truth and realized the destiny of the world on a mountain far away.

Sitting at his closed laptop, the writer shook his head. "Let's not play games, lady, I'm never going to change my mind about UFOs, flying saucers, aliens and alien abductions or things that go bump in the night. They are all bunk! Nonsense! A conning of the general public. Understand?"

Alison nodded. "Mr. Rowan, you made that clear in your book. You are the Prince of Debunkers." She paused, then added: "The seer in Buffalo: remember what she said and carry a candle."

"If it makes you happy, I will think about it," he said and flashing a smile added: "Of one thing I am certain. It's warm to have an intelligent woman in this place."

"Thanks," she said. "It feels right to be here. Tomorrow morning I will catch the bus for Maidenhead and take the train to London. I think I have said enough." Reaching over she kissed his forehead and clutched his hands in hers. "Goodnight, David. May the Creator bestow abundant blessings upon you."

It was the first time she had used his name and for some unknown reason he felt a tremor of energy surge through his body, but he quickly shrugged it off. It really did not mean anything so he booted the laptop and as it warmed up he mulled over the rest of what the Buffalo medium had said but he had not revealed to Alison.

"There will be total darkness in your world and you will run for your life." The psychic had said it pedantically as if every word counted.

David Rowan had no intention of believing any of this until the seeress added: "A woman sends her love. She says her name is Carla.

It was at that particular moment that David Rowan's debunking crusade started to show cracks and a desperate voice inside called out: "Patch up the bastions. Patch up the cracks."

3

PENNI SINGLETON HATED AIRPORTS and JFK in New York was no exception. Her normally pale face was even paler this early afternoon. Fists clenched reflecting her slim wiry body taut under a blouse and slacks, she stared as the last of the people pulling their wheeled baggage, computers, heavy bags hustled from the Customs area and departed into the arms of loved ones, friends and cabs. But there was no Peter.

"Dan, there has to be a mistake," she grated.

"The Royal Air Morocco's Boeing 777 arrived and the 239 passengers took almost an hour to get off and clear customs and immigration," snapped her husband. "Something must be wrong."

"That's the other thing, we haven't seen any of the flight crew come through," she said.

Her fingers clasped his shirt sleeve. "Something is wrong, Dan. It's in my heart. I sense something is terribly wrong."

Just as they were about to search for the Customer Service office, a short well cut man wearing a light grey suit emerged from a side door and zeroed in on the fraught couple. "Daniel and Penni Singleton?"

They both stared at the man. His appearance confirmed that something was drastically wrong. They both nodded nervously.

"You are the parents of one named Peter Singleton?"

"My God! Is something wrong? Is he all right," she cried as she reached out and clung to the stranger's jacket. "Tell me he's all right."

"Please follow me," he said.

Dan Singleton slipped ahead of the man. "Hey, who the hell are you?" he roared.

"Let's just say I'm a Security Officer. So please follow me."

They hurried down a corridor and entered a small meeting office. Two Royal Maroc flight officers and two female attendants were seated round a long table. They all stood up.

"What the blazes is this?" snapped Singleton.

"Dan, let me handle this. It's no use blowing your top when anything seems wrong," she said quickly. The woman took a deep breath as she stared questioningly at the flight crew. "I'd like to know the whereabouts of our son Peter Singleton? We had a call from the American Embassy in Rabat that he had been placed on a direct flight to JFK. What happened? Where is he?"

The senior officer stepped forward. "I am Captain Laurent and I'm sorry to report that somewhere during the flight your son left the aircraft."

"What's that supposed to mean? Someone just doesn't leave an aircraft while it is flying over the Atlantic?

The officer felt uneasy and shrugged. Well, one time he was there and the next minute he was not there. He simply disappeared."

"What?" Dan Singleton's face flared red with sudden anger. "People just don't disappear off a jet plane in mid-Atlantic. What crap are you trying to pull."

The senior attendant flashed an apologetic glance at the captain. "Madame.. monsieur... if I may," she said. "Your son was seated in first class and the seat next to him was empty. It's a long flight. We served him luncheon and offered him wine, but he refused. He told us he was tired and wished to sleep, so we left him alone."

The attendant appearing tired flashed another glance at the captain, then continued. "We had a call from another passenger and as we passed your son's row we noticed he was no longer there. It was strange because neither of us noticed your son going to the rest rooms."

The captain spoke: "The attendants scanned the entire aircraft, checked the restrooms and came to the most unusual conclusion that a passenger was missing."

"Oh, damn it!" snarled Singleton, "that's a load of crap."

It was at this point that Penni Singleton gave a piercing shriek that jarred everyone including nearby windows and collapsed on the floor. Airport attendants rushed her to a small clinic where a medical officer attempted to administer a sedative but she quickly came to her full senses, staggered to her feet, brushed everyone aside and stomped out.

The well-attired fellow who said he was a security officer found another office and using his cell phone made a call to Langley.

"You're not going to believe this, sir, but the Singleton boy our people put on a plane in Rabat disappeared in mid-flight over the Atlantic. Can you believe it?"

"Mack, there's something really weird going on," said the voice at Langley. "We've had two reports in the last hour of passengers disappearing in mid-flights. A young married couple returning from a Mexican honeymoon to L.A. and a former ambassador to South Africa going to Quebec for a U.N. conference."

Stunned the CIA operative walked down the corridor and was met by the Moroccan airline captain. "You might be interested in this," said the officer. "The flight steward has just reported finding two sandals under the seat where the Singleton boy sat. He also left a backpack and this book. You're not going to believe the title. It's all about debunking UFOs."

Just then Penni Singleton, her reddish brown hair seemingly aflame, came storming back to where everyone was gathered. "Listen, I don't know what you people are trying to do but I'm going to find Peter and I may turn the whole bloody world upside down to do it."

The woman seized the book and stuffed it into the backpack. She glanced at her husband. "Dan, you are totally hopeless. Go back to your teen-age hussy. I'm going to find my son." The two stomped away in entirely different directions.

"Wow!" muttered the CIA man to no one in particular. "That gal is sure a ranging lion."

4

KATE ROWAN FELT GOOD this Sunday morning as her slim, trim figure jogged along the road lining the sand and shingle beach with its bundles of sun-bleached driftwood. To her creative mind they appeared like strange ethereal white statues. A cool morning summer breeze born in the still snow-covered peaks of the Olympic Peninsula swept across the Puget Sound and caressed and freshened her body as her feet pounded the roadway. Her long dark hair caught in a clasp bobbed up and down as she ran towards the Keystone Ferry Dock at Admiralty Inlet on Whidbey Island.

Mark was a student in WSU's College of Engineering and Kate was in the Edward R. Murrow College of Communication and they would not have crossed paths except they both loved jazz and met at Dimitriou's Jazz Alley in Seattle when Kenny G was there. The mellow sax worked magic in cementing a special link between them.

The ship swung in from Port Townsend and she had no difficulty recognizing his vintage yellow Volkswagen as it emerged off the ferry ramp, swung over the bridge and stopped beside her in the parking lot.

"Hi Kate!"

"Hi Mark!" she said slipping into the car.

Five minutes later they were lying on the sofa in the cottage clutched in each other's arms as if the world were about to end.

"Heavens!" she called out gasping for air. "You can tell you're an engineer."

"Can we go to bed?"

Kate flashed a reprimanding glance as she sat up. "Sex maniac too!"

An easy grin spread across the broad clean-shaven face. "You drive me crazy, woman."

"Ease up on the gas pedal there," she said quietly as she pushed herself up. "You'll burn yourself out." Moving across the room to the oak desk and a laptop she flicked it on then turned and said: "Breakfast?"

They cooked side by side, Mark fetched things while Kate cooked eggs, sausages with fried onions and mushrooms and after they had finished eating she announced: "I have to check the mail. Dad doesn't like to be kept waiting too long."

"Do you work for him?"

"Secretary. Unpaid," she replied. "But he does take me on some of his trips when I'm not at WSU. His work is always interesting especially in paranormal and UFO stuff."

"Does he really believe in that junk?"

"Junk, it may be," she said becoming a little distant, "but he does make a lucrative living. His latest book in which he debunks the phenomena has become an instant best seller."

"Title?"

"THE UFO FILE: Fact, Fiction or Mass Hysteria?" she replied, and picking up a copy from the shelf dropped it on Mark's lap.

"So he doesn't believe in the paranormal or psychic stuff?"

Kate shook her head. "Try not to judge too soon, Mark. Some days I think he is adamantly opposed and some days I think he supports the UFO theories. He's somewhere in between. He makes a great target for both sides and that sells books." She paused and reached for his arm. "Mark, come and take a look at this picture?"

Together they peered at the photograph of the rock plateau in Morocco with the ghostly image of a pyramid.

"It's from Dad. It's from a place called Tikiout He wants me to find out if there have been other encounters with ghost pyramids when and where," she said with a frown. "I guess I'm going to be tied up for a while."

"How do you find such things from a cottage on Whidbey Island?"

"It's the knack of knowing where to look," said Kate, her voice resounding with efficiency. "That's why I'm in communications."

Kate worked quietly and diligently for over an hour while Mark took the book, walked outside and lounged on cushions padding a wooden chair and for a while watched a Holland America cruise ship sail along the sound towards the open Pacific.

Skype broke her thoughts. David Rowan came on the screen.

"Did you find anything on the Tikiout pyramid in Morocco?"

Kate shook her head. "I've got something better, Dad."

"That's my girl. Spill the beans."

"Some Japanese fishermen spotted a ghost pyramid on the tiny volcanic island of Kuchino-Shima. It's in the northern part of the Ryukyu Islands. They saw it briefly in morning mists about a week ago," she said. "It lasted about 30 seconds then vanished."

"Source?"

"Tokyo Newswire."

"Good. Anything else."

"The second incident mentioned briefly in the English language Shanghai Daily reported university students hiking in the mountains near Hangzhou -- the place Marco Polo raved about. They claim to have spotted a ghost pyramid on a plateau overlooking the Yangtze River some miles south-west of the city. One actually took a digital photo but when they tried to download it the picture disappeared," she said. "Totally weird. They claimed they spotted it in some smoke coming from a nearby kiln."

"You're doing well, Kate lass."

"The third and last one has occurred in a place called Umm Qusr. It's a busy port right on the Iraqi-Kuwait border. It featured in the First Gulf War. Anyway, it happened on the Kuwait side. A British commercial consultant saw what resembled a pyramid in the moonlight. Both he and an American partner spotted the appearance. This was reported in the English language Egyptian Gazette just yesterday," she said. "I'll send you the document."

"Good Lord!" said Rowan. "The plot thickens. The question now is: What's happening and who's playing games with ghostly images of pyramids."

Kate spun round to see who was coming up behind her. "Oh, Mark...you surprised me."

"You have somebody there?" asked her father.

"Mark, the young engineer I told you about. He's over here for the day."

"Oh, all right," said Rowan. "I had forgotten..."

"Dad, Mark has his tablet open and there's a news item on Twitter. "Peter Singleton, the hiker picked up near the Tikiout pyramid has disappeared," she said quickly. "Wait, there's a link."

"I'm waiting,"

"His mother said the American Embassy people in Rabat put him on a direct flight to JFK Airport in New York and he failed to arrive," added Mark.

David Rowan shook his head. "Follow this one for me, Kate dear," he said. "I'm heading out to New York for a day with my publisher then heading southwest to Taos, New Mexico for the UFO Conference."

"Dad," she called out quickly. "Who is the woman standing behind you?"

"Oh," said her father with a chuckle. "This is Alice. An expert on languages, she's a translator I met at the book signing. Very intelligent." The words came uneasily with an obvious feeling of embarrassment.

"Beautiful, too," said Mark.

"Mark, you'll go far young man," quipped Rowan. "Alison will be catching the bus to London."

Everyone laughed as the Skype closed down.

5

"WHEN YOU'VE FINISHED AT the UFO thing at Taos drop in on the pyramid expert," said Alison over a coffee as they took breakfast on the patio overlooking the river.

David Rowan peered at the woman. "You sure are pushing the boat for me to see this archaeologist fellow. Are you his spin-doctor?"

Alison smiled and shrugged. Not a bit. "Last evening I suggested you meet with him and after listening to your daughter's report on what you call ghost pyramids, I think it's urgent that you call on him."

The writer paused while spreading strawberry preserves on rye toast. "So who is Hugh Geraint-Jones?"

Alison nodded. "In a nutshell, Hugh was the big attraction for teaching classical archaeology thirty years ago. Then while he and his archaeologist wife Chloe were visiting Giza in Egypt they heard of the work of Joseph A. Seiss who wrote The Great Pyramid: A Miracle in Stone. It was then they realized they had to get students to unlearn the academic norms."

"Unlearn? How unlearn?" Rowan flashed an inquisitive frown.

"The accepted teachings on Egyptology were that the pyramids were built to house the bodies and spirits of the pharaohs," she said. "Giza, the great pyramid which triggered the craze of pyramid building among the kings was not. It was and is unique. No one in mainstream science has ever figured out why it was built and who truly built it."

"Something tells me you know," he said. "Why can't you say? Do you have a block?"

The woman smiled lightly. "Geraint-Jones. He has all the information you require."

Rowan stared at the woman. "Without being rude," he said tersely. "What are you getting at."

"Your next book."

"I have no plans. Reaction from my current book is enough to send me into hiding. UFO-ites can get pretty ugly if one publicly undermines their ideology too much. Beliefs are delicate phenomena. More people have died because they sabotaged someone else's beliefs than in any aspect of life."

The writer's sharp come-back failed to bother the woman at all.

"Geraint-Jones and Chloe have all the background you need for your next book," said Alison peering over the rim of the coffee mug. "Put it this way, they will hand you all the research necessary on a golden platter."

"Alison, my dear, you're a sweet young woman, but you are starting to bother me. Give me their address," he said controlling his annoyance.

"I gave it to you last night."

"Damn! I've misplaced it."

"Typical absent-minded writer," she said. "I'll email Kate."

"You don't know her email."

"I peered over your shoulder when you were on Skype. Remember?" she said with a tantalizing laugh.

They sat and ate breakfast in silence for several minutes, enjoying the delicately fresh summer morning by the Thames both in deep thought. Kate's report on the growing number of spectral pyramids had taken them both by surprise.

"One illusion from a person spending a night in the Moroccan desert and getting dehydrated in the presence of a pyramid I can understand but now," he exclaimed opening his hands, " three more spread around the planet – Japan, China and Kuwait,"

"It's weird because there's no connection except for the fact they were all illusions," said Alison as she finished her coffee.

One thing is for sure," he said, "they're all illusions but is there a connection and if so what is it? There are too many damned questions. I'm still trying to fathom out the logic of the UFOs."

"Does there have to be logic, David?"

The writer shrugged. "For all we know they might be just a bunch of observers from different planetary systems keeping an eye on us earthlings. Flying saucers have become obsolete so now they're floating around in ghostly pyramids." He flashed a mischievous grin at the woman. "Sometimes I think the UFOs are like people watching the activities of occupants in a goldfish bowl."

"David, that's not a very nice analogy," Alison muttered with a forced grin. "But getting back to the pyramids, illusory or not, there is no connection between those and UFOs. Right?"

"Who is to say? There might well be a connection, but right now I have no idea," he said pausing to take a bite of an English biscuit. "To suggest there is a connection would get the UFO believers community up in arms. They protect their stand on unidentified flying objects with a dedication that borders classical religion."

Alison laughed lightly. "I can understand why," she said easily. "In your book you suggest that all the aliens, the ones with strange faces, black eyes, commonly known as *greys* are nothing more than humanoid robots, highly developed computerized beings whose job is to observe and report to higher beings sitting on some other planets."

"True! They have no spirit, no soul and their intelligence is subject to programming," he said, finishing his breakfast and sitting back. "If you could communicate orally with one of the greys, you would quickly drive them crazy with human logic. It's a natural fault in artificial intelligence."

Alison stood up, collected the breakfast trays and took them into the cottage. A moment later she returned. "So if the greys are humanoid robots who is pulling the strings?"

"Good question! Not only who but where are they and why?" said David. As he spoke the phone buzzed with a new text message. "It's Kate and she's telling me to check my email," he said rising.

In a few seconds they were reading the message on the laptop:

Ghost pyramids have been reported at three locations in the southern hemisphere.

(1) South of La Serena, the cruise ship port in the Coquimbo Region of Chile. Newspaper reports pyramid seen by villagers before it faded.

(2) Porto Alegre on the Atlantic coast of Brazil. Observed by two airline pilots. The pyramid appeared to float on a lake near the airport. It was raining at the time.

(3) Brief appearance of pyramid south of Brisbane, Australia near the King Konrad Mine. A photographer visiting the Minehead spotted and got a picture which is attached. Love, Kate.

David glanced at Alison standing beside him. "It would be nice if we had a wall map and made some marks on it as to the locations of these visions. Perhaps the fellow who owns this place has an atlas. Let's look around."

Then his cell phone buzzed.

"Hello, Kate. Thanks for the news."

"Dad, my friend Mark and I have been up all night. He's been putting flags on your wall map hanging in the verandah and something weird has come up?"

"You mean more than all these pyramid sightings?"

"Absolutely! The earlier ones I gave you including the Morocco sighting are all on 30 degrees latitude in the northern hemisphere, and the last lot in the southern hemisphere are in the 30 degrees south latitude."

Rowan paused and frowned. "Wow! That's ominous."

"Mark just handed me reports of two more sightings," she said, her young voice tightening with growing excitement. "Both are in the United States. We're getting details."

It was as if a brand new phenomenon was coming to roost in David Rowan's life and the problem was he really did not know the key, the fulcrum, the reason for all of this and that bothered him. Alison felt she had to go to catch the bus but David drove her into Maidenhead where she would get a direct train to Paddington in London.

Alison gave David a kiss on the lips and a warm hug. "Don't forget. After Taos, get over to Oregon and visit the Geraint-Jones couple," she said. Then turning towards the open carriage door of the train, she turned and softly dropped a bombshell.

"You have already started work on your next book so now you need to know about those who from another planet came."

"What?"

"They are expecting you!"

6

THE FIRST DAY OF THE annual gathering of the American Society for UFO and Paranormal Studies in Taos, New Mexico was gripped with excitement, tension and a fusillade of contradictory arguments. The convention theme posted over the grand entrance to the deluxe Anasazi Resort Hotel proclaimed "Invasion from Space Imminent."

Talk of UFOs was a natural drawing card for many folk from all over the south-west and even beyond but this year's theme struck at the very fear inherent in humankind – an invasion by aliens! British writer H.G. Wells opened the dark door to human phobia in 1898 and Orson Wells dramatically intensified human fears in the 1938 radio drama *The War of the Worlds*.

In Taos it was like tossing a couple of steaks into a starving lion's den. The UFO fanatics descended on the northern New Mexico town with a voracious appetite and most attendees were keen and eager to hear something that would tantalize then quell their fears.

Emotions were stoked to a new high when Grace, the over-worked, under paid chairperson of the ASUFOS revealed that someone had stolen the Society's membership list complete with email addresses the week before the conference.

This revelation along with the controversial Invasion theme drew the curious and anxious from far and wide and included supporters, defenders, rejecters, curious media crews, religious representatives, atheists and two smartly attired young men in beige summer suits which most flying saucer enthusiasts recognized as reps from the Albuquerque office of the Central Intelligence Agency.

David Rowan checked into the hotel, turned and almost collided with a heavily built tawny haired woman he recognized as the founder of the UFO society. "Grace, how good to see you. Still smoking I see. That'll get you into the next world fast."

"If the end is coming I might as well enjoy it," said the rotund woman with a short laugh. "We have a vendor table for your books, and you're on at eleven before lunch," she cried almost gleefully, then added: "If you live that long."

Rowan raised a stern eyebrow.

"Some of our members are quite irate with your latest book. In fact irate is a modification," she said quickly then leaning forward she muttered: "At tonight's barbecue one member wants to see you burned in effigy."

The writer mustered a grin. "But I was only telling the truth. Ufology has become dogmatic almost like a religion. Your society is telling people what to believe or not believe and that in my book is religious dogma."

Grace stared in silence for a moment then broke away. "I have to go -- work calls!"

David watched her go, shrugged and was about to head over to the elevator when a young voice said behind him: "I couldn't help but overhear. Are you the writer that everyone including my mother is mad about?"

The writer turned back and came face to face with a vision that immediately caught his eye. "Is Grace your mother?"

The oval face atop a neatly formed body smiled openly. The hazel eyes under two perfectly formed brows glittered with a childish merriment. Rowan observed that her hands were clasped almost in a prayer-form above her neatly formed bosom enclosed in a light yellow blouse. Her slim well formed legs appeared below tan shorts concluded in neat Indian turquoise embroidered sandals.

"Young woman are you praying for me or your mother?" he asked, attempting to maintain a serious visage.

"Both I guess," she said in a honey voice he found soothing. "Last night at the pre-convention meeting the executive committee was bent out of shape over the news that mother had invited you. They called you a heretic, crank, maverick and one director said you were the anti-Christ and prayers should be said before you speak."

"Really?"

She nodded. "He's the spiritual director. A southern Baptist minister."

"And he believes in UFOs?"

She grinned. "He claims UFOs are messengers from God."

"Wow! Heavy duty!" The writer shook his head then put out his hand. "David Rowan."

"Molly Thomsen," said the well formed lips easily. "Do you need help with books? I have a set of muscles that need a workout."

In the next hour while they set up the writer's table in the broad well lit corridor decorated with potted palms David Rowan discovered an interesting and vibrant personality. When two heavy duty characters in Star Wars tee-shirts accosted him with some obscene expletives Molly intervened and scolded them for being "narrow minded" and using "vulgar gutter words," they both took off for the bar.

"Must go and help mother," she said suddenly with a smile. Her hand reached out and clenched his arm. "You have a supporter, David."

"Really? Where?" he replied with mock surprise and a straight face.

"Me, silly!" A grin flashed easily across her face then she swept away.

David finally checked into his room, showered and changed. After the two hour drive from Albuquerque's International Sunport and the grit picked up from a commuter air flight a wash and brush up was always refreshing. Flipping open his tablet he spotted an email from Kate.

"Two calls last night. Both from a man named Frederick. Said it's urgent he see you in Taos. No, he had a protected number. Really an odd-ball character."

Rowan grinned. The nooks and crannies of metaphysics were loaded with odd characters. So-called mediums, psychics, soothsayers, dowsers, UFO spotters, abductees, flying saucer witnesses were always crawling out of the woodwork. So here was another. It was little wonder the New Mexican media in Santa Fe and Albuquerque chose to ignore the gathering of 300 people at the Anasazi Hotel and Convention Center. For the most part such conventions were repetitive and old hat. Even the Convention theme of Invasion from Space Imminent had no appeal in the minds of media assignment desk editors.

News reporting styles of three decades ago – the news media in the times of his stepfather, Paul Rowan and his long time buddy in radio, Tom Halerte had gone the way of the Dodo bird. Tim McCoy the dedicated publisher of Verity Magazine had watched in dismay as circulation dwindled with the advent of instant internet news. Consequently along with countless numbers of other top flight news magazines had been sold or become extinct. McCoy refused to convert to cyber-news and that had triggered an early death of both his publishing empire and himself. He pushed such thoughts aside.

"Frederick." He mulled over the name. Why would he call home base in Washington State if he was going to be here in Taos?

A knock at the door severed his thoughts and yielded two neatly attired youngish men perhaps in their twenties. Attired in light tan linen suits they sported identical brief cases.

"Mister Rowan? David Rowan?" asked the taller of the two men.

Rowan grinned with that cheeky smile he had maintained as long as he could remember. "You boys left your black suits at home?" he quipped as he stepped back and waved them into the room. "You forgot your gats too?"

"Gats?" said the tall man frowning.

"Before your time," commented the writer easily. "A year or so ago I wrote a mob novel of the 1920s. Those were the days when they called their weapons gats – a slang term from the old Gatling, one of the early rapid fire weapons." Rowan always enjoyed testing young men on history. It gave him a kick. "Sit down and relax. What can I do for you?"

"Jackson Devenport sends his regards."

"Jax? How is he doing?"

"His gout bothers him."

Rowan nodded and sat down on the edge of the bed and waved to the visitors to sit down. It was the old CIA man's method of showing the messengers were legitimate. Devenport was a fascinating mine of information on early American intelligence operations prior to 1947. His father had been with the Office of Strategic Services in World War II and Jax had assisted Rowan with information and photographs for his book *In Pursuit of Intelligence.*

The tall operative whose name was Jenkins seemed to be in charge. Glancing round the room his pale almost hypnotic eyes settled on Rowan. "Sir, what do you know about these people claiming that an invasion from Space is imminent? Are you a member?"

"Question two: No," said Rowan easily. "Question one: Honestly, I have no idea. I think it is the Society's angle for marketing their annual conference. It draws strange people." He flashed a cheeky smile. "It drew you guys."

"That's not why we are here," said Jenkins waving his hand as if to ward off a fly. "Have you ever heard of a young man named Peter Singleton?"

Rowan shrugged quickly. "No, should I."

"The young man had a strange encounter in southern Morocco," explained Jenkins. "The gendarme in a small coastal village of Tikiout saw the teenager one day and he was healthy and fine while exploring the beaches for the study of shells…"

"Conchology," nodded Rowan.

Jenkins continued. "Less than two days later some French honeymooners found him on the beach, seriously dehydrated and in poor shape. He claimed to have lost everything to some people he described as Egyptians in a pyramid."

"A pyramid in Morocco," muttered Rowan. "No such creature."

"Precisely! Our people in Rabat say he was the victim of hallucinations and put him on a Moroccan plane heading for JFK," said Jenkins. "Well, he never arrived. Somehow he disappeared in mid-flight."

"You're kidding!"

Jenkins shook his head. "The problem now becomes more complex. Apart from a change of shirt and pants, he had no property outside a backpack and a book."

"Book?"

"Your book, Mr. Rowan," said the CIA man. "The UFO File: Fact, Fiction or Mass Hysteria. Inside was your signature."

Rowan felt like quipping "Oh, a collector's copy," but he sensed the intense dedication to duty of the two young operatives and said with a shrug: "I sign a lot of my books. I'm an author and that's what authors do."

The other agent who had been carrying a dark brown briefcase pulled out some papers and gave them to his partner.

"When Singleton disappeared from the aircraft your book was left in the next seat," said the CIA man. "What concerns us is the page where you mention pyramids and someone, presumably the young man underlined a section." He gave the faxed sheet to Rowan who was now deeply interested.

It had been sent from the U.S. Commission in Morocco and highlighted was a paragraph: *There is a growing concern among UFO adherents that ancient pyramids scattered about the world, notably in Egypt, Eastern Europe, Central and South America are homing beacons for invaders from space. Archaeologists and many scientists have generally panned the theory stating that pyramids are nothing more than memorials, burial tombs, piles of rock from another age. It's an idea that has been listed as crazy, if not infantile. Besides, the United States has the technology and the fire power to challenge any invaders from Outer Space.*

David shrugged. "Nothing wrong with that. It's a valid statement," he said and handed the sheet back to Jenkins.

The two CIA men stood up and prepared to leave. "Oh, yes, Mr. Rowan," said Jenkins returning the sheet to the writer. "If you look at the bottom of the page you'll see there is a notation. Someone, presumably Singleton wrote *Les pyramides au-delà de l'eau claire* and then added: *Not thirty*." Jenkins peered inquisitively at Rowan. "What do you think that means?"

"It's French for the pyramids beyond the clear water," said Rowan. "Thirty? Well, I have no idea. When you catch up with Peter Singleton make a point of asking him." He flashed an easy smile to cover his thinking. Thirty degrees north was the number given to him by Kate and Mark on the location of the spectral pyramids and he was not about to divulge that information. The CIA could work that one out for themselves. Besides Jenkins was a cold faced CIA agent. "What do you suppose it means?" he said at length

"That's what we are asking you," said Jenkins smoothly.

"Well, I have no idea," Rowan shot back. "Give my regards to Jax."

Jenkins was just about to make a comment when his iPad buzzed. He paused for a moment, then glanced at Rowan and handed him a card. "If you meet a man named Klassen at the conference, call us. It's urgent."

The writer shook his head. "I'll call Devenport. What's Klassen's problem."

"He's a person of interest," said the other.

"What's Klassen's first name? Most people here don't have last names, just familiar names."

Jenkins glanced at his iPad. "Frederick," he said simply. "Frederick Klassen."

Ten seconds later Rowan was alone and totally puzzled about what was happening.

7

DAVID ROWAN DETESTED CONVENTIONS. Always had and he assumed he always would. For a while he sat as a vendor at his table positioned in the main foyer. A young woman hired by his publisher to assist in sales complained that "business is really quiet" and promptly disappeared for a ten minute break. It was a chance to call Kate.

"Two things," she said. "Your step-parents are headed this way – Paul and Natalie. They said you invited them. They'll be here mid-week."

"Wow! I completely forgot," he said quickly. "Okay. So I'll be there. They said something about visiting Mom and Saks up in British Columbia. Okay, that's fine. We'll entertain them." He paused then added: "Who else?"

"Frederick! He's really hot under the collar," she said. "He cannot understand why you are not here at Whidbey."

"It's none of his damned business where I am," grated Rowan. He detested being told by readers or fans that he should be at home or in the office. "Did he leave a phone number?"

"Oh, no! He's quite adamant about that and I refused to give him yours."

"Good girl!"

"One thing I did discover," she added. "The phone he used belongs to an Erich Steiner."

"Steiner? You're kidding!"

"Why should I do that?"

"Steiner is speaking at this Convention. In fact he's on stage right now," Rowan stood up and started a fast walk down the hall. "Talk to you later, Katie."

The spacious auditorium was loaded with at least 300 people of all ages and varieties. Most were dressed casually in colorful light shirts, pants or shorts. Some wore illustrated tee-shirts that proclaimed: "UFOs are Real!" "Roswell is Mecca" "Aliens are Welcome" "We Come in Peace" and "My Parents are Aliens." One scrawny fellow whose ragged attire was laced with drooping sunflowers resembled an aging hippy from the 1960s. A large silver flying saucer that served as a hat was clamped to his head leaving bleak watery eyes to peer uncertainly from under the saucer's brim. Several people sitting quietly wore grey suits and resembled plain-clothed police or CIA or FBI. One never knew these days. Strangely Jenkins and his buddy had disappeared.

Rowan attempting to be inconspicuous slid into a spare seat in the back row. On stage Grace had just finished introducing Steiner, an easy going wiry fellow in his thirties who had his hands tucked into his trouser pockets.

The convention brochure branded him as "famous movie producer and director" and listed productions most people had never heard about. One documentary on a West African spiritual healer was nominated for an Academy Award. Rowan recalled that Steiner's real claim to fame was a brief marriage to a fading Italian movie actress who claimed to resemble Gloria Swanson and whose great ambition was to star in a remake of *Sunset Boulevard*. Mariana, almost 20 years his senior, performed a fast exit when she discovered Steiner's focus was extraterrestrial, aliens, UFOs, and abductions. Screaming "Weirdo!" she departed and sailed across the Pacific to find renewed fame and fortune with the budding Chinese film industry.

Now Steiner was on stage at Taos. There were no notes and that appealed to Rowan. He disliked speakers who read speeches or worked from prepared statements. Steiner was an ad-libber with a sharp and clear voice.

"Things are happening of which you should all be aware," he said leaning towards the microphone hands still in his pockets. His sharp dark eyes demanded attention as they scanned the audience. Now, everyone was listening.

"Flying saucers and UFO-gazing have not changed much since the late 1940s. Lights and unexplainable things in the sky really started when someone put war on a nuclear footing. Thousands of books have been written, hundreds of movies made and people still stand on hilltops waiting for glimpses of UFOs," he said quietly.

"What are they looking for? Something to jump out and cry *Earthlings, we are here*! Well, it hasn't happened. Not yet anyway."

Steiner stepped away from the microphone then came back like a rock-singer. Seizing the microphone he cried: "Let's take a look around and see what's going on. You may pooh-pooh the folks who run around chasing crop-circles, those intricate designs appearing on farmers' fields. You may take the easy way out and side with the debunkers."

The dark brown eyes focused on a little lady smirking in the front row. "There's a farmer in England who stood helplessly by and watched while a fantastic crop circle developed in his wheatfield in less than ninety seconds," he said softly. "Now the bureaucrats and academics have the gall to proclaim it was the work of pranksters. So I tell them and I'll repeat it for you: Get new glasses!"

A murmur swept through the listeners.

"Crop circles have been registered in fifty-eight countries of the world and most are works of art. They're symbols. Now let's face the damned cold truth," he said softly. "The bottom line – whether we like it or not -- is we haven't got a clue as to what they mean or from where they originate," he shouted.

"The genetic engineers – the characters who manipulate our agriculture -- have not yet trained plants to lie flat at a moment's notice," he said with a forced grin, then added: "At least not yet."

Steiner raised his right arm and pointed to the roof. "So who, why or what is beaming down these patterns from outer space? If it's not the military, not the satellite system, it can only be one source. Extraterrestrials!"

Reaching out and pulling the microphone until it almost touched his lips, he whispered: "Are we so fucked up in our thinking that we honestly believe there's no superior civilization in God's Universe that can create crop circles – graffiti – on someone else's planet?" Dark eyes scanned the all-attentive group. "The gurus, the philosophers down through the ages have proclaimed that humanity is asleep. They were right."

A wave of applause and cheers thundered across the group.

"Are we so bound up in our own corporate-spirituality, the totally stupid belief that God, the Creator made a wonderful mind-boggling universe full of stars, galaxies, nebulae and lots of cozy little planets and decided that only one should be a breeding ground for creatures called Homo sapiens? Folks, if you really believe that, you're really in the stone age."

Another wave of applause and various people stood up and cheered. The speaker nodded and reached for a glass of water. He ceremoniously extracted a pink handkerchief from a pocket and dried his lips. Replacing it he peered at various faces in the front rows and opened his hands.

"Next, there has been a proliferation of UFO sightings. The latest being an appearance several times over a Chilean Air Force Base while a squadron was flying by. The whole episode was caught on tape."

Steiner then described claims from Pentagon and various officials in authority that many observations were "weather balloons" and other "weak-minded solutions."

The movie man paused, took a deep breath and leaning over the microphone called out: "Now hear this, one thing is very obvious and it's this. Some intelligence is flying around Earth's skies and they really don't care whether they are seen or not so we must admit this over-powering fact that if a UFO can flip around a squadron of Chilean Air Force fighters they must have (1) superior flying power and (2) superior intelligence to Earth people."

"The nitty gritty is this: The human ego is such that we do not like to think there is a superior power out there in the Universe. That a power or consciousness infinitely more advanced than ours actually exists and is watching us."

Steiner wandered across the stage seemingly in deep thought with his hands holding the sides of his face. Then, turning back to the audience he said:

"Sooner or later this Planet Earth can expect visitors from somewhere out there. The big question is this: Are we going to receive them in peace or war?"

Steiner paused to allow the question to seep into the minds of the audience.

"My thoughts are this: For many decades movie goers world-wide have been systematically programmed to fight any invaders from space with total rejection and total violence."

A projector flashed a list on the screen: *Earth versus Flying Saucers, It Came from Outer Space, War of the Worlds, Predator, The Day of the Triffids, The Day the Earth Stood Still, Skyline, Kronos, The Thing from Another World* and *Independence Day.*

"Movies have programmed audiences world-wide to reject with violence and signs of visitors from outer space. Now, we are damned sure that the Pentagon folks can be listed among the movie watchers and they are holding the big guns."

Steiner paused for another sip of water.

"Recently, the BBC in London listed the world's largest employers. Topping the list was the United States Department of Defense with 3.2 million employees. We should note the United States has military forces stationed in over 150 countries and the number of units exceeds 1,000. The Department's Defense budget is more than the defense budgets of all other countries of the world combined."

Steiner turned away and gave a mocking laugh. "Surely this is not in case some puny country like Iran or North Korea might one day flex their muscles and threaten to join the nuclear club. The great powers of the world have much too much at stake in each other's economies to trigger a conflagration requiring an immense military machine."

Raising his hand and pointing his forefinger at the ceiling he cried: In down to earth terms we can only assume that the Pentagon's intelligence folks – the ones who gave us the Iraqi debacle with so called weapons of mass destruction -- are secretly concerned about an invasion from outer space."

Carrying the microphone from its stand, Steiner walked to the edge of the stage and peered down. "If these UFOs -- space voyagers with the ability to zap around the Universe and our planet – are for real, then they must be far more advanced than the expensive stage-coach era rockets NASA has been messing around with."

"Over the years we have programmed so many Americans to believe -- particularly gun-toting Americans -- that should this country be invaded from outer space they must retaliate and shoot. This means that any chance of a peaceful welcome is aborted, finished, gone down the drain. Extinct!"

"I would like to think that our human leaders are ready to extend the hands of peace and friendship, recognize the real benefits of demonstrating Cosmic love and put away any thoughts of aggression and war."

The audience burst into a roar of cheers and applause.

As the sounds died down, Steiner concluded: So the question is: "When space gods call how do we react? I hope to hell someone gives the military the day off and asks a woman to handle the reception." Almost choking with emotions, the movie man cried: "Because our very existence, our lives, our future depends on it and I'm doubtful that men can peacefully handle the arrival of extraterrestrials."

The audience erupted, especially the women members. Some broke out cheering while some men, particularly older ones, sat and frowned as if in abject misery.

As Steiner waved and was moving to leave the stage, a lean and withered man in a light brown suit that had seen better days, his graying hair bedraggled and unkempt, staggered across the boards and grasped the microphone.

"People! Everyone! Listen. The war has already started. We shot down a UFO last week"

The room froze, conversation stopped. All eyes were on the stage.

Two burly young stewards lunged in from the side and gripping both arms of the unannounced visitor started to drag the protesting intruder away.

Grace, the Society's red haired secretary charged across the stage followed by Erich Steiner.

"Hey, wait!" cried Grace as she jerked the unfortunate man away from the stewards. "Everyone has a right to speak here."

The intruder pulled himself together and stared across at Steiner. "I'm ready to say what happened."

Steiner picked up the microphone which had fallen to the floor, looked back at the audience now breaking up and moving around. "Please be seated. You may wish to hear what my friend has to say."

In the furor David Rowan had moved down the right aisle and now seated himself in the front row.

Steiner nodded at the writer. "David Rowan, you predicted this in your book then went on to shoot down the idea. Well, things have changed," he said and gazed back across the audience.

"Ladies and gentlemen, I'd like you to meet Frederick Klassen. Until a few days ago he was employed as a civilian at the 10th Space Warning Squadron at Cavalier Air Force Station, North Dakota. The squadron operates and maintains the world's most capable phased-array radar system known as PARCS. This system monitors and tracks over half of the 23,000 earth-orbiting satellites and reports directly to the Secretary of Defense and the President."

He paused and surveyed the silent faces in the room.

"Fred Klassen was reluctant to say anything because he is in hiding. But he feels you people should know," he said with a go-ahead nod to the man.

"Three months ago, the Hubble telescope picked up a new unidentified object in the middle of nowhere. It became brighter with the passing of each day," said Klassen slowly, deliberately picking the right words to say. "Then it stopped moving and disappeared without a trace."

Klassen paused and reached for a glass of water. "Our people in North Dakota scanned the immediate area and after four days spotted the object. It resembled something similar to an earth station which orbits at a height of 240 miles or 400 kilometers," he said. "This one assumed a geosynchronous orbit – in other words it appears to stand still – at over 22,000 miles out or 36,000 kilometers."

Various people gasped.

"Its position was in the Clarke belt so named after Arthur C. Clarke the sci-fi writer and science visionary. The belt is an important area for communications satellites," explained Klassen.

"Fred, get to the meat," urged Steiner softly.

"Well, the President apparently sent a stream of messages in 52 languages to this unidentified object. Everyone assumed it was intelligent. This continued for seven days and there was no reply, in fact the UFO actually disappeared for several hours only to return to its original position and maintain a silence."

Klassen stared at Steiner as if seeking permission to continue.

"Five days ago the President sent a repeated message stating that if there was no communication between the party in space and Washington, the United States and its NATO partners would be forced to eliminate what was taken to be a threat against the welfare of this planet," said Klassen with a distinct touch of nervousness. Pausing to cough, he continued: "There was no response and two days ago an EKV was launched from Vandenberg Air Force Base."

David Rowan felt the tension growing in the group.

"EKV?" cried someone.

"An Exoatmospheric Kill Vehicle," said Klassen. "It's designed to operate outside the earth's atmosphere."

"Did it kill?" asked Steiner.

"Absolutely! The EKV flies at 22,000 miles an hour and an explosion was reported on time," said Klassen. "That's when I said enough! And left! Because I now believe we are at war with an unknown people in space."

Uproar broke out in the Convention. Secretary Grace called for silence but no one seemed to hear. Rowan edged through the crowd onto the stage towards Steiner and Klassen. It was at that particular moment the large double doors at the back of the auditorium were flung open and heavily armed police heavily clad in bullet-proof vests and helmets swept in followed by plain clothes officers.

"Rowan, help me get Klassen out of here," cried Steiner.

Moments later the trio raced helter-skelter through the hotel kitchen.

"Where the hell are we going?" cried the writer.

"Hell's a great word," cried Steiner. "Gotta get Fred to a safe spot."

"You're kidding!"

They came out into the almost blinding New Mexican sunlight and found themselves among a fleet of vendor vehicles. Grace sprang from nowhere: "The model UFO," she cried. "We call it Roswell. There's a trapdoor in the back."

Within a few seconds Klassen was hidden in a ten foot diameter silver flying saucer parked on the back of a flat deck truck.

"Listen, Steiner," whenever I get caught up with you I finish being a wanted person," muttered Rowan.

"It's for a good cause," cried the other and turning back he tapped on the panel of the flying saucer and whispered: "Fred, we'll be back for you when everything is clear." Turning to Rowan he said: "I'll buy you a beer. Come!"

Just then a big grey SUV burning rubber, roared through the parking lot and for a moment Rowan thought he spotted Molly, Grace's daughter behind the wheel. It appeared she had a passenger. The SUV zipped by the police cars and trucks parked by the Anasazi entrance and disappeared in the direction of downtown Taos. Word must have got inside because a minute later the police squad rushed out, climbed into their cars and trucks and with sirens howling gave pursuit. By then, Molly and the mysterious passenger were long gone.

Steiner grinned. "It was one of the dummy ETs. That'll fool the CIA for a while. Let's get that beer."

8

THE SUMMER SUN HIT 90 degrees Fahrenheit by mid-afternoon. The two CIA agents and State Troopers discovered the dehydrated body of Frederick Klassen when a considerate Grace opened up the UFO model to give the withered man water and food. They were not going to be fooled twice. Jenkins called an ambulance and the crowd of UFO enthusiasts watched silently as the vehicle followed by police cars joined traffic heading south along the Paseo de Pueblo Sur and headed for Santa Fe.

David Rowan and Erich Steiner watched from the patio then turned back into the cool of the hotel.

"So this country has destroyed the first legitimate UFO," Steiner remarked as he emptied his beer glass and ordered another round.

"And it happened two days ago?" quizzed Rowan. "What have we got? A cover-up? Is the media asleep?"

"It won't be after today," replied Steiner. "There was a reporter from the Santa Fe daily sitting at the back. I bet it's all over the wires right now."

A barman moving by quipped: "It was on Twitter over an hour ago."

Steiner tapped the table. "I bet the mainstream media is flocking to the White House seeking permission to use."

"Just like they did when WikiLeaks in 2011 exposed the story that China and the United States were shooting down each other's weather satellites because someone thought they were spies in the sky. Again the mainline media was asleep at the post," commented Rowan.

Steiner shook his head. "The problem is fear, David. The big corporations run the mainline media and news directors have to toe the line set by the Pentagon and the White House."

Rowan froze. "You know what you've just said?"

"It's bloody obvious. We are living in a closed society. The news isn't being censored, it doesn't even surface long enough to be censored."

"Ever since Roswell in forty-seven we have been living in a closed society," cried Grace as she approached. "Thought you guys would like to know Molly is back. I really get worried about that girl. She's a live wire."

Molly approached smiling like nothing had happened. "ET dummies come in useful at times," she said moving to Rowan's side. I get a kick out of teasing the high and the mighty."

Steiner bought beers for the women while Grace stepped aside to answer her cellphone. The heavy but vibrant woman frowned initially then nodded enthusiastically. Finishing, she closed in on the others then peered round to look for anyone in range.

"Listen, that was Cecil Maguire one of our former directors. Cecil is a rancher living in south Texas. He claims he and one of his ranch hands were out looking for stray cattle last night and in the evening light they spotted a UFO hovering over a huge pyramid…"

"Pyramid?" Rowan's eyes shone with sudden interest.

"It was there on a desert plateau for almost a minute," she said quickly. "Now, here's the clincher. He says they both spotted a UFO hovering close by. Then in a flash, both disappeared."

Steiner peered at Grace. "Where?"

"Hey, I have the address. High Sierra Ranch. It's south of a place called Marfa."

"Marfa?" put in Rowan. "Isn't that the place where they're always seeing strange lights?"

"The same. But this is a handful of miles south of there," said Grace. "One other thing. Maguire says they also hear people's voices in the same area and there's no one around for miles."

Steiner broke away. "I'm heading south, David. I'd like to video this fellow for a show I'm doing."

"That is 600 miles south of here," cried Grace. "That's a ten hour drive through Albuquerque and El Paso."

Steiner laughed briefly. "Who's talking about driving?"

"Holy dingbats! I forgot. You have a little thing called a Cessna Caravan," cried Molly jubilantly. "It's a quiet afternoon at the Convention and mother can look after the action. Can I come?"

Steiner nodded then glanced at Rowan. "Are you in?"

"Me? Wouldn't miss this for the world," he said enthusiastically, but his inner self was sensing trouble. Too many things were happening in too short a space of time. UFOs, crop circles, pyramids that appeared in the mist then disappeared and now the United States has done what he and Steiner feared the most: Reacted to a UFO with violence which could well have sounded the trumpets of a cosmic war.

"Maybe it's the start of the war of the worlds near Marfa, Texas," cried Molly.

"Don't be too glib about that," said Rowan. "The shooting has already started out in space. That's what Klassen's announcement was all about."

9

BY LATE AFTERNOON THE trio was over Marfa a small town with a big reputation in south-west Texas. Created in the 1880s as a railroad community, it was the home of a USAF training squadron in World War II, then Hollywood discovered the place and for two months in 1956 it was the set for the movie "Giant" with Elizabeth Taylor, Rock Hudson, James Dean, Carroll Baker and Dennis Hopper. Several movies were subsequently filmed there and eventually someone hit on the idea of a movie festival which has since become an annual event. It's also a gathering place for budding artists seeking galleries to hang their canvasses.

But for paranormal enthusiasts it is the Marfa Lights that attracts thousands each year. The phenomenon started in 1883 and on clear nights it can be viewed south-west between the town and Paisano Pass.

"They shine in various colors and twinkle," Molly leaned forward and told Rowan sitting in the co-pilot's seat. "They jump about, split, move together, frequently disappear and when you think they're done for the night they reappear. I think they're cheeky. Presidio County built a viewing station east of town on U.S. 67 near the site of the old air base," she cried over the hum of the Pratt and Whitney turboprop engine. The whole place has energy – metaphysical energy.

The High Sierra Ranch is close to the Big Bend National Park a high desert area laced with mountain ridges and sierras loaded with ample grasslands. A controversial region it sits on the border between the United States and Mexico and is separated only by the Rio Grande River. A nice easy landing, the Cessna churned up clouds of white dust as it trundled along the unpaved airstrip leading to a large wooden sign that had seen better days. "Welcome to the High Sierra." Close by basking in the afternoon sunshine was a cluster of ranch houses and a large barn topped with an array of solar panels and surrounded by a scattering of oak, pinion and juniper.

The Cessna swung to a standstill by two tall figures leaning against a dusty light blue SUV. As the trio climbed down a lean cowboy stepped forward and hugged Molly who promptly introduced him as Cecil Maguire. "He's one of the Society's longest members," she said. "He used to be a great board director until he bought this ranch."

Rowan nodded an introduction. Maguire resembled the young Clint Eastwood when he starred in *Rawhide* back in the early 1960s. The rancher's Texas drawl eased itself over every sentence that came forth as he introduced his dark-skinned manager named Chuck, a sturdy looking young man of Mexican-Spanish origin.

"Heck of an investment: UFO aficionado buys a ranch then sees UFOs on the property," said Steiner flashing a grin.

"Sure thing. May be they're jest followin us," drawled Maguire. "Need help with your camera gadgetry?"

Steiner shook his head. "It's a portable video-sound unit. Just right for desert stuff," he said handing the case and tripod to Chuck. "Now where did you make the sighting?"

"About two miles up the draw. We had a few head of cattle up there but they moved to a lower level which is strange because they normally like the feed up there. Funny thing, we both heard a faint hum, a tone coming from up there. But there was nothing to see – until we got there."

Fifteen minutes later the SUV stopped on the edge of a grasslands plateau. A trickling stream almost dried up, flanked the edge and a sharp rocky ridge protected the far side of the plateau. Several squatting fat junipers broke the plateau's monotony.

Rowan and Molly walked across the rough grass and found cattle hoofmarks and droppings. "There's nothing that would show that either a pyramid or even a UFO were here," he said to her. They turned back to Steiner setting up the camera unit on the tripod. "There's not even an indentation."

Molly stared at the tall grass long and parched in clumps from the hot summer sun. "Look David, the tall grass over there near the rocks is bent towards the north-east. The prevailing winds are from the south-west." She gripped his arm and said slowly: "Look at the tall grass in the middle. It's bent southwards which means there was a force coming in from the north."

Steiner came up and stared. "Heck, you're right, Molly. You must have been an Indian tracker in a past life," he retorted easily. "But you're right. There was a force or something here."

"Not was," said the woman slowly, shading her eyes from the sun. "It's still here."

"You're kidding," laughed Rowan.

Maguire stood watching the trio. "Molly's a great intuitive. I was supposed to buy this place on a Friday and Molly urged me to settle on a Wednesday. Good thing I did because the seller died next day."

A tension in the air. Rowan suddenly felt it and his skin tightened and felt distinctly itchy. He glanced at the others and spotted a similar reaction. Steiner walked quickly back to the camera, set it on wide angle and hit the "record" button. "Insurance," he said hustling through his baggage. "If anything happens I want it on tape."

Steiner ran towards the group clasping a canister. "Rowan, you said that pyramids have normally been spotted in the twilight or in a mist or smoke. Well, I have the smoke." He placed it on a small rock among the bunch of tall grass bending towards the south.

"Hey, Erich," Molly yelled, "Are you crazy?"

"It doesn't burn. It just bellows smoke. Lots and lots of smoke."

A jet of white smoke spouted high into the air. The group instinctively pulled back. The two ranchers moved behind the SUV while Rowan and Molly walked quietly to the side. Steiner stayed in front of the rolling camera. Within a minute a cloud of grayish white smoke floated slowly across the plateau energized by a slight breeze from the south-west. As the cloud grew bigger it revealed distinctive lines towering up into the sky.

"Oh, shit," yelled Steiner. "I should have brought a panorama lens. The thing's too damned big for my angle." Even as he fiddled with the camera the smoke revealed a huge section of slanting walls towering up to a peak. "It's a bloody pyramid, Rowan. A bloody great pyramid!"

"Oh, mother of god," cried Molly. "I don't believe this.

Rowan hastily pulled out a digital camera and started pulling back to get as much of the pyramid into the picture as possible. "We are too damned close," he cried to no one in particular.

Steiner seized the video cameras with the tripod and started running back toward the edge of the plateau to find a better all embracing view. "It's too big, much too big."

Suddenly he stopped. His ears picked up a sound that was out of sync with this desert location. Frowning, he peered through the afternoon sun and thinning smoke at the mountain silhouettes. "Look there's a UFO coming."

Over the distant ridge a dark spot hedge-hopped across rocks and ridges and swept across the grassland of the plateau seemingly oblivious of the pyramid.

"It's a black helicopter," cried Rowan. "Probably CIA or Homeland Security."

Steiner panned the camera and zoomed into the oncoming helicopter for a close-up.

"A Sikorsky UH60-M," cried Rowan then suddenly he stopped realizing the helicopter was heading straight for the pyramid and disaster. "The stupid pilot hasn't seen it."

"The guy is blind. Everyone is going to die," cried Molly wringing her hands. 'He just can't see it."

Even as she spoke, the helicopter sliced into the image of the great building and everyone waited for an explosion. But nothing happened. Not a sound. Not even the sound of a helicopter engine. The entire helicopter has disappeared. Molly stood beside the men on the desert rock waiting for the explosion.

"It's actually gone inside," cried Steiner excitement running high. "The bloody pyramid must have gobbled them up. Nobody's going to believe this."

Suddenly, the throbbing sound of the helicopter came again and the flying machine emerged from the nearest wall of the pyramid. The black machine flew dangerously close to the group then slowly veered to the left careening into a dive. It crashed into a rocky ridge below the plateau. A thunderous explosion slammed through the air and each one felt the vibrations. Each one knew they had witnessed a deadly disaster.

"Oh, those poor people aboard that thing," choked Molly.

"Did you get that, Erich?" cried Rowan.

"Got it coming out. Sure, but I missed the crash though," he called out pulling his camera unit off the tripod. "Let's get over there."

Molly and the two ranchers intent on giving help to any survivors were already running down the slope towards the burning machine, its blades tangled hideously among the rocks. Steiner ran with the video and Rowan followed. A mushroom cloud of white and orange smoke hung over the scene and flames were spluttering out of the tangled wreckage strewn between several boulders. Steiner stopped, raised the camera and started filming. Rowan walked to the side and took stills.

Then above the crackling helicopter fire there came a new sound.

They all heard it at the same time. A second helicopter! Another black Sikorsky skirted the west ridge and hurtled towards them completely oblivious of the now fading pyramid. The crew members had spotted the crash and were now heading for that location.

The next few minutes were chaotic. Armed police and homeland security officers leapt from the helicopter and hustled around the burning ruins of the ill-fated machine. One officer took photos while others peered inside the tangled wreckage.

As the ranchers and the group turned up two armed police held them back. "Did you witness this accident?" said one. "The director has some questions."

"I bet he does," growled Steiner. "This one is going to take some explaining."

"Try me," said a new voice coming up from the wreckage. "First of all, we need to borrow your video camera to examine your tapes. We'll see you get them back once they're cleared."

David recognized the voice from Washington, DC.

"Jackson Devenport. He's CIA. Director for the Investigation of the Paranormal," he said and introduced each one. "He's also known as Jax."

The heavily built Devenport removed his helmet and wiped the beads of perspiration from his forehead. "For a city writer, Mr. Rowan you sure are a long way from home."

"It wasn't planned, I can assure you."

Two officers took Steiner's camera, placed it in a box marked "Evidence." They left the tripod and the accessories bag. Steiner was about to protest when Molly held a finger to her lips and said: "Erich, silence is golden."

Devenport looked around and finally said to Rowan: "What the hell happened here?"

Cecil Maguire intervened. "Why don't we go over to the ranch and talk about it."

"Well, I hope you've got some damned good answers," muttered Devenport. "When that Sikorsky crashed eight officers were supposed to be on board."

"Supposed to be?" quizzed Rowan

"When our bird crashed there was no one on board. Not even a bloody pilot."

10

THE NEXT MORNING DAVID Rowan dived into the deep end of the open-air swimming pool at the Anasazi Resort Hotel and performed ten laps before he spotted someone watching so he stopped, brushed the water from his eyes and looked up.

It was Molly in a very neat white bikini style swimming outfit that seemed to match her streamlined and well defined body. Some of the UFO crowd liked to brand her as an Amazon, one of those Greek mythological women warriors that appealed to so many writers down the ages. If one was into mythology, Rowan thought of her as a Greek goddess, perhaps an Aphrodite who had spent some of her days not on a sandy shore but in a Grecian gymnasium pumping iron. Her light brown hair touched with delicate blonde streaks was well kept and framed a beautiful face that was always expressive, usually happy although it could turn cold when angry. It was one of those photogenic faces beloved by movie directors, in other words Molly's visage was easy to read.

But her assets were not in just looks. Her mind was intellectual, amazingly warm and understanding in spite of her hurts. Upon returning from the violent pyramid experience near Marfa the night before they had dined together in a comfortable Byzantine-style restaurant in downtown Taos where they ate mussels simmered in an exquisite garlic and herb sauce. Somehow as two energies are often brought together by the Cosmic Law of Attraction they found their lives strangely coincidental.

Molly was born to a Buffalo, New York couple. Clark Thomsen was a Canadian-born welder who specialized in oil rigging construction and maintenance while Grace Thomsen was a high school teacher. "We never knew when dad was going to be home and mom gave up trying to figure things out. She built her own social life. When not teaching she was a ten-pin bowler and later when she saw the light, she became involved in searching for extraterrestrials and UFOs. She always liked being active and still does."

Molly paused to sip a Californian Merlot and for a few moments it enriched the shape and beauty of her lips but then a serious frown flickered across her brow.

"When I was four, tropical storm Claudette swept through the Gulf of Mexico and instead of evacuating with the others Dad stayed behind on the rig. It was July 1979. They said he drowned in a boat that capsized heading for the Texas shore. They never found his body. He used to call tropical storms – Gnat's piss." Molly shrugged as if trying to throw off the hurtful memories.

"Mom eventually got herself a new boyfriend and he had his eyes on me from the day he stepped into the house. Something inside me, a voice told me to get a weapon. At a second-hand store on Main Street I bought a British policeman's old wooden truncheon – a nightstick. The man said it was loaded with lead and to be careful. You might hurt someone, he said."

The frown increased on her forehead and David wanted her to stop but when he tried to interrupt she shook her head.

"A week later the boyfriend sneaked into my room and started undressing. When he hadn't got a stitch on I brought the truncheon down onto his head," she said with a touch of anger. "It was like hitting a pumpkin. There were brains everywhere. The worst part was mom complaining about having to clean up the room."

"What did the police say?" asked Rowan overly curious.

"Nothing! They said he was a convicted sex offender, besides they failed to find the weapon. The coroner said the man was intoxicated and sustained fatal injuries when his head struck a concrete fireplace."

"What happened to the weapon?"

Molly flashed a mischievous grin. "I hid it. It was an old brass bed and if you took the knobs off the main legs you could hide things like a truncheon inside. It slipped all the way to the bottom. They never found it. Mom sold the bed and if it is still being used somewhere the owners are probably unaware that the deadly nightstick is there."

"You're a devious little thing."

"Little? I was then. Afterwards I started thinking well of myself and when I was twelve I started bodybuilding then switched to martial arts and by the time I was twenty-five I had so many cups and ribbons to fill a whole room, so I quit."

Rowan tilted a glass of wine. "You're quite a woman, Molly. Quite a woman!"

Molly's hazel eyes scanned the writer's face carefully. "Your bio – the one on your book cover -- is about as shallow as a dried up fish pond."

"Me? Oh, I was a bastard. Illegitimate. My biological dad was a Quebecer named Monk. He ditched mom the day I was born up in Canada. They say he died trafficking drugs out of Mexico," he said with a shrug. "Something like that."

"And mom?"

"Oh, she's a neat little woman named Jenny. Lives in the wilds of British Columbia with a heck of a great Indian fellow named Saks – Saks Bellefleur. A great guy, he teaches young kids to play the Indian pentatonic flute. Has trouble walking. He broke both legs in the cataclysm of '79 and the bones failed to set properly. He doesn't have time for doctors."

"Wow!"

"Yes, wow!" he grinned. "My stepfather is Paul Rowan, retired international newsman, and my stepmother is a honey-blonde named Natalie. A great couple. Took me with them all over the world. Consequently I was home schooled mostly. When they put me into the Alexander Mackenzie University in British Columbia to study Journalism, the professor thought I was a know-it-all until he found out about Paul, then we got on like a house on fire."

"That's a quaint expression."

"What? House on fire? It's as old as the hills. That's another," he said and they both laughed easily.

Then David told her about Carla, a rising concert pianist, how they had lived in Washington, DC and were graced with a beautiful daughter named Kate. "We thought life was perfect. Carla's music was in demand everywhere and she performed at the Lincoln Center, the Albert Hall in London and the Sydney Opera House in Australia." The writer paused and looked at the water. "Then three years ago while driving home from New York – it was a terrible night. A late snowstorm hit the New Jersey Turnpike. They said it was a white out. A multi-vehicle pile-up. She died on the way to hospital and the bottom fell out of my life."

Molly reached out and touched his arm. "Damn it, David, I can feel your hurt," she said quickly. "I'm sorry I intruded."

He patted her hand and felt her vibrant energy and it felt good. "You're a kinesthetic. You read psychic energy?"

"A little. Some years back I followed the Rosicrucians for a couple of summers." Her eyes met his and in that moment David knew Molly was becoming a force in his life. "So how did you come to move to the west coast?"

"We had enough of Washington DC so one day Kate and I packed our stuff and moved across the country to Washington State and a place called Admiral's Cove on Whidbey Island. It's part of the famous Puget Sound so it's beautiful and quiet – mostly."

Molly's hand stayed on David's arm and her beautiful hazel eyes searched his face and dark brown wavy hair. "Does Carla's passing still bother you?"

A slight frown simmered on his brow. "Yes. I suppose it does. You know, I've met several beautiful and talented women I would like to know better and each time a hand, perhaps a wall of invisible energy sets up and blocks any movement on my part."

"Perhaps you are trying too hard, David.

"It's not the sex, the love-making," he said quickly. "It's making a commitment for living, loving and enjoying life together. That's important to me."

"Me, too," said Molly. "That's why I've never married. All the possible candidates were too busy. Texting at breakfast, texting while having sex, texting while having a shower…you name it they were busy. Once I had a short relationship with an air force drone controller. He couldn't sleep, kept on waking up with nightmares. Technology is the sin of the world. It's going to wreck the so-called civilized world."

David took Molly's hand and looking into her eyes, shook his head gently. "I may be nuts saying this, but do you think you could get me started? Just come to my room, share a hot chocolate and share a bed. I sense you have warmth in your body that appeals to my soul."

"Just good friends?"

"Absolutely."

"No sex?" she said softly.

"Not tonight. Not yet."

"David, ever since I met you I have the feeling that we must have been soul mates in a past life."

He laughed. "You believe in that stuff?"

"After what happened this afternoon with the helicopter I'm starting to believe a lot of new things."

And so Molly Thomsen and David Rowan shared a deluxe bed at the Taos Anasazi Resort and the next morning he rose early and went swimming and that was where Molly came and found him.

"David, we have a visitor," she said.

"Who?"

"Erich Steiner. He's not in good shape. He's in your room waiting for you."

11

"ROWAN," SNAPPED THE FILM maker as soon as the writer still in swimming trunks but wrapped in a large white towel entered the room along with Molly. "The CIA thinks the pyramid thing is an elaborate hoax."

"Oh, give me strength," cried Rowan as he grabbed some clothes and went into the bathroom to dress. "It doesn't make sense."

"Try telling that to Devenport and his cronies."

"He is supposed to be director of metaphysical stuff at spymaster central," called out Rowan.

"Well, he says the whole pyramid thing was a set up and we used it to kidnap eight CIA storm troopers and wreck a helicopter all for movie purposes."

"When did these accusations happen?"

"Late last night. They were looking for you at the Convention."

"They got your film, right?" said Rowan coming back into the room, pushing his white shirt tails into his slacks and then flipping a zip.

"Well, yes and no."

"What's that supposed to mean."

"On my camera rig, I have the main 16mm film sound camera. They confiscated the reels and had them processed and printed in Albuquerque and sent back about midnight.

It showed exactly what I had shot, the pyramid, the chopper coming in, disappearing and then coming out again and crashing." Steiner took a fast breath. "No problem."

"Then what is the problem?" put in Molly as she poured coffee and handed it out.

"Well, it's an old trick," said Steiner. "The pan and tilt head is designed to hold the master camera and a small copy camera. The copy camera is digital and it films everything the master camera shoots."

Rowan peered over the rim of his coffee mug. "There's a difference between the movie film and the video?"

"You've been hanging around too many psychics," muttered Steiner. "But the answer is yes. The video is not quite identical." He flipped open his laptop and watched as the unit booted up.

The video started playing. The trio stood watching the appearance of the pyramid in the smoke, then the arrival of the first helicopter. They watched as it disappeared and then started to re-appear.

Steiner stopped the video. "Now just before I pan to follow the pilotless helicopter, something appears. Watch!"

The video continued and in the split second before the camera pans away, an energy form appears right outside the pyramid walls. "It's a person," cried Molly excitedly. "Look, he's standing there watching."

"Roll it back a frame to where he appears," Rowan's voice was suddenly tight with excitement. As Steiner did so the writer pushed through his brief case and extracted several photographs.

"Take a look. These shots were taken in a little town named Tikiout in southern Morocco. A British gal took the picture of a spectral pyramid and her husband, a professional photographer, took this picture in the gendarme's office. It's a young man suffering dehydration. His name is Peter Singleton."

Molly and Steiner stared at the photograph, then at the image on the video taken at Marfa, Texas. "It's the same person," Molly announced while her face contorted in sheer mystery. "It can't be."

"Now, here's the kicker," muttered Rowan. "The American Foreign Service placed Peter Singleton on board a plane at Agadir heading for JFK. The crew claimed he simply disappeared in mid-flight."

Steiner tossed his arms in the air. "So what's this kid doing outside a pyramid in Marfa, Texas?"

"The mystery thickens," said Rowan. "The CIA says a copy of my book *The UFO File: Fact, Fiction or Hysteria* was found in his backpack where Singleton was slumped by the Tikiout pyramid. Inside was a scrawled note which said: Les pyramides au-delà de l'eau claire." Why would this mystery kid have a copy of my book?"

"Which translated means?" put in Steiner.

Rowan thought for a moment then said: "The pyramids beyond the clear water."

"That sure doesn't answer why this strange mystery kid should have a copy of my book when I really don't believe in metaphysics."

Molly's eyes sparkled. "No wonder the CIA are taking a good look at both of you. There's a conspiracy afoot."

The exhausted Steiner flopped out in the deep leather arm chair while Molly performed Reiki healing on his head and shoulders. Rowan called Kate at the Whidbey Island home base and found her all excited about the upcoming Whidbey Island Annual Fair in Langley. "You missed it last summer Dad but you could take it in this year. It's the end of next week. Mark and I will take you."

"Hey I thought it was a dad's job to take his kids out," snipped Rowan.

"Dad, you're past that now, behave," chipped Kate authoritatively. "Where are you? I have several messages for you?"

"Taos. The UFO Convention."

"Boring, I suppose"

"Like a burning bush! It's starting to steam if I may use the expression."

Kate laughed and her father mentally cringed. It was just like Carla. "When will I let her go and get on with my life?" he thought. It felt utterly cruel to be haunted by memories of a woman he loved so much.

"Dad, here's what's new. Lee and Erica Freemont, they are wine experts…"

"Inveterate boozers," he chipped in.

"They want you over early next week for lunch," Kate continued regardless. "John Christian wants you to do a lecture at the Island Book Club and Mike Boulter, the retired auto-mechanic who lives two doors down, collects antique cars, well he wants you to see the 1939 Dodge pick-up Paul and Natalie drove…"

"Wow! Diesel Boulter! I knew he was restoring it. Has he finished?"

"Apparently," she said, her voice sounding so incredibly efficient.

"Maybe he could take us for a ride in it and we can get some pictures," he said. "Your Grandmother Jenny would love that."

Kate ignored the comment. "Listen, Hugh Geraint-Jones called. You asked me to send him a copy of the Tikiout pyramid in Morocco. Well, he's all worked up about it and says he needs to see you urgently at Nehalem, Oregon. I've emailed his address."

"That's strange," muttered David. "A woman I met in London said it was vitally important for me to meet Geraint-Jones for information to be used in my next book. Now the archaeologist himself wants to see me."

"Geraint-Jones says if he's right, there's absolutely no chance of you writing another book," she said as if picking her words carefully. "He maintains these pyramids are spectral replicas of the Great Pyramid at Giza in Egypt and the images are an omen of the coming Doomsday."

"Oh, crap! I wanted some hard information on the Giza pyramid not some wisecracker predicting the end of the bloody Earth," Rowan snapped.

"Well, I did reel off the list of pyramid appearances and he almost had a fit," cried Kate. "He said he caught the Frederick Klassen at Taos fiasco on Twitter. Apparently someone videotaped the action and it's running on YouTube. Geraint-Jones claims it's the Doomsday scenario being played out and he can explain it to you."

12

DAVID ROWAN WAS ALL set to enthusiastically drive the 1,400 miles across New Mexico, Colorado, Utah, Montana to Oregon in two days until Molly made him see sense and travel by regular air from Albuquerque via Los Angeles and then to Salem, Oregon. "My teaching job is dead until September," she told him. "I would love to see what this fellow Geraint-Jones has to say."

"Hey, people," cried Steiner, "I adore archaeologists and guess what? I have a plane sitting on the tarmac at Taos Airport. This Doomsday fellow is intriguing."

"You just want to get away from the CIA gang," said Molly giving Steiner a playful jab.

By mid-afternoon the trio had flown North West, circled the Pacific Ocean with its white capped waves racing across the wide stretch of golden sand beach lining the Oregon shore. The Cessna Caravan touched down on the strip at the beautifully tree-lined Nehalem Bay State Airport and half an hour later Rowan was paying off a cab outside a Bavarian-style chalet that must have been old during World War I. Extremely picturesque with an English country rose garden dominating the landscape the house perched majestically on a rocky tor that overlooked the ocean to the west and the scarred forest lands of the Cascade Mountains to the east.

"Scarred! That's a good word snarled Geraint-Jones shaking his head vigorously. "The damned bloody loggers clear-cut everything then planted flimsy little seedlings claiming they will grow and replace the old forests. Ha! Not in my lifetime."

"Hughey!" snapped Chloe with a frown. "You know your blood pressure skyrockets every time you talk about that. Besides these folk are not here for the forests."

"Aye! I'm sorry," said the old professor with a smirk. "Have to please the little woman."

Hugh Geraint-Jones was one of those elderly people who maintain a youthful image. This was in spite of a mop of bushy sandy gray hair atop a square face that was half hidden by a bristle beard and a close trimmed moustache. Attired in a white linen short-sleeved shirt with baggy beige cotton slacks, well worn brown leather sandals completed the image.

"Tea everyone?" cried Chloe, her pale blue eyes dancing happily.

Before anyone could answer her husband chipped in: "Would a nip of Scotch be more appropriate?"

"Hughey, the sun has not gone down yet."

They all settled for iced tea and while the two were in the kitchen they all agreed Hugh and Chloe were something else.

"He's a young spirit in an aging body," Rowan muttered softly to Steiner.

"Or vice versa," replied the other. "For documentary movies he's a natural."

Molly laughed lightly. "He's the sort I would like to have as a grandfather," but I can't wait to hear what he has to say.

Within a couple of minutes they were sipping cool ice tea and comfortably installed in the spacious living room which like a museum was adorned with framed ancient photos on the walls along with old swords, religious icons, tribal masks and other artifacts.

Rowan with a keen desire to discover why they had come to Oregon popped the question: "Hugh, what did you make of the picture of the Tikiout pyramid? My daughter Kate said you found it quite exciting?"

"Exciting? My God! It's incredible!"

"Why?"

"It's a replica of the one and only, the unique Great Pyramid at Giza. All the other pyramids are inferior, devoid of intellectuality and mysticism. In effect they are bungling imitations of the Great One."

"I understood it was built as the last resting place of Cheops," suggested Steiner reaching for his bag and pulling out his camera.

"Not yet Mr. Demille," growled the professor then shaking his heavy mop of sandy gray hair added: "The Great Pyramid was not built as a tomb, a mausoleum, and certainly not as some so-called experts suggest, a monument or a cenotaph. That's lazy academic speculation when they have nothing else to say." He paused. "No, in fact the Great Pyramid of Giza was a directional and homing beacon for incoming spacecraft."

Rowan blinked. "What makes it so different from the other 130-plus Egyptian pyramids?"

"Ah, lad!" snapped Geraint-Jones breaking into a classroom mode, "It was the only one designed with an upward gallery, all the rest are downward," he said. "It's also the only pyramid with pure sacred geometry. It has a nine to ten design. For every ten feet that its corners retreat diagonally they rise upward to salute the sun by nine feet – nine being the prime number of the Universe. Nine keeps on coming up in anything one measures at Giza."

Steiner opened his laptop and brought up the movie he had shot near Marfa in Texas. "Is this pyramid identical to the one in southern Morocco?"

The professor peered intently at the screen. "Ah, it's better than the Tikiout pyramid."

"How?" Rowan opened his hands for an explanation.

"The spectral image is floating just above the desert," cried the scholar easily. "Look at the corner base. What's that?" He pointed to the screen.

"A shoe?"

"Absolutely! It's a construction socket," he said peering triumphantly back at Rowan and Steiner. "Each corner of the Great Pyramid has such sockets. It's one of the aspects that make the Great Pyramid unique." Pausing, he sipped the honey and lemon iced tea. "The builders of the Giza pyramid knew Earth alignments. They knew the poles and they knew exactly where to position the Great Pyramid half way between the equator and the North Pole. They set it at latitude 30 degrees north."

Rowan suddenly came to life. "Wait a minute, Hugh. All these spectral images of pyramids – Tikiout, Umm Qasr in Iraq, Zhejiang south of Shanghai, China, Kuchino-Shima, a small island off Japan..."

"Don't forget the two in the United States – Kingsley Lake, Florida and the one in the Big Bend Desert south of Marfa, Texas," chipped in Steiner enthusiastically, "They're all on 30 degrees latitude north."

Rowan placed the laptop on the table. "And now we are getting reports of pyramids in Brazil, South Africa and even south of Brisbane, Australia," he commented as he stood up. "They're all on a latitude of 30 degrees south."

"So where is all this leading?" asked Molly standing by the railings. "What is someone or something trying to prove? We had reports from the rancher Maguire that he and his hand spotted a UFO and heard mysterious voices in the vicinity of the Marfa pyramid."

The old professor was quiet as if mulling over his thoughts. Then he sighed briefly and said quietly: "I may be wrong but I have a distinct feeling they are coming back?"

"Who?" asked Steiner.

"The people who built the Great Pyramid."

"Didn't the Egyptians?" asked Rowan.

The archaeologist shook his head.

Rowan insisted. "All the pundits, all the books say it was the Egyptians."

"They were the manpower, slaves if you like. The architecture of the Great Pyramid is so perfect that even today modern engineers with super-technology cannot repeat the construction of the Great Pyramid. Japan and others tried and failed miserably."

"So who created – designed if you like -- the Great Pyramid?" cried Steiner.

"A line of people known as Nefilim," said Geraint-Jones. "They are also known as the Anunnaki -- those who from Heaven to Earth came. They arrived on earth from another planet 430,000 years ago and their presence changed the way the human race developed. In fact the legacy they left is still with us today in many of the things we do. For instance there is the metric system."

"So why the spectral pyramids?" quizzed Rowan, his skeptical mind trying to grasp what he had heard.

Geraint-Jones shrugged. "They're coming back and from what I hear they are not getting a good reception."

"You mean the Klassen revelation?" put in Steiner quickly.

"Absolutely! When the gods knock on your door the last thing you do is shoot them to pieces," said the professor with a tight grimace. "The problem is we've brought up several generations of Americans with a gun-slinger Billy-the-Kid mentality. For years we have been entertained and indoctrinated through movies, theater and media. The message has taken root in the average American mind: If you want to live shoot first, ask questions after."

The archaeologist stared at each one of the visitors. "The problem is the gun-slingers are in the Pentagon and they have their fingers on the triggers of the world's largest arsenal – the American Defense System."

Before anyone could say anything, a voice called from the deck outside. "Supper?" cried Chloe. "We are eating on the patio. The view of the Pacific is beautiful from here..."

Suddenly, Rowan felt as if the whole thing he was thinking was wrong. Terribly wrong. This wasn't something that he could easily debunk. Somewhere deep inside he wanted to tell Geraint-Jones that talk of space visitors with superior knowledge coming and building a perfect pyramid was totally stupid. Unscientific. Unreasonable. And the idea that they might be coming back, well that was as cock-eyed as flying saucers. But then what was the Marfa pyramid hovering above the desert? Was that a UFO? Suddenly he felt confused.

"I'll tell you more after supper," said the professor leading the way onto the deck.

"There's more?" grated Steiner.

"Oh, he's only just started," commented Chloe with a dainty smile.

13

IT WAS MID-AFTERNOON in Taos when the CIA team at Taos realized that certain key people they were supposed to be observing had disappeared.

"A staffer from Enterprise came and picked up Rowan's rental and the Thomsen woman's car is still on the lot but she was missing from this afternoon's convention sessions," Jenkins told the director. "Her mother pleads ignorance and says her daughter is a high flyer. Whatever that means."

Devenport had absolutely no desire to hear such annoying totally useless trivia. A bowl of chili and a Mexican beer in the Anasazi Lounge had prompted a late afternoon siesta. Now he had a hangover. From what? A beer? He paced nervously across the apartment while cleaning his thick tortoise shell horn rimmed glasses with a handkerchief.

"And the movie fellow? Steiner?"

"Gone! The Cessna took off with a flight plan to Dallas."

Wise the other agent living up to his name put in: "That's strange. Is Dallas north-west of Taos? The plane took off and headed towards Utah."

"Oh, crap!" muttered Devenport angrily. Frustrated he picked up the hotel phone. "Is Molly Thomsen still registered here?" He paused then slammed down the receiver. "She's bolted too."

Impatiently, he booted up his laptop. "Did either of you check the bugs in Rowan's room?"

"If Rowan's checked out we should go and get them back," said Jenkins. "Neither of them worked. The guy with the van and the technology stuff hightailed it back to L.A." He glanced uneasily at the director who was known to emotionally hit the roof over staff incompetence.

Devenport walked across to the window and stared down at the UFO enthusiasts taking a break and milling outside the convention center. "This place is screwed up and haunted or something. All I want is some positive news."

After washing his face, cleaning his horn-rimmed glasses and checking his balding head he led his team downstairs. As they stepped from the elevator

Jenkins' cell phone buzzed. Twenty seconds later he told the others. "Langley photo analysis has identified the person standing outside the Marfa pyramid as Peter Singleton," he said closing the phone. "The kid from Morocco who disappeared on a flight..."

"Yeah! Yeah!" growled Devenport. "So now he turns up in Texas. What is he, a spook?"

Wise normally an agent of few words suddenly spoke up. "It could be the image Steiner filmed out in the Big Bend Desert is part of the pyramid projection and the kid is not really there at all."

The CIA director stared at the agent. "What makes you think that?"

"Well, the ranchers did say they had seen a UFO circling the pyramid when they first saw it," Wise said quickly.

"Wait, you think these pyramids are spectral UFOs?" muttered Devenport his beady eyes behind the thick glasses scrutinizing the agent.

Jenkins stepped in. "Jax, there is a theory that most of the crop circles appearing in some 55 countries of the world can only be projected on the planet from Outer Space. In other words from UFOs." He took a breath. "These pyramids could also be projections."

Devenport thought for half a minute. "That is something I really don't want to hear, but as you have raised the subject, let's go for the next question. Why? Why are they doing this?"

Both agents shrugged.

"One thing really bothers me," continued Devenport, "the presence of David Rowan. "I've known the writer for years and he's a dogged type. Doesn't let go. He did a history on the early days of the CIA and my father's role in it and I helped him out."

"It's weird but his name keeps cropping up," said Jenkins. "The kid was reading an author-signed copy of Rowan's book at the Tikiout pyramid scene in southern Morocco. The kid disappears off a trans-Atlantic flight and leaves the book on the plane. Rowan is present when Steiner films the Big Bend Desert pyramid in Texas."

Wise chipped in: "Rowan is here at the conference selling his books..."

"And he sees Frederick Klassen trying to blow the whistle..." added Jenkins.

"Okay! Let's not get excited," said Devenport. "You guys pack up and make your way back to the L.A. bureau. I'm going to head north-west to Washington State and see if I can find David Rowan at his place in Puget Sound." He turned away and started to walk towards the Desk.

"Jax," cried Jenkins, quickly stepping across the foyer. "Something you should know."

Devenport froze and stared at the agent. "There's more?"

"The kid's mother, Mrs. Penni Singleton has been hanging out in Washington for any news of her son. She was at Langley when they identified the mysterious image outside the pyramid as her son. She confirmed it."

"You're kidding!"

"Do I ever kid?" muttered Jenkins slightly annoyed. "Anyway, she told a secretary she was going to track down David Rowan and find out – in her words – what the hell is going on."

Devenport rubbed his bald patch. "Crap! I need to migrate to another Department or even retire."

14

THEY HAD FINISHED EATING and watched the golden sun drop steadily from a pink sky into the now dark Pacific Ocean before Geraint-Jones picked up the story again.

"The whole of human kind, whether in America, Europe, Russia, China, Australia or South America all stem from one tiny family living in South Africa about 160,000 years ago," he said easily. "They have all been scientifically traced through their DNA which is the molecular record implanted in each one of us. A few years back the National Geographic people set up a plan called the Genographic Project under Dr. Spencer Wells, a geneticist and anthropologist. The Project took DNA samples – genes -- from couples all over the world."

"Genes?" Steiner frowned inquisitively.

"Deoxyribonucleic Acid," replied the archaeologist without pausing. "The human genome contains about 30,000 genes. They determine your skin color, your physique, the way you stand, think and act, your height and even your inclination to disease. The DNA contains your family history and it shows where you came from in the human race. It's like a history book."

Chloe poured French Cognac for everyone, then placing the stopper on the buffalo head decanter she said: "Segments of DNA rarely change but can be affected by occasional mutations or errors in the genetic code. Such errors or mistakes are passed down to succeeding generations and stand out as milestones or markers of descent."

Both Rowan and Steiner looked up in surprise.

"Oh, Chloe is my partner in archaeology. Her favorite digs are in Israel and Jordan," said Geraint-Jones reaching out and holding her hand. "Various populations have different genetic markers and when scientists like Dr. Wells followed them they identify the different branches of the human tree. Wells traced the origin of human sapiens all the way back to their common root in Africa."

"So what has this got to do with pyramids?" protested Rowan mildly.

"Everything," said Chloe easily. "But this is where the scientists stop investigating. Wells did a great television production called *The Journey of Man: A Genetic Odyssey* for the National Geographic and PBS and the BBC in Britain produced *The Incredible Human Journey* with Dr. Alice Roberts. Both stopped short on the African Family's doorstep when they suggested the unique pair of Adam and Eve."

"The big question in the minds of millions of viewers was – how did they get there?" cried Geraint-Jones. "It was like reading a thrilling novel to find the last page of the book missing. It was a total downer."

Totally fascinated, Molly, Rowan and Steiner stared at the couple. "So how did they get there?" asked David.

"God?" suggested Molly hesitantly.

Chloe laughed lightly. "This is where angels fear to tread. Think of it as god without capitalization."

"Okay," snapped Steiner. "Fill us in. Please."

"It's late," said Geraint-Jones. "Tomorrow I will tell you about the coming of the gods. It was a long, long time ago and most academicians, historians, theologians and text book publishers conveniently turn a blind eye, show a cold shoulder on the entire business."

"Why? What's the problem?" cried Steiner shaking his head.

Geraint-Jones gave a short laugh. "Well, a whole lot of books would have to be rewritten; courses in universities and colleges would suffer major revision and restructuring, while theologians would be at the mercy of the fundamentalists."

"What you are going to share is a theory then," suggested Molly.

Chloe shook her head briskly. "Oh, no! Deary me, no! It's a fact that a whole lot of people do not wish to know or talk about. It's an open secret."

Rowan's cell phone buzzed and interrupted. "It's Kate," he muttered and standing up he nimbly moved inside the house only to return several minutes later. "Remember Frederick Klassen?"

"Our friend the whistleblower?" said Steiner.

"Well, he was being held under guard in what they claimed was a safe clinic in Los Angeles. Klassen was being treated for severe dehydration and was incapable of walking," said Rowan softly. "Anyway, he disappeared at 1:00 this afternoon."

"Gone?" muttered Steiner in sheer disbelief.

"Without a trace."

15

IT WAS A LONG time before David Rowan fell asleep at the Geraint-Jones home in Oregon. Too many people were suddenly disappearing such as the CIA team aboard the helicopter at the Big Bend Desert near Marfa, Texas. Devenport had mentioned several others and of course there was the Peter Singleton phenomenon. The teenager who reportedly had a confrontation with a spectral pyramid at Tikiout in southern Morocco, then disappeared while on a trans-Atlantic flight to the United States, only to be filmed again standing outside the Marfa pyramid.

Now it was Frederick Klassen, the scientist who revealed the United States had destroyed a silent UFO parked in a geosynchronous orbit 22,000 miles out from Earth in the Clarke Belt who had disappeared – while in CIA custody.

That was a double whammy, he thought. First, we have sent a strong, undeniable message into the Cosmos that Planet Earth is not a friendly rock in the solar system, an attitude that could reap all sorts of repercussions from any space community, and second, the messenger Frederick Klassen was now on the growing list of mysteriously disappeared people.

Let's not forget another puzzle manifesting itself: the strings of spectral pyramids all resembling the Great Pyramid at Giza in Egypt, all appearing at latitudes of 30 degrees north or south. What is their purpose?

Rowan's mind moved on. "Then there was Geraint-Jones' remark "Tomorrow I will tell you about the coming of the gods. It was a long, long time ago." What was all that about?

The writer shook his head. There were too many questions for which his usually inquisitive mind had no answers and so, unable to sleep he decided he needed some fresh air to clear his mind. Wearing only his jade green cotton shorts he made his way onto the deck and found Molly perched on a wooden stool, her arms resting on the deck railing as she watched the vast expanse of the moonlit Pacific.

"Couldn't sleep?"

"Things are cluttering up my mind," he said softly as he stood beside her body attired only in a soft white negligee.

"The whole place, the wide sandy beaches, the rocks, and the wide ocean look so beautiful under a full moon. It's like being on a desert island." She laughed easily. "When I was a kid I always wondered what it would be like on a desert island. One could go swimming every day."

"This place is similar," he noted. "Sweeping panoramas of sandy beaches."

"My thoughts exactly," she said softly.

Rowan touched her shoulder. "Now?"

"Oh, yes. Let's." Then she hesitated. "I'm not really dressed."

Pensive for a moment. "Neither am I," he replied. "But I'll race you."

Within seconds the writer knew he had lost. In spite of an early morning jog wherever his work took him he was still no match for the sprightly Amazonian figure of Molly Thomsen. As if equipped with wings she sailed down the track to the beach and then once there headed across the golden sand towards the water which was a couple of hundred yards away.

When Rowan arrived and plunged into the waves, he realized Molly had left her negligee on the dry beach so he slipped out of his shorts and joined her.

"Now this is real Adam and Eve stuff," she said happily as she watched him get his breath back. "The sea is so beautiful in the moonlight, I feel as if we could swim to Japan...or somewhere."

"Somewhere is closer," he said pausing to watch her graceful swimming backstroke style, her slim arms lifting effortlessly out of the water, her strong well defined legs propelling her body. For the first time he felt an acute desire to be with this woman. Molly was different. Down to earth she was energetic and vivacious, possessing a warm elegance that magnetized his body and mind.

Later he would realize Molly must be a thought-reader because as he mulled over these positive thoughts in the water she turned and came towards him like a homing torpedo. Her well formed slender arms slipped round his neck and her eyes stared into his. "Are you home, David Rowan?"

For a moment he was frozen in the past but in a flash that old feeling was gone, washed away by a Pacific wave. "Of course, Molly. You're beautiful and very welcome."

For a while they swam easily and effortlessly side by side, making small talk and challenging the incoming waves that lifted their bodies high for a noisy joyous moment and then after they had passed allowed the couple to continue swimming in the moonlight.

Finally they came together again and clung in each other's arms as one, feeling each other's body, allowing the waves to carry them towards the shore. Finally, he scooped up that well defined body, held her close and waded through the water to the beach where the sand was still warm from the 90 degree heat of the day. And so it came to pass on that warm and spacious moonlit beach at Nehalem, Oregon that David and Molly kissed and became as one, their wet bodies intertwined in ecstatic love making.

Gasping and lying on their backs they rested on the sand and gazed at the countless stars shining and the full moon coming from the south. "Do you think the gods are watching us," Molly murmured softly in his ear.

"Who knows? I've quit considering what they might be doing."

Half a mile out on the Pacific a standard 41 foot US Coastguard Utility Boat sat quietly riding the waves, its two powerful Cummins diesel engines switched off. A pilot officer handed his night-glasses to the seaman. "Just a couple of lovers having a midnight fling and screwing around," he remarked. "They're harmless."

16

HUGH GERAINT-JONES WAS in top form the following morning. "Listen my friends, try wrapping your minds around this idea. A NASA mission from Earth after traveling some months lands on a distant planet. Conditions are great for human life and habitation but work needs to be done. The only help on the planet comes in the form of some long armed apes that are friendly enough. They stand erect and are known as Homo erectus but they don't have the intelligence of Homo sapiens."

The archaeologist talks while setting up a projector. "Well, NASA figures they would have to do some breeding so they included some human semen on board. The astronauts impregnate half a dozen of the female species of the long armed apes. The gestation period is eight to nine months similar to Homo sapiens. The first results are not great, so the astronauts experiment and finally achieve primitive workers in our image." He paused then added: For the lack of a better name they call it the Adam and Eve Project.

The group sat frozen. Nobody said anything for perhaps thirty seconds while Geraint-Jones continued to set up the projector.

Rowan broke the silence. "Hugh, can that really happen?"

"Absolutely!" The archaeologist nodded quickly. "Scientists in recent years have found that human beings -- Homo sapiens -- share some 98 per cent of their DNA with apes and chimpanzees. A biologist among the astronauts would probably have to do some juggling, but yes, an intelligent fully functional Homo sapien could be produced."

Erich Steiner suddenly came to life. "Hey, I once read something like that happening on Earth. It was called The Lost Book of Enki...

The archaeologist nodded. "Zecharia Sitchin was one of the leading writers on the subject."

Molly frowned. "You mean a similar storyline happened here on Earth?"

"Happened? Oh, yes! And here on Earth about 160,000 years ago in South Africa," said the archaeologist enthusiastically.

A skeptical frown flickered on Rowan's face. This was something way beyond Roswell, flying saucers, UFOs, abductions and the stuff he had been debunking. Hugh and Chloe Geraint-Jones were internationally acknowledged archaeologists and specialists in ancient history. They had a reputation for working outside the academic norms but this was wild. He stared across at Molly who appeared to be enjoying the revelations so he shrugged and sat back, completely unaware of what the archaeologists would say next.

Geraint-Jones continued: "About 443,000 years ago the first of the space travelers from a planet named Nibiru came to Earth in search of gold. They were called Anunnaki after the Niburian King Anu. Once they found the ore, initially in South Africa, they transported volunteer workers – usually fifty at a time – from their own planet to Earth to work in the mines."

Color pictures of mining operations in the Rand of South Africa flashed onto a large screen. "The gold mines are still operating there incidentally and after being exploited for thousands of years they are still the world's fourth largest gold producer."

Pictures of the Middle East flickered on the screen. "In Mesopotamia which is now Iraq they built a Mission Control Center, mining and processing plants, smelters and spaceports for the spaceships to land and take off. They even had a way station built on the planet Mars."

Rowan looked up from making notes. "How do we know these things?"

"The Sumerians, the people who lived in Sumer – Babylon, now Iraq -- wrote it all down," replied Geraint-Jones. This occurred after the Deluge otherwise known as the great flood which struck some 13,000 years ago. For simplicity's sake we will divide the story into Pre-flood and Post-flood."

"How did the Deluge happen?" asked Molly. "The Bible claims God was angry with the way humankind was developing."

Chloe butted in: "That's the theologians for you. The home planet Nibiru has an extensive orbit around the sun taking about 3,600 years. When it's close to the sun it provides easy access for space travel to the closest planets. The problem was 13,000 years ago it came very close to Earth and created a disaster in the ecosystem with tremendous floods, tidal waves and storms."

"Most of the work the Anunnaki had done was destroyed," said Geraint-Jones, so the Anunnaki started rebuilding their smelters and processing plants in Mespotamia which is now Iraq. They build a spaceport in the Sinai Peninsula, a landmark for incoming space flights at Baalbek in Lebanon and the Great Pyramid at Giza which contained their beacons.

Chloe stood holding a mug of coffee. "With Anunnaki industry growing in Mesopotamia, survivors of the flood gathered to work and develop their culture into what became known as Sumeria and the Babylonian region. After the Deluge the space visitors apparently had a change of heart towards Earth people. They actually went out of their way to help civilization and society advance." There was a pause and she added: "At least some of them helped."

Geraint-Jones nodded vigorously. "Over many years the good Anunnaki taught the Sumerians the practice of writing, mathematics, medical science, music, government, construction and civil organization. The language was Cuneiform which means wedge writing. It was written very well on clay tablets. The Sumerians along with the Assyrians, Akkadians and Hittites all wrote in Cuneiform on clay tablets their knowledge of the Anunnaki."

"And now just a few," quipped Chloe. "Archaeologists have discovered some 50,000 clay tablets and the search still goes on. It's quite incredible because some of these clay documents date back 7,000 years."

The archaeologist switched on the projector and the large image of a light brown clay cylinder flashed onto the screen. "Welcome to Cuneiform," he said waving his hand to introduce it. "The first tablets were discovered in the early 19th century and were taken to various museums around the world but notably the British Museum. No one had the slightest notion of what they meant until 1835 when a British Army officer, Henry Rawlinson discovered some inscriptions on a cliff at a place called Behistun in Persia."

The archaeologist glanced at the trio. "Behistun or Bagastana as it is in Old Persian means the Place of God." Several slides of ruins and mountains in western Iran came onto the screen.

"Carved in the reign of King Darius of Persia the inscriptions showed identical texts in three languages. Ancient Persian, Babylonian and Elamite which was an ancient language in present day Iran. These were the keys to Cuneiform. Rawlinson, a real tiger for exploration, set to work and by 1851 had established the meanings of 200 Babylonian signs."

Geraint-Jones paused for a moment, sipped some lemonade then holding up his hand, his eyes twinkling with undisguised merriment as he announced: "I'm off track. You really need to know how these Anunnaki became gods." He grinned mischievously at the trio. "Remember the little story I told earlier about NASA astronauts landing on a planet and needing workers, well, that happened here on Earth. The Anunnaki astronauts needed some primitive workers to mine the gold because the workers they had brought from Nibiru were totally uncomfortable and rebelled."

"They desperately needed help," said Chloe. "In a word – workers!"

Amid detailed illustrations the archaeologists described how the astronauts found a dark ape-like creature with long arms that stood up – a Homo erectus -- and through a long and grueling process of genetic engineering mixed their own DNA with the DNA of the creatures. Initially the process failed to produce creatures that were intelligent enough to take orders, perform tasks in the gold mines and possess the ability to talk. The Babylonian tablets revealed that genetic engineering at first produced some hideous results such as a person with two heads, a creature with the inability to talk only grunt, malformed hands unable to handle mining tools, another possessed arms with hands too short to eat food, another had malformed lungs and liver and yet another had clogged eyes.

Molly winced at the thought and glanced at David who shook his head and whispered: "I'm having trouble believing most of this."

"The key players in this strange drama were three people," said Geraint-Jones. Enlil and Enki who were half brothers of their father Anu, king of the planet Nibiru. The medical officer who conducted the experiments was named Ninmah, a half sister of Enlil and Enki. She eventually became the key to their success."

"How?" It was the question on the minds of Rowan, Steiner and Molly.

"She gave her own body," put in Chloe with a smile.

"They took an ovum, the egg of a female Homo erectus from Earth and brought it together with male sperm from an Anunnaki," said Geraint-Jones. "They inserted the fertilized egg into Ninmah's womb. Conception followed."

Chloe took up the story. "Ninmah gave birth to a boy who appeared perfect in every way. Everything worked, including the ability to speak. There was only one thing different. Unlike the Anunnaki penis the Earth child had a foreskin. It was Enki who declared that the Earth children should be distinguished by their foreskin."

There was silence as this information sank in. Suddenly Erich Steiner jumped up. "Hell! My father always wanted me circumcised but my mother vehemently protested so it never happened. Is that why the Jewish people practice circumcision because they wanted to be like the Anunnaki?"

Geraint-Jones shook his mop of silver gray hair. "Oh, no, I think that originally they wanted to be like the gods."

"The Earthlings thought the Anunnaki were gods?" queried Rowan quickly.

"Absolutely," said Chloe. "The astronauts from Nibiru came down out of the sky. They could fly here and there and do incredible things that Earthlings could not. They had chariots of fire which are mentioned in the Book of Kings where Elijah is taken up by a chariot of fire with horses of fire and they are still mentioned in song to this day in the hymn called *Jerusalem*. The whole of Earth's religious practices today are based on Anunnaki teachings and philosophy because the early Homo sapiens made the mistake of thinking the Anunnaki were gods and they lived in a place called Heaven."

"Which in fact was the planet Nibiru," put in Steiner.

The archaeologist nodded. "The story of the Creation was written by the Sumerians at least one thousand years before the Children of Israel picked it up and brought it back from their 70-year captivity in Babylon. Hence they wrote the first five books of the *Old Testament*," said Geraint-Jones. "Go back and browse Genesis through to Deuteronomy."

"Wait a minute," cried Rowan getting up and walking over to the archeologist, "what did these space gods call this new Earth child? Adam?"

Geraint-Jones grinned. "Yep! Actually it was Adamu. Eve came shortly after. Enki and the doctor Ninmah asked and received seven female Anunnaki volunteers. Ninmah then took their ovas placed them in vessels – test tubes probably. She extracted life essence from Adamu – sperm that included his DNA – and inserted it into the test tubes. Then she took blood from Adamu and dropped parts into each of the vessels."

The archaeologist smiled softly from his jagged jaw. "Ninmah then planted the fertilized eggs into the seven Anunnaki volunteers. This was recorded by a nursing assistant named Ningishzidda."

"The seven new births were all males," said Chloe. "They realized they needed a female Earthling so they arranged for Enki's spouse Ninki to be impregnated. The gestation period was longer than nine months so Ninmah the biological scientist cut into the womb: we would call it a cesarean procedure and freed a female which was perfect in every way." She smiled easily and added: "They called her Ti-Amat, the Mother of Life."

The group stared in silence at Hugh and Chloe.

"That's beautiful," murmured Molly at last. "Let's drink to that."

They all toasted the story with wine and voiced different thoughts until Rowan asked a question: "The Anunnaki knew all about DNA?"

"Of course! They knew about it 430,000 years ago," said Geraint Jones. "When the Anunnaki explained it to the Sumerian cuneiform writers they called it simply the Tree of Life. Even today, the average person has little or no comprehension of chromosomes and the DNA. In fact it was not until a Swiss fellow, Johann Friedrich Miescher conducting research in the late 1800s separated out what he called nuclien from human cells and declared it was a unique molecule unlike anything known at the time. It was in fact the molecule of life and it would have to wait some seventy-five years before Watson and Crick unveiled the true story of the DNA and revealed the blueprint for life."

Geraint-Jones picked up his pipe and saw it was empty. While searching for his tobacco pouch he glanced across the room and said: "What really confounds me is that the Sumerians knew of the existence of chromosomes in the human structure more than 6,000 years ago but somewhere along the path of human development the information became lost for several thousand years.

"Another point that became lost in the mists of time was the fact the Anunnaki knew of the importance of clay in the human body," said Chloe.

"In what way?" asked Molly.

"The Babylonian tablets state that Ninmah in preparing the essence for the creation of Homo sapiens used earth or clay," replied Chloe. "In Genesis chapter two it says *And the Lord God formed man of the dust of the ground*. Dust is an easy word for clay, a material that is plentiful and inexpensive on Earth. That sentence always bothered us until we heard that researchers at North Dakota State University in Fargo and elsewhere are making great strides in tissue engineering using nanoclay."

"In other words nanoclays coax new bone growth," said her husband. "For people with bone disease and bone loss this can have far-reaching applications. You see the Anunnaki, the Sumerians and the Bible describe phenomena that humanity is only just beginning to realize and understand thousands of years later."

Rowan was fascinated. "So this Adamu and Tia-Amat created at Enki's gold mining base in south-east Africa became the popular Adam and Eve?"

"Exactly," said Geraint-Jones and he flashed a picture onto the screen. "This is a representation of the Sumerian cylinder seal showing the creation of Adamu which in our terms would be the first test tube baby." The tablet showed a goddess holding the baby Adamu while laboratory technicians prepared the DNA mixture and are seen holding a vial or test-tube. The Tree-of-Life is clearly displayed nearby.

"So if this was South Africa," said Rowan. "Where did the Garden of Eden come in?"

"Oh, that!" said Geraint-Jones easily. "They moved the youngsters up to Mesopotamia which is now mainly Iraq and settled them to breed in a place called E.Din in Sumer territory. This was one of the first places established by the Anunnaki as a permanent settlement. It was of course the biblical Eden."

"There are some very interesting texts in Genesis that point to a physical god as opposed to the cosmic god," said Chloe. "It talks about god walking in the garden looking for Adam and Eve. That was an Anunnaki god, probably Enki who was considered Lord of the Earth at that time."

"Which raises the question what about the fruit they ate that got them expelled?" Steiner leaned forward curiously.

Geraint-Jones smiled. "The Tree of Life. They started trying to find out about their DNA, the genomes that made them like the Anunnaki. You remember in Genesis 3:7 it says: Then the eyes of both of them were opened, and they realized they were naked. The Sumerian tablet writers were trying to say the activities opened their higher consciousness. They became aware of themselves. It's called mindfulness these days."

"This is what is called down to Earth thinking," said Chloe with a demure smile. "Enlil, Enki's senior brother ordered them deported from E.Din to the gold mine area known as Abzu in South Africa. It is there they bred and became slaves – primitive workers -- for the Anunnaki."

Geraint-Jones broke in: "And about 160,000 years ago their breeding multiplied and their descendants started spreading around the world to where we are today – all of us. It's a pity the National Geographic and the TV people didn't follow through on their history of Humankind and discuss the Sumerian tablets."

"Why not?" quizzed Molly.

"Many people still have difficulty accepting the Babylonian tablets as true in spite of the fact the first five books of the Bible are based on those tablets," said Geraint-Jones. "They'd have to re-write massive amounts of history books, and a herd of religious teachers and fundamentalists would get bent out of shape." Flashing a beaming smile at Molly he added: "But evidence and the truth is gradually coming to light."

"What about?" said Rowan.

"The fact that human beings are different from all other forms of animal life on this planet," said Geraint-Jones. "We do have some DNA in us that came from Nibiru, the Anunnaki or Outer Space."

"There's proof?" Steiner was keenly alert.

Geraint Jones nodded. "In November 2012 researchers announced the finding of a new gene – called miR-941 – which appears to have played a crucial role in human brain development, particularly how we learned tools and language."

"That was two of the requirements of the Anunnaki in South Africa," said Rowan.

Geraint-Jones nodded. "Researchers say mirR-941 is carried only by humans and not by apes," he said. "A team at Edinburgh University compared the human genome to eleven other species of mammals to find the differences. And the new genome makes human sapiens unique."

"Incredible!" muttered Molly walking out onto the deck. It was raining lightly.

"Well, if you think that what Chloe and I have told you so far is incredible, wait until after lunch and we'll show you what helped the Anunnaki fly around and how the first atomic bombs on Planet Earth did not happen in World War II," said Geraint-Jones. "Nuclear war happened on Planet Earth 4000 years ago a fact that demonstrates Anunnaki bad blood runs through our veins."

17

BUD BERRINGER DROPPED HIS briefcase and laptop onto the passenger seat of the black Mercedes Benz S-Class saloon, waved a hand to other departing officers and slipped behind the steering wheel. A deep sigh of relief broke through the tight jaw muscles. It had been a grueling week at the George C. Marshall European Center for Security Studies. Meeting policy-makers from different NATO countries was always mentally and physically demanding. Of course, the location at Garmisch-Partenkirchen high in the beautiful Bavarian Alps marginally reduced some stress.

"Colonel!"

A woman's smoky voice. He turned and spotted the slim wiry French secretary coming in fast at ninety degrees. "Oh! Crap!" he whispered as the window slid open.

The sharp angular face, the dark shining eyes and her well groomed body looked different in daylight under a slink and professional navy blue suit. It was her bedside manner that appealed to his primeval nature. Berringer peered into the frowning face.

"Monsieur le Colonel," came the hurt voice. "You forgot to say au revoir."

"So sorry Anouk. My unit at Wiesbaden. They want me back like yesterday."

The woman shrugged. "We still have a rendezvous in Brussels next week?"

"Of course, ma chérie. Of course."

Anouk leaned through the window and attempted a passionate French kiss.

Berringer broke away and the car moved forward. He reached out and waved an arm. "See you in Brussels."

It was a lie. Next week he would be stateside at the Pentagon in Washington for a debriefing on the American project at Tel Aviv and then heading home to Irene and the kids – well, kids in college.

The Mercedes Benz purred along the autobahn heading for Wiesbaden some four hours distant. At Stuttgart, Berringer took the 831 Rosental exit and headed for a late lunch and a Scotch. A number of happy teenage tourists were coming down the street by the restaurant. They appeared Scandinavian, chatted excitedly and snapped photos as they approached.

Berringer paused outside the Mercedes and watched the young women. One with long blonde hair grinned and took his picture.

Click. The camera flashed in spite of the sunshine.

It was at that precise moment that Colonel Bud Berringer of the U.S. Army Corps of Engineers disappeared. One moment he was there, the next moment the space where he had stood by the car was empty.

The small crowd of Scandinavians gasped. The young girl with the camera collapsed in a faint. Then all the others started screaming.

During the investigation the German police examined the girl's camera.

"Correct us if we are wrong. You say there was one American standing by the car who disappeared a moment after you took the photograph," said the police officer in English.

One of the girls chipped in: "That's right. There was one American in a light tan suit."

"What about the other man with him? Where did he go?"

"There was only one man. An American," insisted one of the other girls.

The policeman shook his head. "I'm looking at the camera and I can see two men. The American and standing next to him is a tall man who looks like a Middle Eastern fellow in a white suit and a gold belt."

The girls pushed forward to look and the policeman held up the camera for them to see.

"Looks like an Egyptian to me," said one and at that point three of the young women flaked out on the sidewalk.

18

THE LITTLE HAMLET OF Ravensbrook is located at the foot of the Pocono Mountains just off U.S. Route 209 in Pennsylvania. In the first part of the 20th century it was a vibrant anthracite-mining village but in 1972 with changing times it closed. Many of the small homes which had seen better days were torn down; others were restored and sold as luxury cottages to retired and affluent couples from Philadelphia.

The only two stores that exist in Ravensbrook rely on summer tourism for their existence. Visitors on their way to neighboring Lansford to ride and view the train that runs through the historic coalmine tunnels frequently stop in the village. Tourists like to view and photograph the picturesque creek that forms below a cascading waterfall and runs parallel to the main street.

One remaining store is the Ravensbrook Hardware and Fishing Tackle store, the other is a bakery combined with a tea and home-made pastries café. The owner of the latter is known to the locals as Fat Phyllis but no one ever calls her that because being short tempered she often retaliates by slinging a pie.

On this lovely June day two linesmen Art and Casey from the Pennsylvania Power and Light were seated on the bench outside Phyllis' teashop. As usual on work days they brought their own lunch buckets complete with drinks but here in Ravensbrook Phyllis brought out mugs of fresh coffee laced with sugar and cream.

"Thanks, Phyllis," said Art who always believed in being polite although he resorted to obscene expletives when things went wrong. "Planning your end-of-season vacation yet?"

The heavy set woman peered up and down the street. "The rate we're going this year I'll be lucky to afford gas to get to Philly let alone Florida. Six pastries, two donuts and three teas in three hours."

Casey tore some bread off a loaf and was about to push it into his mouth when he spotted a small van with at least half a dozen children and two adults coming up the street. "Your economy is starting to bristle," he said.

"I'll bristle you, Casey-boy!" she cried and started to trundle back into the shop. It was at that precise moment the lights went out. The stove and coffee pot lights went out and the air conditioner in the side window stopped working.

"Casey!" screamed Phyllis, "We're off the air. Power's gone."

"Check your breakers," cried the linesman.

"I'm doing that right now! They're fine."

An irate male's voice came from the hardware store. "Did you monkeys do anything stupid with the lines? The power's out."

Art stared down the road at the small bus loaded with kids and the car behind. Both vehicles had stopped and the owners were now looking under the hoods.

"Casey, call the depot,"

"Can't. The line's dead."

"Oh, crap! It must be a regional outage. Somewhere up the line," Art said as he slowly got to his feet. "Two vehicles both stop in the middle of a street because of a power outage. That's one heck of a coincidence."

"Art, my watch has stopped," said Casey. "It was brand new only last weekend."

"Phyllis has a landline," cried the other. He ran into the pastry shop, spotted the dial-phone and lifted it. Dead!

Then as if nothing had happened the power started flowing again.

In reporting the incident to management back at the depot both Casey and Art figured the outage had lasted about eleven minutes. "The peculiar thing was that everything else on independent power also stopped. The auto engines, our watches, landline phones, anything that works on batteries failed."

The manager stared at the linesmen. "You guys been drinking again?"

Back at Ravensbrook Fat Phyllis called a cousin in King of Prussia whose husband works at a Philadelphia daily. Next day a small shoulder item ran under the head: "Mysterious power outage strikes village."

The following day there was a second story of something else that happened in the village. One of the youngsters in the van had taken a photo with an old Kodak Instamatic of the picturesque Ravensbrook Creek. It included the two linesmen by the bench and standing beside them was a spectral image of a tall man in a white suit with a gold belt.

19

HUGH GERAINT-JONES UNLOCKED the door to a place he called "Corkscrew Cellar" tucked underneath the cottage. The heavy wooden steps led down to a long and spacious room cluttered by a horde of objects most of which were covered in dust sheets. The array of lights revealed to David Rowan, Erich Steiner and Molly Thomsen that it was not just a run of the mill basement with a few bottles of wine thrown in but a large warehouse built into the rocks below and behind the house. The end of the depository appeared as a large stone cavern.

"One thing you need to know is that the Anunnaki were expert space travelers. They knew all about the Earth being a globe and part of the solar system. They told the Sumerians all about the other planets and the Universe beyond and they wrote it down on the tablets," he said, then paused and glanced at Chloe. "The German fellow...the Assyriologist my father knew?"

"Friedrich Ernst Weidner," Chloe replied instantly.

"Yes, Weidner wrote a *Handbook on Babylonian Astronomy* based on tablets found in Mesopotamia and it's become known as *The Great Star List*. It's a fabulous collection of data on seventy-one celestial bodies and their positions in the skies. There are some errors because the Sumerian scriptors really did not understand that the solar system revolves round the sun – heliocentric, is the word."

Chloe broke in. "In spite of the Anunnaki teachings recorded so many centuries ago, humankind insisted on claiming a Flat Earth – which the British Historical Association listed in 1945 as one of the greatest myths of all time. Sad to say but it took humankind millennia to catch up with records left by the Anunnaki space visitors thousands of years ago."

"For those entrenched in modern-day pronouncements of academics it is difficult to believe," said Rowan standing by a case of replicas of tablets from the Library of Ashurbanipal at Nineveh in Sumeria.

"It's like Planet Earth has skeletons in the closet and modern folk are largely in a state of denial," said Molly.

"Including me – somewhat," said Rowan.

"Ah, yes, many find it difficult to accept," agreed Chloe. "The authority of our culture does not wish to update history. The costs to change thousands of books and data banks would be enormous."

"Let alone people's minds," put in Steiner standing by with his camera.

Geraint-Jones shrugged as if tired of trying to update the human race on its own history. "Let's get back to the flying accomplishments of the Anunnaki. The Sumerians indicate very strongly in the tablets that the gods of Heaven and Earth were special because they could roam the skies whenever they wished – and they did it frequently."

"That's why simple people called them gods – with a small g," said Chloe.

Look at this," said Geraint-Jones. He pointed to replicas of tablets showing figures equipped with wings. Then he promptly moved to another display and called out: "This illustration was found showing a rocket head above ground in an area growing date trees. The main rocket assembly is shown here stored in a silo underground. This occurred many millennia before Americans and Soviets caught on to the idea in the mid-20th century."

"How come humanity lost knowledge of all this until the Babylonian tablets were found in the mid-19th century?" Rowan expressed the thought.

"Ah, good question, David" said the archaeologist with a smile. "It's called the Cosmic Dark Ages. Originally the term Dark Ages characterized the period between the 6th and 13th centuries. It was a time of intellectual darkness. But there was an even greater period of darkness initiated and enforced by the growth of religion in India and the Middle East. In reality the Dark Ages lasted over a millennium and much information on Earth history was lost."

"Some history was carried through," exclaimed Chloe quickly. "The Jews while in captivity in Babylon for seventy years were exposed to the Creation story that features Adamu and Ti-Amat in E.din. Even then the that story was over 1,000 years old so the Jewish scribes returning from Babylon rewrote it with names slightly changed and created the first part of the Old Testament as we know it today. That's why it still contains references to god as I said earlier."

Rowan shook his head and flashed a tight grin. "This means that if you see the Old Testament god as a human being what you are really seeing is an Anunnaki – a creature in our likeness."

David, you said that," said Chloe her eyes sparkling with merriment.

"God walking in the Garden of Eden was really an Anunnaki god," suggested Steiner with an understanding shrug."

"Absolutely!" nodded Geraint-Jones.

"Did you ever find out how they flew around?"

"Oh, yes," said Geraint-Jones eagerly. "I mentioned rockets which the ancient humans called chariots and sometimes chariots of fire. When Moses went up to see god – with a small g – he saw a burning bush which in reality was one of the Anunnaki flying machines. There are many examples of people being taken up in the Bible."

Steiner suddenly caught on. "When we had Exodus in Sunday school and the teacher read the line: The angel of the LORD appeared to him in a blazing fire from the midst of a bush; and he looked, and behold, the bush was burning with fire, yet the bush was not consumed."

"Great memory, Erich," muttered Molly.

"Was that again an Anunnaki flying machine?"

"Absolutely," said Geraint-Jones with a vigorous nod. "The True God does not need burning bushes, chariots of fire and all that physical stuff. The True God is much more sophisticated.

"Exodus says that Moses was on the mountain forty days and forty nights," said Steiner. "Forty days seems a favorite time of the Anunnaki gods."

"You're right," chipped in Chloe. "Practically speaking the Anunnaki astronauts took Moses to Nibiru – which was also called Heaven – from where he returned an enlightened man. Exodus says his face shone and people were afraid to go near him."

Chloe came forward. "I like the story on the Prophet Elijah and Elisha which says *As they were walking along and talking together, suddenly a chariot of fire and horses of fire appeared and separated the two of them and Elijah went up to heaven in a whirlwind.*" She paused. "Of course, we mentioned that earlier."

"That's in the second Book of Kings, 2:11," said Geraint Jones clasping his hands as if in prayer. "The one I really like is in Genesis Five and concerns Enoch the great-grandfather of Noah *And Enoch walked with God; and he was not, for God took him.*" The archaeologist paused then added: "I like the phrase - *and God took him*. It's like saying *Hey, Enoch would you like a ride in my flying machine?*"

Steiner rubbed his hands while deep in thought. "They taught us in Sunday school that Ezekiel with the Jewish exiles in Babylon had an experience with God that changed his life."

"That was another prophet who was taken up in a rocket ship by the Anunnaki and quite vividly too," agreed Geraint-Jones. "*Then the Spirit lifted me up, and I heard behind me a loud rumbling sound as the glory of the LORD rose from the place where it was standing.* That's Ezekiel 3:12."

"It's truly amazing that when one knows ancient history one can see the Bible in a truly different light," said Molly enthusiastically. "It's quite realistic and believable."

Geraint-Jones lit his pipe and carefully planted the match in a clay pot of sand. "The story that really needs investigating is the life of the historical Jesus," he said slowly. "Forty days and nights in the desert. Biblical scribes assumed he was fighting the devil. A psychotherapist would suggest he was sorting out his ego. A student of the Babylonian texts could suggest he was taken by the Anunnaki gods. Even the words used in Acts on the ascension of Jesus are inclined towards the Nibiru gods. The trio stared as an image appeared on the screen.

And when he had spoken these things, while they beheld, he was taken up; and a cloud received him out of their sight. And while they looked steadfastly toward heaven as he went up, behold, two men stood by them in white apparel.

Rowan stood up slowly and standing by the door nodded pensively then looked at everyone. "I'm beginning to see the light in all of this," he said slowly. The ancient script writers had no idea about astronauts and how they traveled vast distances. They had no idea how to describe a space launch or an inter-space rocket. It was outside their vocabulary, so they used such phrases as chariots of fire, taken up, disappeared into the clouds." He turned to a bookshelf and pulled out a copy of the Holy Bible.

"One of these days I'm going to read over this thing again and it will be in a new consciousness," he said. "In light of the thousands of Babylonian tablets written more than a thousand years before the Bible came about, I would suggest everyone re-read the book, particularly the Old Testament. It's as the Sumerian writers told it, we just haven't been reading it in the right light."

"Absolutely right, David," said Chloe. "Absolutely right. When you apply your knowledge of the Anunnaki while reading the Old Testament you will find the entire book is devoted to mass killings, struggles for power and deception and the acquisition of wealth. That was how the some of the Anunnaki leadership, particularly Enlil manipulated the Earthlings they had created. In effect they hated what they had created in much the same way as Baron Frankenstein hated his monster. Much the same way as some Americans hated the blacks in recent years. There is no mention of loving yourself and your neighbors."

"Wow!" gasped Molly, "That is some indictment."

"People don't know how to read the Bible," said Geraint-Jones with a sigh. "And talking of power, it was the Anunnaki who introduced the monarchy system to humanity. They called them priest-kings. One of the earliest was Melchizedek mentioned in Genesis. It was he who blessed Abraham. At least one priest-king exists today in Rome." The pale blue eyes twinkled inquisitively at the trio and Chloe chipped in: "You didn't know?"

The big archaeologist rubbed his sandy gray hair as if to say "Enough of this." He promptly strode over to a large object hidden by a tarpaulin and with one jerk of his arm pulled off the cover to reveal a large shining sheet of metal measuring eight feet by four and about four inches thick. It appeared incredibly heavy and ancient with strange engravings carved into the sides.

"What is that?" Molly shook her head, her eyes totally fascinated by the piece of metal.

Geraint-Jones gave one of his famous grins. "We found it north of Baalbek buried under 15 feet of mud and sand left by the Great Deluge which means a space vehicle crashed while approaching the first of the beacons," said Geraint-Jones. "There are no markings to suggest what it consists of but there are some strange elements about it."

The trio walked around it puzzled but fully alert.

"Rowan, how are your muscles?" said the archaeologist. "Pick it up."

David moved cautiously towards the shining metal, slowly bent down and started to slide his hands underneath. Suddenly he jerked back. "It moved. The thing actually moved," he cried, suddenly aware that his expectations were way off mark. Even as he spoke the huge sheet of metal floated up to his waist and then gently nudged him as if it were a dog demanding attention.

Startled, he jumped back. "The damned thing is alive!"

Geraint-Jones laughed. "You can pick it up with one hand."

Rowan's hands gingerly reached out and gripped the metal. "Weird! It's as light as the old proverbial feather. What's it made of aluminum?"

The archaeologist grinned. "We have never been able to find out. We had it analyzed but no one could identify it. We imagine the Anunnaki used it extensively on some of their flying machines.

"Why some?" queried Steiner.

"Because it's quite volatile. It is sensitive to human thought."

"You're kidding," muttered Rowan.

"All right, sir," said Geraint-Jones patting the writer on the shoulder, "why don't you sit on the thing."

The metal sheet lowered itself to a few inches of the floor. Rowan climbed aboard and as he did so the metal plate moved forward.

"Now, David," ordered the archaeologist, "you see that white post standing at the far end of the workshop, simply think of being there."

"Just like that? Think?"

"Just think, man. Think you are there and gently touching the post."

Suddenly the sheet of metal raised itself to three feet above the floor and moved quickly towards the post. Erich Steiner gasped. "Heck! I would like to have filmed this."

Molly shook her head. "That's incredible."

"Now David, think in your mind that you should turn round," cried Geraint-Jones. While Rowan was pondering on how to ask the question the big plate of metal turned.

The archeologist picked up a wooden post and stood along the flight path to Chloe. "Now think that you wish to be three feet in front of Chloe."

"But I'm going to hit you and the damned post," cried Rowan nervously.

"Do it, man, do it," urged the archaeologist almost impatiently.

The piece of metal with David Rowan on board started its forty-foot journey. As it approached Geraint Jones holding the pole, it swung sideways, made a semi-circle and continued on to a point just in from of Chloe. It then parked itself on the floor.

"Incredible," muttered Rowan climbing off. "It's unbelievable. It's just like a snowboard except it thinks."

"No, it is sensitive to human thought," said Geraint Jones. "This is what gave the Sumerians and the cultures that followed them the concept of the magic carpet."

Chloe broke into the conversation. "These personal flying chariots were very popular as the Hindi religion developed. They called them vimanas and you can read about them in the Mahabharata. One is referred to as *a marvelous vimana, a crystal ship that flew anywhere at his very thought.*"

"Powerful stuff," said David. "It's little wonder you keep it hidden. I don't think the regular world is ready for that sort of travel."

They took a break while Erich Steiner filmed Chloe riding back and forth on the sheet of strange metal.

"Can't one fall off?" asked the movie maker. "There are no handles."

"Not a bit," responded Chloe. For a moment she pretended to slip off but the metal sheet tilted so that she was forced to move back to a seated position. "It's all in our thinking. Do you understand?"

Steiner felt he should but failed.

Meanwhile Geraint-Jones led David Rowan and Molly upstairs, refilled their coffee mugs and joined them standing on the deck overlooking the Pacific. Rowan desperately wanted to link the Great Pyramid of Giza with the spectral pyramids appearing on 30 degree latitude north and south

"The Anunnaki brought all sorts of gifts to Earth. One was the sexagesimal numbering system with a base of 60. It appeared about 5,000 years ago and has been passed down through the cultures and is still used in modified forms for measuring time – 60 minutes in an hour, sixty seconds in a minute – angles and geographic coordinates. We have the decimal system and our compasses are based on a 360 degree system which is divided into 60 degree components," said the archaeologist as if he had said it to people many times before.

Geraint-Jones escorted David and Molly to a large globe in the corner by the bookcase and his large hands reached for the North and South poles. "From these points to the equator is 60 degrees and half of each one of those is 30 degrees which are called the north and south latitudes.

"They form the half way mark between the equator and the poles," said Rowan.

"Exactly."

"It is on these lines that we have found a string of pyramids – illusory pyramids."

"Kate told me, David. That's just fascinating."

"Any idea as to why they are appearing, Hugh?"

"Honestly? Not much," grinned the archaeologist. "You see spectral images are spectral. They are illusions. They are not physical. The questions you really need to ask is are they influential? Do they have fields that can influence life, notably human life? And if so why?"

"Do you think they originate with the Anunnaki?"

"Well, that's a toughie, young man," muttered the archaeologist stroking his beard. "We know the Anunnaki appreciated the cosmic power of pyramids and built one in Egypt and several in Central and South America along with India.

"You said earlier the Great Pyramid acted as a beacon for incoming space ships," put in David.

Geraint Jones grunted. "A lot of the academicians living in their little conformity boxes will pooh-pooh that suggestion but like the Sumerians reported and the Bible writers copied, the earth is round and floats in space. It took centuries for science to catch up and reach the same conclusions." He started searching for his pipe but continued talking. "Sometimes I can't figure out why the universal church claimed the Earth was flat when in the Bible right under their sniveling noses it was written: *He sits enthroned above the circle of the earth.* That's Isaiah chapter 40, verse 22."

"Why were they so blind?" asked Molly.

"Heaven knows and that's not a pun," said Geraint Jones quickly. "That was a direct pick-up from the Sumerian tablets and it's the reason when you ask a lot of people today where is God, they immediately point to the skies. We cannot get over the fact that the so-called gods – the fathers of humanity as we know it – came in their celestial cruisers from another planet somewhere out there." He shrugged. "Sorry, I get distracted. What was your questions again?"

"Do you think the spectral pyramids originate with the Anunnaki?"

"Zecharia Sitchin and other translators of the Babylonian tablets say the Anunnaki had easy space flights to Earth because of Nibiru's close proximity to Earth. Their planet has an irregular orbit of 3,600 years. Right now it's still a few hundred years out there but there is a catch."

"Catch?"

"If the Anunnaki first visited Earth and started colonizing our piece of rock some 400,000 years ago and at that time were already accomplished space travelers, it is only natural that their civilization is now light years ahead of ours and quite beyond any Earthling's comprehension and understanding." Each word was stated specifically and carried deep thought and feelings.

Both Molly and David were stunned at the idea. "We're not used to thinking there's a vastly superior race operating in our universe," said Rowan trying to feel his way in a maze of confusing thoughts.

The archaeologist moved closer and peered into Rowan's face.

"Take for instance the crop circles. So many scientists try to say they are locally produced hoaxes by kids with planks in spite of the fact they have appeared extensively in 55 countries and many are extremely intricate," he said softly. "Earthlings are so ego-intensive, so neurotically afraid of being second, losing wealth, losing pride, we hate to think there might be an intelligence up there that can out-think, out-perform all the so-called moguls and eggheads on this planet."

He paused for a breath. David, lad," he muttered, "it baffles me why someone has failed to recognize that these phenomena are messages – just like the Egyptian pictographs, the Cuneiform tablets in Mesopotamia – and need translating."

Rowan listened and nodded his head. "What you say makes sense, Hugh. So you think that people like the Anunnaki are sitting out there sending us messages."

"Absolutely."

"Do you think they will invade Earth? After all, the United States has a military defense system that is way too big for any local conflagration."

"That's a childish question, Rowan. Start thinking! Use your intelligence, imagination and your powers of intuition," he cried as he tapped the writer's chest. "You've only discovered a handful of spectral pyramids. What about the others not discovered yet? Perhaps they're all along the 30 degree latitudes both north and south."

"Couldn't some other power, some other space travelers be using these illusory pyramids?"

"Not likely."

"Why are you so sure?"

"Remember that Cecil Maguire owner of the High Sierra Ranch near Marfa reported hearing a distinct hum in the area of the pyramid that he claimed drove the cattle away?"

Rowan frowned. "Yes, I mentioned that to Kate…"

"And the lassie told me," added the archaeologist. "Well, I checked the location of several of the illusory pyramids and they are all manifesting identical tones to each other."

"Tones? What tones?" asked Molly.

"All of them are resonating to the same tone found in the Great Pyramid at Giza."

"And that is?" quizzed Rowan.

"On the music scale an F sharp."

Molly nodded. "I play the piano so what is the importance of F sharp?"

Geraint –Jones moved to a glass cupboard and selected a singing bowl. Allowing it to rest on the palm of his left hand he ran a wooden mallet round the rim. Within seconds a distinct tone filled the room so much so that Steiner and Chloe came up stairs to listen.

"Did you hear the overtones? Like a warbling of the note?" said Geraint-Jones. "That's harmonics and F sharp harmonics are powerful"

The trio stared open faced.

"Your human hearts resonate to F sharp as does our dear old planet Earth," put in Chloe as she moved beside her husband.

The archaeologist obviously enjoying himself added: "The Anunnaki space travelers knew all about sound vibrations thousands of years ago when they built the Great Pyramid at Giza. They designed it to resonate at F sharp to be in harmony with Gaia the life spirit of this planet. Now they have all the spectral pyramids resonating to F sharp."

"So they are here?" suggested Steiner, his face quizzical and expectant.

"Of course."

"You're joking," put in Rowan stiffly, his inborn skepticism coming to the fore.

"Rarely joke," muttered Geraint-Jones. "I'm just trying to think about when and how they will announce their arrival."

"You mean something like H.G. Wells' in his book *The War of the Worlds*."

Geraint-Jones laughed but it was more of a scoff. "Rowan you really do need to get out of your box." The big man stepped out onto the deck took a breath of fresh air then suddenly turned and looked back at the visitors. "We have all been programmed. Wells started it you know."

"How? By having an invading army of mechanical beasts with protruding eyes coming in from Outer Space?"

Geraint-Jones nodded. "H.G. Wells set up the theme in 1898 and writers and movie-makers have been following that line ever since. There's always something coming in from space – a meteorite, an unidentified missile or even a fully loaded flying saucer as in the 1951 movie *The Day the Earth Stood Still*."

"Hugh," muttered Steiner leaning against the door post: "Let me get this right. You're saying the odds are against an invasion from Outer Space."

The archaeologist spun round. "No! No! No! I'm saying the invaders are already here and are just waiting for the right time to explain things." He walked back to Steiner's side, stared at the movie maker then glanced at David and Molly. "You see the Anunnaki colonists who arrived 430,000 years ago never really left.

Well, they planted their paternal seeds in Adamu and Ti-Amat – Adam and Eve if you like. As the Bible records in Genesis the Anunnaki gods also took the daughters of men as wives. The roots of the Anunnaki are so prevalent in our nature and our being that there are some people walking the Earth who are more Anunnaki-Nature than Earth-Nature."

"That's hard to digest," muttered Rowan sourly.

Geraint-Jones ignored the comment. "Their direct offspring are still here today and I sense they are getting worried."

"What about?" quizzed Molly.

"For starters a nuclear conflagration," said Geraint-Jones reaching out for his pipe and slowly lighting the tobacco. "There are too many nuclear threats. Minor league players suddenly possessing weapons of mass destruction and testing in their own backyards triggers alert stations round the clock by major league players. The temperature for nuclear war is increasing day by day. It only needs one false word, one false action, somebody losing their cool.

"In this day and age?" retorted Molly.

"It happened in 2024 BCE," replied Geraint-Jones.

"On Earth?"

"Not only on Earth it spread to the home planet Nibiru," said the archaeologist softly.

The writer looked across the deck to where Molly was standing and suddenly felt an acute fear vibrating in his mind, body and soul. For some reason he was beginning to feel totally helpless, and it was a feeling that would now haunt him for days. Deep inside total skepticism was having a wrestling match with everything he ever believed was right – and it felt like a hound gnawing his stomach.

Geraint-Jones silently puffed on his pipe then looking around at the group said slowly: There is a dark side to the Anunnaki which I think you should know about."

"Let's talk about that after dinner," said Chloe quickly then she added: "Because it really is the dark side."

20

KATE AND HER FRIEND Mark jogged along Keystone Road to where Route 20 comes out of the small hills and winds beside the tall sun-bleached grasses bordering the beach and the countless amounts of driftwoods scattered along it. It had been raining lightly all morning from the same Pacific weather system stretching up from Nehalem in Oregon where her father was meeting Hugh and Chloe Geraint-Jones.

"I wonder why on earth Dad needs an archaeologist?" Kate called out to her partner.

"Something old and dusty, I expect," Mark replied.

That was Mark, she thought, always dry humor. They had been living together for several days and Kate was now impressed by the fact that he enjoyed cooking and being domesticated. In addition he was a great DIY enthusiast. Mark fixed the window frame at the back of the house, re-organized the crazy pavement outside the front door, and surprised her when he did some excellent pencil drawings of some futuristic houses.

"You should be studying architecture," she suggested as they had sat on the tiled floor, drank wine and watched a British drama presentation on PBS television. They slept with each other and loved passionately and Kate was beginning to think he would make a good partner in married life.

As they jogged back along West Keystone they caught site of Mike Boulter working on one of the classic cars he stored in the barn at the back of the house. Kate swerved her form into the driveway.

"Hi Diesel, do you always work on cars in the rain?"

"It's the drizzle, kiddo. Keeps me fresh," he chuckled as he stood up with a wrench in his hand. It's good to see you youngsters keeping fit. I wish you'd go over to the high school and talk to the kids. Apparently the Phys. Ed. teachers have to use dynamite to get them to even run around the track."

"They'll come a time when they will appreciate running," she said easily. "How's Uncle Paul's old station wagon coming on?

"The 1939 Dodge Pick-up? Oh, it's fine and in working order. Having trouble finding an exact match for the blue they used over 70 years back," said Boulter. "I hear Paul and Natalie are dropping by on the way to see your grandmother?"

"Oh, yes, I think the little cottage will be full of life by tomorrow night," she called out as she and Mark jogged off. "See you soon, Diesel."

'Why the name Diesel?" asked Mark as they moved along the road.

"Oh, a couple of reasons," she said. "He's an expert on diesel engines, in fact when one of the big TV stations in Seattle did a history on city buses they did quite an extended interview with him." They pulled into the driveway at the Rowan cottage and paused at the door. "Since then he's been nicknamed Diesel Boulter and I think he likes it."

They had just finished drying themselves off and had changed into dry clothes when the brass knocker broke their reverie.

"It always sound like a cannon going off," she called to Mark as she moved to the front door and swung it open.

The man was short and somewhat heavy, particularly around the face. His light tropical white suit needed pressing and his big eyes behind heavy horn-rimmed glasses peered at her.

"Is that really you, Kate?" The voice matched the body but it was friendly. "You've really grown since you were in D.C."

"Oh...Mr. Devenport...what on earth are you doing here?"

"Looking for your Dad. Who else?"

"Well, please come in. It's wet out there," said Kate pulling the man's left arm and closing the door after him. "Fancy seeing you here."

"Mark," she called. "Come and meet Jackson Devenport. Most people know him as Jax." A grin flickered on her face. "He's also a spymaster."

Mark stepped forward, smiled and shook the outstretched hand.

"Jax helped Dad with a whole lot of historical stuff when he wrote the early history of the CIA," said Kate.

"The Central Intelligence Agency?" Mark sounded uncomfortable.

"Yeah, I work for the Dark Side of the Agency – metaphysical and oddball stuff that no one believes in, like UFOs, alien landings and ETs."

"How long have you worked on the…Dark Side?" asked Mark.

"Since her Dad wrote the book. They said it was a promotion," he said with a short deep laugh. His heavy eyes sparkled behind the horn rimmed glasses. He always enjoyed talking to young kids. He glanced around the cottage. "So where's your Dad, Kate?"

"He'll be here tomorrow night," she said easily. "He's meeting an archaeologist – actually two. Hugh and Chloe Geraint-Jones. They are experts on the Middle East and pyramids."

"Hey, wish I were there," said Devenport. "There's a whole pile of stuff I'd like to know about pyramids." Even as he spoke, his mobile flashed a text. The smile evaporated and grimly he glanced at Kate. "My laptop is in the rental. Can I bring it in? You have Wi-Fi, I suppose?"

The CIA boss had his computer booted up and within seconds he was staring in sheer puzzlement at two pictures. "Listen, young ones, you might as well see these. They're in some of the papers."

Kate and Mark gathered round. The first picture showed Colonel Bud Berringer by the Mercedes Benz in Germany. The specter of an Egyptian was beside him. "This high ranking policy maker disappeared a fraction of a second after the photo was taken." He flipped the computer and the second picture came up.

"This is a place called Ravensbrook in Pennsylvania. The whole village suffered a strange power outage, not just regular power but electricity in cars, trucks, cell phones and even watches," he said. "A young woman took this picture of two linesmen and there is a spectre standing behind them. Looks like a young man."

Kate gasped. "That's Singleton. Peter Singleton," she cried her voice tense with excitement. "That's the teenager at the Tikiout pyramid in Morocco."

"The one who disappeared over the Atlantic and was later taped by Steiner at the Big Ben Desert," snapped Devenport and angrily clenched his fists and brought them together. "This kid has a lot to answer for."

Mark suddenly came to life. "How does he move around so fast?"

"Look," the CIA man stared at Kate. "I'm on the same wavelength as your Dad. I don't believe in UFOs, crop circles, spirits or any of that crap. It's my guess someone is playing tricks to attract our attention from the real problem."

"And what is that, Jax?" Kate appeared totally innocent.

"All this should be in the jurisdiction of Homeland Security," he said with a shrug. "Langley offered me a retirement package a couple of months ago. I should have taken it. My gut is wrenching my body."

"You need an antacid?"

"You kidding? A scotch would do fine."

At Kate's nod Mark disappeared into the kitchen.

"On the rocks," cried Devenport.

The heavy brass knocker shook the cottage door. Kate peered through the window and saw Mr. Boulter standing with a woman. Stepping quickly across the room, she swung open the door.

"Diesel, is there a problem?"

Boulter nodded his head towards the woman. "This lady is lost. She almost collapsed when the cab dropped her at my place but we gave her a strong coffee. She seems fine now." His dark tanned leathery face peered quizzically at Kate. "She's looking for your Dad. Her name is Singleton. Mrs. Penni Singleton."

"Mother of...," Kate started to say.

"Peter Singleton," said the tired woman. "I don't know what I did to deserve this, but I'm sure going to have it out with God when I get to Heaven."

Kate invited the wet and bedraggled woman into the cottage and turned to look at Devenport. The old CIA man was seated in an armchair holding an empty glass. "Listen, folks," he muttered, his hands trembling. "I don't think I can take much more of this. I have a gut condition. Could you spare another scotch?"

21

JOHNNY MANUEL AND CAL Halston had been buddies longer than either could remember. They lived next door to each other and in spite of the fact that Johnny was an Indian of the First Nation Shuswap Band and Cal was a budding guitarist and pianist with ambitions to have a traditional jazz group, tour the world doing gigs and make commercial CDs, they both had an affinity for doing things together.

They lived near Vavenby deep in the heart of British Columbia's North Thompson River region which caters to the logging industry, tourism, fishing, and movie making. In fact Johnny's father was a film location scout along with being an Indian Cultural adviser. An outdoors man he repeatedly encouraged the two boys now 17 to get out into the wilds and "make friends" with the Spirits of Nature as he called them. Cal's father, a retired member of the Royal Canadian Mounted Police was proud that his son possessed the strength to say "No" to drugs so he encouraged the friendship.

For three summers the boys packed their camping gear and generally stayed within the confines of Wells Gray Provincial Park, a 5,000 square kilometer wildlife sanctuary and a home for over 200 species of birds and 56 mammals. The Park appealed to the boys because most of the wilderness is beyond the reach of cars and trucks and can only be explored by canoe or on foot. The Park contains Helmcken Falls one of the most photographed sights in British Columbia. Towering 460 feet or 141 meters in height, it is the 4th tallest waterfall in Canada and three times the height of Niagara Falls. Then there are five major lakes, two large river systems, numerous other spectacular waterfalls and millions of trees.

Normally the teenagers would spend two or three days identifying trees such as Douglas-fir, Engelmann spruce, subalpine fir, western hemlock and western red cedar, black cottonwood, trembling aspen and paper birch and closely watching all manner of wildlife. They frequently encountered deer, moose, black bear, grizzly bear, and caribou plus birds such as osprey, eagle, woodpecker and raven.

But this summer was different. Johnny had suggested it first. "Let's expand our horizons, Cal. I've always wanted to explore the forests and the peaks in the north region."

"We ought to take a week," Cal responded. "It'll be a tough haul."

Cal's father took them along the twisting Clearwater Valley road and across the fast flowing Murtle River. At the drop-off point they struggled into their backpacks which were a little heavier than past years because they carried more rations and also a 12-inch solar panel for charging a cell phone and a GPS for global positioning – thoughts originating with both their mothers.

They both enjoyed eating garlic so they carried a sizable bag of it freshly peeled. "It sure keeps the mossies away," muttered Cal. They had learned early in their lives that the mosquitoes that frequent the North Thompson appear to be among the world's biggest so chewing a couple of cloves a day made a real turn-off for the flying insects and kept them safe.

The first and second days passed without incident and on the third day the rain and mists came in from the Pacific across the Coastal Range and spread into the North Thompson region. Although they carried a small bivouac by sheer luck they discovered a large cave uninhabited for the summer months by animals such as bears and spent the night sitting by a large log fire. Both had brought their Native Indian flutes and for a while they listened to their own music until it was time to sleep. Although they had lightweight space blankets designed by NASA technology to keep them warm, they found the blazing fire warmed up the entire cave.

"Crap! It's still raining," muttered Cal the following morning as he returned from an outside trip to relieve himself. "Maybe we should stay holed up here until the weather breaks." He perched on a boulder behind where the Indian was sitting." 'Johnny, what are you doing?"

"Studying a map," said the other. "There's a plateau north of here that should produce some wildlife when the rain passes. My mother's birthday is next week and I'm sure she'd enjoy having a picture of a moose. They always fascinate her."

"You think it will clear soon?"

They were both looking at the misty valley below the cave when something shot past the entrance. "Wow! Did you see that?"

Both jumped up and rushed to the cave opening. They were just in time to see the silver disk slip across the rough grasslands, hedgehop a cluster of pine and disappear into a tree lined valley.

"There it is! Crap! I don't believe it," cried Cal. "It's some sort of flying machine."

"A UFO?" queried Johnny hesitantly.

"Damned if I know. It sure was hitting the gas at super-speed."

"Wow!" said the Indian boy. "That'll blow my sister's mind."

"They won't believe us," muttered Cal. "That's all spooky stuff. My parents are somewhat religious. Fundamentalists with a capital F."

The weather broke shortly after ten a.m. and the sun came through as the pair trekked up a wildlife trail to the plateau. A soft warm breeze coming over the Coast Mountains provided a refreshing treat from the earlier rain. Tall grasses stretched away for at least two miles and on each side of the alpine meadow a row of aspens trembled in front of fir trees. A cloud of mist still hung over the scene as the boys found a well defined deer trail cutting across the lower part of the meadow.

A soft almost imperceptible humming sound behind drew their attention. Spinning round they saw the shiny silvery object hovering about 200 feet above the ground, a quarter of a mile away.

"Oh, that's sick," cried Cal in shock. "Freakin' awesome!"

"I get a gut feeling that it's watching us!" retorted Johnny.

"Why? What in hell's name have we done?"

"Nothing! I guess it just doesn't like us."

"I heard on one of the TV channels they abduct people," muttered Cal.

"Let's get the heck out of here," cried Johnny feeling distinctly uncomfortable.

Swiftly they realized they had been caught in wide open territory. There was no place to hide. No trees. No caves. No gullies. Just a wide inhospitable plateau. Besides, running with backpacks was neither easy nor practical. But the acute desire for survival gripped both of the teenagers. Feeling totally cornered and with adrenalin pumping their young bodies they were ready to flee in deadly earnest.

Spinning round they turned to run but they both stopped and stared.

"Jeeze!" cried Cal. "What's that?"

"Hell! I don't know," muttered the Indian. "An Egyptian?"

The giant had appeared almost in the blink of an eyelid. Fast and out of nowhere. Standing some eight feet tall and wearing a white suit with a gold belt. His face appeared white, sharp and angular but a light tan gave him life. His arms hung loosely at his side and a white with gold trim brimless circular kofia sat on the man's head.

"Hello, I am An-Nusku," he said in perfect Oxford English. "Please tell me from where do you come?"

The voice put the two teenagers at ease and they realized later that the man spoke with almost an hypnotic lilt. They quickly explained they were high school students on vacation hiking and exploring the wilderness wildlife.

An-Nusku smiled. "Or security observers followed you from the cave and were somewhat concerned."

"What are you doing here?" asked Johnny. "Making a movie?"

The man ignored the question. "We have chosen this plateau for an important meeting of the elders. It is remote and generally inaccessible by land and we can, if necessary block any aerial movements."

The boys stared across the plateau, the mists they had spotted earlier had disappeared and now there was only grass almost as far as they eyes could see. A ridge of mountains broke the view.

"In this place? Why there's nothing here," said Cal.

An-Nusku moved to the boys' side, promptly turned and clapped his hands gently. "Perhaps you need to learn how to see," he said softly. As he spoke images appeared over much of the plateau. Both boys gasped as a long ornate building in white with purple trim resembling a medieval palace opened up before them. At each end a golden pyramid glittered brightly in the sun.

"Is it real?" cried Johnny now feeling totally helpless.

"Of course," said An-Nusku easily. "Once the conference is over it will be removed."

"Say, mister," cried Cal, "who are these elders coming here."

"There are many. Key leaders. Opinion and law makers from different lands," he said. "Too many to name."

"You're inviting them?" asked Cal innocently.

For the first time the man hesitated but then he permitted a hesitant smile to flicker over his angular face. "Inviting is not an operative word. They will simply come and join our elders for a discussion."

For the first time the Indian teenager sensed a negative energy emanating and he knew the stranger was not talking about free will and that bothered him. "When will this discussion, this meeting be?"

"When the sun is at its peak. They call it the summer solstice," said An-Nusku.

"That's June 21st," replied Cal. "That's next Friday."

"Hey, does anyone know about this?" asked the Indian. "We haven't seen any notices, ads, that sort of thing. What's it about?"

"Those who know already know, those who don't know and should know will be brought," he said. Then as if tiring of the conversation he started to turn away but he stopped and looked back.

The dark brown eyes gazed first at the Indian boy. "Where is God?"

Caught completely by surprise the teenager shrugged, tried to grin at the silliness of the question then peered at the stranger and said: "The Great Spirit is in the Earth."

An Nusku nodded then stared at the other boy. "Cal, where is God."

The teenager remembered what his mother had taught him and immediately raised his right arm with a finger pointing directly to the sky."

The stranger shrugged then smiled softly. "Anyway at the Gathering there will be others of your age. Do you wish to attend?"

"Absolutely," cried Cal. "How do we get here? Helicopter?"

An-Nusku smiled at the enthusiasm of the youngsters. "Do you know the Indian elder Saks Bellefleur?"

"Saks?" said Cal. "We both attend his Saturday morning flute and meditation classes at his ranch."

"That is excellent. Saks knows all about us and you can come with him," said the man. Then with a wave of his arm he and the images across the meadow vanished. They turned to look for the UFO but that too had gone.

For at least a minute the two teenagers stood in stunned silence not knowing what to say next. Finally the Indian said: "Deep in my heart the Great Spirit is telling us to return home."

"Yes, I agree," muttered Cal. "There is something here that is distinctly not cool. In fact I have the feeling we should not be here. It's not good."

The boys turned and started to walk back along the way they had come. Cal tried to phone out then realized the closest cell tower was probably ten miles away and out of reach. Johnny pulled out the GPS.

"It's showing a grid reference here," he said and pulling out a notebook from his jacket pocket wrote down the grid reference. "Your father will probably want to know where this happened."

"We should tell my folks?"

Johnny thought. "Let's get to Saks' place and see what he knows. According to this it's about six miles east-south-east of here."

"We'll make it by late afternoon," said Cal and with that the boys started the long and arduous trek down from the plateau. Initially they followed deer tracks, then a dried creek bed and finally they found an old, almost overgrown logging road that took them to an open meadow with several horses. They both recognized the ranch house tucked away among the cedars and aspen. Exhausted and breathless they staggered through the garden.

Jenny sitting on the patio deck looked up from peeling potatoes. "Hi young men, it's not class today. But it's good to see you anyway. What's up?" She peered at the boys as they slumped down on wicker chairs. "My goodness something is wrong. What is it?"

"Is Saks here?" gasped Cal as he looked around.

"Coming," said a voice from the old log barn at the end of the house. "Something tells me you have a problem. Did you meet a bear."

"No. We met a fellow named An-Nusku," cried Cal. "A real strange dude all dressed up like an Egyptian in a white suit and cap."

Saks nodded. An-Nusku was here last winter. Stayed several days."

"He's a wizard," put in Jenny, peering over her glasses and pushing aside her silver-grey hair. "In two days he corrected Sak's injuries that had bothered him for over 30 years. Truly amazing. He's as fit as new now." She laughed softly and her eyes still retained the twinkle Saks had come to love in the cataclysmic days at Amber in British Columbia.

"He claims there's a meeting, a conference or something of the elders," said Johnny eagerly. "It's a fascinating place. They have a palace and a couple of pyramids on the Eagle Plateau. Right above Murtle Lake."

Saks and Jenny both peered intently at the young Indian boy. "The man – he was a giant – said if we were with you on Friday for the Summer Solstice we could come with you to see what goes on."

"You don't think you'll get bored?" queried Saks.

"Oh, no," responded Cal. "He was a real cool dude and he had a UFO with him."

Saks started to clean his old briar pipe. "Hey, fellows, can you keep a secret?"

"Sure," they cried in unison.

"Make sure you don't tell anyone. Not a single soul until Friday."

The two lads stayed for dinner with Saks and Jenny. Shortly after Cal's father picked them up and took them home and as requested neither breathed a word about what they had seen. Both claimed the expedition had been a washout because of the rain.

Jenny and Saks spent the rest of the evening sitting on the cedar deck chatting and listening to the silence of the world around them. Finally she spoke.

"Why Friday? Why should they keep a secret until Friday?"

The dark brown eyes peered from under the heavy Indian brow and a sigh came from the aging face. "Because by Friday it will be too late. Our ancestors will be here to clean up the mess."

"Will you call David?"

"Of course, I will do that now."

22

ERICH STEINER AND DAVID Rowan accompanied by Molly Thomsen decided they needed some exercise and as Steiner succinctly expressed it, "some mind-clearing air," so they spent an hour after dinner walking barefoot along the expansive sandy beach at Nehalem. Steiner felt frustrated like a person who is in range of a pot of gold, the Golden Fleece, but is unable to grasp it. Apart from having Chloe ride up and down on a piece of antique metal which Geraint-Jones claimed was an Anunnaki artifact there was little else to the story. "That'll make five minutes on YouTube and viewers will claim it's a fake, a fraud," muttered the movie man.

"You really need someone with credibility to sit down and interview Hugh and Chloe and conduct a full production piece," said Rowan holding his head high to capture the distinctive aromas of the Pacific.

"The skeptical hordes will create a furor so mainline TV won't touch it because corporate America does not approve," put in Molly. "Regular TV shows won't touch it with a Mississippi bargepole. No one ever wants to go out on a limb and say this is genuine in spite of the odds being that it is."

"Yeah," nodded Steiner reluctantly. "That's the damned trouble. The other thing is Geraint-Jones really does not want any real publicity on his flying carpet – because of commercial or bureaucratic thieves. People like the Lebanese will scream piracy and maintain Geraint-Jones stole it."

Rowan stopped walking and the others turned back to face him. "It's bloody obvious that the world isn't ready for the work of the Babylonian scribes. This is in spite of the fact that the tablets have been gathering dust in various leading museums of the world since the mid-19th century. Our so-called modern cultures simply don't want to hear that their gods were cosmic travelers who came from a rogue planet named Nibiru which earthlings called Heaven."

"That's right on!" cried Molly. "White America doesn't want to hear that their ancestors 160,000 years ago were predominantly black and originated in South Africa. It goes against the grain." She turned her face towards the setting sun and the ocean breeze caught and fluttered through her fair hair like invisible fingers playing. "It doesn't bother me," she said defiantly, "in fact I get a kick out of the possibility that there is a cosmic gene operating in my body."

For a moment, Rowan saw the mischievous twinkle in her eyes and he flashed a smile back. Then as if pulling himself back to his thoughts he plunged his hands deep in his pockets. "One thing has been bothering me for quite a while."

The other two stared at him, their faces quizzical and demanding.

"Why are we chasing pyramids and why are we being briefed so much in detail about who the builders were and how these astral travelers created us Earthlings through genetic engineering? Why do we need to know all this? Is this what the ghost pyramids are all about?"

"Geraint-Jones explained that people like Zecharia Sitchin and others have translated various parts of the Babylonian tablets and many books are already available on the origins of humankind, the Anunnaki gods and the imprint they left on Earth," said Molly slowly as if her mind was searching the words for answers.," Then suddenly she stopped and stared at Rowan.

"David, who set you up for this trek?"

"Set up?"

"Remember the kid – Peter Singleton – the one who was found at the Tikiout pyramid? Well he had a copy of your UFO debunking book."

"That was coincidental," said the writer in a mildly protesting tone.

"Was it?" snapped Molly.

"You told me about that woman – Alison Simonian in London -- urging you to check in with Geraint-Jones," she said slowly, a frown crossing her brow. She stared at Rowan. "Why would she do that?"

"Perhaps she wants me to debunk the whole thing," said Rowan. "Maybe I have to write that this whole aspect of humanity, the Anunnaki reports, the Babylonian tablets is a complete fraud."

"And what about so many people witnessing the spectral pyramids?" snapped Steiner.

"Mass hysteria," retorted Rowan with a shrug. As I wrote in the book thousands of people witness flying saucers or UFOs and yet so few people capture good pictures and good video of these things on camera in spite of us living in the digital-age. You must agree the quality in most cases is inferior and highly questionable."

"Wow," said Molly with a whistle. "It's a good thing they didn't get you on stage at Taos. You'd be severely bruised by the fundamentalists."

Both men smiled and walked on. Some youngsters building a large sandcastle caught their attention and Molly stopped to talk to them. Just then Rowan's cell phone buzzed. It was Kate. He walked towards the incoming tide as he listened and it was not until they were in the relative safety of the Geraint-Jones home that he revealed to everyone what was happening.

"Hugh," said Rowan. "You're right. Apparently the Anunnaki are here on Earth and not only flying around in so-called UFOs, they have established an Earth Mission on a remote plateau in the forests and mountain areas of British Columbia. They say they wish to speak to all the elders – that was the word they used – elders of the world to discuss the current state of the planet – which they describe as their colony."

"Wow!" exclaimed Molly.

"Geraint-Jones and Chloe smiled softly to each other and held hands but no one seemed to notice.

"Crap! I've gotta be there," snapped Steiner, "who knows, maybe I can get an exclusive." He paused then added in an excited tone: "What's the source of this mind-blowing stuff."

"Two teenagers hiking in the high country ran straight into an eight foot tall man named An-Nusku who showed them the outside of the Mission building. It's not visible unless they show it to you."

"Sounds far-fetched to me," snapped Steiner, his initial enthusiasm dwindling.

"Oh, it's genuine all right," said Rowan. "My mother's life-long partner Saks Running Wind – original name Bellefleur – called my daughter Kate and said he had actually had a visit from the Anunnaki earlier this year but was asked to keep silent until Friday."

"What's Friday?" quizzed Steiner.

"Summer Solstice," replied Molly.

"The longest day of the year," added Chloe. "Well, I must say this is totally intriguing."

"Saks Bellefleur?" Molly looked at Rowan. "Is he the Indian runner your father mentioned in his book Cataclysm '79? There were claims he was badly injured in both legs."

Rowan nodded. "Apparently the visiting Anunnaki somehow corrected both his legs and now he's running around – well at least walking without a cane. Miraculously healed after 35 years, but I find it difficult to believe."

"Hey," chipped in Steiner. "This I gotta see. Can I come with you guys?"

Rowan looked at Molly. "Are you on board, Miss Thomsen? I'd be grateful if you came along."

Molly nodded. "I wouldn't miss this for the world."

"Come along, Erich," said Rowan. "You might secure footage to make a movie after all."

Suddenly a new voice popped up. "Can we come? I would love to meet these people." It was Chloe. She looked appealingly first at Rowan and then at her husband. "Hugh?"

"Aren't we a little ancient to be ripping round the country looking for aliens?"

"Shush!" quipped Chloe. "They are our ancestors. You've been talking about them for sixty years, it's about time you said hello."

"We'll take my plane up to Whidbey Island tomorrow morning," said Steiner enthusiastically. "Then we'll figure out how to cross the Canadian border and get into the B.C. interior."

"Let's drink on that," said Chloe producing another bottle of wine and glasses.

They spent the rest of the evening talking and getting ready for next morning's departure. Then Rowan's cell phone buzzed again. He listened intently then looked at everybody.

"There's a distinct feeling that someone – perhaps the Anunnaki – are showing their muscle. Remember I told you earlier about how a small village named Ravenswood in Pennsylvania suffered a mysterious and complete power shutdown?"

They nodded.

"Well, it's happened again," he said. According to Jax Devenport of the CIA – who's waiting to see me at home – it has happened in China. He says the Lanzhou Zhongchuan Airport along with surrounding homes and industrial sites suffered a mysterious power failure similar to the one in Ravenswood. It was so complete a passenger jet lost power on take-off, crashed and left 151 dead."

"Wow?" exclaimed Molly. "How could a power outage on the ground affect a plane taking off?"

"Computer shut down," suggested Rowan. "But how or why, God only knows."

"Could that be a coincidence?" asked Steiner.

"Now here's the kicker," said Rowan grimly. "The CIA claims the Ravenswood and the China incidents occurred at exactly the same time – to the second in fact and lasted the same time to the exact second." His eyes panned the group.

"Think about this," he said quietly. "These power outages are not your run of the mill events, they are shown to be all embracing and deadly. If the Anunnaki are doing this, the big question is why? Then, let's turn it around. If the Anunnaki are not doing this, somebody is capable of wielding some very powerful and killer forces. Are you all sure you want to come to British Columbia?"

They all nodded enthusiastically and Molly's hazel eyes sparkled. "Mother would give her right arm to be with us," she cried. "She'll be quite envious." Turning to Rowan she touched his arm. "David you mentioned the rugged interior of British Columbia. Where exactly are we going?"

The writer became pensive. "The area in question is high in the mountains of the province's interior. To get to there we must travel through the Cascade Range and into the interior which is grasslands – cattle country. Then beyond the city of Kamloops up the Yellowhead route to a town called Clearwater and a wilderness known as Wells Gray Park. Mom's place is beyond that. It's in real rugged country."

Chloe who had been listening intently echoed David's words. "Clearwater and beyond that? What was the inscription that the Singleton boy made in your book? The one he carried at Tikiout in Morocco."

"Les pyramides à l'eau Claire?" he replied quickly.

Chloe nodded. "That's French for the pyramids beyond the clear water."

"Clearwater!" exclaimed Molly excitedly. "This means that Peter Singleton knew all along about The Gathering in British Columbia. Wow! This is fascinating."

"Singleton also wrote Not Thirty," said Geraint-Jones. "These pyramids up there are nowhere near 30 degrees latitude north."

Rowan remained pensive for several moments. "It goes a little deeper than that," he said quietly. "We were all meant to be exactly where we are at this present moment."

"That's ridiculous!" said Steiner quickly.

"Is it?" muttered Rowan. "I have the feeling that we are pawns and the chess masters are the Anunnaki."

"That coming from the great extraterrestrial debunker is one heck of a turn-around," quipped Steiner.

"Is it? The woman Alison Simonian finds me in a London bookshop and urges me to come to Oregon and get a briefing from two archaeologists who are not only knowledgeable about pyramids but also the Babylonian tablets, the Sumerians and the space travelers – the Anunnaki, the creators, the gods of Homo sapiens, the people who were our fathers."

The writer walked to the edge of the deck and gazed across the expanse of water, then turning to the others he declared: "There's something missing. Some element that we have missed or haven't yet heard about."

Everyone was silent.

Geraint-Jones cleared his throat and stroked his beard. "President Bush used the term some years back – weapons of mass destruction. You should know the Anunnaki used them on Earth 4,000 years ago and the scars are still visible today. The year was 2024 BCE. There is a very dark side to the Anunnaki, the people our ancestors called gods. Remind me to talk about that later."

More silence.

"Let's get going to Whidbey Island and British Columbia," said Rowan but the eagerness in his voice had diminished and Molly felt tension growing inside him.

23

PENNI SINGLETON LAY SLEEPING on a comfortable bed in one of the guest rooms at the Rowan "cottage" at Admiral's Cove on Whidbey Island. Mark had made her calming chamomile tea which soon allowed the exhausted mother to slip off into a deep healthy sleep. Occasionally through the night they would hear talking but as Devenport pointed out she was talking in her sleep.

"Although I would sure like to have a heart-to-heart talk and find out why her kid is the way he is," he told Mark and Kate as they sat on the deck in the shade of a mass of grape vines clinging to rafters above the cedar deck. The CIA man's dark brown eyes stared through his heavy spectacles at their drinks. "You enjoy that porcupine piss?"

"Its fresh lemonade," Kate protested with a shallow grin. "Would you like another killer coffee?"

"Nah! The last one ripped my old steam engine apart," said Devenport. "I'm surprised I slept last night." He paused. "Thanks for putting me up. That's good of you."

"Didn't you and Mary put Dad up when he was writing his CIA book?"

"That was some years back."

"Anyway, we have some six bedrooms in the annex and a dormitory upstairs over the barn," she said. "We could house an army if needs be. I don't know why Dad bought such a large place."

"Books," said Mark stoically. "He's got books in every room."

Kate's iPhone beeped. "Dad's on his way – with a small army. Be here at six," she said then taking her leave of the CIA man she said "Mark, I have to drive over to Oak Harbor this morning and load up with groceries at Safeway. Can you help?"

"I'll help too," said Devenport chuckling.

"It'll do me good to get domesticated for a while."

"What about Mrs. Singleton?"

"The chamomile will hold her," said Mark. "I accidentally gave her a triple."

"Mark!" Kate flashed a stern glance as she backed out the SUV. "You're bad!"

It was exactly at six that a sleek black stretch limousine arrived at Admiral's Cove and deposited David Rowan, Molly Thomsen, Erich Steiner plus Hugh and Chloe Geraint-Jones. For almost half an hour everything at the Cove cottage vibrated with chatter and laughter as Kate and Mark guided guests to their rooms.

To add to the chatter a dazed Penni Singleton staggered into their midst and smiled bleakly at everyone then suddenly realizing the presence of the CIA seized Devenport by the shoulder and deftly steered him into the yard. Her sharp voice still loaded with the dryness of prolonged sleep crackled: "Mr. Devenport, where is my son?"

The CIA man grated his teeth. He hated being accosted at the best of times by the male species and when it was a woman, well his stress levels soared like a rocket loaded with irritability.

"Listen, lady," he growled like a bulldog ready to bite, "If I knew that I would have him shackled and in deep interrogation. Peter Singleton is a bloody killer. We have footage showing him calmly watching one of our choppers burning and eight SWAT Team officers gone – who knows where." Devenport glared at the woman. "Are you the creature that spawned this creep?"

Sobbing and frustrated Penni Singleton threw up her arms in sheer disgust, started to walk back into the cottage then suddenly changed direction and stalked off along the beach road. Devenport watched her go then in a moment of growing remorse hurried after her and apologized.

"Hey, lady, I don't know how I can help, but I'll try," he said and in the next little while he heard Penni Singleton's story that started 19 years before in Cairo. As they walked along the road they were oblivious to the passing of a Yellow Cab from Seattle-Tacoma Airport. It stopped outside the Rowan cottage. Paul and Natalie Rowan tired from their long flight from Europe had arrived.

Kate totally thrilled and gleeful gave each enthusiastic hugs. For a few moments David made a valiant attempt to explain that Paul and Natalie were his step-parents. "My guardians, the folks who made me a part of their lives and injected me with the desire to write," he said mastering a bland smile.

"Hey, don't blame us for some of the UFO and alien debunking the kid produced in his latest book," said the elder Rowan with a grin. Ever since he had first met David as a nine year-old at Amber in the Fraser Canyon, Paul had referred to him as kid. He glanced around at the group. "Let's make it clear: I'm on the side of the UFOers."

"That's great!" Molly called out. "My mother runs a UFO spotters group down in New Mexico."

"Good Lord! How is it that you are mixed up with my step-son, the great UFO debunker?" said Natalie accepting a glass of wine from Mark.

Molly laughed lightly. "Listen, I attempted to convert him but I think I'm an abysmal failure."

A chorus of laughter lightened the entire group.

David took the floor. Somewhere along the way of life I ended up with two mothers – and I love each one dearly. This is Natalie who got me sorted out at school and pushed me through university," he said holding her hand. "For those of you coming to British Columbia you'll meet my dearly beloved birth mother Jenny and her husband Saks when we get to their Running Wind Ranch." Pausing briefly he added: "We have to be there by dawn on Friday – that's the summer solstice when things are supposed to happen."

"What things are supposed to happen?" Devenport sounded cynical.

"A UFO is coming to pick up volunteers and take us to something called The Gathering," David said easily then he grinned along with the others.

"Hey, I'll believe that when I see it," put in Steiner.

"Frankly I have no idea," David continued. "Saks says we will actually be meeting some aliens from another world. I'm still trying to get my mind round the idea. To be fully rested and ready for this unique adventure I think we should arrive at the Ranch by mid-day Thursday."

"How far is this Running Wind Ranch from here?" asked Geraint-Jones.

"Just under 400 miles or 630 kilometers," responded David Rowan. "It's about a nine hour drive – if there are no hang-ups."

"Hey, we could fly. I've got wings," said Steiner. "The bird is at the Oak Harbor Airport."

"Good idea," sounded an immediate and enthusiastic chorus.

It was now Monday and darkness closed in on Whidbey Island shortly after nine p.m. and most of the group exhausted through travel had retired for the night. Steiner, an inveterate outdoors man, pulled out some blankets and a pillow and slept curled up on the deck under the grape vines where he could feel the soft night breezes coming across from the distant Olympic Peninsula caressing his face. Devenport tried to sleep but his chat with Penni Singleton disturbed his thinking so he slipped into his slacks and shirt and wandered down to the beach where he found David and Molly drinking Washington State Riesling in the light of a an old brass hurricane oil lamp.

"That Singleton woman," growled Devenport as he sat down on the log beside them. "Now most of these UFO types, ghost-hunters and psychics I can stand but she takes the biscuit and then some."

"Is she strange?" enquired Molly.

"Strange? She's nuttier than a fruit cake. Cuckoo!"

"How so?" asked David.

"Well, some twenty years ago she marries a fellow she calls a Great Guy but it turns out he's a blank cartridge, no lead in the pencil."

"Infertile?" said Molly.

"Bull's eye! That's it. Infertile," quipped the CIA man. "He's also impotent. She finds out he was badly abused as a child so they don't indulge in sex while he attempts to go through therapy." He paused and looked at the two in the growing darkness. "The wife Penni Singleton gets depressed. It happens she is also a frustrated Catholic. Unable to find spirituality in the pews or sex at home she boards a New Age Christian movement in New Jersey. The group organizes Holy Land and Middle East tours every year so she climbs aboard and somehow finds herself feeling sick in a downtown Cairo hotel. Unable to travel she misses a five day cruise on the Nile and stays alone in her suite."

"All by herself? Isn't that dangerous?" asked Molly.

Devenport shrugged. "An Arab who claims to be the hotel medic checks her out says she is suffering from a virus and orders her to drink juice and take some pills. She claims she cannot remember much about the five days. Twice she recalls someone, a tall man in a white coat resembling a doctor coming in and talking with her and each time she felt pleasantly dizzy and dreamed of angels massaging her body."

"How strange," remarked David.

Devenport nods. "This is the weird part. At the end of five days, Mrs. Singleton suddenly feels well, rejoins the group and after sight-seeing in Alexandria the tour returns to New Jersey. Well, it's there she feels the old morning sickness thing and her doctor announces she's pregnant – got one in the oven so to speak. Well, this blows her sanity and she's given a mild sedative."

"Heavens above!" cried Molly with a shudder.

"In spite of the doctor confirming to her flabbergasted husband that his wife is still a virgin, Dan Singleton blows a gasket and heads off home to a pandering mother who gets him to cool down. Eventually he returns to Penni -- the day before she goes into labor. Even with all these doubts and the unanswered question of who fathered the kid, they raise the boy as their own."

"So it all ended happily ever after?" suggested Molly.

"Are you kidding?" snapped Devenport. "The boy is a whizz-kid, a genius. He's walking and talking key words at seven months. At age 12 he's making rings round the local religious gurus. At 17 he quits university saying the professors were teaching outdated material and they should live in the real world. He disappears for several weeks. Penni says it was forty days. She claims she counted each day in torment."

David Rowan frowned. "So where was he?"

"His mother has no idea but when he reappears suddenly in the house all he says he has been called and must go and study in the deserts of the world to await the right time," said Devenport. "The woman is frantic. The kid is only 18 years old."

Nobody spoke for several minutes. They simply watched the moon reflected in the waters of Puget Sound, listened to the waves and sipped their wine. Finally, Devenport spoke.

"So where is this place that you're going to meet the UFO people?"

Rowan shook his head. "It's about ten miles north-west of my mother's ranch and that's in the mountain foothills close to Wells Grey Park off the Yellowhead Highway. It's a large plateau covered by grass and surrounded by mountain ridges," he said slowly. "A couple of teenagers doing a Nature hike said they saw a UFO and spoke to an alien who said they should come back on Friday – the summer solstice to witness an event called The Gathering."

"Would that be a meeting?"

"We honestly don't know," he said. "But my mother says we are all invited. Maybe they have a bus that can take us up there. Ten miles is tough going on foot in that area. It's raw territory."

"Can I come?" Devenport spoke slowly.

"Sure! Why not," said Molly. "It'll do that warped CIA mind of yours some fresh outlook on a different world."

The trio walked back into the cottage and called out good nights. Devenport at the far end of the building closed the door of his room flipped open his cell phone and dialed a 703 area code which would link him to a place in Fairfax County, Virginia and a complex known as the George Bush Center for Intelligence – the home of the CIA.

24

IN THE PREDAWN HOURS of the Tuesday morning some 360 miles to the east of Whidbey Island and the Rowan cottage there was unusual activity at the Fairchild Air Force Base (AFB) south-west of Spokane, Washington. A sleek 1,000 pound Predator-B unmanned aircraft undergoing scheduled tests for U.S.-Canada border surveillance was commissioned for a special late-call reconnaissance flight. It took off on the west-east runway banked over Interstate 90 then headed directly north.

Within the hour it had crossed into Canadian airspace, changed to a nor-nor-west course that took it over Okanagan Lake and the City of Kelowna. It was dawn when the Predator cut through the mountains of the North Thompson Valley changed vector and again headed north for Clearwater. It crossed Wells Gray Park and was over the plateau ten miles North West of the Running Wind Ranch.

For some unfathomable reason the controller back at Fairchild Base was unable to explain, the Predator suddenly tilted forward and performed a nose dive into a heavily forested mountainside. In the nine second gap between losing control of the aircraft and the crash, images were flashed back to base. A photo-analyzer working with video recordings told the officer in charge: "There are six circular objects on the adjoining grassland. About ten meters in diameter."

"Any idea what they might be?"

"No sir. They appear like the lids of large garbage cans. One is suspended in the air as if ready to move."

"All right, Adams," said the officer. "Should I say they are UFOs?"

"You might say that, sir."

Ten miles from where the Predator crashed and burned Jenny was doing her morning chores of milking the goats. She stood up.

"Saks, did you hear that?"

The old Indian nodded as he pulled open a bale of hay. "I have the feeling that someone in high authority has just done something foolish. Just before it happened I saw a strange white aircraft crossing the valley. A low flyer and it was being followed."

"Followed?"

"Shadowed then." Saks looked at his watch. "It's just 7:00 a.m."

On the other side of the continent in Washington D.C. the Homeland Security Secretary called the White House and a short while later the Vice President of the United States was on the line to Ottawa and the Prime Minister of Canada.

Shortly before 11:00 a.m. one ministerial secretary chatted with another on Canada's Parliament Hill. "The Americans told us that one of their drones got lost and accidentally crashed in the mountains of British Columbia. Would we be so good as to pick up any remains, box them up and ship them to the manufacturers?"

"Bloody Americans," snapped the other secretary. "Whatever will they think of next?"

They laughed easily but it was short lived.

It was exactly 11:00 a.m. Eastern Daylight Time that the lights went out in Ottawa.

"Bloody hydro electric people," said the secretary staring from a window. Suddenly she gasped as a large commuter helicopter fell out of the sky crashed onto the lawn at Parliament Hill and promptly exploded sending a ball of gold and black flame billowing skywards.

Then everyone started screaming,shouting and running.

25

THE BLACKOUT STRUCK AT exactly 8:00 a.m. on the west coast. No warning. It just happened. Everything became still in the Rowan cottage on Whidbey Island. Some members of the group were sipping coffee at the picnic table on the deck while others were standing in the yard watching a cruise ship heading for Seattle. Others were still in their rooms hurrying to respond to Kate's breakfast call. Jax Devenport was in the road quietly talking to his superior on the east coast when he suddenly realized his cell phone had gone dead.

Kate and Molly working round the electric stove and a toaster oven suddenly realized the equipment had gone dead and the light bulbs had quietly ceased to function.

"Power failure," muttered David as Molly wandered in barefooted and carrying sandals. He stood up and walked outside where Paul and Natalie were sunning themselves on the deck. "Something's happened to the power. My computer's off."

Erich Steiner was on the beach with Kate's boyfriend Mark both taking photos of gnarled and bleached driftwood.

"My digital still camera just died," said the movie maker.

"Mine's okay," said Mark. "I have an old 35 millimeter Praktika with film. No problem," he said and cranked the film.

Penni Singleton, frail and worn was gaining comfort from Hugh and Chloe Geraint-Jones as they strolled along the road leading to the ferry. They all stopped and gaped.

"The ship," cried Chloe. "It's lost power and is drifting out to sea." Even as she spoke a distress flare arced through the morning sky.

Kate came from the kitchen. "Someone call the Power and Light people," she called out. "My cell phone is as dead as a door nail."

David moved forward and picked up the land line phone on the corner table. "This shouldn't happen. It's dead as well."

"Heck! What's happening?" cried Steiner as he ran back into the cottage followed by Mark. "All the neighbors are checking with each other. Everything is dead. Just along the road two cars just stopped dead and on the hill there's a stalled cop car with two officers peering under the hood and shaking their heads."

Even as he spoke a policeman appeared at the door. "Our car and radios have just gone dead. Could we use your landline, sir?"

David shook his head. "I'm afraid you're out of luck. Everything is dead here."

The officer nodded to Rowan's SUV. "Could we borrow your vehicle?"

The writer walked to the vehicle, opened the door and turned the ignition. Nothing happened.

"Oh, crap!" snapped the policeman starting to feel totally helpless. For some seconds he peered at the people in the cottage then throwing up his hands started walking back up the hill to his own vehicle.

"I'll make some more coffee," said Natalie.

"Yeah. You know some magic?" quizzed Steiner.

"We could light a fire in the barbecue pit," said Kate. "There's an iron kettle in the cupboard."

"The tap doesn't work in the bathroom," said Devenport moving into the living room.

Kate turned the faucet in the kitchen. A dribble emerged.

"The water system pump is powered by electricity," said her father. "In the barn there's a stack of spring water in gallon bottles we could use for cooking."

Molly looked at David. "There's something strange here, dear," she said. "You computer has an eight-hour battery. Why isn't that working?"

David Rowan came over and pushed the power switch. "It's completely dead. It's not just a power failure. It seems that anything powered by electricity is dead. It no longer works."

"How on earth can that be?" cried Kate from the kitchen.

Hugh Geraint-Jones walked into the living room followed by Chloe and Penni Singleton and was just about to speak when a horrendous explosion rattled the windows and a column of fire and smoke pierced the blue sky over Puget Sound.

"Something just hit the water," said the archaeologist. "I think we saw a big airliner coming down low. We didn't think anything of it."

"It must have lost power too," commented Steiner. "Everything driven by electricity has stopped. Even my watch has stopped."

Everyone glanced at their watches and gasped.

"Eight o'clock!" muttered Paul and Natalie Rowan coming in from the deck. "It's damnably crazy. Everything stopped at precisely 8:00 a.m. What the hell is going on?"

For the very first time the people gathered at the Rowan cottage on Whidbey Island began to experience a growing sense of acute fear deep within. There were no explanations and people simply hate that because it stirs the elements of phobia to greater lengths in their minds. And the ultimate fear among human beings is death.

"I think we had better get down on our knees and pray," suggested Natalie.

"Not now, dear," said Paul. "I think we had better try and find out what's happening elsewhere."

It was quickly decided that Kate and Mark should take bicycles and ride over to Coupeville the nearest town, make contact with someone in authority and find out what was happening. Armed with bottles of spring water they headed out while the others gathered in the shade of the grape vines growing over the deck.

"Who is for a drink?" cried David attempting to stimulate the rest to positive action. Then a thought speared his bewildered mind and he suddenly stopped. "My God! I've suddenly realized. Kate and Mark have no way of telling us where and how they are."

The grimness of the situation now provoked frantic fears in the minds of everyone. The growing realization that this was now a regular regional power failure created fear and despondency among the group. For a moment Erich Steiner brightened the situation when he triumphantly produced a 16 millimeter Bell and Howell movie camera with a tri-turret lens. "Guess what! It's clockwork. A wind-up. I had a hunch I should bring it along." He grinned. "Insurance! Just in case we see any action."

Jackson Devenport standing at the cottage door muttered cynically: "You missed the plane crash."

"Ouch!" said Steiner. "That hurt." He flashed a jaded grin.

"Look! There's a hell of a fire over in Port Townsend," said the CIA man and everyone gathered on the deck to see.

"There are several fires in different places," said Molly anxiously reaching for David's arm. "There's something about all of this I don't like."

Then someone saw two cyclists racing down the hill leading into Admiralty Bay. "It's Kate and Mark," cried David suddenly feeling better.

The two young people pushed their bicycles into the barn then came over to the deck where all eyes were upon them.

"Bicycles are in demand," cried Kate slumping down in a recliner. "We were offered a hundred bucks for our bikes by some grown-ups heading to Coupeville. 'They said they were going to raid the supermarket for food."

"There was a whole gang of them," said Mark. "If the two cops who were walking back to Coupeville hadn't come along and pulled their revolvers we would have lost the bikes."

"People panicking! Going crazy!" cried Kate. "We met a teenage girl who was hysterical because she couldn't text her boyfriend in Oak Harbor. She was screaming at everybody and pleading for a cell phone that worked."

"Heavens! I'd like to think you're kidding," snapped Natalie. "It's obvious the situation is deteriorating quickly."

"Hell of a story," said Paul Rowan. "It's one of those days when I wished I was still working for Verity."

"How would you get the story in?" growled Devenport. "Throw a note in a corked bottle?"

"I cannot believe this is happening," said Kate shaking her head. "It's not normal." She peered at her father. "How are we going to get up to Jenny and Saks in British Columbia."

"How far is it?" asked Molly?

"About 350 miles," said David. "Or 550 kilometers in Canadian metric. It's about seven to eight hours driving."

"Except we haven't got wheels," muttered Devenport sourly. "Just a couple of bikes."

"That means we are going to miss the chance of a lifetime on Friday – the summer solstice," cried Molly. "Isn't that the time these aliens or whatever were going to pick up the people at your mother's ranch?"

Penni Singleton suddenly came alive. "We've just got to get there. My son...we've really got to get there. If there are pyramids I'm sure that is where we have to be." She seized David Rowan's arm. "Please! Please do something. I need my boy."

Suddenly the entire group felt lost, totally crippled with nothing to do, nowhere to go except talk and that did not seem to be going anywhere. Just then Hugh and Chloe Geraint-Jones walked up to the cottage from the water where they had been sitting quietly, completely oblivious to everything going on.

"Hugh has a theory," said Chloe accepting a glass of wine from Kate.

"Heck! That's all we need is a theory," muttered Steiner.

"Why don't we listen?" suggested Rowan senior. "It may help us to understand."

"Good idea," said David and everyone stared at the archaeologist.

"This is an abnormal power outage," he said slowly. "The ramifications are slowly sinking in and the situation will worsen. This phenomenon is not just a simple loss of power for domestic appliances, heating homes, air conditioners, television, electric clocks, computers and cell phones, it goes far beyond that."

"Heck! How far can it go Hugh?" snapped Steiner, slightly dazed and irritable.

"We've seen planes falling out of the air, what looks like oil refineries burning, police without any form of communication and automobiles which rely on both DC batteries and generators are now disabled."

"Gangs are already showing signs of violence in Coupeville," put in David. "If the blackout lasts any length of time, they will raid the supermarkets for food and supplies."

Geraint-Jones nodded. "It appears there is an inability to enforce law and order by the authorities," he said pulling out his pipe and fingering it. "This means buses, trains, and all forms of transport, factories, hospitals, are at a standstill, and the news media has no method of communicating in any shape or form. How far this shut down extends we can only guess."

"So what is your theory, sir?" asked Mark.

"There has been indicators," said Geraint-Jones. "Two mysterious blackouts, one at Ravensbrook in Pennsylvania, the other at Lanzhou Zhongchuan Airport in China where a passenger plane lost power during take-off. The CIA people noted they both happened at the same time and for the same duration. That, ladies and gentlemen is our indicator."

"Indicator of what, Hugh?" asked Devenport.

"Someone, somewhere has been able to neutralize the electrical power systems worldwide," he replied slowly. "If two power outages can occur at the same time and for the same duration at two distant points of the globe, it can only be the work of people who are putting crop circles in 55 countries around the world. Probably the same people who are creating illusions of the Great Pyramid of Giza around the world."

"You're kidding, Hugh" said David Rowan now appearing distinctly uncomfortable. "I really cannot get my mind wrapped around such an idea."

"Still in the box, kid," said Paul but it was not meant unkindly. "Simply a comment."

"My theory and I could be wrong is that the Anunnaki, the biblical Nefilim, the people who created the human family in their likeness in South Africa are back," he said.

Gasps of astonishment and dismay came from the listeners.

"Why would they be so barbaric as to neutralize the world's electrical systems?" asked Molly.

"Well, if you recall Frederick Klassen at the Taos Conference," said Steiner. "He did say the United States had destroyed a stationary extraterrestrial space ship positioned in the Clarke Belt."

"And the only people who have shown an interest in Planet Earth for thousands of years are the Anunnaki," said Geraint-Jones.

"And it seems as if they're back," said Paul Rowan solemnly.

The archaeologist smiled grimly. "It's the return of our fathers," he said. "I may be wrong but I strongly believe they are back."

Everyone started talking at once and David raised his hands. "Something has now become very obvious. We need to be at Jenny and Sak's farm by Friday morning. Because I sense something very critical will happen."

A lone voice full of desperation sounded from the doorway leading into the cottage. "Will I ever get my son back?" she called out, her slim, taut figure trembling in the afternoon sun. "He's all I have, you know." She glanced at Kate: "May I borrow your bike? I have almost $200 for a deposit."

The simple plea hit everyone and silence descended upon the group. Finally David spoke.

"That's interesting. How are people going to get money? Get paid?"

"Why?" It was Steiner.

"ATMs don't work without power and neither do most doors of banks," he replied. "They are mostly computer or electronically controlled. We don't know how far this power shutdown extends but it looks as if the whole country, perhaps the world is shut down."

"That's a morbid thought," muttered Paul.

Frustrated and angry David walked out onto the road turned briefly and beckoned to Molly. "Let's go for a walk to think this thing out. There has to be a solution and maybe our lives will depend on it."

26

YOU WOULD EXPECT PEOPLE in high places to be huddled in closed offices, particularly the chiefs of staff accompanied by their strategy gurus at the Pentagon. When two airliners fell out of the sky and crashed into the Potomac River with several hundred people on board, everyone watching assumed it was another September 11th 2001 and that terrorists had struck again.

All office lights had ceased functioning seconds before the aircraft incident as had computers. Even technological instruments such laptops, iPads, texting devices and more, all stopped working as if their batteries had frozen.

"Where's the emergency backup," cried a man with braid on his uniform.

"Dead," came the reply from down the corridor. "Nothing works."

A CNN reporter outside the Pentagon broadcasting live on a routine political agenda suddenly realized to his horror the link was now dead just as a passenger jet simply plummeted from the sky. Nearby, a news photographer with a digital camera attempted to capture the looming disaster. Frantic, he realized to his horror the unit had simply stopped working. Awestruck at the unfolding drama, he screamed in sheer frustration. "All hell broke loose and I had nothing to record it on," he reminisced later.

At the nerve center of the United States Global Defense System all power ceased. As instructed by emergency regulations and countless practice drills everyone bypassed elevators that were not working anyway and rushed to the stairs leading to the bunkers buried deep below the Pentagon. In doing so they realized with the electricity gone they were cut off where they stood.

"Shit! We're trapped," shrieked a man.

Pentagon employees beat on the electronically motivated doors to the bunker but they were solid and refused to budge. The emergency generators, both the main system and the two back-up systems failed to operate and everything on the stairway was now in total darkness.

"Anybody got a light?" cried a general.

"Wait!" responded a secretary. "I have a flashlight." She fumbled in her pocketbook. "Damn! It doesn't work."

"Hey, everyone sit down," said the general. "Let's think this over."

"On the steps?" came a voice in the darkness. "No one ever thinks of putting chairs in an emergency corridor."

"Who is that? Sellers?"

"Yes, sir."

"Well, you're a bloody analyst. What the fuck has happened?"

"The power's off. Not just off but completely stopped."

"That's impossible."

"No sir, it's possible because it's happened."

"Your logic will get you shot one of these days, Sellers."

"It's so dark in here, sir," said a woman her voice trembling. "I just tried to get back to our office floor and the wretched door won't move."

"You mean we're stuck here on an emergency staircase. We can't get into the bunker and we can't get back to our offices," said a male voice in the darkness.

"Who is that? Secombe?" asked the general.

"It might be, sir."

"For crap's sake. Don't you know," hissed the general from somewhere in the darkness.

"Sir, I'm scared."

"You're scared? We're all scared," croaked the general. "We've got the world's biggest and most expensive defense system complete with every bloody piece of fucking hardware imaginable from nuclear bangers to drones that monitor the world. In addition we have military heavyweights and so-called wisdom gurus falling over each other in this the heart of American Defense and we don't know who screwed our power system."

The general gasped for breath, felt his heart for a moment then continued. "Some bastard unplugged our defenses and if it's the last thing I do, I'm going to get that worm, that toad and pack him into solitary confinement for life."

"Here! Here!" said Sellers with obvious approval.

"Look, I've got a gun," said a young male voice in the darkness.

Silence descended on the group on the stairwell.

"You've what?" said the General.

"It's only an old thirty-eight special," said the young man. "It's a Smith and Wesson. Shippenhauer left it in the desk I inherited when I came here a year ago."

"My God!" muttered the General. "Give it to me. I'll take charge…"

"Hell," muttered the young man, "I've tripped over someone's leg."

"Where's the damn gun?"

"On the steps somewhere. It fell."

"Hey, wait a minute," cried Secombe "I've just trodden on it. I'll get it."

A shot was followed by a zinging crackling ricochet that sliced the darkness.

"Oh, my God," growled the General.

"Well, at least we know something works around here," said the analyst.

All was quiet for a few moments until someone in the darkness was heard to give a prolonged gasp followed by an ominous slump on the stairs.

"Who the hell is that," snarled the General.

"Who knows?" remarked the analyst. "I'm an asthmatic and I'm developing an acute feeling the air conditioning is not working and we are getting short of air."

"Just don't die on my watch," muttered the general.

27

DAVID ROWAN AND MOLLY returned from their walk along the beach road totally at a loss to know what to do next. They also found Penni Singleton openly harassing Kate over her bicycle.

"Dad, she desperately wants to cycle 350 miles to grandma's house to be there for Friday's solstice," said Kate. "I've told her she doesn't stand one chance in a million of getting there."

Their return prompted everyone to gather on the deck to hear David explain the options.

"Right now, there aren't any not unless you consider the two bikes and two horses in the meadow up the hill," he said.

"We could find a cart," suggested the CIA man.

"Fifty miles a day if we're lucky," said David's father. "We'd get there in the middle of next week when the meeting with these aliens would be over."

"The greatest story of our lives and we are stymied," muttered Steiner in sheer disgust.

"There's basically nothing we can do," agreed Molly with a distinct tone of despair.

A pall of disappointment fell over the group. Kate, Natalie and Molly rescued some pork and beef steaks from the still cold refrigerator while the two Rowans found matches and got the charcoal briquettes smoldering in the barbecue. Devenport built a log fire in the backyard while Erich Steiner found some old white emergency candles and more matches while Geraint-Jones and his wife sat at the picnic table trying to console Penni Singleton who periodically burst into a flood of tears.

Natalie called out from the barbecue. "Listen everybody, maybe we should pray for help. That is still an option."

"Hey, maybe God has been unplugged too," cried Steiner trying to lighten things up.

"That's blasphemous," retorted Natalie. "You should just try praying."

Steiner shrugged, stood up and with both hands raised called out: "Hey, God! If you are listening could you find it in your heart to send us some hot wheels?" He looked around hoping to hear support but there was no reaction so he added a quiet: "Amen."

"Damned atheist!" cried Natalie. "Erich Steiner you'll go to hell."

The movie maker shrugged. "Maybe hell got unplugged too."

Nobody said anything. The futility of the entire situation, the growing frustration and its cousin depression penetrated the minds of everyone gathered at the cottage. It was not that they were losing a great opportunity for meeting an alien or two and perhaps seeing a flying saucer, but that everything around them – everything powered by any form of electricity was dead and that created frustration laced with growing fears.

They eventually sat down for dinner of steaks, baked potatoes and glazed carrots at the picnic tables on the cedar deck with the grape vines dangling down with growing green fruit. David produced two ancient oil lamps given to him some years back by his mother and Saks and got them going while Paul Rowan poured Washington State Riesling.

In spite of the steaks and the wine the conversation was low key, almost uninspired. An aura, a shroud of growing apprehension was manifesting around the group enhanced by the disappointment they would miss the opportunity of a lifetime – meeting and hopefully conversing with entities from another planet, another dimension. Quite often they heard ominous distant explosions and several times the younger ones ran down to the beach to see distant flames and spiraling smoke illuminating the growing darkness along Puget Sound.

"Normally the sky is lit by all the lights from the metros of Seattle, Tacoma and scores of other communities along the Sound," said David. Several times they heard the plaintiff cry of distant people. Paul Rowan suggested they might be roving vandals scouring the countryside looking for food.

"May be, may be not," said Hugh Geraint-Jones. "In times of famine hungry people head for big towns and cities."

"A good point," said David. "Perhaps, if we get moving and head for Canada we should avoid heavily populated places."

"Do you honestly think we are going to find working wheels beside a horse-drawn stagecoach or a wagon that we haven't found yet?" It was a question from Jax Devenport.

"May be Mr. Steiner can put in another prayer to God," quipped Penni Singleton in one of her rare unemotional utterances.

"Well, the last one failed to work," said Natalie with a soft smile.

When several of the group reflected back on these days they recalled it was in the immediate wake of Natalie's comment that the Cosmic Forces, the Creator, the Source of Our Being answered Steiner's prayer, at least several of the group were so inclined to think that.

A lone figure attired in khaki shorts, a white tee shirt and brown leather sandals emerged slowly from the darkness, his feet crunching on the layers of pebbles covering the front yard. A hurricane lamp was held high as he entered. On his shirt were the words "Got Big Rig?"

"Hello all!" said a deep cultured voice with an obvious English accent. Dark eyes twinkled under a mop of dark brown hair. "Hello Kate, nice lot of quiet people you have here. I thought I'd come over to see what's happening."

"Everyone!" cried Kate enthusiastically coming to the man's side, "This is our neighbor from along the beach -- Derek Boulter. We all know him as Diesel because he was once an auto mechanic in Merry England and he looks after our car and he also collects cars. He has that large red barn down the road – if you're interested in old cars."

"Vintage is the word, Love," the figure corrected Kate with a grin.

"Come and sit down. We have a spare steak and lots of wine," said David Rowan.

Boulter eased his slim wiry figure onto the picnic table seat and sat next to Devenport. "This blackout is a right how-do-you-do," he said sipping wine. "Reminds me of tales my Dad used to tell of England during the Blitz. They used to shutter all the windows every night like everyone else so the Huns couldn't recognize anywhere to drop their bombs." He gave a short laugh. "Dad kept the shutters until he died in case the Jerries ever came back. Never did trust a Jerry."

"Steady there," growled Steiner. "My father came over from Germany after the war. He flew with the Luftwaffe, got shot up by the Brylcreem boys, was invalided out and went into movie making – Otto Steiner. He loved Marlene Dietrich."

"Oh, yes!" cried Diesel enthusiastically. "Remember her singing *Where have all the flowers gone*? I still have a long-play thirty-three rpm by her. Great singer."

"Great looker too," said Steiner. "German, you know."

The car-collector grinned. "Diesel was German too," he added and Steiner laughed then everyone smiled at the dialogue that had just happened. That along with the wine brought some relief to the gloom that had settled over the group.

"Where has all the power gone?" cried David Rowan. "That would be more appropriate. We need a vehicle but all the cars around here work with generators and electricity and not one works. The only vehicles we have are a couple of bikes."

"There are a couple of horses up the hill if we can find a wagon," put in Kate.

"Where do you need to go?" asked Diesel as he cut a piece of steak.

"Do you believe in UFOs, aliens, that sort of stuff?" asked David in a casual voice.

Diesel peered across at David and Molly. "When I was a kid in Maidenhead I once saw a flying saucer flying over the Thames," he said. "A really smooth job. My mother said I was never to tell anyone because they would lock me up. So I didn't." A short laugh followed the end of the sentence. "Do I believe? Why not? I always reckoned there had to be other characters like us on those other planets out there." He raised the piece of steak on the fork and then paused: "So what's the problem? Where do you need to go?"

Suddenly everyone focused on the man with the dark bristle hair, the tanned easy going angular face with dark eyes that seemed to light up whenever he smiled.

"There's a strange UFO occurrence happening at my mother's place up in the British Columbia interior on Friday and we need to be there," said David. "It's a once in a lifetime event."

Boulter stopped chewing. "It's funny you should say that, David. I read your book debunking the UFO phenomena and I agree so now my mind is ticking over and pondering why is a fellow like Rowan chasing UFOs and alien? But then, I say to myself, he's a writer and writers get bent out of shape every now and again," he said with a cheeky smile. "But I know where you are going. Kate told me – your mother lives close to the Yellowhead Highway. Very picturesque! Mountains and all that! Pretty remote!"

"Mom's place is off the Yellowhead between Clearwater and Blue River," said David.

"Know it well," said Diesel. "When the missus was alive we used to go camping up there in the state park."

"Provincial park," Kate corrected softly.

Paul Rowan shaking his head and feeling impatient stood up. "Kate tells me that you have renovated the old 1939 blue Dodge pickup that we used to escape the Fraser River cataclysmic flood of '79. Does that need electricity to work?"

Boulter nodded. "Sure does," he said slowly then added, "However if you want some wheels that move without the electric thing then you need one of the older diesel driven vehicles."

"Diesel vehicles work without electricity?" quipped Kate.

"The first ones did," put in her boyfriend Mark. "This past semester we studied the work of Clessie Cummins. In 1931 he did a promotion to get his engines into the trucking industry. He fitted a diesel into a truck and drove it across the United States to prove it was not only reliable but economical too. The fuel for the total trip was $11.22."

Diesel Boulter stared at the young man. "Listen young man, when you graduate I could use some help like you in the barn. I have several diesel cars and one truck."

"Does one work without electricity?" asked Paul Rowan eagerly.

"Cars? No, they're all relatively modern. Post 1955," he said. "The truck is older. She doesn't need electricity."

"She doesn't need electricity?" echoed Molly with growing excitement.

"Really? Could we borrow it," cried David. "We'll return it safe and sound."

Boulter hesitated. "It's got a hell of a crank. She'll break your arm if you hold on too long. Also she's temperamental on hills. Likes to be kept warm."

"Does it have seats?" asked Natalie quickly.

Diesel shook his head. In the back? No, we'd have to install some cushions, pillows and blankets," he advised.

"When do you need to go?"

"Tomorrow?" replied David. "We need to get moving tomorrow."

Diesel Boulter looked round at the faces peering at him in the flickering lights of the oil lamps. "Is everybody coming?"

They all nodded.

"Good. The truck will hold just about all of you plus some fuel and supplies. You'd better pack some food," he said. "I'm driving and I'd like the young engineer and his girl Kate to sit up front with me. If that's all right with you old folks."

"Do you think we'll make it in one day?" asked Steiner. "It's 350 miles you know."

Diesel Boulter nodded. "It'll be a breeze," he said with a flickering smile but his normally confident face did not reflect any optimism because deep down both he and the two Rowans were well aware of the danger of lawless mobs driven to violence by anger and starvation. "We'll keep to the country roads."

Steiner rubbed his hands gleefully as the prospect of getting movie footage of UFOs and aliens suddenly grew stronger. He caught Natalie's eye: "See, God heard my prayers."

28

WHEN DAVID AND HIS stepfather Paul Rowan came to writing books about the group's trip from Whidbey Island to the Yellowhead region in the interior of British Columbia, they both had serious trouble in creating a title for the chapters on the life and death phenomena that occurred in the High Coquihalla. Not one of the group that departed Admiral's Cove on Whidbey Island had any notion of what was in store for them, in fact David objected to Diesel Boulter's idea of hiding a 12-gauge shotgun under the front seat.

The younger Rowan who was more of an evergreen pacifist objected to carrying weapons of any kind but both Diesel and Geraint-Jones pointed to the wisdom of having at least one weapon of protection so David wisely yielded to the shotgun. In addition Diesel quietly stashed two baseball bats in the tool chest behind the cab seats.

When the renovated 1929 White diesel truck departed Admiral's Cove it resembled something one might see working in an evacuee internment camp in the Middle East. The truck originally painted in fire engine red had long lost its fiery luster. The cargo section was enclosed with wooden slats up to waist level then welded metal bars formed a structure for a canvas canopy over from which flexible panels were installed and tied down. The panels could be rolled up and fastened to allow travelers to view surrounding countryside. A large grey canvas panel enclosed the rear and was tied to a wooden tailgate.

The boxy non-streamlined but practical cab possessed a vertical windshield with two minor side screens. The driver and passenger doors were devoid of glass. A degree of protection from rain was provided by an overlip from the cab roof. A radiator with a round chrome frame headed the front of the engine housing. A round silver metal thermometer with a glass face perched on top. Sturdy metal running boards flanked the sides between the cab floor and the ground. A crank handle protruded from the lower level of the engine housing.

Once Diesel Boulter was on board with Mark and Kate up front, the others attempted to make themselves comfortable in the cargo section but it was obvious conditions were not in any stretch of the imagination going to be deluxe in fact some people envisioned being cramped. The nine in the cargo section were: David Rowan, Molly Thomsen, Hugh and Chloe Geraint-Jones, Erich Steiner, Jax Devenport, Penni Singleton, plus Paul and Natalie Rowan. Kate had thoughtfully packed a wicker hamper of foodstuffs that provided a seat for Natalie and Chloe directly behind the cab. Other seating was provided by the rear-wheel covers while the rest gallantly attempted to find forms of comfort on two single mattresses, along with numerous cushions and blankets from the cottage.

The first part of the journey from Coupeville to Blaine went according to plan. Something they had not expected were the scores of cars, trucks and motor cycles abandoned just as they had stopped when the power failed. Several long-distance freight trucks loaded with foodstuffs had been ripped open already and looted. Other trucks loaded with consumer articles such as stereos, TVs, furniture and others had been cleared and they wondered how looters could use such electrically driven goods. The looters left countless empty boxes littering the highway.

As Diesel's truck zigzagged through the garbage the group spotted vandals hauling boxes and sacks away across fields and down country lanes. Several looters possessed small trolleys and perambulators with goods stacked high and people pushing or pulling their loot would stop to stare at the strange old truck throbbing along while all other transport was dead.

Once a tall gangly youth screaming obscenities attempted to catch up with the rear of the White diesel but Devenport delivered a well aimed kick to the face that readily sent the unfortunate character reeling into the dust still screaming. Various other groups carrying axes and pitchforks attempted to stop the old diesel truck but Boulter gunned the vehicle straight at them and most of them sprang out of the way.

"We're just getting on Interstate Five," he called out when David Rowan poked his head through the canvas opening. It should be clearer than the side roads."

The auto mechanic was dead wrong. The entire freeway as far as the eye could see was dotted with cars, tractors and trailers all dead and abandoned. Some had simply come to a stop on the Interstate while others had skewed off the road and plunged into ditches and fields. Most truck drivers had simply walked away while some, suspecting thieves decided to camp in their vehicles until this "strange crisis" was over. One heavily bearded driver attired in coveralls sat perched on the top of his loaded truck with a loaded shotgun in one hand and two hand grenades attached to his thick leather belt.

As they approached the Salish Way ramps north of Bellingham unknown painters had daubed ominous signs on several trailers. "Looters will be shot!" and "Bellingham hates looters!"

Diesel Boulter took the exit and stopped at Lake Padden Park where everyone got out to stretch their legs and as David Rowan suggested "take a leak." They found volunteers cleaning the stinking and much polluted toilets. Geraint-Jones stood by the lake and lit his old briar pipe and that's where a man wearing a khaki bush jacket and sitting on a white horse came up alongside. A Bushmaster AR-15 rifle slung across his front signified he was in business.

"Good day, officer," said the archaeologist easily.

"Not a cop, if that's what you mean," said the horseman casually pulling on a long grey moustache. "We're self-appointed rangers. We organized the volunteers to clean the shit houses," he said sounding like a bureaucrat. "Also to look after the lake. It originally provided drinking water for old Bellingham but now people are coming here to fill up buckets and containers. The city water system is out." Even as he spoke a couple with mules pulling a small two-wheeled wooden cart loaded with plastic jars came into the park and headed for the boat dock.

"Last night some cretin came and tried to poison the lake," said the horseman. He patted his rifle. "The body's in a garbage bag over by the shit house." He peered at Geraint-Jones who was now accompanied by Diesel. "You folk heading somewhere?"

"Canada," said Boulter. "The Yellowhead Highway beyond Kamloops."

"Best if you avoid Bellingham. They're nervous, trigger-happy and shooting anything that resembles a looter. Take the old roads. Yew Street to Route 542. At Cedarville pick up Route 9 and that'll take you right up to Sumas and the Canadian border."

"Thanks."

"Best of luck," said the horseman. "You'll need it."

As the old truck with its human cargo took the Yew Street turning they heard the sharp rattle of automatic rifles. Steiner looked wistfully at his 16 millimeter camera and muttered: "I should have been in newsreels. I could have made a fortune." Several of the others grinned.

The 29 miles to the Canadian border at Sumas in normal times takes about three quarters of an hour. It took David Rowan and his company of travelers over two hours. Most of them started to feel the heat of the day now hovering around 80 degrees Fahrenheit. They kept the canvas sides rolled up to let the air through but often when travelling through congested areas with gangs roving about it was best to close themselves in. Paul Rowan who, like his son, detested guns reluctantly accepted holding the loaded 12-guage shotgun and riding next to Steiner at the tailgate.

"If we're in danger at any time let them have a blast," said Boulter. "Our lives may depend on it."

"You think so?"

"Absolutely! There's an acute shortage of motorized transport," Boulter said. "Some people may kill to get hands on this truck."

Strangely, they did spot several old diesel vehicles on the move. One was a 1920s bus with "City of Seattle" in faded paint on the side. It was packed with tired faced women and children heading south. Another was a farm tractor and yet another was a World War 1 scout car loaded with gun-toting young men patrolling a small shopping center near the highway. Everywhere along the route they noticed families, many with someone carrying a gun, standing in the doorways or sitting out on the decks and balconies ready to ward off invading thieves. Paul Rowan summed it up: "In times of great crisis America becomes an armed camp."

As they approached Nooksack a small town in the foothills of the Cascade Mountains Diesel suddenly applied the brakes.

"What's the problem," cried David.

"Tanker! Dead ahead," replied Boulter. "It's on fire."

"Is it loaded?" asked Molly. Then she realized it was a dumb question. "Sorry about that. I guess I was saying what I was thinking."

"Can we get round it," asked Natalie nervously.

Kate scanned the map on her lap. "Turn left here. Emerson Road will take us round it."

"Good idea." Diesel touched the accelerator and turned the truck off Route 9. Seconds later they all felt the air being sucked away as the tanker exploded belching a massive column of red, orange and yellow flames and smoke into the blue sky. For a moment the entire vehicle disappeared.

"It's airborne," screamed Steiner leaning out the back.

The burning heavy metal tube that had been the cargo hold of the tanker landed with a terrifying crump on the road where they had just stopped, then rolling sideways as if being spun by an invisible force it started chasing the truck and its pale faced occupants across the single railway line. Diesel hit the accelerator and miraculously moved away while the remains of the tanker slowed after taking out the grade-crossing gates and several power poles. It finally finished up in a small grassy field where it triggered an instant fire.

"Crap!" screamed Steiner in sheer despair. "What a shot! And I missed it!"

Everyone wanted to laugh but the stress levels were too overwhelming. They stopped at the convenience store in Nooksak for ice creams and sodas. The store was in darkness and the owner apologized. "The ice creams are melted and the sodas are warm," he told the group. "I am ruined. Do you know when the power will come back?"

Several bought hard candies, some Tostitos chips and salsa and reloaded the truck. As it headed north Steiner cried out to Paul Rowan: Did you see that great big chicken back there? Must be at least ten feet tall."

"It's harmless" said the other with a grin. "Typically Mexican."

The truck continually swerved round abandoned wreckages of vehicles and trucks on the road. Several times people tried to stop them but Diesel skillfully avoided them pumping his old rubber air horn so that they quickly and angrily scattered.

Shortly after noon they noticed scores of wide open fields on both sides of the border between the United States and Canada. The name "Sumas" appeared on various signs. The name in old Native Indian language means "land without trees" and Kate was quick so observe the landscape and agreed this was so.

There are two Sumas communities, one each side of the border. The nearest good sized town over the border is Abbotsford which straddles Highway 1 also known to older Canadians as the Trans-Canada Highway. Sumas is usually a busy and still relatively easy crossing for vehicles. One of the interesting points about the Canadian side at Sumas is the fact it is a collecting and assembly yard for freight trains coming and going across the border. There is a familiar and constant sound in the region, freight cars clanging and banging into each other. Today the rail yards were quiet and smoke from a burned out hardware store drifted eerily through the border crossing.

A major roadway that crosses through the yards is Vye Street which had achieved notoriety for being the most dangerous railway crossing in Canada. As the Whidbey Island truck approached the Canadian border crossing, Vye Street was going to live up to its reputation.

The three in the cab could easily spot lines of people standing at the offices of the Canadian Border Service Agency, an upgraded name for the old Customs and Immigration Service, waiting to walk across into Canada. Both Mike and Kate wondered how the officers could process border transients without computers. In addition the entire complex was in darkness. All the green or red crossing signal lights were off.

Many pedestrians turned to stare at the vintage truck. A gaunt middle-aged border officer who appeared not to have slept for at least 24 hours stared at the old truck.

"Where did you get that treasure? Must be worth its weight in gold."

"1929 Smith diesel," said Boulter. "Doesn't require electricity."

"Well, isn't that something?"

"Where are you from?"

"Whidbey Island. We're going to Kamloops and beyond."

"Where exactly."

David Rowan jumped off the back. "We are going to see my parents. They have a ranch north of Clearwater. It's their 50th anniversary."

"Are you a Canadian?"

"Absolutely!" he said and offered his passport.

"Everyone got passports and IDs?"

There was a flurry as hands held up documents.

"What's that?" said the officer staring at Devenport.

"CIA credentials."

"What does the CIA want in this country?" asked the officer. "You'd better come inside."

David's enthusiasm for a speedy border crossing evaporated as he heard the order for Devenport to go inside. Instinctively he knew this would take some explaining. But unaware to the group in the old Smith diesel truck energies were happening elsewhere that would assist them.

Along the street some railway workers working with horses were attempting to move a lone rail tanker car off the Vye Street crossing where it had been parked since the blackout. Several tanker cars had been moved to safety by an engineer who miraculously found a vintage farm tractor with a diesel engine that did not require electricity. After two successful moves the tractor belched white and blue smoke and quit working leaving the one and only tanker spread across Vye Street.

Now the problem was this. The tanker contained butadiene a liquid that when exposed turns into a gas which is highly flammable and can be extremely dangerous if inhaled causing serious throat and lung irritation. A railroad foreman warned people standing around that the tanker was packed with 30,000 gallons of the toxic and flammable liquid.

"It's just like propane," warned the railroad man.

Two firemen in uniforms symbolically carrying buckets for no apparent reason said there was no way they could help. Add to this Hazmat crews were not available. "We would normally evacuate everyone within a two-mile radius if a leak occurred," announced one of the firemen, "but we have no way of warning people. Even the siren doesn't work." He shrugged. "No electricity."

"Crap!" muttered the foreman and started to walk away.

Just then a desperate figure raced past the foreman and scrambled up onto the rail car containing the deadly Butadiene. The foreman threw up his arms: "Oh, shit, the bloody looney is here."

Earlier in the day several blocks away a lean Quebecer named Chevalier who had murdered his Vancouver girl friend had escaped from the medical unit at the maximum security unit at the Fraser Valley Penitentiary. Raiding the home of a retired army colonel the escapee had seized an old British World War II Lee Enfield rifle, several loaded magazines along with two unexploded hand grenades with pins intact.

Two armed Royal Canadian Mounted Police officers without cars, motorcycles or even horses pursued the runaway Quebecer on bicycles. Chevalier, known as a skin-head and a contortionist, weaved his way through the light industrial yards flanking the railway that crosses Vye Street. He spotted the crowd of officials gathered around the lone railway car and the horses trying to pull it out of the way. Sprinting across the grass and onto the road he rushed up to the lead horse.

"Sorry, old friend," he cried breathlessly as he patted its face. "Adieu, mes amis."

Glancing at the surprised officials, Chevalier sprang nimbly onto the rail car loaded with butadiene, stood poised alone for a brief second, then calmly extracted the pins from the two grenades and thrust them into the loading cock of the rail car. They exploded simultaneously at the precise moment the Canadian Border officer was asking the CIA director Jax Devenport to come into the office.

There were two explosions. The first when the hand grenades exploded rupturing the loading cock on the rail car and then when the flowing liquid rushed over Chevalier's burning body. The blast knocked flat everyone around including the horses.

Immediately the Canadian Border staff raced out to witness the debacle. Several raced up the street including the officer who had spoken to Steiner. Even the people standing waiting for permission to enter Canada were running helter-skelter in all directions into the country.

"Move it, Diesel!" cried Rowan. "There's something damned wrong up there. Take a side road. Make a detour."

Boulter gunned the truck out of the Customs station, headed north along Sumas Way, swung into the first turn-off into the residential area, zipped east along Boundary Road and eventually swung onto Route 1, the Trans Canada Highway and headed for Hope. All aboard breathed sighs of relief.

"What on earth did we miss?" asked Chloe.

"Looked like something really lethal," said Steiner. "Naturally I missed it."

"The way everyone was standing around that rail tanker," said Paul, "it had to be extremely toxic."

Well, I thought the Anunnaki were dangerous," said David. 'This trip seems to be getting worse all the time."

The 80 year-old truck made good time along Canada's main artery swinging round stalled cars and trucks, eluding people guarding their vehicles and others who were hiking and trying to thumb a lift. Just over an hour after leaving the Sumas Border Point they reached the town of Hope nestling in the high coastal mountains. They found a cafe where a woman was brewing on an open fire and decided to stop for a break.

"Another 230 miles and we'll be with Jenny and Saks in their mountain sanctuary," said David.

"Are we going through the famous Fraser Canyon," asked Chloe.

"Is that the one you wrote about?" asked Steiner looking at Rowan senior.

"Over 30 years ago," replied Paul as he stepped down from the truck. "No, they've built the Coquihalla Highway since then which takes us across the mountains into the interior. It should be plain sailing. We should be at Jenny and Sak's place by nightfall."

Before the sun went down that day Paul Rowan was to discover his earlier statement reflected misplaced optimism. They would spend the night stuck high in the Cascades and one of the group would be fatally shot and David Rowan would start believing in miracles, healing and the paranormal.

29

THE COQUIHALLA HIGHWAY NOT only passes through some of the most beautiful, rugged and spectacular landscapes in British Columbia it also traverses several ecosystems which start with the lush giant coastal cedars that pierce the morning mists around the town of Hope to the tall slender pencil-like firs that form sentinels on dramatic rock faces in the semi-arid high country of the interior. Then the traveler witnesses the appearance of expansive grasslands which have long been the homes of great ranches and herds of roaming Canadian beef cattle.

The highway opened in the 1980s, provides easy access to the interior communities and completely bypasses the unique and tortuous highway through the Canyon where Canada's third largest river the Fraser forces its way through the weather-beaten narrow cliffs flowing at peak run-off at two million gallons a second.

First explored by the great fur-trappers of the Hudson's Bay Company, the original route through the Coquihalla Pass saw a progression of trappers, hunters, fur traders, settlers and in the mid-19th century flocks of gold prospectors came this way. With the advent of the steam era the Pass witnessed the Kettle

Valley railway line until it closed in 1960. Then came construction of two major pipelines and various logging operations before the provincial government said let's build a short-cut to the interior of the province.

Like most other travelers Diesel stopped the truck to allow legs to be stretched and provide time for the group to be tourists and admire the massive granite mountain named Yak Peak that pierces the clouds at 2,000 meters above sea-level.

By the time the group got within a few miles north of Merritt, a renowned cattle center and a favorite with trout fishers, the plan to reach the Running Wind Ranch had changed. Diesel stopped the truck. In the growing darkness they could see looters about a half a mile away unloading a tractor trailer rig sprawled across two lanes. Beyond it sat the frame and wheels of another truck still smoldering from a fire and in the distance columns of black smoke curled up into the darkening sky and drifted ominously across the wide Nicola Valley.

Diesel walked back and peered at the faces staring from the truck. "There's an intersection half a mile back," he said waving his hand. "Maybe we can find a place to stop and camp out for the night. My old crate doesn't have any lights and I don't like driving in the moonlight."

A short while later they found an old motel that had seen better days tucked away on an old roadway overlooking the Coldwater River and the remains of the Kettle Valley Railway track bed now a hiking trail. A sturdy looking woman with grayish blonde hair tied in a bun and wearing brown dungarees and sandals stood outside a shack that still had the word "Office" written on a wooden door that clung to life on one hinge. In her large hands she carried a rifle. She waved it at Diesel and David as they approached.

"You city dwellers?"

"We are mainly Americans. I'm Canadian," said David. "We're heading up to my folks beyond Clearwater. Do you have accommodation for the night?"

"Depends. We don't have light, no water, no showers and half the place, the north wing, got burned down by looters from a liquor truck along the highway," she said. "I winged two and they all took off. Luckily they didn't wreck the whole place."

The woman still carrying the rifle watched as the group came off the truck. "There is water in the river," she said. "That's good drinking water and it's great for bathing. A bit cold though." She allowed a faint smile on her weathered face. "That's why they call it the Coldwater River. Naturally!"

Everyone from the truck started walking about to stretch their legs. The men wandered off to see the wreckage of the north wing while the women gathered around the owner whose name turned out to be Nell O'Connor. Two units were taken by the women and the men were housed in a big red barn that had seen better days but there were plenty of straw. Bales of it. Kate spotted some picnic tables overlooking the river and so joined by Natalie and Chloe they organized salami sandwiches, apples and bottles of warm spring water.

Steiner, Devenport and Kate's boyfriend Mark found some logs and soon had a huge fire burning in a stone barbecue pit and so the group sat around on well-worn picnic tables munching sandwiches. David apologized to everyone. "I didn't figure on making a night stop," he said.

"That's quite all right," said Penni Singleton perched on a disused wooden wine barrel close to the tables. "I'm sorry I showed such bad manners back at Whidbey Island."

"Penni," retorted Kate briskly with an upbeat tone. "Don't you worry. Hopefully we'll find your son."

"You think so?"

"We'll certainly try," said David. "There are no guarantees. Was Peter always interested in things like UFOs?"

"No. Certainly not," said Mrs. Singleton obviously irritated by the slight suggestion. She sat and stared at the burning logs and they could see tears welling in her eyes. "He was a good boy, incredibly intelligent at school but it all started when our Church organized a tour of the Holy Land. Peter was fascinated by the archaeological discoveries at Jericho…"

"Ah, yes," put in Geraint-Jones. "Kathleen Kenyon – the British archaeologist did some incredible work there and also in Jerusalem with the City of David exploration. Unfortunately she got stymied between traditional mainline thinking and material coming out of Sumer."

"Regarding the Anunnaki?" asked Steiner.

Geraint-Jones nodded and turned to Mrs. Singleton. "Apologies my dear. What happened?"

"Peter wanted to go to the south end of the Dead Sea some 40 miles away and spent an afternoon wandering around the salt flats there," she said. "We missed our tour and had to stay at a nearby hotel. Over dinner he made a startling revelation."

Everyone suddenly listened intently.

"Peter said – and I remember his words exactly – This is where they destroyed Sodom and Gomorrah and five other communities. It was a bomb. Nuclear, he said. Then he added: I can feel it."

"How strange," said Kate.

"A sensitive psychometrist can pick up energies and read them, even imprints of energies thousands of years old and produce accurate descriptions," said Geraint-Jones.

"Peter said Lot's wife who according to the Bible turned back and was changed into a pillar of salt was in actual fact caught in the nuclear blast and vaporized," said Mrs. Singleton.

"That's exactly what Zecharia Sitchin discovered when translating the Babylonian tablets at the British Museum," said Geraint-Jones. "Sitchin claimed that if you study photographs of the Dead Sea region and also the Sinai Peninsula from space you can see shadows of nuclear explosions written in the dark sands."

"You mean the Manhattan Project was really old hat when J. Robert Oppenheimer claimed the atomic test in New Mexico was the first atomic explosion," put in Steiner.

Geraint-Jones shook his head. "If you check the records old Oppie never said that. He expressed considerable concern over what the Manhattan team had done."

He turned round and told the group: "Sodom was not the first nuclear explosion on earth. The giant Lonar Crater with a diameter of over 2,000 meters located 400 kilometers north-east of Mumbai is dated at less than 50,000 years and is still radioactive."

"Difficult to believe. Why are there no records?" put in David.

"Oh, there are. There are," said the old archaeologist vigorously nodding his head. "The place itself is still dead after all these years. Also the Mahabharata, the long sacred Indian epic tells of a single projectile charged with the power of the Universe resulting in an incandescent column of smoke and flame as bright as a thousand suns rose in its splendor. He paused then added, "The corpses were so burned as to be unrecognizable. It's a ghastly document but it shows Earth history is still unknown to present day inhabitants. But the records are there."

The group sat in stunned silence.

"That's still difficult to believe," said David Rowan holding a bottle of water.

Paul Rowan chuckled. "My dearly beloved step-son still finds things difficult to believe. I have a feeling you are in for a surprise, David."

"In the Sodom disaster all fingers point to the Anunnaki," said Geraint-Jones, "simply because the Sumerian tablets said that god was angry with the abominable morality of the people at Sodom and Gomorrah and the other cities and wished to destroy them."

The archaeologist held up his hand in the firelight. "You have to know that the ancients believed that these astronauts who came out of the sky on fiery chariots were gods and the place they originated was Nibiru otherwise known as Heaven. You have to remember too that one of the gods was named Enlil who was a strict disciplinarian and often wanted to see the creatures they had created on Earth eliminated. But his half brother Enki actually defended humanity."

"Enlil was the tough vengeful god of the Old Testament?" asked Steiner.

"Absolutely!" Geraint-Jones stroked his beard while his pale eyes watched the people listening. "The Old Testament is a bloody testimonial that the god it portrays is not the True God of the Cosmos, the Creator of the Universe. Even the Anunnaki spiritual teachings refer to the Creator, the Maker of All Things. Somewhere along the way Homo sapiens got caught up in believing the astronauts from Nibiru were gods and that Nibiru was Heaven."

"One heck of a mistake if you're trying to create a religion," said Steiner.

David Rowan looked at Geraint-Jones. "You mentioned in Oregon that the first humans as we know them today, Adamu and Ti-Amat were genetically modified from Homo erectus and encouraged to breed."

"The Anunnaki needed cheap primitive slave workers for the gold mines," said the archaeologist. "The Babylonian tablets describe how Enki – the good god – was fascinated with a specific creature that lived among the tall trees, their front legs as hands they were using. That's a direct quote, incidentally. The used their own blood, their own DNA and created the first Homo sapiens. It all happened in South Africa."

"They genetically modified them to mine for gold?" suggested Steiner.

Geraint-Jones nodded and then looked David, Erich and Molly who had just joined the group. "I mentioned in Oregon that there was a dark side to the Anunnaki and now is a good time to discuss that."

"Dark side?" quizzed David. "Can there be a dark side to god?"

"The Anunnaki? Absolutely!" Geraint-Jones reached into his bush-jacket pocket and pulled out his pipe. "The dark side is the legacy. It's a prevailing part of the human psyche today." He turned and looked at Paul Rowan's hand. "Why do you wear a gold ring?"

Paul shrugged. "Tradition, I suppose."

"But there are more beautiful metals and crystals with which one could make wedding rings and jewelry. Why gold?"

"Frankly, I have no idea. Sentiment?"

"Most people have no idea why they wear gold," said the archaeologist. "Let's go back 160,000 years to that first family in South Africa who we genetically modified to carry Anunnaki blood and Anunnaki genes. "Those first primitive workers were bred to walk upright, talk and converse intelligently, use Anunnaki tools and – hunt and dig for gold."

Molly rose from the table and stood by the fire. "You said earlier that the Anunnaki needed gold to repair the environment around their home planet," she said. "Why was that?"

"The writers of the ancient tablets did not appreciate the scientific principles behind gold," said Geraint-Jones. "Repair of the environment may have been an easy way of describing their needs. Nibiru was a planet where gold was almost totally deficient. It is only in the last few years that we on Earth have discovered the true value of gold and the true reasons the gods wanted it."

"And that is?" asked David.

"First of all one ounce of gold can be drawn into a wire eight kilometers in length. It is among the most electrically conductive of all metals. It works even in harsh cold to boiling temperatures," said the archaeologist smoothly. "Now here's the good stuff: Gold contains a little thing called a nanoparticle. It is so small that even now scientists have difficulty seeing it, but the effects are something else. Nanos are so powerful and they are changing our entire lives, our whole existence in biomedicine, optics, electronics and even how we explore the mystical DNA – the tree of life -- more. The Anunnaki knew all about nanotechnology but their gold supplies were minimal. They were starving for gold and planet Earth had plenty and still does. Their civilization wanted gold so much and they created a colony called Earth and a humanoid species made in their image."

"And you think this has impacted us down the ages?" asked Molly.

"Absolutely!" came the reply. "Permit me to remind you. Throughout history human beings have possessed an insatiable hunger for gold. Gold is mentioned in the Bible 417 times, the word golden 66 times. No other metal comes close to that. The Jews were told to build the Ark of the Covenant in gold and it conveniently disappeared.

"The gods stole it," remarked Steiner to no one in particular.

"The Egyptians loved gold. The mask of Tutankhamen was made of gold, the Spaniards ravaged central and North America for gold. In modern times thousands of ordinary people dropped what they were doing to embark on the great gold rushes such as the Klondike, California and Barkerville events. People scream, panic and kill for gold and yet to tell the truth it is a rather drab looking metal."

Chloe suddenly chipped in: "Back home we mentioned the Anunnaki established the monarchy system on earth," she said. "They called them priest-kings and these people surrounded themselves with gold and if you watch television from Rome you'll see a modern-day replica of the priest-king still surrounded by gold while millions on the planet go starving."

"That's true," agreed Paul Rowan but Natalie seated beside him frowned with obvious annoyance.

"And for that these aliens were called gods," said Paul Rowan who had been listening intently.

"Adam and Eve were told to go out and multiply," said Chloe. "After the Deluge when the close proximity of Nibiru upset the worlds' eco-systems and created the Flood, Enki told Noah and his people to go forth and multiply. Multiply was the operative word."

"And the Church still echoes that to this day," said Geraint-Jones. "In fact most of what civilized men and women do today is a result of the Anunnaki space travelers. "The True God never said anything about multiplication. The Anunnaki did. It's an order, a misguided obsession among some people that is now thousands of years old and it's systematically killing the human occupation of this planet."

"And they say it was the word of God," put in Devenport. "In truth it was the word of the galactic travelers a long time ago."

"It was gold that triggered the dark side of the Anunnaki," said Geraint-Jones. "All through their colonization of Earth which lasted thousands of years they lived and demonstrated excessive greed for power, wealth and dominion, selfishness, anger, jealousy, hatred, retribution, underhandedness and deceit. The Anunnaki leadership spotted these traits in earthlings and so almost 4,000 years ago they gave Hammurabi, the first king of the Babylonian Empire a set of laws for people to live by. The presentation was made by the god Utu otherwise known as Shamash a grandson on Enlil. The sad part is the Anunnaki violated most of them and freely practiced incest."

"Heavens," muttered Natalie, "I really don't want to hear this."

"Shortly after Hammurabi received the Code the Anunnaki edited them down to ten and gave them to Moses on Mount Sinai," said Geraint-Jones. "But while they did much good for planet Earth and their influence spread to all corners of the globe they did leave one tragic and very costly habit tucked away in our genes?"

They all stared expectantly at the big man standing in the light of the burning logs.

"War!" came the reply. "Ever since they created Adamu and Ti-Amat – otherwise known as Adam and Eve – there has not been a time, not even a day of peace on this planet."

The statement was followed by a silence broken only by the crackling of logs on the fire. Finally Kate asked the question: "Why is that, sir?"

War?" Geraint-Jones asked blandly. "War is in our genetic makeup. People are easily programmed for war by political leaders, opinion leaders in the media, universities and various books. When the Christian fathers adopted the Jewish Old Testament they inherited an ideal that says war is right and god supports that ideal. When you have time, take a new look and you'll find the wanton destruction of cities and empires throughout, deaths by the thousands strewn liberally among its pages. The true God never supports war, only the Anunnaki gods."

Paul Rowan nodded: "After years of being a foreign correspondent I have to agree that in a way we are slaves to war much the same as we are slaves to gold."

Geraint-Jones said slowly: "The seed of the fathers is buried deep within us. Adamu and everyone that followed him carried a mental strategy energized by the passion, the greed and the desperation of the Anunnaki: Use whoever you can and employ any strategy and force available to secure gold. Little did the primitive workers realize and understand that they were slaves -- slaves to the space colonists and later as a curse to live by. That is the dark side of the Anunnaki.

"Oh, come on Hugh," cried Natalie stubbornly. "I cannot believe that."

The archaeologist shook his head and held up his right hand to gain attention. "Think about this: Who gave man the idea and the ability for owning another person? It's the most abhorrent act in the human race, everyone condemns it and many practice it."

"God?" David poised the question knowing it was wrong.

"The True God? Never!" snapped Geraint-Jones. "It was the little gods, the gods from up there in the skies who came with their genetic engineering and implanted the damnable idea. Consider this. There are over 130 references to slavery in the Bible. It's the matrix of life. Moses the author of the Book of Leviticus approved of slavery even among the priesthood when he wrote: *Your male and female slaves are to come from nations around you; from them you may buy slaves."* Geraint-Jones looked at each one in the light of the fire. "You see right from the very beginning Homo sapiens – Adam and Eve – were bred into the matrix, the format of the Anunnaki."

Diesel nodded: "You might say we are chips off the old Anunnaki block."

No one laughed but Geraint-Jones nodded briskly. "Mr. Boulter, to quote another adage – you have hit the nail on the head."

"So where does that leave us?" asked David.

Suddenly Molly came to life. "For years my mother and I have been under the impression that if we could catch a UFO and talk to the creatures within, there would be a startling and mind-shattering revelation, but now everything is different." She stood up and walked to the fire and stood by Geraint-Jones.

"It's my firm conviction that we are going to meet the Anunnaki – if that is what they are -- to find out if all the Babylonian tablets and the stories they contain on Anunnaki life, morals and culture are true," she said. "We should regard this expedition as a learning mission to discover and benefit from the truth."

Several people applauded and as she returned to her picnic table David patted her on the shoulder. "Deep down within our hearts and souls I think that is why we are coming, but you, my dear, have said it very well." Molly smiled as David put his arm around and hugged her.

The word shared by Geraint-Jones started many minds thinking and that generated a silence over the group and as they lit their emergency candles and started to move towards their quarters they all heard strange sounds.

"Aliens!" quipped Mark with a grin.

Kate rebuked him with a well aimed finger to his ribs.

"Pssst!" hissed David Rowan as he stood up. "We've got company."

Through the light of the still-burning log fire they saw two dark strangers coming towards them. The group could hardly make out who they were. As they came into the light of the fire and the candles they saw the newcomers were two men, one mature, stocky, barrel-chested and balding, the other young, lean and sallow, perhaps a teenager close to twenty. An old rifle was cradled in the youngster's arms.

David Rowan stepped forward. "Can we help you?"

The older man stopped and coughed. "We saw your truck earlier on. Vintage but good," he said in a raspy smoke-heavy voice. "How come it moves when nothing else does?"

"Diesel," said Rowan. "It's an antique before they had glow plugs and solenoids. It runs differently to gasoline engines. What's your interest?"

"We would like to buy it?" said the teen with the gun.

Rowan shook his head. He could sense Diesel Boulter moving silently towards the truck and the shotgun. The cab door squeaked as it opened. "Sorry," he said softly. "It's not for sale."

"Well, that's a pity," said the smoky voice. "I guess we'll just have to commandeer it. Who's the driver?"

As he spoke Devenport and Steiner moved silently to Rowan's side. Paul Rowan moved in from the far side of the picnic table. The two men stared at the growing opposition in the group. From out of the shadows Molly appeared and moved to the far side of the two men.

"Unless you have some faster artillery than one rifle, I have the feeling that you're not going to get very far," she said softly. "Besides your bootlace is undone. You could trip."

The teenager fell for the ancient distraction line and glanced down. That is all Molly wanted. The wiry Amazon flashed through the darkness seemingly faster than anyone could see. A foot seemed to tap the young man's forehead and as he slumped down, Molly's elbow flashed a lightning jab into the nape of the teenager's neck and he went sprawling.

In the action the rifle went flying in the direction of the older man who deftly snatched it and immediately slid back the bolt. A bullet rammed into the breech. The weapon was cocked and ready. At that precise moment the man caught sight of Diesel Boulter now armed with a baseball bat coming in from the side. The man bellowed something that sounded like bastard, swung the rifle round and fired. Eyes suddenly agog, Diesel gasped, twisted round and slumped to the ground.

Everyone raced for cover behind trees and picnic tables.

"I'm gonna get you bastards for what you done to my son," he cried aiming the gun at Molly. Angrily he slid another round into the breech and stared around.

Another shot more penetrating suddenly cracked the night. Blood spewed from the man's mouth as he slumped backwards. The bullet had gone through his mouth and exited from the back of his neck.

Out of the darkness strode Nell O'Connor. "Hell, do I hate American shit disturbers. This is Canada," she announced softly. "That's the second shit disturber I've shot today."

For the next little while everything seemed chaotic. David Rowan and Erich Steiner carried the injured Diesel into the motel and placed him on a bed.

"He's been shot but I can't see any signs," said David.

"We'll get him undressed and check him out," said Nell. "You men leave us. Molly, you can help me."

Another voice came over. "I'd like to help I'm a nurse," said Penni Singleton. Then she added: "An R.N."

Paul Rowan and Natalie found more logs and built up the fire. A mood of shock and despondency had fallen heavily upon the group. They sat and stood as somber sentinels gathered round the now crackling fire. They had not expected violence and death in any shape or form.

"What do we do with the bodies of the attackers?" asked Devenport.

"I didn't really mean to kill him," said Molly softly but he was going to shoot us.

"Of course not," said Natalie Rowan. "We could drag the bodies down to the river. Somebody will find them." She paused then gazed in stunned amazement at the others. "Did you hear what I said? Could you believe I said that?"

Her husband moved over and put his arm round the trembling body.

David was now at a loss and he peered at the truck then at the others. "The main question now concerns a driver. Whatever Diesel's state of health is tomorrow I think we can rule out his functioning as a driver for the rest of the trek," he said slowly. "For one, I don't even know how to crank the handle to start the damn thing."

Geraint-Jones chipped in: "I once operated a diesel in northern Iraq."

"Like heck you will," snorted Chloe. "Eighty-year olds are not supposed to get into the trucking business."

"Well, I watched Diesel start it," said Steiner. "Perhaps I could get it going in the morning."

"We could get some blankets from the motel and build up a bed for Diesel directly behind the cab," suggested Devenport. "The problem is getting a driver. I've driven army trucks, I could probably drive that one."

Just then Nell O'Connor walked across from the motel followed by Molly. "Folks, we've got some bad news," she said slowly. "Your friend Diesel didn't make it. That's a real pity because he looked such a nice fellow."

30

PENNI SINGLETON SAT QUIETLY in the musty motel room gazing at the lifeless form of Mike Boulter. One small bedside light with a yellowing cracked shade cast a gloomy ethereal aura over the place with its once fading white walls. A cracked mirror was stacked above an old unpainted dresser. A glass wrapped up in sterile plastic sat next to a glass ashtray promoting somebody's beer. Her normally contained and perfect self, her nurse self, felt distinctly uncomfortable here.

"It's not a good place to die," she whispered. "Not a good place at all." Tears welled up under her closed eyelids. In the three days since they met at Whidbey Island, she had come to like him. The label Diesel did not appeal to her so she insisted on calling him by his proper name, Michael or Mike. The auto mechanic was always so quiet and very efficient but always willing to help anyone. At the Rowan cottage he had brought her a drink and accompanied her for a walk for a "breath of fresh air" along the drive. Diesel was a listener more than a talker and when he did speak it was always something pertinent.

"Why, oh why did you have to go?" she sighed with a sob. More tears welled in her pale blue eyes. "Why, oh why did God have to take you?" For several moments she glared at the Gideon Bible lying on the far end of the dresser but then she saw his wallet and key-ring someone had set there when they brought him in. The glare reduced to a softness. Those were his things.

Thinking back, she wished Dan had been more like Diesel. Her husband had changed radically after Peter's birth. Never the same, he was always critical, always wanting to be away on some trip, some mission, meeting new clients and frequently being away at weekends.

Then when Peter was found in Morocco and disappeared on a trans-Atlantic flight, Dan became terribly horrid and declared: "I can't stand any more of this kooky stuff. I'm leaving." Next day he filed for divorce and it was then that Penni knew she had to find her son.

David Rowan was somehow connected to Peter. Why was Peter reading his book on UFOs and all that silly stuff and why had Rowan signed it? The puzzle bothered her. That's why she headed for the writer's cottage on Whidbey Island where she discovered that Rowan and Steiner had been at the pyramid in the Big Bend Dessert near Marfa, Texas and somehow Steiner had filmed the ghostly pyramid with Peter standing close by. What was all that about?

Penni knew from the start that her boy was different. It could not be Dan's child so who was the father? It was a question that stayed and haunted her mind over the years. Memories of that Cairo hotel were as vivid now as they had been almost twenty years ago. She had been sick for five days in Cairo and the only person who had seen her was the Egyptian doctor.

The thoughts triggered a release from her subconscious mind. She saw it all clearly now. Wait! Doctors don't feed their patients! The doctor was feeding me! It's becoming clear. Why? Why wasn't it a nurse or the hotel staff? Why the doctor? Another thought pierced her mind like an arrow. Was that Egyptian really a doctor? The idea sent a jolt of fear racing through her body. She took a deep breath and held it with her diaphragm close in as she had been taught in nurse training many years before. She released the breath slowly and immediately felt a little better.

That was strange, really strange she thought. Why am I remembering this now? Why am I thinking of things that happened so long ago when this poor unfortunate man, Michael is not even cold? The thought of this whole episode made her cry and she leaned back on the armchair and stared at his body. A big circle of blood stained his checkered shirt where the bullet entered.

In the quiet something moved.

Not sure what it was she looked first at the body. It was totally still. Anxious, her eyes scanned the room. "Is there somebody there?" The door was the same as it had been, slightly ajar. No reply. The sound occurred again. Turning her head towards the dresser her eyes caught the movement. The keys! They moved! They were still moving. They continued to move towards her end of the dresser.

Mike? She desperately wanted to say his name but something inside her blocked the energy. Was he now in spirit? No, she did not want to think that. Some months before she had attended a Spiritualist church and watched and listened to the proceedings. The elderly minister was talking about how dying people when they "cross over" into the Spirit World often return to let friends and relatives know that all is well.

"Mike," she whispered suddenly. "If that's you I don't want to know that you are in Heaven or that Spirit place." She stared at the keys. They had stopped moving.

Suddenly she felt extremely strange, quite dizzy, as if her body had just lost a lot of energy. "I must be sick again," she muttered, "just like I was in Cairo those many years ago…it is just like that…but why?" Her head felt unbearably heavy. Her body reeled back in the arm chair. Panicking she struggled to sit up. Somebody...someone was in the room. She tried to look. Her hands reached out for the end of arms of the chair for a grip but she failed to pull herself up. In desperation she tried to see who was in the room.

The figure was dressed in a simple white suit, almost a uniform. No markings only a broad silver belt round the waist. A strange circular boxy hat sat on the figure's head. Perhaps he could be someone from the local hospital, the psychic ward, she thought. Then she realized he was tall almost seven feet. Lean and agile, the stranger looked at Diesel lying on the bed then without turning round said in perfect English: "Woman, sleep!"

"Who are you?" Desperately she tried to sit up.

"Sleep. All is well. This man is only asleep."

With that the stranger spread his fine hands across Diesel's body and started moving them back and forth. As he did so a deep rich tone started to fill the room. Penni found it so deep that it made her body tremble. "Oh, that is so beautiful," she thought to herself as the sound permeated every cell in her body. Now totally frantic she attempted to see what the stranger was doing.

Suddenly the toning ceased and the stranger took Diesel's hand. "Arise Michael Boulter. Arise, you have work to do."

How did this stranger know his name? What was he trying to do? Didn't he know the man was dead and had been dead for maybe an hour? She struggled to get up. Then she stopped unable to believe her eyes.

Diesel moved! His lips shivered for several seconds and then came a soft groan. She heard the rasp of air being drawn in through his nose and mouth. His chest expanded as he started to breathe. Finally his eyes opened and he peered around.

"What happened?" he asked nervously.

"You were asleep, Michael," said the stranger.

"I was shot. I remember being shot," he muttered.

"The bullet is here on the dresser," said the stranger with a wave of his hand. "Your wound is healed. Tomorrow you will be strong enough to drive the vehicle because the witnesses must be at the Gathering point for the Summer Solstice."

The stranger watched as Diesel stood up and flexed his muscles. "Wow! I feel fine," he said cheerfully. "Who are you?"

The visitor ignored the question. "I must leave you now. I must be about my father's work but my mother whom you know will look after you," he said and with a soft smile he turned, revealed his face to Penni and leaning forward he kissed her forehead.

"Peter!" she whispered but it was too late. He had gone.

31

THE GROUP TRIED TO get off to an early start but it was seven o'clock before Diesel got the vintage 80 year-old Smith truck going amidst a cloud of dirty white exhaust smoke. While everyone was joyful that Diesel was restored to life nevertheless a strange uncomfortable air of not knowing what to say descended on most of the people.

"Some folks don't know how to handle metaphysical stuff," said Molly as she stuffed a rolled-up blanket onto the truck.

David stared at her and shrugged. "It's damned difficult for a traditionally skeptical mind to comprehend. Diesel was dead. His heart had stopped. How long was he dead? Almost an hour? We were seriously considering how to bury, cremate or otherwise dispose of the body. Then Penni says a figure in white appears, chants some sounds, waves his hands and the dead man comes back to life. How do we logically explain that to ourselves?"

"There is no logical explanation," she said softly as she reached for his arm to provide comfort. "My old teacher used to say if you attempt to intellectualize spirituality or spiritual events you'll bomb out. Just learn from what you see and note the experience."

David grinned meekly. "Hey, I'm supposed to be the philosophical writer around here."

"You'll make out just fine," said Molly. "Just keep an open mind."

Paul Rowan overheard the last of the conversation and chipped in: "I used to tell the kid, keep an open mind and learn everything you can and resist judging particularly on things you know nothing about." He shrugged and flashed a grin at Molly. "I read his UFO book and he hasn't learned a damned thing."

"Hey, Dad," growled David. "Whose side are you on?"

"Right now, this good looking creature who adores you," he said putting his hand on Molly's shoulder.

"Listen, old timer," chipped in Natalie from behind, "stop handling the goods."

Everyone laughed which broke some of the tension. As the group prepared to move Erich Steiner took movies with his 16 millimeter camera. "What happened to the two invaders who were lying in the bushes last night?" he asked.

"That's another mystery," replied David. "When Dad and I went looking for them at dawn they were nowhere in sight."

"Perhaps it never happened," suggested Natalie. "Maybe it was all in our imagination. Perhaps the alien took them."

"Peter is not an alien," snapped Penni with a frown. "He's my son."

Nell O'Connor found a box of early Okanagan peaches which everyone welcomed and relished and that got everyone going. Penni Singleton decided she wanted to stay in the cab and be close to Diesel who smiled at that idea. Steiner joined them with the idea of capturing more movie material. As the old truck moved off and headed for the highway Chloe and Hugh Geraint-Jones started singing old western songs. Hugh gave an impersonation of Johnny Cash singing *Ghost Riders in the Sky* which made everyone laugh including Kate and Mark who claimed they had never heard it before.

Apart from deserted cars, trucks and debris left behind by looters the Coquihalla Highway was a good ride for the group. The air was fresh and filled with the aroma of pine trees that scattered the valley and hills. They rolled up the canvas sides to stare at the burning fires in the historic cattle-town of Merrit in the Nicola Valley. Only once did a group of looters attempt to stop the truck but Diesel just ploughed through them as if they didn't exist and he had a new lease on life. For a few minutes they had an unexpected passenger who sat on the tailboard clinging to a bicycle. He was Tom Fedorak a sergeant from the Royal Canadian Mounted Police bleary-eyed and tired riding home to Nicola Lake.

"It's so peculiar," he said. "There's just no communication anywhere. No radio, no phones, no wireless, no TV, no power for lights. We know we should be out there but we have no force, no back-up. One of our members got killed last night. What do we do with the body? The hospital, the mortuary, the funeral people have no methods for keeping a body cool – especially in the middle of summer. It's damnably weird. Also no one sees it ending anytime soon."

"Where did you finally put the body?" asked a curious Molly.

"Oh, in the cemetery. Where else?" he said as he got off the truck. "The corporal nabbed a couple of looters and instead of incarcerating them put them to work digging a grave."

"Did they do it all right?"

"Oh, yes," nodded Fedorak with a glum grimace. "They not only buried the man, they disappeared with our shovels."

The highway wound its way north through parched grasslands and rolling hills dotted with pine trees and grassy slopes. Diesel told Penni and Steiner about the famous Douglas Lake Cattle Ranch tucked away in the hills beyond the highway. The movie man wanted to take a look but Diesel shook his head.

"We have to keep going," he said. "I don't know how long this old bird will keep flying. She's over 80 years old."

Incidents seemed to be getting fewer as the truck carrying its special group swung through the hills overlooking the City of Kamloops. A large grass fire burning out of control on the hills flanking Peterson Creek created a dangerous smoke screen as Diesel weaved the old truck through scores of vehicles littering the highway.

"In a moment we'll cross the bridge that will take us on our last leg," cried David to the others sitting and standing in the back. "The Yellowhead Highway."

Diesel aimed the truck for the center lanes of the four-lane bridge spanning the South Thompson River then suddenly called out: "What the blazes is that?" He waved an arm to the right and they spotted a huge parking lot with a circular low-lying arena.

Paul Rowan stood up and looked. "It's the Kamloops First Nation Indian Pow Wow Center. Every year in early August the Native Indians stage one of the largest celebrations of First Nations' culture and heritage in Western Canada. The Pow Wow is a great exhibition of storytelling, song and dance in traditional regalia," he said then added, "Saks and Jenny came last year."

"But it's not August," cried Chloe. "What are all those people doing there?"

"Ugh-oh!" muttered Diesel, "we have company."

Several Indians wearing shirts and jeans and mounted on horses were on the highway. Two of them waved for the truck to stop. "We're on Indian lands," said David.

The Indian horsemen looked over the truck as if they had never seen such a vehicle. A somber heavy set man who appeared to be in charged rode up to the cab.

"There are not too many vehicles these days?" he said slowly. "Where are you all going?"

David explained they were going to Elks Head Valley Road beyond Clearwater.

"You know Saks and Jenny then?"

"My mother."

"Saks taught my son to play the flute," said the man with a smile.

"What's happening here?" David waved a hand toward the Pow-Wow Center.

The man explained that since the blackout the Tk'emlups Indian Band had been feeding hungry people from the area. "We slaughtered several steers, built log fires and cooked beef and potatoes. So far we've fed close to 5,000 people in three days. A full stomach keeps everybody peaceful until the power comes back."

"A great idea," said David. "The Great Spirit will love you all."

"Maybe," said the Indian. "Can you stay for a bite?"

David explained the urgency so a horseman disappeared down the road to the Pow Wow grounds and returned with a basket of freshly cooked bread, beef and potatoes. "This will keep you going," said the Indian. "Good travelling."

They got under way again and to the relief of all aboard some two hours later the truck wound its way through the thick forest lining the dusty Elks Head Valley Road. Diesel swung the veteran vehicle through the gateway of the Running Wind Ranch, stopped in the parking area, a feat which prompted everyone to let up a huge resounding cheer.

"We made it," David said as he jumped off and made his way to the cab. "Diesel you're one champion driver. It's great to have you with us." As he pumped the man's hand he noticed the other hand was being held by Penni. "We made it. I always believed you would do it for us."

Diesel grinned. "In spite of the fact I was at death's door and saw angels?"

"Now you'll be able to write a book: *How I drove an 80-year old truck to Heaven.*"

"Hey," cried Penni quickly. "He's not there yet."

They laughed, but their laughter was short lived.

After greeting and introducing everyone and providing cold drinks and biscuits on the terrace outside, Saks stood up and announced some bad news.

"The plateau, the place high up in the mountains where we are supposed to meet the Anunnaki people tomorrow?" he paused to take a breath, "Well, something is wrong. The early morning of the day the power stopped coming, an aeroplane without humans scouted the area…"

"A drone?" said Paul Rowan.

"Yes, a drone attacked one of the Anunnaki shuttles," said Saks, "and was instantly destroyed. The remains are in our upper meadow."

Everyone started talking but Saks held up his hands.

"There have been dark clouds gathering over the plateau and we have not had any communication from any one including our friend and contact An-Nusku." he said slowly, his dark brown eyes scanning the group. "It appears someone gave information to the American war people. Now, I don't know if they will come for us tomorrow which is the summer solstice."

"Oh, crap!" muttered Steiner and a barrage of disappointed sighs and comments came from the crowd. Jax Devenport started cleaning his horn rimmed glasses and remained silent.

The big Indian shrugged. His dark brown eyes scanned the group as he and Jenny were introduced. Finally he stopped searching and smiled softly as Jenny made everyone welcome.

The CIA man suddenly felt distinctly uncomfortable and afraid.

32

THE ANNOUNCEMENT BY SAKS Running Wind that he had lost contact with the Anunnaki contact An-Nusku created an air of deep disappointment among the group. Steiner became depressed as visions of capturing a movie scoop shattered in an instant and Jax Devenport became totally disillusioned and wandered around Jenny's garden with a long guilty face. Originally the CIA director had envisioned an action that would upend all the many critics of his Department in Washington but it had failed to happen. Instead of finding an alien outpost on Earth the drone had been destroyed before it reached its target. In Devenport's mind that was a costly and total waste of time. The others showed their disappointment over Sak's announcement in various ways mainly through talking with each other.

"We could wait and see if the aliens return," suggested Penni who kept looking at the mountains obviously hoping her son would reappear. "It is so very strange I cannot understand my son's connection with these aliens."

Jenny attempted to make everyone comfortable by serving fresh lemonade, tea and coffee and then started allotting spaces for guests to spend the night. Saks announced that dinner would be served in an hour.

In the late afternoon sun David and Molly walked up to the meadow and were quickly followed by Kate, Mark and Jax Devenport who all expressed a desire to hike the forest trails that lead to the upper grasslands and view the remains of the drone aircraft. Erich Steiner realizing the opportunity for getting some movie footage ran after them.

David and Molly stopped walking by the three horses in the upper meadow and watched while the others climbed the trail into the trees.

"Are you thinking what I'm thinking?" she asked.

"That our friend Jax called his boss at the CIA and revealed the location of the Anunnaki mission center?" he said softly. "I'm pretty sure. After all he's only doing his duty as a paid employee of the CIA." Turning he placed his hands on her arm and added: "While Jax gave them information to protect his backside, I don't think he ever imagined the military would send a drone to check it out and worse, get attacked by one of the Anunnaki defense craft."

Molly took David's hands. "You are a bit of a softy, are you not?"

David suddenly felt defensive. "All right, supposing he hadn't informed them and they had later found out, he'd find himself in the deep hole of trouble and would probably lose both a job and a pension. The CIA is quite demanding when it comes to loyalty in its employees."

While he spoke he found himself gazing into her light hazel eyes. "The immediate problem dominating my mind is this: Are we still welcome to see what happens at the solstice tomorrow?"

"That peculiar statement made by Penni Singleton's son about us being witnesses," she said. "What do you suppose that's all about?"

"Oh, they're going to show us the latest thing in space travel," he quipped.

Molly flipped a playful punch to his chest. "Comedian! You have no idea have you? You also have no idea how we are going to get to the plateau high in the mountains where the Anunnaki are alleged to have their mission center, have you?"

"They'll send a bus or a helicopter or a space shuttle," he said with a soft grin. "We could even hike it. Those two local kids did it."

On the way back to the ranch house they met Jenny treading lightly through the vegetable garden full of smiles her eyes twinkling as David always remembered her.

"Is this that special person you told me about in your email?" For a moment the eyes lost their glitter as she scanned the figure but they hastily resumed their twinkling. "Molly looks pretty demure and glamorous to me."

"That's a beautiful illusion," said David. "The UFO radicals call her an Amazon. In reality she's as tough as nails while covered in mink. Well versed in martial arts she has a deadly kick."

"You're not sleeping with her are you, dear David," said Jenny adjusting his shirt collar. "She might get restless leg syndrome and all that stuff."

"Mother, you still have a wicked tongue," laughed David.

"Are you going to marry her?"

"She hasn't asked me yet." He raised his eyebrows and flashed a grin at his friend.

"Beware!" she said turning to look at Molly. "His mind is a little warped. Writing makes it so."

They laughed and moved towards the deck where Chloe and Geraint-Jones were trying to explain the Babylonian tablets and the Anunnaki to Penni Singleton, Diesel Boulter along with Paul and Natalie Rowan.

The archaeologist was deep in discussion on gold. "You only have to look around at the human race to realize that we have been programmed for the most part to hunt for gold and everything that means wealth," said the archaeologist occasionally puffing on a briar pipe.

"Strange," said Molly, "I am allergic to gold, so I like silver."

"That was the second metal enjoyed by the space travelers," said Geraint-Jones. "But it was always gold that dominated the objectives of the Anunnaki – gold in the Abzu otherwise known as South Africa. They started mining it just after their arrival 430,000 years ago."

"Specifically the gold fields are in the West Rand," said Paul Rowan nodding. "They are still very much in production today. Some years back I did a story for Verity Magazine but nobody told me of its far-reaching historic aspects."

"Modern science is loathed to accept the fact there are more intelligent and advanced people in the cosmos than ourselves and that they actually colonized Earth so long ago," said Geraint-Jones. "When they created the so-called primitive workers they created a matrix, a way of living from which one can never escape: A civilization driven with an obsession for gold."

"Hey," muttered Diesel. "Isn't that being crude?"

The archaeologist shook his head. "Throughout history kings and power lords have been overwhelmed by the greed for gold. They saw it and still do see it as sacred and most don't know why, because they fail to realize the Anunnaki spirits planted long ago are still as greedy today as they were when they created those primitive workers."

For several moments he chewed on his pipe stem. "You must remember that humans were born as slaves and they are still slaves today in acquiring gold and its brothers wealth, money, power and prestige."

Geraint-Jones watched as Jenny appeared carrying juice and wine and Molly helped distribute filled glasses, then he said: "Don't you believe me? Take a look at the stock markets, the financial investment houses, the oil companies, the giant corporation that manufacture and prosper from foods that make people obese and sick so that other corporations can produce and prosper from medication to remedy sickness, and all the players make gold while doing it. Greed is just as rampant today as when the kings and war lords killed and looted in many regions of the world."

"Well, I have several gold medals for performance in martial arts?" said Molly.

"Would you have competed for medals in bronze, steel or tin?" returned Geraint-Jones.

Molly thought for a moment and then shrugged. "Hugh, I see you point."

The archaeologist sighed. "Humans are told from the cradle to be ambitious and go for the gold. For example: all sports and competitions including the Olympic Games immortalize gold medals. Marriage partners normally wear gold rings."

"But gold has always been something special to human beings," said Paul Rowan.

"Ah, that's just it," he said with a touch of triumph in his voice. The matrix implemented by the Anunnaki in our ancestors is still very evident today."

"One doesn't hear of the primitive workers, the slaves in the South African gold mines rebelling and building empires," said Paul Rowan.

"Ah, that's just it," said Geraint Jones. "For thousands of years gold had no intrinsic value to the uneducated workers but the moment they became educated, well the world changed drastically."

"When was this?" asked David.

"About 7,000 years ago there was a change of heart in Nibiru regarding its Earth colony. The leadership decided to introduce a basic civilization to the Sumerians. The people of Sumer basked in the cradle of learning as the Anunnaki teachers shared a basic language called Cuneiform. Suddenly they were able to write, count and conduct business. With this came the knowledge and practice of mathematics, detailed astronomical data, the practice of medicine and surgery, how to set up a dating system which the Jewish people still use to this day, the practice of municipal government, setting up codes of law and more. In less than a thousand years the Anunnaki set up an instant civilization that still influences the world today."

Chloe came forward and gave her husband a glass of wine and he held it up in the sunlight and the group saw that it was golden. While he sipped the wine Chloe took up the story. "As the new civilization spread through to the Akkadians and Hittites nations gold took on a new meaning, it was proclaimed sacred. Possession of it became godly and divine. To possess it was to possess power and influence. Slaves who toiled over mining and processing the ore were frequently told that gold is the property of the gods. Ultimately gold among the educated classes became a symbol of wealth and social standing."

Geraint-Jones relit his pipe. "Wanting something you cannot have is the major cause of unhappiness in the world," he said slowly. "Kings and war lords wanted gold and they spared no expense to get it. They created huge armies that destroyed nations, decimated cities, wiped out entire populations of men, women and children. Why? Because they wanted gold and the power and prestige with which it comes. It's all in Genesis chapter 14." He waved his pipe and shook his head. "It is also why history for the last 6,000 years has been littered with the casualties of war. The insatiable creed for power and wealth."

Molly nodded vigorously. "And it is still that way today."

"Gold translates into money and business," said Paul Rowan. "We noticed just recently that China, India and Brazil are building up their gold reserves."

Geraint-Jones beamed. "It's all about power, sir. Those who have the gold have power."

"America started losing its power when President Nixon took the country off the gold standard in 1971," commented Natalie.

. When a country no longer holds itself to the gold standard it has to exercise muscle in other ways," said Paul Rowan. "Such as building a mammoth defense system and doing police work around the world."

Natalie opened her hands. "In all of this history where were the Jews, the Children of Israel.?

"If you haven't read it lately go back to Exodus where the Anannuki god gives Moses instructions how to build the Ark of the Covenant and overlay it with gold both inside and out, provide gold molding, cast four gold rings to carry the Ark along with cherubins of pure gold. Instructions included a mercy seat to be made of pure gold and set on the top of the Ark from which god would give instructions to the Israelites," he said, then added "With each paragraph you will realize the power and the influence of the Anunnaki gods."

"My gosh," cried Penni, "that must have required a tremendous amount of gold."

"Almost two tons," remarked Geraint-Jones.

Chloe chipped in. "Michael Tellinger in his book *Slave Species of God* suggests the Ark of the Covenant was a communications device mainly because the instructions given for its construction were so precise

"It all makes sense," agreed Paul, "but where does it leave God, the True God the one we pray to?"

Geraint-Jones walked across the deck and looked back. "The gods of the Old Testament were not the true gods of the Cosmos – they were our fathers whom the simple minded Earthlings considered and branded as gods. The so-called god of the Old Testament was a ruthless manipulator of wars and destruction. Unfortunately it set the stage for every war and conflagration ever since."

Diesel Boulter said: "Of course, I was brought up to be a god-fearing man. My mother used to tell me that the streets of Heaven were paved with gold."

"I recall that too," said Molly. "But I can see where the professor is coming from. Over the many years these space people hauled away countless tons of gold for the home planet Nibiru. It's little wonder people were taken in by the streets of gold suggestion."

"I'm feeling quite giddy," said Natalie. "This is all very upsetting in my mind."

"Why is that, Natalie?" asked Chloe.

"Because when we were at the Vatican in Rome we saw all the things made of gold – gold chalices, gold candelabra, gold seats, gold trim round the Pope's robes," she said and looking at Geraint-Jones she held up her hand and clenched her fist. "All through the years we have been intimidated into being slaves to the threats and the dogmas of the church. The whole idea of slavery is embedded in our DNA. We are slaves to our work, our ideals, our limitations and even our religions." She stared at those around her. "And some of the people here are looking forward to meeting these aliens? We should spit in their faces."

Paul stared at his wife. "Wow! Where did that come from Natalie?"

The woman shrugged. "The idea of meeting these thugs makes me cringe."

Geraint-Jones sat on a bench and fiddled with his pipe. "Listen, there is something we have not discussed," he said his pale gray eyes watching the others. "It is this. While the Anunnaki taught Earth people many valuable gifts they introduced an unsavory aspect which I call the dark side."

"The dark side?" David was curious. "Wasn't slavery a part of their dark side?"

Geraint-Jones shook his head. "You must remember they walked and influenced Earthlings for thousands of years. They brought with them a culture that contained a grotesque record of treachery, war, corruption, infighting, incest, anger, revenge, jealousy along with murder, torture and the indiscriminate killing of innocent people including their own."

"Wow!" Molly shook her head in total shock. "That's hard to believe."

"Is it?" quizzed the archaeologist with a frown. "The Anunnaki planted their own seeds with the introduction of monarchies and religion which instantly bred tribes of greedy warlords seeking power – and gold."

"The problem was," said Chloe, "the Anunnaki suggested a system of kings be established and elders or priests be appointed to implement religion which they saw as a form of control."

"By intimidation?" suggested Paul.

"Right," said the archaeologist. It all started with a fellow named Sargon who saw the powers inherent in the religion so he murdered the first king and assumed the throne and created the Akkad Dynasty in northern Babylonia. Sargon with his army through destruction conquered most of the central Middle East area. In fact his wars were so devastating that according to one scribe, not a branch was left for a bird to perch on."

Chloe nodded enthusiastically. "Sargon realized the power of women too. Enheduanna, his daughter became a high priestess and created the Sumerian Temple Hymns and Songs to each of the central temples in Sumer. The hymns which are some 4,000 years old are contained in the Sumerian tablets at the British Museum in London."

Geraint-Jones continued by saying it was not until Naram-Sin, Sargon's grandson assumed power that religion really started to spread. "The grandson called himself King of the Four Corners of the Universe and a living god." With a brief laugh he quipped: "Didn't do him much good. The Anunnaki god Marduk who was the son of Enki and recognized in Egypt as Ra, got all bent out of shape and caused a famine and effectively crushed the empire. Incidentally there's a victory stele – a pillar – at the Louvre showing Naram-Sin wearing a horned helmet, a symbol of his divinity."

"So Naram-Sin is acknowledged as the first real proponent of a religious cult?" asked Natalie.

"That was some 22 centuries before the birth of Jesus," replied Geraint-Jones. "This was over 200 years before the coming of Abraham who was also a Sumerian and lived in the desert near the city of Ur. Abraham of course is recognized as the father of Judaism, Christianity and Islam and worked for the Anunnaki as a spy."

Natalie was surprised. "Spy? You're kidding!"

"Absolutely," said the archaeologist. "Go and read Genesis 18 and 19 and see how Abraham bargained with god for the people he knew were good in Sodom and Gomorrah. The Sodom crowd wanted to kill Abraham but two men – probably Anunnaki aides – struck the attackers with blindness. The entire destruction of the two cities is not the work of the True God, but the gods known as the Anunnaki – and this ladies and gentlemen, leads to the really dark side of the Anunnaki -- nuclear war!"

David shook his head and whispered to Molly: "I find this difficult to believe."

Geraint-Jones heard the comment and stared at the writer. "Perhaps you need to learn Cuneiform and read some of the thousands of Babylonian tablets that exist today for anyone to read. There's enough material for thousands of books." He nodded to his wife. "Please tell them more about Marduk the Lord of the Earth."

"The great flood was caused by the close proximity of the home planet Nibiru," said Chloe. "The Anunnaki watched the devastation from out in space. Afterwards, they returned and the rivalry became so great between the sons of the Anannuki that war between the gods was inevitable. It was all over succession rights. Ninurta was the son of Enlil the god of the Old Testament who hated what they had created on Earth while Marduk was the eldest son of Enki who favored educated Earthlings."

"It all happened in the year 2024 BCE," said Geraint-Jones. "Marduk who was totally power hungry designated himself Ruler of the Earth. Enlil started a devastating nuclear and biological war directed against Marduk and his supporters. Marduk sought refuge in the Egyptian space beacon known today as the Great Pyramid of Giza. Nuclear explosions resulted in a vast tract of the fertile Middle East, Sinai and North Africa being turned into desolate wastelands or deserts which still exist in part today. The radioactive clouds known as the Evil Winds drifted east causing terrible and gruesome death and systematically wiped out all life in Babylon and all the surrounding cities of Ur, Eridu, Lagash, Umma, Sippar and of course E.Din. The Sumerian civilization became virtually extinct except for one thing." The archaeologist paused then added: "The thousands of clay tablets which tell us the history of the early civilized world. They exist!"

"The Anunnaki rulers concluded that the Middle East was no longer habitable," said Chloe. "They moved to Central and South America where they continued their gold mining until the home planet's orbit took it away from the proximity of Earth and made interplanetary space travel at that time no longer possible."

"But that was a long time ago and the Anunnaki are back," said Molly. "Do you think they have changed in their warlike culture?"

Geraint-Jones nodded. "One can only hope that they have drastically altered their ways," he said. "Because if they haven't I think Earth is heading for a rough ride."

Jenny and Saks appeared. "Dinner is served," she cried out.

Molly reached out to hold David's hand. "Suddenly I sense a fear, a state of mind I have never experienced before," she said as her hazel eyes turned towards the upper meadows and the mountains. "The sun is dropping down and it will be dark in a couple of hours. I wonder what happened to the others.

33

THE SEVEN HORSEMEN APPEARED to come out of nowhere. One moment the natural meadow lying in the foothills of the heavily forested mountains existed quietly pastoral, the next moment heavy thumping on the earth broke the silence with snorts of animals breathing heavily. The horsemen looked impatient and extremely wary. None resembled cowboys or traditional ranchmen because they were all dressed in informal urban wear, tee-shirts, jeans and runners except two wore leather western boots. Only one sat under a dark dirty brown Stetson, the others wore baseball caps with various sports and beer logos including the Vancouver Canucks emblem. Three of them carried rifles or shotguns and one had a revolver. Five were lean and mature, one appeared as a teenager and one was broad shouldered and heavily built.

Erich Steiner filmed them coming up the draw to where Kate, Mark and Jax Devenport were standing.

"Hey, no pictures!" cried the big framed man under the Stetson as he reined in his snorting animal. "We don't want any pictures."

"We're shooting for personal records," said Steiner.

"Who the heck are you people and where's the UFO crash site?"

"It's back there on the edge of the pine." Kate pointed her hand.

"It's not a UFO," said Devenport. "It's a drone. Unarmed."

"How do you know? Are you an expert?"

"No. I just recognize drones," he replied.

"That's strange. I hadn't heard of drones in Canada," said the big man.

"It's NATO," said Davenport not wishing to bring the United States into the discussion. "Incidentally who are you people? I'm Jax Devenport and these are my friends Kate, Mark and Eric."

"Well, my name is Halston," said the big man. "Retired police sergeant. RCMP. We're up here to check the place out and also the drone." His sharp eyes scanned the four. "You wouldn't be looters, would you? We shot and killed a couple in the town earlier today."

"Is there a lot of looting?" asked Kate curiously.

"This morning the mayor called for a dusk to dawn curfew," said Halston. "The local force is now on horseback so they are mobile." He peered at the four again. "I don't recognize you people. Where are you from?"

"The States," said Steiner. "We're visiting some friends down the way – Saks Running Wind and his wife Jenny."

Halston nodded and seemed surprised. Turning to the teenager on horseback, he called out: "Cal, have you seen any of these people at the Indian's place?"

The youngster shook his head. "Saks said there were some people coming."

"Oh, so you're here for the aliens, the UFO invasion," said Halston. "My boy told me what happened here."

"Dad, you forced it out of me."

"Shush your mouth, son," snapped the big man. "We are heading over to the plateau where my son and his friend an Indian kid named Johnny Manuel claim they saw a huge medieval palace with golden pyramids. Personally, I think it's a load of horse manure."

Steiner shrugged. "Have you any idea who caused the power blackout? It's pretty extensive. We came up from the Lower Mainland and Washington State and everywhere was blacked out. No power."

"Halston shrugged. "It's those bloody terrorists," he snarled. "I lost a close buddy in NYPD at the nine-eleven massacre. We should exterminate all terrorists and sympathizers." He glanced up at the mountains. "My kid says the palace he saw with the pyramids was Arabic which means Moslems."

"Damn it, Dad," cried the teenager, "I never said no such thing. You've got it all wrong."

Halston shook his head with a tired smirk. "Anyway, we're heading up to see if there are any terrorists up on the plateau," he said. "If there are we're not bringing them in alive. That's for damned sure."

The four watched as the group of seven reined their horses round and moved up the draw to where the remains of the drone were scattered among the trees.

"Do you think they mean what they say?" asked Kate anxiously.

"The way that ex-cop was chaffing at the bit, I wouldn't be surprised," said Devenport.

Steiner looked at him. "I'm surprised you didn't flash your CIA badge. He would have been impressed."

"Yeah," grinned the other. "It would have triggered an international incident. That's why I said the drone was a NATO thing. No need for America to get involved."

"There's something wrong there somewhere," said Mark quietly. "Royal Canadian Mounted Police are usually not that radical, even retired ones. I have the feeling he was retired early."

"In other words, booted out," said Kate reaching for her water bottle. "It's getting late. I think we should head back and tell Saks and Jenny of the encounter."

They stood and watched as the seven horsemen made their way up the grade and then moved single file along the edge of the forest until they disappeared over the brow of the hill. Turning they walked down across the meadow, stopped for several minutes while Steiner filmed a shot of the North

Thompson Valley with the river winding its way south towards Clearwater. The fires and smoke that had been burning when they passed the town earlier were no longer evident. Mark thought the authorities must be getting some sort of control in spite of the lack of electricity.

"People are learning to live without power," remarked Devenport.

They all heard it. Galloping hooves beating the ground. A lone solitary horseman as if being chased by the devil hurtled over the brow a quarter of a mile behind them.

"It's the cop's kid!" cried Mike.

Cal Halston his eyes wide and fearful, gripped the reins and pulled the sweating horse to a stop.

"UFOs! UFOs!" he screamed. "They took us all by surprise. They came out of nowhere. They surrounded everyone. Three or four of them hovering a few feet above the ground. They had Dad and the others corralled." The teenager twisted in the saddle and looked back. "Mom's going to be so mad. She told Dad to stay home until the power comes back on."

"How did you get away?" asked Kate as the lad slipped off the horse.

The boy looked embarrassed. "I had to crap in the bushes," he said. "The others went on. They were some distance ahead of me and as I got back on the horse. Then I potted the UFOs. Oh, heck. I should have stayed."

"Why? It's good that you got away, young fellah," said Steiner.

"There's nothing we can do," said Devenport quickly. "Let's get back to base."

Suddenly more sounds of thundering hooves over hard ground split the air. They all spun round to stare as six terrified horses, their long legs pacing across the grass, their manes flowing, and their nostrils wide and blasting air as they hurtled towards them. In a moment they had flashed past and galloping down the valley trail.

"Heck, looks as if they're being chased by the devil," cried Steiner. Gripped by an overwhelming fear the teenager's horse reared up, broke free from the lad's grip and snorting harshly it raced after the others.

As they watched completely dumbfounded they all realized the saddles on the seven horses were empty.

34

IT WAS DARK WHEN Kate, Mark, Erich Steiner and Jax Devenport accompanied by Cal Halston staggered wearily onto the candle and oil lamp illuminated deck at the cottage. Jenny and Natalie brought them wine, juices and food and listened in stunned silence to the strange story of the six lost men.

"They must have been abducted right off the horses," suggested Steiner as he alternated between taking bites of a cheese and tomato sandwich and dusting off his camera from the excursion.

"We scoured the band of fir surrounding the plateau," said Kate.

"That was the place where we met the alien fellow a couple of days ago," said Cal. "Now he was nowhere to be seen."

"The buildings?" asked Saks.

"Not a thing. There was nothing there," said the teenager.

"We just kept on looking until it started getting dark," said Mark. "Those men and Cal's Dad have disappeared off the face of the earth."

"This changes things, I think," said Paul Rowan slowly. "Is it possible the Anunnaki have been delayed or simply retreated because of the power failure?"

"You mean they didn't trigger the blackout?" put in Devenport.

"The Anunnaki are not the only alien life form in the Cosmos," put in David. "There could be other entities flexing their muscles and neutralizing the U.S. power grids."

"And perhaps the world," said Steiner quickly.

"Come on," said Natalie. "No alien force could pull that one off. You guys are imagining things."

"Wait a minute," cried David Rowan standing up. "Think about this. We know the power is out in Washington State and also British Columbia. Not even simple things like cell phones work, computers, flash lights work at all – and they're all equipped with batteries which suddenly do not work. In fact, anything that demands electricity – AC and DC --doesn't work." He held up his hand to take the floor. "There's something else missing."

"Yeah?" It was Steiner.

"Ever since we started this trek in Whidbey Island we have not seen a single aircraft," he said. "Not one."

Several people nodded.

"This can only mean one thing. The power outage is world wide," said David. "And if this is the case we may be on the battle lines of a cosmic war involving planet Earth in which case the Anunnaki are being challenged by other invaders from outer space."

"For someone who only a few days ago was the epitome of skepticism when it comes to aliens and alien invasions," said Steiner, "you sure have changed, David."

Molly stepped up to David's side. "Listen, folks," she said. "There's been a lot happening in just a few short days. "We've had reports of strange replicas of the Giza pyramid appearing all over the world and then Frederick Klassen a civilian at the 10th Space Warning Squadron at Cavalier Air Force Station, North Dakota revealed how the Pentagon ordered the destruction of a UFO observer ship in the Clarke Belt. There's more: numerous people have mysteriously disappeared including Penni Singleton's son." She turned and looked at David. "What else?"

"The two local teenagers," he said, "Cal here and his friend Johnny Manuel had an encounter with what appeared to be an Anunnaki spokesperson named An-Nusku and saw a large building that resembled a palace flanked by two pyramids."

"Then an American drone apparently unarmed and on an observation mission over Canadian territory is shot down presumably by one of the UFOs reportedly guarding the plateau," said Molly. "Then this kid's father and five of his colleagues disappeared on the mountain without trace. This is getting to be a terrible circus."

The CIA man moved closer to the lights. "Both Saks and Jenny here report that An-Nusku a representative of the Anunnaki spent some time here recently but did not say what is going on," said Devenport staring at the Indian. "Are you sure you've told us everything, sir?"

Saks clutching an Indian flute sat still in the old cedar chair and finally nodded. "He said he would come for us when everything is ready. The time of the solstice. That is tomorrow morning."

"Well, it looks as if all of this was for nothing," said Mark.

"Have heart, kiddo. Just because you didn't find the alien's buildings up on the plateau," Molly said quickly, "it doesn't mean they've gone. They may have changed vibrations in light of so many people taking an interest in their location."

"How do you figure that one, Molly?" Paul Rowan looked at her inquisitively in the candle light.

"Simple," she said placing her hands on Cal's shoulders. "Where's this young man's father and the other five horsemen? They seem to have joined the long list of people who have suddenly disappeared. In other words – abducted!"

"Where is Mrs. Singleton?" asked Kate looking around for faces in the candle lights.. "Also where are the Geraint-Jones couple and Diesel?"

"They all went for a walk," said Natalie. "In the moonlight. Chloe said they needed exercise after sitting in Diesel's truck for two days. It certainly was not the most comfortable ride in the world.

"David looked at his daughter and Mark. "Did you find anything that resembles a track or a road up towards the plateau?"

Kate shook her head. "After Saks and Jenny's upper meadow there's nothing but deer and moose tracks and they're not too clear."

Saks leaned forward in the wooden cedar chair. "There is an old logging road that branches off to the north down our road and winds its way up into the mountains but it's a winding route used by loggers twenty years ago. There have been rock falls over the years so I don't think Diesel's truck would make it."

Just then they heard approaching footsteps on the gravel. They all turned to see in the darkness Hugh and Chloe Geraint-Jones coming along the path to the deck followed by Diesel Boulter and Penni Singleton. As they came onto the deck and were illuminated by the candle lights, Hugh turned back.

"We have another visitor for our jolly clan," said the archaeologist. "We found her walking in the moonlight. She says she is a friend of David Rowan's and was responsible for him coming here."

The figure of a woman dressed in a white suite and a carrying a sunhat and a yellow travel-bag came out of the darkness. David stared as if he could not believe his eyes. Memories of the London bookshop, the cottage at Bourne End and the peculiar night with a woman by the Thames came flooding back.

Geraint-Jones continued: "She says her name is …

David Rowan gasped: "It's Alice Simonian from London, England."

35

IN SPITE OF BEING miles away in the country on a dusty road, and in spite of the soft flickering oil lamps and candles the woman came into the light appearing with the aplomb of a fashion model. Well presented, she wore a white suit, carried a large sunhat in one hand and a small pocketbook slung over her shoulder.

"Hello, David," she said in a soft and distinctive voice.

"Alice!" For a moment, the writer was stunned. This was not supposed to happen. He had almost forgotten spending a day and a night with this slim attractive woman who seemed to be about his age. There was something incredibly attractive about her but it was elusive and he felt hard pressed to pin it down.

"Come on in and meet everyone," he said and taking an arm guided her round the group which had become very quiet for some strange reason. All the men greeted her with big smiles and hearty handshakes and the women – well, as someone pointed out after everything was over – the feminine aura was indeed powerful and electrifying.

Steiner whispered to Devenport: "This is like some ordinary suburbanites having a steak and barbecue party and a movie actress like Ava Gardner dropping in."

"You should have been a movie gossip writer, Steiner," whispered Devenport drily.

Paul Rowan was trying to figure things out. Molly immediately sensed competition and her pale eyes watched every move and everyone sensed a sudden upsurge in the energy on the deck.

"And this is my partner, my lover and bodyguard," David found himself blurting out as Alison approached. "This is Molly."

A slender well manicured hand reached for Molly's hand and held it briefly as if both were trying to make up their minds, then a warm energetic shake occurred between the two.

"Good choice, David," murmured Alison with a knowing smile that could not be missed.

"We met in Taos," said David. "At the UFO Conference. Molly was told about our encounter in London."

"Ah, yes Taos," said the other. "That's where Mr. Klassen revealed the atrocious actions of the American defense systems in destroying that observation station in the Clarke Belt."

"Observation station?" said Molly quickly. "I thought Mr. Klassen said it was a communications ship from somewhere in space."

"Probably the same thing," said David in a diplomatic tone. "The two roles go together. At least I would think so."

Natalie came into the light with glasses of wine and gave one to Alison who spotted Erich Steiner packing away his movie camera and moved across.

Molly pulled David aside into the quiet of the kitchen and hissed: "And you spent the night with that goddess and let her sleep alone?"

"Carla," he replied. "She haunted me. That's my excuse. Dumb, isn't it."

"She didn't haunt you when we were together on the Oregon beach that evening," she said softly.

"You are different," he said. "I think Carla would approve of you."

Molly stared at him and a smile simmered gently on her face. "David," she muttered, "I didn't realize that one of your hidden assets is diplomacy."

A kiss on the lips and as she took his hand they returned to the deck where everyone was engrossed about what would happen the next day, the summer solstice. An air of tension had grown and now enshrouded everyone particularly Cal, the teenager who was at a loss to account for his missing father and friends.

Jenny and Natalie tried to console the lad. "I'm sure he'll come back on foot," said Jenny. "Something must have spooked the horses."

"All of them?" muttered Cal staring around. "I always saw my Dad as a tough guy, being a police sergeant and all that."

"What happened to your friend, the Indian boy?" asked Jenny.

"Johnny Manuel?" said Saks standing in the shadows. "He said he'll be coming first thing in the morning."

David came over and looked at Saks. "How is all this supposed to happen? The only thing we have is a 1929 diesel truck and a couple of horses."

"Three horses," put in Saks.

"We could all walk," suggested Steiner eagerly, but he was greeted by several disappointing boos. He shrugged and added: "Well, I tried."

"Well, I don't mind walking." Penni Singleton came forward into the light. "I have to find Peter. I've heard so many things about him."

"I don't mind walking," said Diesel and David noticed that he was holding Penni's hand. "The old truck is useless to go any further. There are no real roads or tracks that pass for roads."

Jax Devenport sitting in a cedar armchair shook his head. "Heck, I've been as enthusiastic as the rest of you to see what gives with this UFO stuff. We didn't see any kind of a palace and two pyramids like the kids said." He stared around looking for support, but seeing none, he said: "Maybe because of the drone attack the aliens pulled out."

Silence descended on the group.

Natalie jumped in. "I think we are all a little tired," she said looking around at everyone. "It's time we all lit our candles and got a good night's sleep."

Mark who had been sitting quietly near Kate, stood up and looking about said: "I have something that bothers me. A question."

"Shoot," said David easily. "Let's hear it?"

Mark stared across at Alison sitting next to Steiner and said: "With a lack of general transport and all that sort of stuff, how on earth did that lady get here?"

A silence came over the groups and several started to say something then stopped.

"Well," replied Alison with a meek smile, "I came early before the black-out."

"That makes sense," said Steiner by her side.

"How did you know there was going to be a black-out?" asked Molly.

"That's a difficult situation," she said slowly almost picking her words.

Hugh Geraint Jones paused from sucking on his briar pipe. "You see Alison is psychic."

A titter of laughter ran through the group.

"That's a good question you have Mark," said David. "Just how did you get here, Alison?" All eyes turned to the woman.

"Look, I've always been interested in the Anunnaki," she started to say.

Geraint-Jones cut her off. "Only 200 people in the world can read Cuneiform. Alison is perhaps the only woman who can speak it."

"From where did Cuneiform originate?" snapped David.

"It was one of the lower languages on the planet Nibiru," she said. "So the fathers, Enlil and Enki considered it appropriate to introduce it to the Earthlings. After all they had no written language."

Devenport shook his head. "Miss Alison Simonian you seem to know a lot about these aliens. "Just why are they of interest to you? I gather you set David

Rowan on a course that you knew would take him to Geraint-Jones who in turn would guide him to here."

"That's quite an assumption, Mr. Devenport," said Paul Rowan. "There were a lot of things happening such as the mysterious pyramids perched on the 30 degree latitudes around the world, but I don't see how that could be blamed on this lady."

"It still doesn't answer how she got here when nobody else can," snapped Penni Singleton. "She didn't have a horse or an old diesel car the two modalities that work in a black-out."

Alison appeared to be distinctly uncomfortable.

"Look, Alison, I have the strange idea that you set me up when we met in England for this train of events that would get us here in the remote mountains of British Columbia," said David. "There are too many coincidences."

"Sound's like a wild goose chase to me," snapped Devenport. "I'm of the distinct opinion that nothing will happen tomorrow. We've all been led astray."

Paul Ryan shook his head. "So here we are in the middle of nowhere – the mountain country of western Canada -- with no communications, no transport except an 80 year-old diesel truck and three horses, no electricity and the only lights we have are emergency candles and some oil lamps."

"And there's no guarantee that we are going to see any of the Anunnaki – aliens, space people, UFOs whatever," said Steiner. "That's a bum deal if ever I heard one."

Suddenly a woman's voice broke through.

"Hello, may I say a few words," said Alison Simonian. "All indications are that everything is working the way it should be. We will all be attending the Gathering tomorrow. That is for sure." She smiled softly as the faces, some agog, some frowning, some smiling heard her words.

"Lady," snapped Steiner feeling angry. "How can you say that? Do you have the privilege of an inside track?"

"Our host here, Saks Running-Wind was informed by An-Nusku that we will be collected at the time of the summer solstice," said Alison.

Jenny suddenly moved forward, a frown on her normally friendly face. "How do you know that? You weren't here when Saks told the group when they first arrived," she said. "And you were not here when An-Nusku visited us and healed my husband's legs."

Jenny's small figure walked round the lady in white, then her face and eyes peered up at the beautiful ivory features. "And while we are at it, you never gave an answer to Mark's question: how did you get here so well dressed, ready for a party or a ceremonial and not even a speck of dust on you. What sort of traveler are you?"

David walked to Alison's side. "With all her lingual attributes including Cuneiform, I think she's one of them. She came to that bookshop in London to ensure that I would get here along with some other key people such as Steiner, Geraint-Jones and possibly Devenport."

"We call them witnesses," said Alison standing now to her full height. "We need reliable witnesses to record and tell the people of your world what is occurring at this time. The message is very important." Suddenly, she turned and faced Penni Singleton. "Your boy is safe and will be with us tomorrow."

Jenny was insistent. "How did you get here?"

"An-Nusku dropped me off outside your gateway," she said simply. "He wanted me to come and reduce any concerns you might have about tomorrow."

"You know An-Nusku?" asked Saks from the back.

"An-Nusku is my husband," she said simply. "We have been married a long time. In your years almost 900. In Nibiru time perhaps a little while."

"Good God," said Steiner with a whistle. "I wish to hell I'd captured this whole damned thing on film."

"So tomorrow is a go?" chipped in Devenport appearing excited behind his heavy glasses.

David Rowan sat stunned until Molly came by, tapped his forehead and said "Let's all have something to drink. It's been a strange day."

"Can tomorrow be even stranger?" he asked.

36

MOST OF THE 13 visitors spent restless periods of sleep, tossing and turning, occasionally getting up and listening to the forest and the mountains for any unusual noises. Except for the periodic mournful hoot of an owl and the distant cry of a moose all was quiet. Overwhelmingly quiet. The mixed feelings of curiosity and fascination that they could actually meet some famous aliens from another world stuck in their minds with a vice-like grip. The idea that they might lose their lives or even be abducted by aliens was subservient to their overwhelming desire to see and experience at first hand space travelers from the vast reaches of space.

Out of the visitors Hugh and Chloe Geraint-Jones both in their mid-eighties slept the best because they had been immersed for most of their lives in the incredible history revealed by the 6,000 years-old Sumerian tablets found in the remains of the old Babylonian empire.

"Chloe, we're on the final leg of our journey," Hugh said to his wife as they lay side by side. What could happen tomorrow that might surprise us?"

"Nothing, my dear. Now blow out the candle and get some sleep."

The old archaeologist grinned. That was typical Chloe.

Saks and Jenny after seeing everyone with a comfortable place to sleep retired to their bedroom they had known for so many years. Since the time of the great Cataclysm in 1979 when they had finally declared their love for each other and had come to Elks Head Valley and the ranch bequeathed to Saks by his uncle, Jenny had cared for the Indian until he was well enough to walk around with a cane. Saks taught Indian flute lessons to local children regardless of ethnic background and it produced a slim income. If a child was unable to pay the 25 cents a lesson, Jenny would give the kid a dollar and say: "Pay Saks next time." The child inevitably did. Occasionally, students would bring baskets or boxes of plums and apples and Jenny would send the students home with jars filled with preserves and tied with neat blue and white ribbons.

Then one day almost a year ago a tall well attired man who called himself An-Nusku arrived. He stayed with the couple and told them many stories of a place far away called Nibiru and warned them not to share the things he had told them. Then one day just before An-Nisku departed he placed Saks into a deep sleep for over an hour and when the Indian returned to full consciousness his legs were totally healed.

"Maybe I can run again," he said with a smile.

"Over my dead body," cried Jenny.

Before he left, An-Nusku revealed to the couple that his people would be bringing a large number of people to the mountain plateau beyond Elk Head Valley and it would take place at the summer solstice. "It is all being arranged and a group of witnesses chosen by us will meet here for transport to the plateau," said An-Nusku. "Naturally you are both invited."

"How will people get to the plateau?" asked Jenny.

An-Nusku smiled easily. "We will arrange that," he said and after drinking a cup of jasmine tea he walked out onto the deck and simply disappeared.

"Can you sleep, dear Saks?" she said.

"It doesn't matter what will happen tomorrow. We will simply live and learn," he said as he placed an arm around her small body and pulled it to him. "Let us sleep."

Most of the others eventually found sleep in the cool mountain air freshly scented by pine and cedars. Diesel got up to relieve himself and found Penni Singleton asleep in a cedar chair so he found a blanket and covered her and went back to bed.

Jax Devenport so used to "being in touch" with everyone at the CIA stared at his dead cell phone and wondered how everyone was doing back at base. "Probably having coronaries," he said. "There's nothing like a frustrated general who cannot communicate with his troops. It's the ultimate military impotency." As he slipped off to sleep the cell phone slipped out of his fingers onto the floor.

Jenny being Jenny and greatly image conscious insisted that Kate and Mark have separate rooms. Of course in the overwhelming darkness it was easy for Mark to slip along the corridor to Kate's room where she was waiting with a lonely candle.

"Everyone's worried about how we are all going to get to the Anunnaki place on the plateau," said Kate as they sat side by side on the bed, propped up by ample pillows.

"You dad was telling me how that Geraint-Jones fellow demonstrated a magic carpet," replied Mark. "Maybe they'll send a fleet of them for us."

"That will be cute," said Kate giving Mark a nudge. "You'll have to come on my carpet of course."

"Just to keep you from falling off?" he quipped.

"Ha!" she puffed. "I'm sure it will be the other way round."

They laughed lightly until Kate put her forefinger to her lips. "Shush! We don't want to wake anyone. Let's sleep."

Across the hall Molly and David were tossing restlessly, peering into the darkness, the see-through drapes on the one window were silhouetted against the stars in the night sky. An owl hooted, almost mockingly, he thought. Finally the writer got up and sat on the edge of the bed found a match and lit the candle.

"What's wrong, David?" Her hand reached out and gently massaged his back.

"There's something we've been missing," he said slowly. "The power failure. We have no idea how widespread it is. The absence of aircraft in the skies suggests it might be worldwide." He turned to face her. "In which case the world is currently in a chaotic and deadly shambles. The economy is gutted. Kaput!"

"How?"

"Life without electricity! Somehow we are surviving but there must be one hell of a lot of people who aren't surviving. We witnessed looting, riots and burning on the way here and it never once dawned on us that this blackout could be global. In the big cities – New York, London, Paris, Athens – I can well imagine lawless mobs armed with every means of artillery searching for loot, terrified people gathering together and setting up fortified communes, or simply evacuating, leaving the battlegrounds and heading for the countryside."

He paused and then leaned towards her. "Everyone depends on electricity for their lives, their work and their wellbeing. A world without electricity means factories and production lines are dead. Transportation – air, land and sea – is virtually nonexistent which means no one can get to a job that no longer exists. Communications are dead. No television, no phones, no texting, no emails, no web, no way of communicating beyond talking to each other. Facebook and Twitter are nonexistent. Supply chains for food, water and commodities are dead."

Molly suddenly sat up. "My God! That goes for hospitals too. The chaos in such places must be tortuous and horrific. Thousands, perhaps several million people lying in hospitals and clinics on life support systems must be clinging desperately to life on their own resources or simply have passed away."

David stood up and walked to the window and gazed at the dark mountains in the east across the North Thompson Valley silhouetted against the star-studded night sky. "It is now Friday and it'll be dawn in a few hours," he said softly. "Friday! The blackout started Tuesday. It is now early Friday, the day of the summer solstice. "The world has been without electricity for five days. Someone or something has created a hell on Earth."

The writer paused then continued. "It's the perfect hell. Torture. Someone has effectively killed the one thing on which Homo sapiens live – communications. Talking, exchanging thoughts, opinions, views on life keeps people alive, gives them strength and confidence. Deprive them of that in one foul stroke and humanity is plunged into the depths of hell. It would have been better to have sent a flock of nuclear missiles and destroyed all traces of humanity. No hurts, no crying, no not knowing if loved ones are alive. Just blackness. Complete! Gone!"

"David!" Molly started to say but he continued.

"By closing down the global electrical systems they have brought life on this planet to an horrific standstill."

"The Anunnaki?" said Molly coming to his side.

"Who knows? There may be a cosmic war occurring between two alien forces and little old Earth is stuck in between. Who knows?"

"The woman," said Molly. "Alice Simonian does not seem concerned."

"That, my dear lady is probably the only stabilizing factor in this crazy adventure," he replied. "But there is another thing."

"More?"

"Earth has been invaded and we don't even know it," David said grimly. "Homo sapiens are generally and incredibly oblivious. They're so entrenched in their boxes, their lives, their beliefs, their thinking, most of them usually turn a deaf ear when someone talks about life on other planets." He gave a short skeptical laugh. "Oh, my God. When they hear that their dear old planet was once a colony of talented but crazy gods that gave them Adam and Eve, their laws, their ways of life and their religion, people will again turn a deaf ear. It's too much for the average mind to grasp." He turned and faced Molly standing by the candle. "Or they'll decide it's too much to comprehend, promptly panic and throw themselves off the nearest cliff."

"Isn't that a little extreme?" asked Molly.

"Think so? Americans are so scared of losing a buck, their dollar life-line, their piece of gold they'll go to extremes. When the Stock Market crashed in 1929 there were rumors of suicides and heart attacks but no one ever produced statistics. Same thing happened in 1937 when Orson Wells dramatized on network radio H.G. Well's novel *The War of the Worlds*. People were so naïve they actually believed Earth was under attack and started building fortifications around their homes."

"Hey, people even worry when we tell them about UFO sightings," said Molly. "You have to hear the frantic calls Mother and the other directors receive. Some even offer to bring their rifles and shoot the invaders."

"So how is the public going to react when they hear that these Anunnaki, the creators of Adam and Eve who have a history of tossing nuclear bombs around are actually here on planet Earth?" asked David. "They'll flock to church and pray to God."

"Which God?"

"Ah! That's one of the problems," said Molly. "If you find you cannot believe the 50,000 Babylonian tablets that tell of the Anunnaki creating the so-called primitive workers – Adam and Eve – in South Africa 160,000 years ago, how is one expected to believe the Bible?"

"Exactly," muttered David. "Who the hell is one to believe? That is the great question."

They stood together by the bedroom window and watched the stars shining in the night sky like a diamond-studded carpet. Suddenly a shooting star flashed across the astral panorama and they both gazed in wonder.

"Earthlings – that's us – have been so programmed that the only invasion we can expect from outer space comprises huge machines with long mechanical legs brandishing ray guns and stomping through town demolishing buildings as they go. People don't want to consider that space people like the Anunnaki are now so far ahead in their evolution that nuclear weapons have become passé, very old fashioned in fact stage coach thinking."

"There's something more powerful?"

David nodded. "My senses tell me that somehow they have developed a neutralizing system where they can shut down the entire electrical power system on a planet," he said simply. "Unless a planet has a blockage defense system there's nothing the residents can do about it.

"That is a terrifying thought," whispered Molly clinging to his arm."

"Take it one step further," he said, and she noticed the tightness developing in his voice. "They must possess a control system that allows their neutralizing system the ability to be selective."

"Why?"

"The human body with its neuro system runs on electricity," he muttered. "Every school kid knows that. Now, if their control system was all-embracing it could also shut down all life as we know it on the planet. Life would be totally defunct, nonexistent. We would not know a thing about it. Earth would be totally unplugged!"

Neither spoke for several minutes. They simply stood watching the night sky and holding hands. Finally Molly spoke: "David, after what you said I feel so terribly small, so awfully insignificant."

"Me too," said David. "I'm beginning to detest the Anunnaki with a vengeance. I damn well hope they have a good argument when we meet them."

"If we meet them," she remarked.

"If?" he whispered. "That's a big if. Let's get some sleep."

37

WHILE THE GROUP AT Saks and Jenny's place in the remote wilderness region of the Yellowhead in western Canada were sleeping it was late in the day -- shortly after 9.00 p.m. -- on Friday the day of the summer solstice in Melbourne, Australia. Everything in the city and suburbs was ragged and tense as it had been since the start of the blackout five days before. Situated at the south-eastern part of mainland Australia the city started as a pastoral village in 1835 until the mid-1850s when the great Victorian gold rush transformed the place into one of the largest and wealthiest cities in the world. In fact The Economist frequently ranks Melbourne as one of the World's Most Livable Cities.

For the Prime Minister of Australia Melbourne was the best place to be if there was to be a complete blackout, a complete shutdown of everything including government. As the world became unplugged Charles Rafferty found himself staying with his sister on one of the islands in the Patterson Lakes region. A comfortable slightly upscale place with homes surrounded by Silver Wattle, Red River Gum trees and some palms. Access is across a short bridge. The area is a favorite of Australia TV movie producers and a van, loaded with equipment was parked on one street, guarded by two armed security fellows.

Completely isolated from the rest of the country and the world, Rafferty decided to go for a late evening walk before retiring. Smoke from riots that had taken place over the last few days were all from the north so Rafferty assured his sister he would stay in the vicinity and not wander too far away. Australia's winter prevailed in fact it was 43 degrees Fahrenheit on the weather gauge outside the garage so he buckled up with an old Navy duffle coat and an English Scally cap on his head.

For a few minutes he stopped on the small bridge, leaned on the metal railings and in the moonlight pondered the homes flanking the lake. It was totally eerie. Not a thing moved anywhere. No cars, no aircraft, no boats. Faint lights probably oil lamps or candles glimmered in some of the house windows.

Rafferty occasionally suffered pangs of guilt that he was not in his office handling the crisis, but how do you manage a country or a world in virtual suspended animation. An ADC riding a horse came every day from the Victoria State offices with messages and good advice that it was safer to stay out of Canberra until power had been restored.

Just then a boy perhaps elevenish came by peddling a bicycle. The youngster stopped, propped his bike on the curb and joined Rafferty to stare at the still water in the moonlight

"Do you ever go fishing?" Rafferty asked the lad.

"In the summer. When it's warm," he replied. "My Dad takes me on his boat on the water..."

"Port Phillip Bay?"

"Yes. Snapper is dead easy in September and stays until around March. Mom likes whiting so we have to catch some of those," said the boy. "In three months we'll be out there..."

Something was missing.

Frowning, the lad stopped talking and looked around. The man had just vanished. Gone without a trace, not even a murmur.

At home the boy told his father: "This bloke I was talking to on the bridge...well, he disappeared."

"Strewth! 'ave you been into my tinnie."

"Dad, I don't touch beer."

At exactly the same moment in other capitals of the world, presidents, prime ministers, dictators and various heads of state disappeared one after the other. As several witnesses said later it was as if they were snatched by invisible hands, an invisible force. The phenomena occurred with a minimum of feeling. Most heads of state simply felt their whole body, their whole being becoming totally relaxed. Some described and recognized it as an hypnotic trance. Ten seconds later they simply disappeared. If they were asleep they failed to feel anything as their bodies were taken up.

To be snatched from a host of various activities shocked those around them. Loved ones, relatives, civil servants, guards and others shrieked and attempted to give the alarm. Apart from screaming and running about in sheer panic there was really nothing anyone could do because nothing worked. There was absolutely no power at all. The entire world had come to a standstill. The entire planet might just have well been frozen which in a way it was.

Later, in her biography the Italian movie actress Francesca Megalatonni told of her affair with the President of Italy. "Alberto was a great lover. He was just coming deep inside me when he simply vanished. The scare gave me non-stop orgasms for hours."

The Israeli Prime Minister narrowly missed being assassinated by a runaway camel carrying a live U.S. manufactured M26 fragmentation hand grenade. A nimble Arab driver pulled the pin and leaving the grenade attached to the camel goaded it towards the Israeli leader. The leader was snatched a split second before the camel crashed into his bodyguards and the grenade exploded. Survivors claimed it was a miracle that the Prime Minister was "taken up" just before the grenade exploded. As a friend commented drily "God took him and he wasn't even a prophet."

And so it was that while the group at the Running Wind Ranch generally spent a restless night in sleep the global blackout continued and almost 200 country leaders from Afghanistan to Zimbabwe suddenly disappeared. In addition a number of selected opinion leaders from around the world, people with voice at CNN, BBC, Reuters, Associated Press, Bloomberg, Al Jazeera and others suddenly felt the invisible and totally irresistible force that caused them to vanish.

The greatest news story to occur on planet Earth since the Creation had no life because all electronic communication systems were off. As one New York Times editor commented later the story was, to use an ancient newspaper word, embargoed! Not because of any corporate giant saying "Hold this story!" it was simply because the world was now without electricity and had become totally unplugged. There was however one area where electricity still flowed.

38

JOHNNY MANUEL ARRIVED AT the cottage shortly after dawn following a one hour trek up the Elks Head Valley road and he immediately helped Saks milk the goats.

"Down in the valley we could see strange lights around the plateau in the higher range," he said. "Is that what we are going to see?"

Saks shrugged. "I think they are getting ready for the Gathering," he said. "Don't let it bother you. Nothing will hurt you. In fact there'll probably be much to learn about the world in which you live."

"Dad was really worried last night and didn't want me to come," he said picking up the bucket of milk and walking towards the house. "So I snuck out."

Jenny and Natalie had a fire going in the pit beyond the cedar deck with a cauldron of water boiling. "Who wants tea?" she called out as different figures emerged. Several of the group headed over to the hand operated water pump and cleansed the sleep from their heads. Others made themselves mugs of tea and coffee while others ate bowls of a form of Kashi cereal made by local Indians laced with goat's milk.

Conversation was sparse and terse. "It's not knowing what the hell is happening," muttered David to his father.

"We are all gathered here to find out what makes UFO ticks," muttered Steiner. "It'll probably be similar to the UFO confab in Taos, nothing really sensational."

"Klassen was sensational," said David.

"The mainline media wouldn't touch it," said the movie man.

"Touch what?" asked Paul Rowan curiously.

"A rebel scientist named Frederick Klassen revealed to the Taos Conference that the United States had deliberately destroyed an unidentified space vehicle parked amid the Earth's communications satellites in the Clarke Belt," said David and pointing to the sky added: "its orbit was 22,000 plus miles up there. Klassen was hauled away into oblivion by the CIA."

"None of my doing," put in Devenport defensively. "Blame the White House."

"Anyway he too disappeared from a safe clinic in L.A.," David added.

Suddenly Alison Simonian loomed among them. "I've just heard from An-Nusku. They are ready for our group. Please follow me." The tall white figure walked out onto the grass area beyond the cedar deck. "Please form a circle."

"How the heck is that going to help," muttered Davenport suspiciously. "I thought there would be a truck or something to take us up to the plateau."

"Get out of your box, Mr. Devenport," said the woman with a condescending smile as she watched members of the group move to stand around her.

Alison's voice was laced with impatience a facet David had not heard before in the woman.

"Come on, Molly, come with me," he called out and once she was at his side he glanced around.

"Don't we have to dress for this thing?" asked Kate easily.

"It's a come as you are," said Paul with an obvious shrug. "Relaxed dress is a good code to adopt when meeting aliens.

Alison winced.

Erich Steiner's face appeared strained and confused; Hugh and Chloe Geraint-Jones were at the circle along with Kate and Mark. Penni Singleton looking extremely nervous clutched Diesel's hand, Jax Devenport continually shook his head with an obvious feeling he should not be here, Paul and Natalie Rowan closed into the group followed by Saks and Jenny and finally the two local teenagers Johnny Manuel and his friend Cal Halston.

"We have thirty seconds," said Alison standing in the center.

"Where's your watch?" asked someone. The woman ignored the question.

"Where's the UFO? Or are we going to walk?" asked Mark then promptly gasped as he received a sharp poke to the chest from Kate.

"Heck!" cried Steiner waving his arms in a helpless gesture. "My camera's on the bloody chair." His slim legs propelled him across the ten yards to the chair and as he reached out for the camera and the film bag, his hands only a few inches away, he felt the totally relaxed as the invisible force irresistibly started pulling his body.

Everyone in the group felt the electrifying power that swept round the circle. For a couple of seconds it was as if they were injected with a rapid relaxation drug totally calming and extremely pleasant. Molly later described it as orgasmic. David felt the pull as if a thousand hands were occupying every bone, every muscle, every gland, and every cell in his body. There was nothing anyone could do. The force embraced the group and everyone was taken up firmly and gently including Steiner now minus his camera.

One moment there were 17 people including Alice Simonian standing on the grass outside the ranch house, the next moment the site was completely empty. Five minutes later when Lance Manuel rode into the ranch on a horse looking for his son he called out but there was no reply. Dismounting, the Indian movie scout walked over to the chair on which Erich Steiner had left his camera and bag and stared at it. It was at that precise moment the 16 millimeter camera along with the bag disappeared -- and so did Lance.

Manuel's horse suddenly wide-eyed and breathing heavily, reared up and seconds later bolted down the Elks Head Valley Road.

The goats watched then went on nibbling grass.

39

DAVID ROWAN NEVER REALLY discovered if the Anunnaki complex was real or simply and illusion because although the plateau on which the two teenagers had seen the palace flanked by two pyramids was only two miles across, this complex covered infinitely more space than the plateau. Horizontally, the main corridors were vast and ended much further than the eye could see. For several moments both David and Molly seriously considered that they had been transported to another planet but both the Geraint-Jones suggested the theory was impossible because everyone was still breathing oxygen.

The group was fascinated by the sets of flying armchairs that zipped along corridors oblivious of gravitational forces and with no visible means of propulsion. Geraint Jones was inclined to think they had evolved from the flying carpet unit he had hidden away in the basement. "Remember, the Hindu gods had vimanas too," he said.

"Look! Aliens!" Mark proclaimed to Kate.

"They're people," she said with a sniff. "Can't you tell the difference?"

"They're Anunnaki," said Geraint-Jones with a grin.

"Well, they look like people," protested Mark.

"They made us in their image," said Chloe with a knowing smile. "When they first created us, that is Adamu and Ti-Amat better known as Adam and Eve, the only major difference was the Adamu had a foreskin and the Anunnaki didn't."

Natalie standing nearby choked but then caught her breath.

Geraint-Jones jumped in: "Certain Homo sapien tribes have been promoting circumcision all these years because they wanted to be like their creators – in this case the gods otherwise known as the Anunnaki."

They paused to watch three Anunnaki walk past. Uniformly dressed in white Nehru-style cotton suits with red belts their attire was complete with kofias, brimless cylindrical caps with flat tops on their heads.

One nodded politely to the group as they marched softly by.

"Wow! They're big!" muttered Cal Halston, nudging his Indian friend.

Chloe heard the comment. "Yes, Anunnaki have always been taller than most Earthlings, but not much perhaps a foot or so. It's little wonder the ancients in Babylon called them giants because the average height of a Sumerian 6,000 years ago was well under five feet."

"There were giants in the earth in those days," said Geraint-Jones. "Genesis chapter six. Good stuff!"

Alison Simonian came up and apologized for the delay. Gathering the group together she explained the three young Anunnaki with red belts had been security agents. Taking the group through the main concourse she explained there were three different levels in the complex. Stairs were noticeable by their absence but there existed a strange form of invisible elevator, one that apparently read thoughts. They watched as an Anunnaki woman wearing a white uniform with a blue belt came by and stepped onto a simple blue marker set in the floor. "Blue is Information Assistant," said Alison as they watched the woman who was immediately lifted off the ground and stopped two floors up where she stepped off from apparently nothing onto the hard floor.

Alison explained the existence of a green marker close by was for people coming down, but David wondered what could one see for coming down. There were no floating markers. Two Anunnaki stepped off the second floor into apparently empty space and descended quite easily onto the green marker on the ground floor.

"You wouldn't get claustrophobia going up and down on those lifts," he said to Alison. "Once you get the idea of stepping off onto nothing."

"You might suffer astrophobia," suggested Chloe softly to no one in particular.

The woman stared at Rowan. "You're wondering how this works if electricity has been neutralized on your planet," she said.

"Damned woman!" he snapped with a faint smile. "Reading thoughts. You're dangerous."

Alison ignored the comment. "We have learned to harness gravity," she said. "Fairly easy actually."

Geraint-Jones standing close by overheard her statement. "That's the same as the flying carpet we have in our cellar at home," he said. "Works on gravity and thought projection."

From across the hall a slim young Anunnaki girl dressed in white and wearing a yellow belt signifying administration appeared and marched straight up to Erich Steiner and presented him with his camera and bag. With a brief smile she simply walked away.

"How?" muttered the movie man completely surprised. "How did she know that I had left my equipment behind, and how did she know they belonged to me?"

Everyone stared at Alison.

"Nis-Aba is an energy reader," she said. "When you arrived she noticed you were upset about missing your camera and she promptly retrieved them for you." Even as she spoke a dazed Indian walked up to Saks and Jenny and muttered: "Where am I? What's this movie set doing here?"

Everyone laughed. "This is Lance Manuel a movie talent and location scout who lives near us," said Jenny. "His son Johnny is coming this way."

"Well, I arrived at the ranch and was looking at the movie camera when something grabbed me, the camera and the bag," he said staring around. "So where are we?

"Lance, you are with the folks who gave Native Indians a free shave?" said Chloe easily.

"What's that supposed to mean, lady?" asked the movie scout.

"Adam and Eve's first son Cain killed his brother Abel," she replied. "Well, according to the ancient tablets god assigned Cain and his descendants to a life of migration and because men in the old days were proud of their beards, he punished Cain with a genetic marker, absence of facial hair. Thus American Indians are and I quote: *doomed to walk the Earth in sorrow.*" Chloe smiled. "Sorrow is an old word. I think it should be doomed to walk the Earth in meditation."

Manuel stared at the woman. "Isn't that something? This world is full of surprises."

"Now you know why other men envy you guys – you save a fortune on razor blades," quipped Steiner as he checked his camera.

Alison Simonian checked the group then held up her left hand. "Hello, everyone, welcome to the Nibiru Space Mission to Earth," she said in professional and clipped words. "Let me show you your sphere. That's where you'll observe the event."

"Event?" quizzed Paul Rowan.

"The Gathering," said Alison.

"Thanks for my camera and bag," remarked Steiner moving in. "So what's the gathering? Can we film it?"

"From the sphere of course but first my husband will be coming and he will brief you on everything. Please follow me," she said and promptly led the group across the large hallway which was rapidly filling up with Earthlings being brought as witnesses. Various Anunnaki paused to watch David and Molly's group as it passed and made comments in a language nobody understood, except Alison and several times she frowned at the aliens who suddenly stopped their chattering.

The sphere appeared like an earthly ecosphere, a plastic balloon held up by air in which gardeners maintain plant growth except the wall was not made of plastic but something else because Alison leading the way walked right through it as did the 18 in the group. The sphere's walls trembled for several seconds then immediately closed after them.

"It's an illusion," Alison told David in response to his thoughts.

Several dozen earthlings were already inside the sphere, all chatting quietly with hesitant smiles wondering why they had suddenly been abducted and transported to a palatial complex set between two pyramids. All seemed generally quiet and most of the group settled themselves into plush theater-style seats until Devenport spotted a group of men in SWAT uniforms. "Damn it! I don't believe it," he cried. "That's the crew from the helicopter – the one that went through the pyramid at Big Bend near Marfa – then came out empty and crashed."

"Our people lifted them out before the aircraft crashed," said Alison with hardly a blink. "It's normal procedure."

Finding it hard to believe David Rowan shook his head as the CIA man zeroed in on the group and started an animated discussion. Suddenly David turned to Alison. "You people sure have a neat way of abducting Homo sapiens," he said. "Don't they ever rebel?"

Alison shook her head. "Once they know they are safe, we get them to relax and enjoy Anunnaki hospitality with a promise that they will be returned to their homes sooner or later."

"How soon is soon?"

"You do have a lot of questions, David." Alison peered off into the distance as if searching for something or someone. "Come, follow me. An-Nusku is waiting. You do have questions, don't you?"

David looked at Molly and Steiner and they both nodded. "That would be fine," he said and escorting the trio the woman weaved her way through the crowd and led them into a small comfortable adjoining sphere.

Rowan noted that young Anunnaki were very neatly attired in white Nehru-style suits and with circular caps perched on their heads that gave them a halo appearance, were serving drinks and cocktails. They wore blue belts.

"These are information students learning a career in space travel," said Alison. Her dark eyes looked at one and must have conveyed a telepathic message, because the young Anunnaki suddenly swung round and entered the sphere and offered drinks and strange pieces of something that resembled sugared fruit. It seemed that every moment there was something new, something unexpected.

Then An-Nusku simply appeared. A tall slender man standing at least seven feet tall, he towered over David's six and Molly and Steiner's five and a half feet. Wearing the traditional white suit, the man seemed to glide through the air, almost as if his body was any weight at all and then David realized Alison was like that. An-Nusku's face was smooth, the skin a light tan and his wiry steel-grey hair, closely cropped. A round hat was on his head. Round his waist was an embroidered gold belt. An-Nusku's eyes were a dark blue tinged with red, almost purple.

With a wave of an elegant hand he invited everyone including Alison to sit down on what appeared to be large mushrooms in ivory cupolas. He sipped from the glass goblet and the others did likewise. David thought it was a mixture of mango and date and said so.

An-Nusku nodded. "The mango was already here when our fathers arrived," he said. "The date and the palm originated on our home planet Nibiru. It was one of the many things our fathers brought to Earth. Others were the cauliflower and sheep." He waved a nonchalant hand. "Of course you know all this."

It was an assumption that annoyed David and raised the question in his mind: Had the two archaeologists, Hugh and Chloe Geraint-Jones been primed to brief him? Had everything that had happened since that meeting with Alison Simonian in London been set up, pre-arranged? "Damn it!" he thought. "She said I would write a book on this."

Immediately another thought speared his mind. Was his relationship with Molly pre-arranged? The idea annoyed him intensely. He caught sight of Alison's face always statuesque but her eyes sparkled with child-like merriment. Her head shook gently as she answered his question. "Damn it, she's reading my thoughts." He turned his attention back to An-Nusku.

Molly clasped her hands and forefingers together below her chin. "We've had an excellent briefing on how the Anunnaki colonized the Earth and created Homo sapiens, so now I have a question. Why and how have you brought all human life on this planet to a standstill?"

Amazon-thinking thought David. Straight to the jugular.

An-Nusku smiled easily. "How do you know without communication that we have done as you suggest, brought all human life to a standstill?"

"Guessing," snapped Molly, her hazel eyes intense under a trimmed mop of fair hair. "Nothing is moving. No cars, no electrical machinery, no aeroplanes, jets, anything which means it has to be widespread. It's not normal."

"Once upon a time Earthlings used to welcome our people from Nibiru or Heaven as they called it," said An-Nusku in almost a monotone. "But in recent times our monitors, those orbital units, the ones you call UFOs which are operated by intelligent robots, have detected an aggressiveness that we find obnoxious. From our systematic monitoring we frequently detect a tendency to violent reaction to any people approaching Earth from the outer realms. It appears you have all been programmed to manifest a hostile reaction to any intelligent object coming into your territory."

"Not everyone," said Molly defensively. "There are some who welcome..."

An-Nusku shook his head. "I speak of your leaders, your representatives, your tribal heads," he said quickly. "And of course the plebeians who wear mantles of fear."

"It's a fear of the unknown," said David.

"But it's a phobia that has been intensified by your cultures and writers. For instance for well over a century ago Herbert George Wells in 1898 published the book *The War of the Worlds* which your own scholars recognize as one of the earliest stories that details a conflict between humankind and extraterrestrial neighbors. It was such writings that released a flurry of dramatic presentations all inspiring fears among the readers that any visitors from other planets automatically brought death and destruction."

"That's true," said David nodding. "Humans are inherently greedy and extremely protective of their castles and lifestyles. From what I gather from Geraint-Jones your people genetically engineered this aspect when you produced the first Homo sapiens in South Africa – the primitive workers – Adamu and Ti-Amat, the original Adam and Eve."

"Your knowledge of our original labors on your planet is interesting," said An-Nusku. "We needed to replace our own workers who found it difficult to labor in the mines because of your gravity and shorter days than on Nibiru. At that time our people were much like your Earthlings today, greedy, possessive and extremely war conscious. We too had what you call an industrial-military society where the kings, the leaders offered protection to ensure capitalists could trade confidently in different regions of the world."

"Is that why the Anunnaki came to Earth, created primitive workers to dig for gold because they were motivated by greed?" asked Steiner.

"There was an urgency to acquire gold," said An-Nusku.

"To rebuild your eco-system which was growing weaker because of population growth and industrial pollution?" said David.

"That was the message we left in the Sumerian tablets," he replied. "But as your scientists have recently discovered and something that was difficult to describe to the Sumerian scribes is nanoparticles and nanotechnology. Gold nanoparticles are tremendously powerful in many aspects of our lives. We had little gold and the Earth was abundant and still is hence our coming here."

David suddenly recalled a trip he had made to Paul and Natalie, his stepparents in France and how they had met a Swiss university researcher who after explaining the many uses that had been made for nanoparticles such as many domestic and consumer products, communication facilities, packaging food, had suddenly told them of developments in exploring the human body.

"Not just medical and health developments but in the structure of Homo sapiens," he said. "Research has discovered that gold nanoparticles have an excellent use in unzipping and manipulating the human DNA. Envisionaries see science circumventing disease and prolonging human life to not just a few years but hundreds of years."

David's thoughts recalled Geraint-Jones telling of how the early patriarchs such as Adam lived for 930 years, Noah for 900, Abraham 175 and Moses for 120 years. Then the Anunnaki re-genetically engineered Homo sapiens to live shorter lives.

An-Nusku had stopped talking and was looking at David. We needed gold for its nanoparticles...and yes, we were forced to reduce the average life-span on earth. However, you will note that in these times it is naturally expanding. Today there are over 55,000 people over 100 years in the United States and the total world population of centenarians is in excess of 200,000."

David flinched. "The Anunnaki is reading my thoughts," he told himself then defensively he responded: "Can gold nanoparticles help people read thoughts?"

The dark eyes twinkled but the man did not reply. He simply moved on and David instinctively knew that the answer was in the affirmative.

"We on Nibiru feel deeply responsible for our colonization of Earth and in recent times, principally since your invention of the atomic bomb and nuclear development we have felt the need to communicate and warn your leaders of the extreme consequences that occur when Homo sapiens are endowed with nuclear powers," said An-Nusku.

"You knew all this?" Steiner appeared amazed.

"We have people on your planet who communicate with us constantly," he replied and nodded towards Alison. "Several times you have come close to nuclear war and several times we have been forced to neutralize your weapons systems."

"Neutralize?" David was intensely curious.

"We neutralized the Russian missiles in Cuba and at the same time neutralized specific American missiles so that if war had developed, it would be like throwing rocks at each other."

"Did our governments know this?" demanded Molly.

"Certain people did," said An-Nusku. "We neutralized them. Many of your missiles, which your governments claim are old and ineffective, have long been neutralized."

The trio appeared shocked by this revelation and for some time sat in deep thought. Before any of them could ask the question on how neutralization works, An-Nusku continued. "The Anunnaki who first came to Earth had their differences and as descendants we saw how this was negatively impacting development of the new civilization. There were civil and regional wars, inclinations to acquire slaves, displays of greed and mindless debauchery. The monarchial priest programs deteriorated under tyrants whose sole objectives were the acquisition of lands, people and wealth. Certain communities became totally negative and mutinous so they were exterminated."

"How and where?" asked Molly.

"Seven communities close to our Space Mission Center," said An-Nisku with a nonchalant wave of a hand. "The two major ones were Sodom and Gomorrah. Our forefather Enlil, the one your Bible refers to as Yahweh, ordered the annihilation with the use of nuclear devices. Abraham of our mission center at Ur was Enlil's emissary and intelligence communicator. Even today there is little more than salt in the region below the Dead Sea. Incidentally there was another nuclear explosion in India and again not much survives in that region."

Molly was inquisitive. "That part of the Bible which Geraint-Jones says was a pick-up from the Sumerian tablets gives no indication it was a nuclear explosion."

"Go back and read your Bible again," said An-Nusku, "and you will see it in a different light."

David Rowan had been making notes and now appeared somewhat angry. "So what I am hearing is that you neutralized all nuclear defense weapons…"

"That is correct, Mister Rowan."

"Then how did you neutralize the world so that electricity does not work?"

For the first time An-Nusku hesitated and looked across at Alison who shrugged briefly. "All I can say is a device equipped with an energy neutralization facility works through slave-units that effectively close down everything that operates by electrical current."

"Slave-units?" asked David.

"Pyramids," said the Anunnaki. "We strategically located pyramids on thirty-degree latitudes north and south around your planet and when the time was correct, they became functional. We tested them with minor power outages in various locations. You know about the one in Pennsylvania. Those were tests."

David Rowan stood up and stared first at Alison and then at An-Nusku. "Why did you have to stop all electrical activity around the Earth. Do you know the infinite amount of harm and discomfort you have brought on ordinary people? Do you know how many people caught up by fears of the unknown actually killed themselves because they feared the end of the world was here? Do you know your black-outs triggered riots, looting and riots in which people died?"

An-Nusku nodded. "It is unfortunate that some must die for the majority to live in peace and harmony."

"Peace and fucking harmony?" snarled David. "You've got to be kidding."

"We brought you and various other writers and opinion-leaders here to a safe and remote area of Canada for you to witness a Gathering. There is no instant media coverage, no mass hysteria, no scoops or exclusives. The public out there has no idea of what is happening here today because there are no communication systems anywhere. Understand we could not have organized the Gathering with rampant rumors and irresponsible reporting. Tonight we will cease neutralizing and life on Earth will continue. Perhaps people will be wiser; perhaps you will help in your books with what you learn today."

"There's more?" asked Molly.

An-Nusku nodded. "There are still elements on Nibiru that urge the total annihilation of the Earth experiment, the Earth colony. The sons of the sons of Enlil call for this, but Enki, the good god of the New Testament, the Father of many spiritual beings, has effectively blocked the urge and once again saved the Earth colony, hence today's event."

"How would you destroy human life on Earth? By nuclear missiles?" she asked.

David butted in: "Or have nuclear missiles become passé in your modern times?"

The Anunnaki smiled tolerantly. "Our neutralizer device when extended would effectively block all electrical systems in the human body. As perhaps you understand, your body's neuro-systems work like ours – on electricity. We have the power to neutralize every human being on Earth."

"Oh, crap!" snapped Steiner. "You bastards sure know how to play god!"

"According to the Galactic Council which was in power long before our fathers came here 430,000 years ago, we were made responsible for the safety and wellbeing of your planet," said An-Nusku. "It is for that purpose you are here today?"

"Us?" gasped Molly.

"You're kidding," snapped David.

The Anunnaki shook his head. "There are almost 200 heads of different countries in the world, members of your United Nations. Each and everyone is being enlightened. You are a small but important part of that enlightenment. Come with us."

An-Nusku rose took Alison by the hand and led the trio back into the main foyer and pushing through the crowd of observers he led the way to another observation sphere which resembled a theater. Below on a huge stage were rows of seats which resembled the main concourse of the United Nations.

Even as they walked in they suddenly realized what was happening. Every world leader was in attendance. David grabbed Paul's arm. Standing together and looking up towards them were two famous faces. One was the British Prime Minister and the other was the President of the United States.

"Abductees!" whispered David. "Hell's bells! They've abducted the President. Wait until Devenport hears this. He'll have a coronary."

"Along with a lot of others," said Molly. "It's crazy!"

David shook his head. "No, I have the feeling it is foolproof strategy at work."

40

ERICH STEINER MIND WAS to say the least befogged. In this huge auditorium were all or most of the world leaders gathered together. No secretaries, no aides, no armed security guards, no PR support agents, no ceremony just once powerful leaders now existing in simple bodies waiting. Many were like Steiner and others in the group, befogged.

"They are now just ordinary human beings," said Paul Rowan at his side. "No cheering and adoring fans, no political hoop-la, no bowing and scraping, just frail human beings wondering what the hell is going on."

Molly moved closer and in a soft voice said: "Imagine you are a senator visiting the Oval Office and talking with the President of the United States. He's there one moment and gone the next. Can you imagine the uproar? The panic? Everyone within range must be suffering coronaries right now because there are no buttons, no phones, no functioning security systems to trigger an alarm or a rescue."

"Ever since the power black-out he would have been in the War Room," said Devenport. "Problem is once you're there how do you connect with the outside world? Like nothing works including the air conditioners, oxygen supply units and so on."

"Perhaps no one could get into the War Room if the door is electrically operated," observed Molly with a shrug.

David flashed a grin. "Once you manage to get your mind wrapped round these mass abductions like the Gathering it's one powerful method of attracting attention. Chances are none of the Pentagon war lords ever dreamed that aliens could neutralize the electrical systems of the world," he said then added: "Regardless of why they planned this event it's certainly a spectacular show."

"Trouble is," muttered Steiner with a prolonged sigh, "I don't have enough film. Just enough for a minute. Right from the beginning, I didn't realize we were being set up to witness the greatest event since the Creation."

Paul grinned. "Nice line, Erich. Well, I still have my old Leica and film and it doesn't need a battery to work. He leaned towards the movie man. "Think of it this way. On that one minute of film you will have the only record of what's going to happen today. It will be priceless. You'll be made. Old Tom Halerte would have given his right arm to be with us today."

"The radio reporter? The one who covered the Cataclysm of '79?"

Rowan nodded. "Tom vacated the world with a mike in one hand and a cigarette in the other. His heart. It just stopped pumping. Great guy."

"Heck! Luckily I never smoked," muttered Steiner. "I just need some 16 millimeter film."

Alison came up from behind. "Perhaps we can help," she said with one of those knowing smiles which either pleased or irritated people around. "Where could we pick up some film for you?"

"My office in Santa Monica, California." A forced grin appeared on the tanned face. "It's a long hike from here."

"Come, oh man of little faith," she said and taking the movie man by the hand led him into a domed booth where a transparent orb sat perched on a table. "Open Elijah," she said and in less than ten seconds the stunned Steiner followed by a curious Paul Rowan was being shown the inside of the Santa Monica office.

"There," said Steiner. "The fridge. I keep new film cool."

Suddenly they were looking inside the refrigerator at several 100 foot rolls of Fuji 16 millimeter movie stock. "The fridge has been off for five days but it's still relatively cool inside," said Alison. "That should not affect the film, should it?'

"You're kidding me," whispered the movie man. "That's my office, my fridge and my film stock. How the heck do you do that?"

Alison ignored the question. "Six rolls," she said then focusing on the orb she said something in a language that neither Paul Rowan nor Steiner recognized. She glanced at the two men. "Be patient. The system is retrieving."

The orb clouded over amid flashes of various colors and ten seconds later on a tray next to the desk appeared six rolls of 16mm movie film.

The two men stood in stunned silence.

"How did you do that?" muttered Paul. "That's impossible."

"Really?" said the woman with a short laugh. "How do you think we acquired the presence of almost 200 world leaders for the Gathering?

"Just like that?"

"Just like that. Remember, the Anunnaki were flying across the Universe in their Celestial Chariots 430,000 years ago when your ancestors Homo erectus were still perched on branches in the jungle," she said quietly. "We have moved on. Our civilization can reveal many exciting things. We did it for the Sumerians in such things as writing, language, mathematics, clothing manufacture, medicine, agriculture, building construction and civic law."

"Geraint-Jones told us," said Steiner.

Across the sphere, Diesel Boulter, Penni Singleton and Natalie were taking refreshments offered by the Anunnaki young people while Hugh and Chloe Geraint-Jones were nearby in conversation with a slim sharp faced Anunnaki with neat curly black hair who turned out to be an engineer specializing in thermodynamics.

"Our fathers introduced the wheel to the Sumerians of Mesopotamia," he said. "While we instructed them in rim and spoked wheels they initially insisted on solid wheels which they used in pottery. You see, our people did not need wheel transportation because we had sky chariots and airborne discs."

Geraint Jones looked at his wife and held a forefinger to his lips. He did not wish to inform them of his plate, the magic carpet, which they would surely confiscate. He was about to ask a question when a sudden disturbance occurred. David Rowan came up and announced: "The Anunnaki cops are trying to arrest Jax Devenport."

"The CIA fellow?" said Paul. 'What for?"

The group members suddenly flocked round as two red belted Anunnaki security officers attempted peacefully to take the aging American away but the wily Devenport protested and nimbly swirled about, slipped behind Kate, Mark, Saks and Jenny. Then seizing the opportunity he darted away and took shelter behind the SWAT team standing on the far side of the sphere.

The two Anunnaki split up and came in from either side. The Special Weapons and Tactics team who were enjoying the break simply stood and watched with undisguised amusement.

"Mister Devenport," cried a woman's voice. "Are you crazy? You cannot escape from here." They all recognized the commanding voice of Alison Simonian.

Wild eyed and desperately thinking there had to be a way out, Devenport reached for his back pocket and extracted a dark object.

"He's got a gun," cried Paul and immediately pushed forward to protect Natalie who was now at the front of the crowd standing by Penni Singleton and Diesel Boulter. But even as he moved the two Anunnaki security people made a fast dash and attempted to seize Devenport who in turned sensed their move and started to push through the SWAT team. It was at that precise moment that the CIA man tripped. A shot shattered above the sounds of the crowd and its echo reverberated through the building. The brutal crack of the gun and its echo triggered total chaos. Everyone was either shouting or screaming. The Anunnaki chasers doggedly pursued and nabbed Devenport in a dual flying tackle which prompted more screaming.

David recognized the gun as an Italian Beretta 92 as the weapon slid silently across the floor and stopped right by a fallen body. As he pulled Molly aside he caught sight of Penni Singleton's face as she gasped her last breath and succumbed.

In a moment, Saks, Natalie and Molly were at her side. Molly held Penni's head for a few moments then shouted: "There's no pulse."

"Get a doctor or something," cried David to Alison.

Several Anunnaki attendants who had gathered round cleared the way. A young broad-shouldered Anunnaki who appeared to be a medical orderly came forward and in five seconds pronounced Penni dead. A strange an uncanny silence descended eerily upon the group. The security people hastily led the shivering and distraught Devenport away.

"Why on earth did that dumb CIA man bring a gun to this place?" muttered Paul Rowan. "Did you know him, David?"

"Yes, he helped me write the history of the CIA," replied the other.

"Damned bloody gunslingers!" said the older Rowan.

"Most CIA agents sit at desks analyzing," replied David unable to think of anything to say. "Most don't carry guns."

"Well, this one did," said Paul.

Just then a slim wiry figure dressed in Anunnaki white pushed through the group and stared down at the body. Everyone recognized the young teenager, Peter Singleton, her son who now knelt down at her side and caressed her white lifeless face.

"Can you help her?" asked Diesel kneeling beside the young man, his face wrought with worry his voice pleading for help. "Your mother is my friend. She's done so much for me. We were enjoying being together." His shaking hand reached out and touched the young man's arm. "Can't you help? You did it once..."

The young man turned to Diesel. "What I did for you was allowed by Cosmic Laws," he said. "I cannot do the same for a blood relative – that is my mother."

"Couldn't you try?" asked Molly.

"Just try," said several others in chorus.

"There is one who can help," he said and turning they saw Alison coming in with her husband An-Nusku.

"Perhaps, I can help your mother, Peter," he said and waving everybody back he proceeded to sit down cross-legged by the side of the woman. For perhaps half a minute, An-Nusku sat with closed eyes. Many thought he had gone into a deep trance. Then raising his hands he made several passes over her body.

Still nothing happened. Onlookers began to fear the worse.

Then the Anunnaki became quite still. It seemed from the depths of the earth that a deep rich tone came up and embraced the scene. Staring at the Anunnaki they realized the deep throated tone was coming from his mouth and lips that hardly moved. First it was so deep that it caused shivers in the people watching. The tone started fluctuating and rose to a high shrill, sometimes falling to a low trembling tone. It was as if An-Nusku was singing in another language. Molly thought he resembled a shaman and had gone in search of Penni's spirit in the astral states. David thought he sounded like the Colorado sound healer Jonathan Goldman while others simply had no idea of what was happening and simply prayed.

Several minutes passed before the healer placed his right hand on the dead woman's chest. The long slender fingers came together, clasped an object and as he lifted his hand and opened it those close by saw it contained a bullet. Then the bloodstains where the bullet had entered started to dry and seemingly the blood re-entered her body.

Still the woman did not move.

The Anunnaki stood up then reaching down took her limp right hand and called out: "Penni Singleton…In the name of the Creator, the Source of Our Being it is time to continue living."

Nothing happened for perhaps ten seconds. Then as everyone watched the woman opened her eyes, took in a long deep breath and as she breathed out a faint smile flickered on her white face. "What happened? Why am I on the floor?"

Then she spotted her son. "Peter! You came."

An-Nusku nodded to the young man to take over. He then calmly rubbed his hands and as if nothing had happened pushed through the onlookers to Alison's side where he started talking about the Gathering as if nothing had happened.

Peter helped his mother to her feet and when she started apologizing he quickly told her there was no need. "Come with me," he said taking her arm.

"We'll find you a new blouse to wear." Turning back he called out: "You too, Diesel man." He then escorted the two to another sphere.

Everyone breathed a sigh of relief. "Wow!" muttered Steiner triumphantly. "I got it all on film! What a deal!"

41

THE ANUNNAKI WORKERS IN white with blue belts brought more refreshments and the group stunned by the incredible healing they had just witnessed, broke up into twos and threes, chatted quietly and waited for the event to start. Molly and David armed with questions cornered Alison and her husband An-Nusku.

The Anunnaki healer smiled at David. "You have a question about divinity." It was a statement made in a matter-of-fact voice. Pondering this much later, David realized that as well as being an accomplished healer An-Nusku was also an excellent clairvoyant and thought-reader. Regardless the writer pressed on with a nod.

"Since time immemorial humankind has regarded people from Nibiru – the Anunnaki –as gods, in fact it was your ancestor Enlil who ordered Abraham and the Israelites not to have any gods before him." David said in a prologue. "In fact all through the Babylonian tablets the writers refer to the Anunnaki as gods. So where does the Creator come in? Who is the Creator?"

"Well, first of all Enlil was the Yahweh of the Old Testament and Abraham was one of those people who had an Earth Mother and an Anunnaki father," said An-Nusku. "A phenomenon Earthlings mistakenly entitle a miraculous birth or virgin birth. It was an ancient technique we possessed and still use when it is necessary to have an enhanced philosopher, an ascended teacher with divine consciousness that will assist Earthlings to develop spiritually."

The Anunnaki sipped a glass of nectar offered by a passing server.

"Our people believe that there is a fully functioning Creator responsible for all Creation. It is the spirit that is within all living creatures, a bird, a flower, a tree, a monkey along with you and me. We are all creations of the Cosmic God who is Spirit and that Spirit lives within us all. That spirit, the Holy Spirit is the life pulse of the Universe and the countless other universes that exist beyond. We know it as the Cosmos. It has neither beginning nor end."

An-Nusku took in a deep breath and expelled it slowly. "The air we breathe is the life force of the Creator. That life force allows my people and your people to possess extra powers to assist people such as healing. When the healing force comes through us we are pawns, servants of the Creator. It only works if it is the will of the Creator but one does have to ask." An-Nusku paused and stared at the writer, then at Molly. "Ask and you shall receive. You understand that?

"I'm working on it," said David. "It makes sense."

"Your next question concerns religion," he said softly, "so I will answer that by saying the people of Nibiru are spiritually aware and reliant to the Creator, not to the church nor priests nor any dictatorial body. Religion comes from your Latin word Ligari which means to bind. That is unfortunate because in a sense ligari means one who is enslaved. Spirituality is a much better word because it allows you to have choice. You can choose to attain whatever level in spirituality with which you are comfortable."

Molly stepped in. "Wait a minute, sir," she said sharply. "Our friend Geraint-Jones who is an archaeologist says the Anunnaki introduced religion as one of its gifts to the Earthlings, the Sumerians."

"It was not a gift but a way of life," said An-Nusku. "The first Earthlings heard of Anu who lived on Nibiru and because we were importing large quantities of gold from Earth, they assumed wrongly that Anu was the main god and he lived in Heaven where the streets are paved with gold." He gave a thin smile. "This was in spite of the fact we shared our knowledge and understanding that a Creator existed who was and is responsible for us all, but sadly the aspect of a Cosmic Creator was overlooked and theologians and priests have persisted in portraying and worshipping a god-man even to this day."

"I think the word you need is henotheism," said Geraint-Jones joining the group.

An-Nusku nodded. "It's a term that describes the practice of worshipping one god while believing in the existence of other gods but not worshipping them. Enlil or Yahweh in your Bible says *thou shall have no other gods before me,* which means he knew well there were other gods.

"Trouble was the religion you planted with the priest-kings went very wrong," commented Geraint-Jones. "Men – and I use the noun specifically – created their own male-dominated regimes, their own promises or threats of salvation and used it to enrich and empower themselves. The Old Testatment is full of death and destruction in the name of god and over recent centuries and through the fanaticism of religion millions of innocent people have been killed – witness the Inquisitions that terrorized Europe for centuries, civilizations such as the Incas and Mayans virtually exterminated. Religion has killed countless people in Palestine and Northern Ireland. There has not been a day of peace in the world for two thousand years because of the religious methods of control you people implanted. Religion does not enhance its followers spiritually, it keeps them enslaved to earthly teachers."

An-Nusku nodded. "We did make some grievous errors and this was one," he said. "We created primitive workers with a mindset of mining and obtaining gold. The programming produced not only humans with a slave complex but addicted to a greed for wealth and power. The mistake was when we suggested a combined monarchy and religious system – the priest kings. That is when the matrix went wrong and the result was rivalry and wars."

"Sir, that is one hell of an admission," snapped David.

An-Nusku held up his hands. "Over the years – the centuries -- through selective breeding we have brought teachers to various parts of the world."

"Selective breeding? Would that be what they call mysterious or miraculous births – the real name for which is intracervical insemination," chipped Geraint-Jones.

An-Nusku's dark eyes stared at the archaeologist and he nodded. "Yes, I believe that is the Earth name for the procedure." A mischievous smile lingered on his sharp face. "People who fail to understand such operations describe clinical techniques as miraculous." Turning he said to David. "Regarding the inherent violent nature of powerful elements on Earth our people who live among you keep us abreast of such tragic inclinations. However, there is light on the horizon."

"Really," said David suddenly feeling better. "What is that?"

"You will hear when the Gathering starts," said Alison, "and that will be shortly."

"One more question," said David. "Where did you learn so much about the human condition?"

"Oxford and Cambridge," said the An-Nusku. "I had a friend named John Donne who was a free-thinker so we spent time together. We both refused the Oath of Supremacy that is recognizing the king as head of the church so we never acquired degrees. However it was quite a learning experience. Later in his life John and his friend Izaak Walton spent forty days on Nibiru – that was after we had developed convenient and much faster inter-planetary travel."

Geraint-Jones stared in complete shock. "You were alive on Earth in the 16th century?"

"Do you have a problem with that?" asked An-Nusku with a grin. "When the fathers first came and shared their blood and DNA – the tree of life -- many people lived seven, eight even nine hundred years. So we had to put a stop to that. We changed the DNA and prevented a leaning towards over-population." As he started to walk away with Alison, he paused, turned and called back: "Tell your scientists there are some great secrets in the DNA they stupidly call junk. You only have to look and you shall find."

An-Nusku's dark eyes shone and David wondered if the adjective to use was mockingly or in merriment.

42

IF ONE GOES INTO the rotunda of St. Paul's Cathedral in London and sits by the wall you can hear people talking on the far side. It's an eerie experience if you have not heard of this phenomenon before going and many people taken by surprise initially think they are hearing spirit voices. David Rowan recalled a visit as a boy many years before with his stepfather Paul.

"St. Paul's was an auditory phenomenon when I was a kid," he commented to his stepfather. "The central auditorium here is similar but powerfully weird. There are dozens of dignitaries talking on the far side of this rotunda, but if your eyes select someone speaking, even whispering you can actually hear what he or she is saying. Try it, Dad."

Paul Rowan focused and listened intently for several seconds then smiled. "I wonder how on earth they do this? The fellow from Iceland is speaking in Danish and yet I hear it in English."

"The President of Afghanistan is thinking – thinking, mark you! – that this is all a big CIA event," muttered Molly. "Wow! I'm suddenly clairaudient."

"You know what this means," said Geraint-Jones from behind, "None of these world dignitaries can keep any thoughts to themselves. In other words there are no secrets."

"That could be quite deadly," muttered David. "This place is an auditory miracle."

"It's part of the pyramid mystique," said the archaeologist easily. "Remember I told you back home that the Great Pyramid of Giza is attuned to the F Sharp which is also the tone of planet Earth or Gaia? "Well, I sense this whole structure, this central auditorium is attuned to F Sharp."

Molly's expression was one of deep thought. "I wonder how they achieve that. If only we could discover their techniques."

"Stay around, Molly," said Chloe softly. "It's a hunch but I think we are going to find out a stack of things to blow our minds."

They sat in their chairs watching almost 300 dignitaries, representatives from countries and nations all over the world moving around, seeking others they knew, standing together in small groups, all wondering, all speculating what this unparalleled event was all about. Several bull-headed characters tried to exit but were firmly and politely prevented by numerous attendants in white with red belts.

The central auditorium featured several large circles of white seating units to accommodate each head of state. Each seating unit appeared like an orb sliced in half while suspended over each dignitary sitting inside was a small dome which Paul figured was an auditory arrangement to replace old fashioned headsets or ear buds. Each head of state was equipped with a small white desk with something that resembled a spherical computer tablet. The seating units were set on different levels to enable occupants to see and hear what was happening on a circular dais where there was a small glass presentation unit. The background contained a large panel that appeared like falling rain. The entire presentation area was set in a large and very beautiful conchological shell.

"Aphrodite would have loved that," said Chloe to her husband.

A young Anunnaki female wearing a yellow belt announced she was an attendant to service the group and explained that each dignitary would sit under an acoustic orb and hear everything spoken in his or her own language and they could record if they wished everything that was said.

"Are there any microphones for allowing heads of state to speak," David Rowan asked the attendant.

The Anunnaki smiled blandly. "We doubt they will have anything to say that may contribute to the declaration."

"Declaration? That's ominous," David said quietly to Molly. "What declaration could the Anunnaki make? A declaration of war?"

Molly moved closer. "Perhaps, they're asking for world surrender."

David stared at her beautiful hazel eyes. "You do have a way of stating what most people don't want to think about."

Molly shrugged. "Look at it like this," she said softly. "For years and years people have always feared an invasion from outer space like as old H.G. Wells wrote about. It's become a tradition. People's minds are in a rut that says any invasion from out there has to be by ugly creatures with boggling angry eyes, creepy, crawly giant legs and everyone with a gun shoots them until the invaders catch some earthly bug that wipes them out. That's the embedded belief. Hollywood and sci-fi writers have programmed people to believe that."

"And?" asked David shaking his head.

"However, no one really imagined that Earth could be invaded by people who are just like us in shape and thinking, and what is more are thousands of years ahead of us in thinking, technology and invading places," said Molly. "For instance, they developed a technology that neutralizes every electrical system on the third rock from the sun. Who would have thought electricity was our Achilles heel?"

"Earth got unplugged," nodded Rowan. "With all the gadgets we use on this planet we couldn't visualize that one day some power would come along and switch it off effectively bringing the world to a halt."

"Meanwhile like a giant with an invisible hand they abduct every head of state put them into one place minus bodyguards, secretaries, counselors and hangers on and deliver a message," she said. "So what is the message? Listen Earthlings: You are still a colony of Nibiru and you will take your orders from Heaven?"

"Sounds Gestapoish!" Rowan shook his head. "No, I don't think that will happen. The Anunnaki are too far advanced. They have evolved."

"Perhaps," said Molly.

Natalie and Jenny came through the crowds being assigned to the sphere to watch the Gathering. "There are scores of spheres with a whole variety of opinion leaders, journalists, editorialists, several generals, community dignitaries, scientists, university people and more," said Natalie tapping David's arm. "It's quite an event."

"Like Versailles in 1918 or the USS Missouri in 1945?" he quipped.

"Don't be such a pessimist, David," snapped Jenny. "It doesn't become you."

"Sorry, mother. I'm still trying to figure out why we are here," he said with a bland smile.

"So where's Kate and that young man who adores her?" asked Jenny. "We walked through several of the English speaking spheres and couldn't see them anywhere."

Steiner accompanied by Hugh and Chloe Geraint-Jones pushed through the crowd and joined them.

"We spotted them in a huddle with several other young people," said Erich quickly. Two of Sak's music students, Johnny Manuel and Cal Halston were there too. They were all focused on a presentation being given by one of the more mature Anunnaki who looked like a Prof. I may be wrong."

David frowned. "Young people," he growled. "I wish they would tell someone where they were going."

"Come now, David," said Jenny. "Your daughter is a very responsible young woman. She's not going to do anything rash."

Natalie smiled. "What could one do up here that might be termed rash?"

"Get shot for one thing," said Steiner quickly and then before anyone could criticize his cynical sense of humor he added: "We spotted Mrs. Singleton and Diesel in one of the lounges. Looks like they are making a happy couple."

Suddenly a voice came from nowhere and everywhere. "Please take positions that have been allocated to you."

"Sounds like the voice of god," chuckled Steiner.

Molly frowned. "You're going to finish up in front of an Anunnaki firing squad."

Geraint-Jones moved next to them. "Couldn't help overhearing," he said. "One of their people was telling us they not only banned guns on Nibiru, they gathered millions of weapons, melted them all down and cast the residue into a volcano. Powerful stuff."

"Well, old An-Nusku sure knew how to extract a bullet out of Mrs. Singleton's chest and bring her back to life," said David. "I still can't fathom that out."

Geraint-Jones laughed briefly. "Millions of people have read John 11 over the centuries and most can't figure out how Lazarus was raised from the dead also."

43

THE GATHERING COMMENCED WITH no fanfare, no drums, no red carpets and no pomp or circumstance. David Rowan considered the event possessed the simplicity of a village hall meeting to discuss a church fete. Lights without any apparent source appeared in and around the crystal podium and illuminated the strange drapes that looked like falling rain except now the rain was coming down in multi-pastel colors.

"Could be an illusion," whispered Paul. "They don't look real."

"What are we waiting for?" whispered Steiner who was seated behind David and Molly. "The vicar of Nibiru?"

Geraint-Jones sitting with Chloe leaned forward. "This isn't like the old Anunnaki. If you check some of the pictures from Ashurbanipal's library in Babylonia they were always dressed to the hilt with heavy robes, beards, treated curly hair and wearing crowns."

David glanced back. "Now they look more like something out of New Delhi with those Nehru suits," he whispered. "It's not one of those happy days."

"Everyone seems very polite and extremely helpful," said Natalie.

"Yeah, like before an execution," nodded David. "I wonder who's getting the chop?"

Natalie flashed a reprimanding glance.

"Sorry, Aunt Natalie," he said like a young boy. "This whole thing is getting boring. I'm sure all these heads of state must be wondering what's going on. Incidentally, we haven't spotted the Pope among the heads of state."

"Oh, but he is," snapped Natalie. "He's on the far side wearing a regular suit."

"Left the gold one at home," chuckled Steiner.

"That's the trouble with instant abductions," said David quietly. "It's all come as you are."

As he spoke a slim figure attired in the traditional Anunnaki white suit with a gold belt and wearing a circular cap emerged on the stage. With a curt bow to the audience he stood behind the lectern.

A strange voice started coming over the sound system and was immediately replaced by English to the listeners in the sphere. Alison returned and sat with the group. "Each head of state is listening in their audio chamber in their own language," she whispered.

"We are Nibirians from the planet Nibiru which is the twelfth body of our solar system," said the voice softly and informatively. "For your purposes, my name is An-Kunin and I am a direct descendant of Enki, son of An. It is because of this that you – whatever shade of life you possess, whatever language you claim – you are all my brothers and sisters."

Someone in an unidentified audio chamber shouted something and was immediately silenced by an invisible force.

"Looks as if there is no freedom of speech here," whispered Paul Rowan.

"Heckler suppression system," muttered Steiner standing up to film the event. "Pity I haven't got sound."

An-Kunin's voice continued. "When our people first arrived on your planet some 430,000 of your years ago, our civilization was much like yours is today except we could move astronauts from one world to another provided the planets were reasonably close and accessible."

The panel that presented an illusion of falling rain suddenly came to life. Several pictures appeared in quick succession showing factories, congested highways, urban and suburban communities.

"We were much like your planet today but we suffered from over-population combined with an industrial complex that sabotaged our eco-system, the environment," he said in a matter-of-fact voice that was neither praising nor condemning. "We needed gold to repair our atmosphere and your Earth was and is rich in this ore. This was mentioned in the Assyrian tablets from the Library of Ashurbanipal which are in Britain's National Museum."

Images of gold smelters operating in Babylonia with many black-headed slaves carrying crates and working at the fires flashed to the side of An-Kunin. "Gold, as you Earth people have only recently discovered is rich in nanoparticles that are important for ongoing development in electro technology such as audio communicators, telecommunicators, time pieces and in healing. Nanotechnology will help you conquer diseases such as the many forms of cancer. It helped us considerably."

The Anunnaki smiled. "We tried explaining this to the ancient people of Sumeria and indeed they produced your first stained glass with nanoparticles but they failed to comprehend how it worked. They thought it was magic."

Paul Rowan leaned over to David. "Have you got any idea where this is going?"

The other Rowan shook his head. "No and that's what worries me."

"While we initially came to Earth with the sole purpose of mining gold and shipping it back to our home planet Nibiru, several things occurred that changed our thinking about this planet as a colony," he said. "The major event occurred when our Nibiru which is a planet substantially larger than yours, came between the sun and Earth. It largely disrupted the oceans and the entire ecology of your planet and created catastrophic flooding, The Deluge as some people call it."

Images showing the coming of the planet Nibiru with storms of winds and rains ravaging homes and buildings, forests and entire communities. Tidal waves raced across various landscapes.

"Ziusudra was a son of the demigod Ubar-Tutu," said An-Kunin. "Prince Enki ordered him to build a wooden boat in seven days. It was more like a submarine than a traditional boat and to gather his family, relatives and provisions plus many four-legged creatures and birds and to ride out the storms and floods. It should be pointed out that Ziusudra was the Noah of your Bible."

The images flashed to showing Earth from space. "For their own safety all the Anunnaki pioneers evacuated Earth in their space vehicles. I recall the Sumerian writers called them celestial chariots. It was after the floods receded that we looked kindly upon the few survivors and introduced the Earthlings to Niburian technology and culture. As Prince Enki pointed out: Earthlings have our blood and our genes therefore they are like us."

"So the gods felt sorry for us," snapped David. "Somewhere along the way I was taught that God was angry with the world and wanted to wipe it out."

"That was your Sunday school teacher, old Fergus Doone at the English Church in Japan," whispered Paul Rowan. "He loved intimidating the kids with hell and brimstone stuff."

"It sure left a dent in my thinking about religion," replied David.

"Shush!" hissed Molly with a reprimanding tap on David's wrist. "Let's listen. I'm curious."

An-Kunin accompanied by a kaleidoscope of images showed how the Anunnaki provided seeds of grain imported from Nibiru and taught Earthlings how to create terraced farmlands on the hillsides above the mud-caked lowlands. They also introduced sheep and cauliflower to Earth.

"Over the centuries we brought many gifts to the Sumerians who are in fact your ancestors," he said in a matter-of-fact voice which both David and Molly thought was the fault of the computerized translator. "Following the Deluge, the great flood we gave you the Cuneiform texting and language which ultimately provided the base for Sanskrit and that led to most of the many languages throughout your world. We taught your ancestors to read and write, introduced them to numbers, mathematics and a calendar which the Jewish people still use to this day 57 centuries later. As the floods subsided we taught the Sumerians how to run communities, produce crops through agriculture, farming and harvesting."

An-Kunin paused to sip a drink.

"Because most of you attending here are lawmakers in your own countries perhaps you should know that we introduced a basic code of laws which the priest-king Hammurabi enforced. Talking of that, the Nibirians introduced the system of monarchies – kings and nobilities along with a basic and organized form of religion that included priests."

A large image of Planet Earth appeared on the screen and lines of latitude and longitude appeared. "We introduced the global grid to the Sumerians in a numbering system which uses 60 as its base some 5,000 of your Earth years ago. In a modified form you measure time, angles and as I said, geographic coordinates. This explains why you have 60 seconds in a minute, 60 seconds in an hour. We note that your people now use a global positioning system – GPS – which is based on our geographic coordinates.

Geraint-Jones leaned forward and tapped David on the shoulder. "We told you about this in Oregon. It's called the sexagesimal system. That's why they built the Great Pyramid at Giza on 30 degrees north. It was not only the guiding light for incoming space missions it was also a latitude marker from which they mapped the world."

"Is that why we have heard of so many ghost images of pyramids at 30 degrees north and south?" he asked. "Do you think they are using them to radiate neutralizing rays covering the entire globe?"

"A high probability," agreed the archaeologist quickly. "The majority of Earthlings can't see or detect them. Pyramids built on a different energy vibration actually relaying and transmitting neutralizing fields."

Steiner, who had been listening, leaned across Molly. "Something in my bones tells me that they've got us licked," he said. "We're doomed!"

"Jeeze!" exclaimed Molly. "You've been watching too many of those Hollywood B flicks."

Everyone within hearing smiled politely but many of the facial and whispered expressions were tight and reflected growing stress.

It was time for an intermission and the stretching of legs, a time to mull over what was happening. For David and his mother Jenny an energy form was homing in on them and they had no desire to hear it.

44

DAVID'S WHIDBEY ISLAND GROUP split up and roamed around the sphere exercising legs, visiting rest rooms, enjoying exotic delicacies and fruit drinks from the Anunnaki staff that seemed to hover everywhere. David and Molly found themselves standing and holding hands on a balcony on the far side of the auditorium. Beyond was a magnificent view of the Coastal Range of western Canada.

"So we are still on the plateau," Molly remarked as Saks and Jenny came up. "We are still close to your home. I could have sworn we would have been somewhere near Proxima Centauri by now."

"You and Jules Verne," whispered David giving Molly a nudge.

"Well, I have absolutely no idea why we are here and why we are being subjected to some sort of geography lesson," said Jenny. "Geography and history were at the bottom of my things to study at school in Ottawa."

Just then they all spotted the young people coming back into the sphere. Kate and Mark followed by Cal and Johnny zeroed in on the elders.

"Dad, do you think I should go to Nibiru?" Kate panted almost out of breath. "It's only for 40 days."

David gulped then stared at his daughter. "You what?"

"It's all right," she cried enthusiastically. "Mark will come with me and the two boys Cal and Johnny have put their names to go down as well. They are inviting 120 young people to spend time on Nibiru to be briefed on all the latest inter-stellar technology, cultural and historical stuff. It'll be like attending university."

"Who's organizing this?" asked Molly completely baffled.

"An-Nisku, the fellow who was here earlier."

"Well folks, I just heard they're abducting my kid and I'm madder than a hornet," said a tall man wearing a Stetson.

"This is my Dad," said Cal. "He claims he was abducted with some other men right off their horses."

"Damned right," said the man. "When I get out of this floating penitentiary I'm gonna create hell in Ottawa for allowing these invaders onto our land."

Paul Rowan who had been listening quietly suddenly butted in. "Mister Halston, if you look down into the auditorium you'll see the Prime Minister of Canada engrossed in conversation with the Presidents of the United States and Mexico."

Halston turned and stared then hesitated: "Well, I'd better wait for a better opportunity."

"Dad, will it be all right if I go?" pleaded the young teenager. "Johnny's found his dad Mr. Manuel and he says his boy can go if you say I can go."

"Lance is here?"

"He was abducted along with Mr. Steiner's movie camera," said Cal.

Mr. Halston was now in a fix not really knowing what to do. It was the arrival of Saks and Jenny that brought a solution to his dilemma. "If it makes any difference," said the old Indian, Jenny and I are going as chaperones. They are looking for several other elders to help out. It'll be a wonderful learning experience for those who come. It's only for 40 days."

Geraint-Jones looked at his wife who nodded. "Count us in, we'll go if we are wanted," she said with a broad smile. "I always wanted to be an octogenarian astronaut."

An-Nusku suddenly materialized. "We'd be happy to have an expert on the Sumerian tablets and culture come along. Alison Simonian, who is my beloved wife, is also coming along."

"How far is Nibiru from Earth?" asked Paul.

"One day by our Celestial Voyager."

"That's ridiculous!" put in Steiner. "I heard that Nibiru is currently positioned beyond the planet Pluto and that's three billion miles and you claim to make it in a day. You're nuts!"

An-Nusku smiled patiently. "Mister Steiner you need to broaden your horizons. Our people were ahead of Earthlings some 430,000 years ago. Believe me, we have developed some interesting technologies since then. This is why we'd like to take some young people with us for 40 days." He paused to point his hand at the auditorium, he said: "An-Kunin will give an overview of space travel in the next little while." He flashed another smile. "You have to remember we are a little more advanced than you but we are willing to help your people because after all we are your fathers."

"I'll be a chaperone if you'll let me," said Steiner quickly.

"I'll program your tag," he said politely.

"Okay," said Halston. "My boy would like to go along, and I hear Johnny's father has approved. "I have no idea what our wives will say, that is if we ever get out of the palace."

"You will be returned after the final presentation," said Alison.

Suddenly a shot cracked the relative quiet of the space mission.

Everyone froze the as the realization of a shooting sank in everyone seemed to move in different directions. Some rushed to the edge of the sphere overlooking the auditorium. A frameless opening appeared in the wall and An-Nusku followed by Alison rushed through into the auditorium. David and Molly who were standing right there spotted the opportunity and hastily followed them.

"I hope you know what you're doing, David," cried Molly as they ran down the aisle towards the shooting.

"It's the American," cried someone. "He's been shot!"

Unable to believe his ears Rowan pressed on through the crowd.

Suddenly through all the chaos a small, heavily built man carrying a revolver pushed through the heads of state and headed for the upper parts of the auditorium. Molly and the man collided. The man staggered sideways and raised the gun.

"Molly! Get down!" screamed David but the woman was not the least inclined to obey. The collision with the man triggered her resident fighting prowess.

With mind-boggling lightning speed Molly's training in Muay Thai otherwise known as The Art of Eight Limbs flashed into action. No time for thought or consideration. Her body simply reacted the way it had been trained to do. A swift knee to the jaw produced a deep cracking sound. Almost simultaneously her right hand chopped the man's neck sending the body hurtling into the aisle. Totally unconscious the man collapsed at Rowan's feet, his right hand still holding the gun, his left hand clutching an Anunnaki ID tag. The writer bent down and relieved the man of the gun and the tag.

Alison came back up the aisle and looked first at the now still figure on the floor and then at Molly. "Thank you," she said. "We do not like violence here. That is the new President of North Korea."

Two Anunnaki medical workers arrived, inspected the prone figure and promptly covered him with a silver sheet and then stood back. The sheet and the body promptly disappeared. A red belted security officer came and took the gun from David.

"Unfortunately the President of North Korea is dead," Alison announced to no one in particular. He attacked the American President but thankfully the bullet went high."

For several minutes chaos reigned in the auditorium. Blue belted administrative staff advised everyone to sit down and take refreshments just as if nothing had happened. A well-dressed Arab – someone said it was the King of Jordan. -- gave Rowan a tag and said: "You dropped this in the scuffle."

The writer looked at the two ID tags but there was nothing obvious to differentiate the two. He placed one in the breast pocket of his shirt and held onto the other one. For a couple of minutes there was quiet in the lower levels then Molly and David spotted the President of the United States standing on his feet among a small group of sympathizers.

Alison brushed past and as she did so remarked: "The North Korean fellow, he's going to be all right."

David looked at Molly. "The Anunnaki must have a copyright on bringing people back from the dead," he said. "People aren't going to believe all this."

Molly nodded. "Nothing seems dead for very long with the Anunnaki," she said.

"Did you mean to kill?"

"Not really," she said. "It's a matter of imperfection. I allowed myself to become emotional, in other words I just got carried away with the Art of Eight Limbs."

David stared. "Damn it, I'd better be careful with you." As he spoke he felt someone tapping his arm. He turned and found himself looking into the face of the President of the United States."

"Hello Mister Rowan, I read your book entitled The Winds of Death," he said. "Totally agree with much of it. Solar farming is the way to go." Then he glanced at Molly. "I hear your wife apprehended the fellow who took a shot me," he said and leaning across shook her hand. You'll have to come and have tea one day soon at the White House."

The President turned back to David and held his arm. "Rowan, do you have any idea what these fellows are up to?"

"That's the question that has been on the minds of all the observers," David replied easily. "But I have the impression that we are going to get a reason very soon and it's going to go over like a lead balloon."

45

A HEAVY SOUNDING GONG resonated across the entire complex signaling everyone to take their seats and focus on the audio orbs above their heads. An-Kunin returned to the podium with amazing simplicity. No bows, no hand waves, no acknowledgement of anyone. He had a job to do and was about to do it.

"It has become apparent that various leading nations on this planet are making efforts to probe and survey other bodies in the solar system," he said. "Your technology is heavy, expensive and yields very little information."

Images of a variety of elegant, pencil-like space vehicles filled the screen.

"Our Universe contrary to the ancient and accepted view of one entity, comprises string nets of energy, simply stated as lights and electrons. A one point observer can only witness one view but with omni-stratal vision one can witness layers of string nets not only above and below, but also sideways," he went on. The Universe is neither simply a plane nor a multi-depth formation, it is a multi-layered body existing on a variety of levels in different time dimensions."

"What in heck's name is he talking about?" muttered Steiner in disgust.

"Think of a fish in the ocean," whispered Geraint-Jones. "Depending on its existence it sees multi levels as it goes up and down. For us the Universe is multi-layered. If you stand down in Antarctica and look out the vision is different from the Arctic." The Archaeologist shrugged. "Quit thinking of the Universe as a plane – a flat plate of stars, nebulae and such."

The screen showed space vessels disappearing not into the distance but disappearing as they changed vibrations with new ones coming into the Earth vibration almost out of nowhere. The images brought many gasps of amazement from the audience. "When we have a space mission we focus on the net manifested by a particular star. Light has its own gravity - if we can call it that. Our celestial cruisers use various stars to travel, even stars that cannot be viewed from our present stratus. For a long journey we swing through various stars. We move much faster than your traditionally acclaimed light standard of 186,000 miles a second. That is another of your limitations. Once in motion our system eliminates seemingly long voyages by allowing a space vessel to slip into another vibration on the Omni-Strata Network. In this way a celestial cruiser can safely traverse a great distance in a short space of your time."

An-Kunin surveyed many of the quizzical faces in the audience. "Nibirean celestial cruisers regularly attain 333,000 miles a second or 120 million miles an hour and cover three billion miles in 24 hours which is the current distance between our planet and yours."

David leaned over to Alison "This puts Einstein and the academics back into the stage coach era. They've been adamant there is no such thing faster than the speed of light."

"That's Earth people - they have a habit of boxing and entrenchment that bars cosmic development," she whispered.

An-Kunin smiled briefly. "Now, if you will make room for it in your minds, we will eventually show your engineers and scientists how to build space vehicles that will provide instant mobility through the solar system and the galaxy you call the Milky Way."

The Anunnaki speaker then revealed that some 100 young students accompanied by Earth chaperones will shortly be leaving for Nibiru for education and training in inter-planetary and inter-galactic space travel. They will be returned in 40 days and will be available as resource teams to assist countries interested in space travel and cosmic learning.

"Some 160,000 of your years ago our people took Homo erectus from the caves and jungles and through cross-breeding with our own people -- our own DNA -- created Homo sapiens – primitive workers."

As the speaker went on to explain the process, Paul Rowan leaned forward. "David, you may have missed it. This ties in with a study conducted in 2012 by a University of Edinburgh team who discovered in the human genome a gene miR-941 that is unique and makes us different from eleven other species of mammals including chimpanzees, apes, gorillas and others. The gene gives humans the ability to be conscious of decision making and the ability to formulate languages. I'll forward the news clip."

An-Kunin continued: "We originally required primitive workers who could think, take orders and provide an intelligent communication. There were two reasons for this. One was to obtain gold for our own development and the other was to comply with a wish from the Creator, the Great Father of Our being."

The speaker walked across the stage carrying a glass of juice and said nothing for half a minute. A feeling of tension manifested in the listeners and many realized that they would now be told the real reason for the return of the Anunnaki.

"As we discovered the primitive workers were created with several objectives, some might call them obsessions," he said. "One was an inherent urge to find and possess gold along with its brother money; Two the primitive worker was bred to progress and obey and this resulted in a performance-based industrial economy which subsequently produces an unbalanced society of rich and poor. You may also call it the haves and have nots, a global society where in spite of an abundance of food, many people are living in poverty and starving. The third obsession came into being following the devastation of the Deluge when we asked the survivors to go forth and multiply. You allowed the natural process, the natural gift of procreation to become an acute obsession, a mania that infects all decent standards of living, imperils the purity of your political systems and undermines the education of your children. This was never intended."

The speaker shrugged. "These obsessions, traits if you like, were in our blood, our consciousness, our genes and we shared them with you," said An-Kunin.

Geraint-Jones leaned forward his head between David and Molly. "He's getting into the dark side of the Anunnaki. I didn't think they would ever admit it."

An-Kunin continued: "In recent years your industrial economy based on corporate greed encouraged many of your leading nations to pursue an existence of possession and control which always resulted in physical and mental conflict – otherwise known as war."

Gory images of countless victims being brutally tortured flashed upon the screen followed by drones firing missiles into innocent residential areas and missiles destroying cars as they travelled along roads.

"We observe there are both visible and invisible armies at work on your planet. They are both responsible for the torture and crimes against humanity on a global basis. When innocent people are abducted and hidden in obscure countries with no recourse to justice then something is critically wrong with humanity. There is extensive evidence that the so-called intelligence agencies of Britain, France, the United States, Iran, Russia, North Korea and China have conducted extensive and prolonged crimes against humanity. We know who and where you are and those responsible will be taken out and brought to justice."

"Your scientists discovered nuclear fusion. It immediately offered many positive benefits to humanity but you ignored them and because of your power conflicts and your inherent obsession for power and revenge you developed the ultimate machine for war and destruction – the atomic bomb. That brought you into the nuclear age."

The audience was visibly shaken as 3-D images showed the raging infernos and thousands of people being vaporized as nuclear weapons devastated communities in Japan.

"The nuclear age brought fear, hatred, international power struggles and global intimidation. It triggered mass fears that produced excessive nuclear arsenals along with totally unnecessary defense systems and war machines. Our observers living on your planet report that this has produced an international trading systems ensured by a strong military presence," he said then shaking his head he lowered his tone as if speaking confidentially. "You might call it a military protection racket."

"Many years ago this was performed on much smaller levels. Unsavory racketeers called gangsters armed with hand guns operated protection rackets for merchants in their areas. Nothing has changed, only the size. The weapons now are atomic bombs."

"Some four millennia ago our leaders on earth were very uneducated in nuclear war. They also suffered within their own ranks from extreme egos with ambitions for power and control, jealousy, envy, distrust, corruption and anger," he said.

"For instance we failed to understand that radioactive fallout would be spread by the prevailing winds. The Sumerian scribes described this phenomenon as an Evil Wind. The nuclear explosions were in Sinai where we had our Earth Mission Base and in the seven cities in the region of the Salt Sea also known as the Dead Sea. The radioactive fallout, the evil wind floated east and brought death to all people, all animals and all flora. Like a plague it arrived silently and killed every living thing. It wiped out the entire population of the Sumerian and Akkadian cities that we had helped create. The year was 2024 BCE in other words over 4,000 of your years ago."

An-Kunin turned and pointed to the powerful images flashing on the shimmering 3-D screen. "The war with its awesome weapons that we started here on Earth triggered a nuclear war on our own planet Nibiru. Communities, countries whole races of people were obliterated in a few days. We who were seen as gods by your people were at war with ourselves. The elders of Nibiru had repeatedly warned our leaders about our violent inclinations. Our leaders laughed. They warned of what your people call Karma – the law of cause of effect. It proved correct. What we had sown we reaped. The bombs stopped the laughing. The bombs stopped much of the life on Nibiru. Even those who escaped the bomb blasts were subsequently killed by the Evil Wind. The devastation was immense the extermination of life was almost complete."

As An-Kunin spoke panoramas of nuclear desolation on Nibiru flowed on the 3-D screen with mind-jarring soul-wrenching intensity

"Some of our people survived and commenced rebuilding. All the survivors took an oath that never again would nuclear fusion be used as a weapon for solving our differences."

So it was you," and he stared across the many faces staring back, you, our children, our descendants on planet Earth learned of nuclear power." As he spoke images of the first atomic bomb test at the Trinity Site in New Mexico flashed onto the screen followed by the extermination of two Japanese cities, Hiroshima and Nagasaki. The speaker paused to watch the screen

"It is a well known cosmic adage that says history repeats itself. Our fathers saw evil in the seven cities in and around Sodom and Gomorrah and they were exterminated. The United States saw evil in two cities of Japan, Hiroshima and Nagasaki and they were exterminated. These events changed life on our home planet of Nibiru and they changed life on your planet Earth."

The speaker moved forward and peered across at the world leaders closest to him. "When you commenced using nuclear power -- the atomic bomb -- it is then we started patrolling your planet more intensely and monitoring your activities more closely. The so-called UFOs which your authorities frequently denied existed were not operated by Anunnaki people, but sophisticated robots with a high degree of artificial intelligence. It is interesting that some of your people mistakenly considered these mechanicals to be extra-terrestrial life forms.

Molly nudged David and whispered: "Strange, that's what I used to tell my mother – high thinking robots. She rebuked me, scorned me for being an oddball."

"The so-called Nuclear Age created diseased minds, dangerous mega-egos..Once again the haves and they have nots were evident. The have nots desperately wanted to become haves and be members of the nuclear club. The haves, fearful of their own standing, their own security, their own possessions created massive defense arsenals and as they did so, fear and uncertainty spread like a disease."

The screen was flooded with images of rioting, assassinations, overthrow of rulers and governments and the breakdown of law and order. The great modern empires that possess nuclear arms are being undermined by a fifth column of anarchists, saboteurs, activists who work stealthily through mass communication systems known as the internet," he said. "The problem is elected governments, elected leaders feel threatened and security increases and so does the fear of being the target of a nuclear attack."

"Wars are no longer being fought on demarcated lines that were set honorably by agreement, all honor has gone and they are being fought everywhere humans exist. If one regards Earth objectively one realizes the rise in negativity, nationally and internationally has to eventually result in nuclear conflagration.

An-Kunin clasped his hands together as if in prayer and the observers in the spheres sensed that the Anunnaki speaker was moving towards the whole point of his presentation. David glanced at Alison who looked back and shook her head. There was no smile.

"In spite of these nuclear based mega-defense systems you failed to see their vulnerability," he said. "Apart from fire which was given to your ancestors many years ago the one power that you took for granted and never even considered was the vulnerability of electricity."

The Anunnaki speaker took a deep breath. "We feel responsible for you. Our people had hoped that the people on Earth would become our trading partners, sharing in cultures, technologies and philosophies. Our fears for your safety and livelihood are very real. We realized some time ago that your nations, your peoples are on a course of global self-destruction much like we suffered 4,000 years ago.

An-Kunin shook his head and moved to the front of the dais and surveyed the strained faces. "Therefore the Council of the Cosmic Fathers and Mothers has instructed us to remedy the situation in any way possible. Your weakest link is the very energy on which everyone relies - electricity."

Images of communities and highways at a standstill or in darkness flooded the screen.

"Observe they are not showing rioting crowds, fighting, blood and gore," whispered Molly. "It's clean destruction of buildings."

"Censorship!" Rowan muttered back. "They're not entirely stupid."

An-Kunin continued: "As you will all know, we conducted a global neutralization of all power systems on the planet. Everything that is mobilized with electricity from your satellites down to the smallest instruments in your lives is neutralized. All nuclear power stations across the world have been safely neutralized, their functioning and radiation points have been neutralized as well. In other words we have been forced to bring your planet to a full stop."

An-Kunin held up his hand. "There is one more requirement the Cosmic Council requires of your planet. "All weapons used in warfare and acts of violence such as tanks, field artillery and all rapid fire automatic weapons will be gathered and melted down. This occurred on our home planet and immediately reduced all forms of minor warfare," he said. "You have one month from today to achieve this requirement. David sensed the increased tension growing in the auditorium. Heads of state for China, Russia, the United States, France, Brazil, Britain, Iran and India all showed some form of agitation, a brave smile, a shaking of a head, or sitting up straight or exchanging a brief comment with a neighbor. The President of the United States looked down to hide a faint smile.

An-Kunin unfolded his hands, then walked back and held the sides of the rostrum. "Because we are your fathers and you are all leaders and law makers of your respective lands, we are requesting you return to your people and immediately commence the dismantling and destruction of all weapons that cause wholesale death and destruction. This includes all weapons of war from automatic rifles, machine guns, field guns, tanks, missiles and of course your nuclear arsenals. Our sensors will monitor any aberrations any major or minor acts of war and aggression. Violators will be detained or neutralized. Incidentally your nuclear power stations that work for the good of humanity will be returned to you in working order."

The Anunnaki speaker paused then added: "You have one year of your time to complete this work."

"C'est totalement absurde!" cried the French leader as a chorus of protests echoed across the auditorium but An-Kunin shrugged as if they were of no consequence.

"We will establish a Communications Center close to the United Nations in New York and it will be serviced by monitors, people who have been trained to advise and assist in the requirements of the Council of Cosmic Fathers and Mothers," he said. Its purpose is twofold. One, it will transmit on the internet, television and radio information for children and adults on the ideals and benefits of positive and peaceful living. Two, we will train doctors and scientists how to re-activate the DNA that governs prolonged longevity and introduce changes to the DNA that will secure healthier lifestyles for people.

Of course the students coming to visit Nibiru for 40 days will bring back various benefits for Planet Earth."

An-Kunin watched the reactions of various heads of state, most of which were frowns and lively gesticulations as they talked to people around them.

Then the Anunnaki spokesman walked across the stage and beckoned to someone in the wings.

"The director of the Center will be Peter who is the son of an Earth mother Mrs. Singleton and myself. Peter is my son.

The slim well attired figure of Peter Singleton walked towards the dais, smiled pleasantly and bowed. For several moments he glanced at the many faces looking back at him then he gave a brief description of the role of the monitors and the function of the Center.

David leaned back towards Penni Singleton who's pale blue eyes were wide open, totally stupefied by the statement. "When did you meet An-Kunin?"

The woman kept staring at the speaker and her son on the auditorium stage. "In Cairo – twenty years ago – when I wasn't feeling well. He was the Egyptian doctor who came to my hotel room but…we never did anything." She turned to Rowan. "How could this be?"

"Were you conscious all the time he was in the room?"

"Not really. Looking back, I remember being in a daze, perhaps a trance. Something funny happened and I recall laughing, laughing a lot, in fact," she said. "He was the strangest doctor. Smooth. For a while there I called him an angel and he told me to go to sleep, so I did."

Penni turned first to Diesel then leaned across to David. "In all these years I knew there was something special about Peter. A ten-month pregnancy. He was speaking intelligently and reading at age one, studying the ancient mystics and their philosophies at five. The grade school sent him home because he accused the teacher of being ignorant and incompetent. In high school he started studying archaeology and during summer breaks would spend days in the British Museum studying their massive collection of the Babylonian tablets. Peter learned Cuneiform in six weeks and one day he announced he had a mission."

"A mission?"

"The strangest thing," she said. "Peter claimed he had to spend time in the deserts of the Middle East and find his father," she said. "It seems he was searching for An-Kunin.

With tears welling in her eyes Penni made an excuse to visit the ladies rest room and the group watched her go.

David glanced at Geraint-Jones. "Hugh, what's your take on this? Miraculous birth or the Anunnaki giving her intracervical insemination in a Cairo hotel room?"

The archaeologist nodded. "Most of their representatives on Earth have been incurred by artificial insemination from the time of Adamu and Ti-Amat right the way down to Peter Singleton," he said, then added: "I have the feeling that Mrs. Singleton and her son have been under observation for almost twenty years. The lad is scheduled to be a major player on the future of Earth."

"Let's hope he doesn't get crucified like the dozen or so other saviors who preceded him," said Paul Rowan who promptly received a nudge and a frown from Natalie.

An-Kunin was back at the lectern.

"In a few minutes we will be returning all of you to the places where you were picked up morning. Staff members are currently giving out data scrolls containing all the information you need to know on our plans to bring Earth into line with other members of the Cosmic Council."

"Is there no room for discussion," cried the Prime Minister of Australia. "There's a lot of objectionable material here that is likely to trigger controversy and even violence on an international level."

An-Kunin continued as if he had not heard. "Further to our announcement that all nations who maintain a nuclear arsenal must erase them within one year, we would like to add that as of this moment all nuclear missiles and warheads on your planet have been neutralized and we have reset your world to the way it was in 1945, before the advent of your nuclear age. It is imperative that you must find ways with which to live with this decree."

Several heads of state from Africa and South America applauded the announcement while the presidents of the United States and Russia shook their heads.

David planted his right fist in the palm of his left hand. They've circumnavigated a nuclear war on Planet Earth, reduced a lot of political egos, and clipped a thing called free will."

An-Kunin continued: "In exchange for this our people will train your people in much the same way as we did the Sumerians long ago. We will show you how to develop and explore the Universe and beyond in real time. We will show you many of the secrets contained in your DNA such as longevity and perfect health. We expect complete cooperation from all countries, big and small and indeed radical groups." A short pause was followed by a five word sentence: "There will be no exceptions."

In their sphere above the auditorium the group was now standing up. White uniformed staff members were handing out the Anunnaki data scrolls to all who wanted them.

David looked at the cover. The title was: "Peace on Earth. Moving into a Safe Future."

Paul leaned over: "You might call this an Enforced Peace on Earth. Do you think it will work?"

"I'd hate to think of the consequences if it doesn't work," said David. "The entire planet including human beings will get unplugged.

Geraint-Jones standing close by with Chloe said softly: There's something that was written years ago and it went like this: Nothing could have been more obvious to the people of the earlier twentieth century than the rapidity with which war was becoming impossible... but they did not see it until the atomic bombs burst in their fumbling hands".

"The writer?" asked David.

"The fellow who wrote *The War of the Worlds* – H.G. Wells."

It was at that precise moment that the entire Anunnaki complex shook as if an earthquake had suddenly erupted. A blast of energy from the bowels of the earth shot up and visibly shook the center and everyone gathered there.

46

IF DAVID AND MOLLY ever considered that the strange and unique Gathering was drawing to a close and they could all make their way home they were very much off center. The moment the huge complex with its hundreds of observers and some 200 heads of state shook from the vibrations everyone froze. Steiner noted it was as if some giant armed with a great camera ready to take a photograph bellowed "Freeze!" But that lasted merely a second.

"Everyone, please remain seated," came the cool voice of An-Nusku. As if on cue – or perhaps magic – the fifty or so yellow and red belted attendants disappeared from the spheres and the auditorium.

"What the hell was that?" shouted Steiner, his face taught, eyes open and alert, the movie camera gripped tightly in white knuckled hands.

"Sound's either like the end of the world or the second coming," commented David who promptly received a jab in the ribs from Molly.

"Not funny," she said.

"It wasn't meant to be funny," protested the writer.

Another explosion quickly followed by a second blast shook the building again.

"Please be seated!" It was an order from An-Nusku standing nearby with Alison.

"Can we see outside," cried Steiner. "I'm a cameraman."

"And I'm a writer," put in David.

"Hey, don't forget me," cried Paul moving in.

An-Nusku shrugged. "It's against my better judgment. Simply do not step outside the main doors." Waving a long arm he strode away to the exit ramp followed by the trio. Geraint-Jones started to follow but Chloe seized his arm. "Not this time, superman."

On the ground floor a small Anunnaki army had gathered. Circular hats were replaced by white protective helmets fitted with goggles and breathing tubes. An officer briefly explained the goggles allowed the wearers to see through any wood, metal and rock. The oxygenated breathing tubes assisted the Anunnakis who were not used to the heavy gravity of Earth to move quickly. Each person was armed with a gold covered disc much like a discus thrown in athletics. The disc was gripped from behind on what appeared to be a leather strap. Even as An-Nusku and the trio arrived the main doors were sliding open leaving a yellow line marking the entrance.

"Look at the fog," cried Steiner.

"It's not fog, it's smoke," muttered David moving forward. "Whoever is attacking knew that they could view this place by creating a mist or smoke. Even as he spoke another smoke bomb landed near the entrance.

An Anunnaki figure the visitors had not seen before stepped forward and surveyed the outside. They noticed he was wearing a helmet with gold and orange tints. On his white sleeve he had three pips, supposedly a rank of some sort, an officer of the guard thought David. In a jarring guttural voice the officer gave an order because immediately a dozen attendants formed a column and raised their gold discs.

Steiner's camera started filming and he performed a walking track up to the officer's side for a close-up.

"You wish to die so soon?" An-Nusku seized Steiner's arm and dragged him back.

"Awe! Crap! I was getting great footage!"

Suddenly a whistling sound hissed through the mountain area.

Both David and Paul stood there aghast as the incoming missile heading straight for the doorway suddenly veered up and away. It soared over the top of the complex and exploded on the mountain ridge behind.

"Hand-held missile deflectors," said An-Nusku softly. He listened for a moment as the officer barked in Nibiruan then turned and said: "The commander has just given the order for the deflectors to completely reverse the incoming missiles."

"What sort of missiles are they? Are we being attacked by alien forces?"

An-Nusku smiled. "No. The attackers are Earthlings and they are using what your people call grenades from a launcher. Like a rifle."

"Who the hell would be attacking this place?" cried Paul attempting to peer through the fog.

An-Nusku removed his dark glasses and handed them over. "These will help you see through the smoke," he said.

Paul Rowan stared from behind the heavy lenses. "There's at least forty, maybe fifty people spread all over the plateau. There's a couple of people who look like soldiers but the others are raggle-taggle people, young and old. Some are carrying placards: *Death to the Aliens* and *Invaders go home*." He passed the glasses to David.

"There's some idiot goading them on," muttered the writer. "They're armed with pitch-forks, axes, clubs, sticks and stones. It's a rough looking bunch and they're all angry."

Then he stopped talking as his focus sharpened. "Hey, wait a minute!" he snapped. "It's the fellow..." He turned and stared at An-Nusku. "I thought you had Devenport arrested this morning."

The Anunnaki nodded. "He was returned to the ranch from where he was picked up."

"Well, he's back," snapped David, "and he's recruited some sort of ragged army that includes two soldiers, both in some sort of American uniforms."

"Deserters probably," cried Steiner.

"Davenport is out in front calling the mob to accompany him," put in Paul. "I guess that's why they haven't fired the grenade-launcher again."

"Let me talk to him," snapped David as he tugged An-Nusku's arm. "He'll listen to me."

"It's too late," the Anunnaki started to say but Rowan had darted off, slipped round the commander and the Anunnaki guards and was out on the plateau heading for the CIA man.

"Devenport," he cried as he ran across the rough grassland. "For heaven's sake…"

"Rowan, it's too late! We are taking charge of this place. They're invaders. A breach of a sovereign state."

"What the hell do you know about a sovereign state?" shouted Rowan as he ran across the grassland. "This is Canada and you're a bloody American."

Another fifty yards to go and Rowan knew he would have to grapple with the fanatical CIA agent.

A shadow flicked across the plateau. Then another. They came in from the west, silently, almost unnoticeably as birds on the wing. Now there was a distant hum. It sounded distant but the two Anunnaki flyers were directly overhead, hovering about fifty feet above the mob. People started screaming obscenities at the two circular discs floating above them.

The hum intensified for two seconds and it was almost as if the entire group of attackers had been suddenly asked to lie down. Devenport stopped. His legs crumpled. Finally he fell back in a heap.

One of the craft came and hovered over the writer. "Mister Rowan, please return to the Center immediately. You are in grave danger."

"You fucking bastards," he snarled as he started back. "You killed them because they were only looking after their rights."

"They are not dead," said the voice in the sky. "They will recover and they will remember nothing of this."

It was in that very moment that David Rowan suddenly came to appreciate how the Sumerians felt when they heard a voice – a voice they assumed was god -- speaking from the sky. He stopped and shook his head. No time to philosophize. He stared at the invaders lying in heaps in the grass. It was as if the Anunnaki were playing chess and they knew all the moves. He watched as the flying machines slid away silently over the far mountains towards the sun now moving westwards.

Throwing up his hands he turned to return to the complex – but it had disappeared.

"Oh, crap!" he snarled angrily as he realized the smoke had cleared and the plateau was now empty. Where the hell was everyone? How was he going to get back? Guess where the entrance was? A feeling of annoyance laced with fear flooded his body. He was not like his stepfather Paul Rowan who seemingly showed no fear in any war zone. Just about every war and major conflagration in the sixties and seventies, Paul Rowan had been there for the dynamic Verity Magazine owned by his long-time friend and publisher Tim McCoy. David envied his stepfather for all his apparent bravery in getting the big stories. It was little wonder he was awarded the Pulitzer Prize for International Journalism.

When David graduated from the Alexander Mackenzie University in Vancouver and was looking for work Paul had told him: "There are sticks in writing. Stick to writing books. It's safer because in journalism everyone is carrying sticks with bombs on the end."

David had followed his stepfather's advice and started writing articles for local magazines, then features for the glossies like National Geographic and finally books. The only time he had been forced to run for his life is when an enraged Spanish plutocrat in Madrid had read his book Winds of Death, a work totally against wind turbines, chased him with a Lamborghini and almost killed him.

Why was he thinking these things? He turned and gazed back at the apparently lifeless heaps of attackers in the grass then wondered how he was going to get back to the Complex and the group. Why didn't they come out and find him? Didn't the Anunnaki know they were now invisible? He ferreted in his shirt and pants. Where were those glasses An-Nusku had given him? He must have lost them when he was running, he thought. He started searching. The glasses would help him get back.

An object in the grass! He had walked right by it. He bent down. An unexploded smoke canister with the pin not fully pulled out lay in the grass. "Dippi-dee-doo-dah! Somebody up there's looking after me," he muttered quickly. "I'll create some smoke and find my way back." He pulled the pin and let go of the handle and promptly skipped aside as the canister belched green smoke in all directions.

Then he saw the Anunnaki Center fifty yards away. Relief! The doors were still open and people were shouting. A warning? He spun round. One of the soldiers with Devenport's group had somehow survived and was staggering across the grass behind him – clutching a live grenade!

Wild eyed and determined the soldier wearing a muddied army combat uniform with the universal camouflaged pattern in tan, grey and green came towards him.

"Where are you heading, soldier?"

"We're under attack, sir," gasped the man. "Aliens, sir. We were commissioned by the CIA to defend this country?"

"Canada?"

"We're in Canada? The CIA guy claimed we were outside Seattle."

"Well you sure got things muddled up," said Rowan. "Go back and report to base."

"If you say so, sir."

"Hey, let me have the thing in your hand," said David. "I don't think you need it now."

"Well, okay," said the soldier. "Just make sure you keep the handle down."

"Where's the pin?"

"It got lost."

"You're kidding."

"Nah!"

On the spur of the moment David decided he didn't want anything to do with the grenade, so defensively he spun away and it was at that precise moment the soldier reached over to put the grenade into the writer's hand but it was no longer there.

"Run!" screamed David.

"Run?"

"Damn it! Run!"

They both raced off in opposite directions.

Rowan heard the blast. He felt the air rip past his running body. Then something sliced into his legs and he crashed to the ground feeling as if life had been extracted from his body and a crushing all-empowered numbness was sucking everything that mattered from his body and mind.

47

DAVID ROWAN RECOVERED CONSCIOUSNESS in a first aid room in the Anunnaki Center. Alison was seated nearby with Molly. "This is our healing room," she said as his eyes focused slowly on the two."

"What happened? I feel as if I have been mauled by a gorilla."

"You sustained shrapnel cuts in both legs," said Molly moving over and holding his hands. "An-Nusku worked some magic and did some instant healing. He says you should be all right in a few minutes."

David enquired about the soldier.

"Oh, he was fine," said Alison. "He came back and checked you out and when our people picked you up he said he was returning to base."

"He found your ID card and said he'd keep it as a souvenir," said Alison. "We can get you another."

An attendant dropped by and offered everyone some of the Anunnaki nectar. "It'll build your strength up," said Alison.

Molly frowned. "He's got enough strength now to get into deadly escapades so let's not push it."

As David stood up he realized his pants had gone. "There are some fine Anunnaki white cotton pants on the chair," said Alison. "We'll wait for you outside."

Five minutes later David was in the main concourse and realized that everything appeared to be an air of chaos but eventually it assumed a form of organized chaos. The Anunnaki announced that everyone would be taken back to the places they originated in the early morning. Moving would start with the heads of state at 6:00 p.m. said a voice over the audio system. Observers will follow shortly after. "It is all done automatically by our master transporters," said Alison.

"Hey, Rowan" cried Steiner. "There's some great footage in my camera on you facing the mob out there."

"Did you get the grenade?"

"Absolutely," he chuckled. "You should have been a stunt actor." Then he stopped and took Rowan's arm. "I've got a packet of film here. I'm going to be away for forty days could you mail it down to my office in L.A.?"

David took the packet. "And if they call?"

"Heck, just tell them I'm out of this world," he cried. "They'll know I'm on a story."

Saks and Jenny were next. Jenny taking David's hand asked if he and Molly would look after the ranch and feed the goats, water the vegetables until they got back from Nibiru.

"Sure, I'll be able to write a book from your place," said David. "It's been my home for so many years between living with Paul and Natalie in France and you two in British Columbia." He turned to Molly. "Can you hack that?"

"Sure, it'll be an extended vacation," said Molly. "Anyway somebody has to look after this writer. He occasionally thinks he's a hero or something."

Saks and Jenny both smiled easily. "Look after my flutes," said the Indian. "They need a workout every day. Give them air and they'll play themselves."

Kate, Mark and the two teenagers Cal and Johnny said they were all packed and looking forward to the trip to Nibiru.

"Hey young people," said David, you realize that your view of the world will be considerably changed when you get back. What you learn will put you head and shoulders above the people here on Earth so when you walk in for heaven's sake treat us gently."

"I'll be just the same old office secretary, Dad," said Kate. "Making coffee, taking phone calls, doing research, et cetera et cetera."

David shook his head. "You'll want to write a book about your experiences and make a name for yourself."

"Don't think so, Dad. Forty days is nothing in a lifetime."

"Au contraire!" said Paul Rowan. "You'll be talking about it for the rest of your days."

Geraint Jones and Chloe moved in.

"Hey! Look there. Take a peek at those heads of state," he said. "What do you see."

Kate stared at the auditorium. "They're all talking with one another."

"That's right, lassie," said the archaeologist. "They're all talking. The barriers are coming down. Perhaps they're frightened. Perhaps they don't know how to explain to their people the very thing they have put off for years – UFOs are no longer Unidentified Flying Objects. It's a challenge. They cannot afford to have barriers, international boundaries, cold wars, hot wars any more. They have been given an ultimatum -- some will say by God. And in some way they're right. That's what the Sumerian folk out in Mesopotamia – now Iraq – said so many, many years ago when the Anunnaki started living here –- they must be gods. And to some extent they still are."

"This event sure has started the leaders talking together and that is great news," said Paul Rowan. 'The United Nations has existed for over sixty years and failed to achieve what has happened here today."

"Someone somewhere once claimed that human beings always possessed free will," said David.

"It's a free will as long as you do what the boss is saying," said Geraint-Jones with a faint smile. "The Anunnaki bred us Homo sapiens to dig for gold and we have been slaves to gold and its cousin money ever since. It's the DNA for greed and it's all around us."

"Can we get out of it – this DNA for gold and greed?" asked Paul.

"Perhaps, if we use the Anunnaki world, its culture, its philosophies to improve our own world, we might be able to change or own DNA and break free from the chains of gold," said the archaeologist.

"You're talking Utopia," said David. The 16th century book by Sir Thomas More that describes an imaginary ideal society free of poverty and suffering."

Geraint-Jones grinned. "Ah, yes. Utopia! It comes from the Greek and means no place. Perhaps we will give Utopia a home after all."

"Impossibly idealistic!" said the older Rowan.

"It's worth trying," said David. "Perhaps the Anunnaki hold the keys because we sure don't have a world free of poverty and suffering right now."

Geraint-Jones held David's arm. "Listen young man, write a piece on the slavery of humanity. When the Anunnaki took us out of the jungle they implanted their DNA in our bodies to create a specific entity. By working to understand the Anunnaki we might just be able to fathom the exit from our own misunderstandings of god and focus on the True God."

For a moment their eyes connected and a form of deep understanding was created between their two minds.

An attendant moved in and asked the people going to Nibiru to move to the next sphere so they each said their farewells. David and the others watched as Saks and Jenny, Hugh and Chloe Geraint-Jones, followed by Kate and Mark and then the two teenagers Cal and Johnny moved away. Finally the last of the group to go was Erich Steiner.

"David, call the folks down in Oak Harbor, Washington and tell them to look after my wings for 40 days," he called out as he waved his camera and raced after the others.

Alison came up behind them. "Our numbers are dwindling," she said with a smile. The couple turned and looked and saw that the heads of state disappearing in ones and twos. It was as if someone with a magic eraser was simply wiping them out of the auditorium.

"It is kind of mind-blowing to watch all these powerful people, politicians and war lords of various countries simply disappearing as we watch," said Molly.

Always remember," said Alison quietly. "It's only energy. When you can move a living energy form safely and easily from one part of the world to another, you have achieved some power. The Anunnaki scientists are working on a plan that will move humans from one planet to another safely and completely intact. Think of that: space vehicles will be like the stage coach – in a museum."

She looked at David and passed him an object. "This is your ID tag, it will get you back safely to the ranch," she said. "I will be coming back just to make sure you're all okay."

Penni Singleton and Diesel Boulter came from across the sphere. "We have to get back to Whidbey Island as soon as possible," she said happily. "My son Peter is coming to stay with us for a week before he starts his duties in New York. I'm so happy."

"We hope the old 1929 White truck is still capable of running," said Diesel.

"You might be able to find other transport," said Alison. "The power on Earth was restored exactly at six p.m. – that's five minutes ago."

"That's good news," said Paul and Natalie Rowan in chorus.

"We are processed to return to the ranch in exactly five minutes," said Alison. "Collect any clothing and papers and simply stand here. We don't have to go anywhere."

"That's good news again," said Paul.

The group stood watching the heads of state disappearing. The President of the United States, the Prime Minister of Great Britain and the President of Russia were the last to go.

The auditorium was now empty.

"One minute to go," said Alison.

"Sixty seconds and we'll be at my other home, all safe and sound and it will be just like any other day," said David holding Molly's hand.

In less than one minute Paul and Natalie Rowan, Penni Singleton and Diesel Boulter along with Molly Thomsen and David Rowan would arrive at that little ranch tucked away in the highlands of British Columbia for another surprise than none could predict.

48

WHEN DAVID LOOKED BACK the transfer of their bodies from one point to another was like passing through an MRI – a magnetic resonance imaging device – that so many detest in clinics, except there was no threatening claustrophobic tunnel or tube. In fact when he thought about there was nothing to feel not even a tinge of discomfort or elation. One moment he was standing in the Anannuki Center and the next he was standing on the grass outside the ranch home. The only thing he could say upon reflection was that the transfer was totally relaxing for the few seconds it lasted.

For a fraction of a second he was alone. He blinked and the rest of the group appeared beside him. Paul and Natalie Rowan, Penni Singleton, Diesel Boulter, Molly and finally Alison.

"All here," said Alison with a smile.

"Fascinating stuff," put in Molly. "You sure know how to move folks around."

Suddenly a familiar voice crackled from the end of the deck. "I'm not so sure. I think someone on the alien side screwed up."

They all peered round to see Jax Devenport sitting in the wooden Adirondak recliner. "I just got here," he said rising to his feet. "I walked down. Got here ten minutes ago."

"You sound as if you have a problem, Jax," said David.

"Well, I think the Anunnaki have a problem," he said with a sour grin. "There's a nice guy wandering around the meadow watching the horses and he looks very much like the President of the United States."

A stunned silence descended on the group.

"You're kidding!" cried David.

"Take a look," said the CIA man. "He's coming this way."

The next few seconds were totally unreal. The familiar figure came across the lawn, his jacket slung over his arm, his collar open and his tie hanging loose.

He flashed a simple smile. "Hello! Anyone any idea where we are? I appear to be lost," he said. Then he caught sight of David.

"Mister Rowan," he said moving across the deck. "What is going on? I expected to be back in Washington. It's been such an unusual day, I would really like some rest."

Alison came forward. "Sir, I believe your ID tag may have been damaged. That would account for this unfortunate deviation."

David shook his head. "In the uproar in the auditorium earlier today, I do believe our ID tags may have been swapped. I recall something of that nature…"

"We can soon correct the situation, sir," said Alison working to minimize the error. "I'll make a call to base and get you picked up."

The President looked at Devenport then at David. "This fellow says he's a CIA director but he appears to have lost it. Is he genuine?"

Devenport flinched.

"Truly, I understand he is genuine," said the writer. "He was assigned to investigate the pyramid phenomena which led to this event. Incidentally, he did muster a mob that included two soldiers to attack the Anunnaki Center this afternoon."

The President looked balefully at the CIA man. "What on earth would you do that for? Did you think we were in any form of danger?"

Devenport shrugged. "Langley would expect me to do just that, attack, sir."

"Sometimes I wonder how this country survives," he said to David then he turned and looked at Alison. "Can you get me back without too much fuss?"

"Absolutely," she said pressing the gold bracelet on her arm. "The coordinates are being programmed at this very moment. An-Kunin sends his deepest and most heart-felt apologies."

"Can I tag along, sir?" It was Devenport now looking quite miserable.

The President nodded and Alison again spoke into her bracelet and in a few seconds nodded to Devenport. Then she produced an ID tag from her pocketbook and gave it to the CIA man. "Would you please both stand together?"

Devenport turned to David and Molly. "Thanks for all your help and understanding," he said with a faint tired smile. Then he stepped across and stood by the President.

"Mister Rowan, when you get back to base and have recovered would you give me a call in Washington," said the President. "My first initial reaction is that I'm going to have one hell of a time with Congress, but the Chiefs of

Staff…well, they're going to really hate losing their nuclear toys. Perhaps you can give me some ideas." Then he stared across at Saks and Jenny's home. "I see the lights are on again. Things are getting back to normal."

David smiled and wanted to add: "Nothing is going to be normal for a long time, sir," but he resisted. While he was thinking, the President and the CIA man simply disappeared. Gone in the blink of an eyelid.

"Maybe we can get some dinner going," he said smiling at the others. "There's some wine in the house. It won't have chilled yet…"

That evening the five remaining from the original group ate a mixture of Canadian ham, cheese, macaroni and baked potatoes. "It'll be some time before the stores replenish supplies so we'll have to make do," said David.

Diesel nodded. "It'll take days, perhaps weeks before the grocery stores are back in full business. Thank goodness for canned stuff. I never did like it but I guess we'll have to make do." He smiled at the others then at Penni. "We have enough fuel in the truck we should probably hit the track tomorrow morning. Are you coming?"

"Wouldn't miss it for the world," she said holding his hand.

"I'm heading out too," said Alison. "An-Nusku has just informed me that I have ten minutes to make the celestial cruiser heading for Nibiru." Those were the last words David heard from Alison Simonian and he never did find out why when they had first met in London she had spun a yarn about being the daughter of an Armenian professor who lost his home in the 1974 Turkish invasion of North. Now she was gone.

"Stop dreaming, hero," snapped Molly. "We're going to stay here until Saks and Jenny come home – and play farmers, looking after the horses and the goats…"

"And chickens," said David. "It'll give us a break."

So they sat around a log fire in the pit like reminiscent of when they first arrived. But it was different now. Colored lights from Jenny's house gave a spirited aura to the scene and it felt warm. They relaxed, sat and drank wine and chatted and for the first time for a long time started laughing.

But each one knew in their hearts that in a few hours as the world population started recovering from a blackout lasting five days and the news got out that Earth was now under Cosmic Law for its own good that a lot of people would not be laughing.

Diesel and Penni along with Paul and Natalie left at five the next morning after a lot of hugs and best wishes. David and Molly watched as the old 1929

Smith diesel truck chugged gallantly down the Elks Head Valley Road until it turned the corner and was gone.

At this point the couple found themselves alone. After farming chores and breakfast they saddled up the two horses Colonel and Jollie and headed for the high country. When they reached the grassy plateau there was no sign of the Anunnaki or their spacious Gathering Center set between two pyramids. In fact where the Anunnaki had stationed their complex the grass and the bushes showed no sign of an imprint.

"Could it have all been an illusion?" said David peering across the plateau.

"Everyone has gone to Nibiru," said Molly. "I think they'll have their eyes opened and come back with lots of information that will help us Earthlings understand there is a better future without guns and tanks…"

"And atomic bombs."

They passed on through a thick forest and came to another plateau where some deer were browsing by a perfectly blue Elks Head Lake. It was here they stripped naked and plunged into the cool mountain-fresh water. They swam and splashed and their laughter echoed through the tall purple mountains. Soon they climbed onto the grass, spread a blanket and lay in the warm Canadian sun. They kissed and hugged each other's body for a long time, then finally the dam broke and they made wild passionate love.

"Wait," cried Molly gasping for air. She raised her arm and pointed. "There's a UFO!"

"You've got to be kidding," he whispered. "There's no such thing."

THE END

Or the Beginning?

Sources for Further Information

For those interested in pursuing information regarding the topics mentioned in this book, the author suggests the following.

Slave Species of God: The story of humankind from the cradle of humankind by Michael Tellinger (2005-2010)

Gods of Eden, by William Bramley (1993)

The Lost Book of Enki, by Zecharia Sitchin (2002)

Any of the Earth Chronicles by Zecharia Sitchin

The Babylonian Talmud by Gustav Karpeles (1895 & 2012)

The Seven Tablets of Creation / Enuma Elish by Leonard William King (1902 & 2010)

The Great Pyramid: A Miracle in Stone by Joseph A. Seiss (1973)

The Babylonian Legends of the Creation by the British Museum (2010)

The Babylonian Legends of the Creation by Sir Ernest Wallis.Budge (1890?)

The Journey of Man: A Genetic Odyssey by Dr. Spencer Wells (2004)

The Mahabharata, a modern rendering by Ramesh Menon

Anunnaki Chronology and their Remnants on Earth from 1,250,000 BC to the Present Day by Maximillien de Lafayette

The Holy Scriptures English version from Hebrew by Alexander Harkavy (1916)

www.britishmuseum.org and check for Room 56, Mesopotamia 6000-1500 BC.

DVD: The Incredible Human Journey with Dr. Alice Roberts (2010) (BBC/Amazon)

DVD: Journey of Man with Dr. Spencer Wells (PBS Home Video / Amazon)